COMMUNITY ORGANIZING
AND
SOCIAL MOVEMENT

COMMUNITY ORGANIZING AND SOCIAL MOVEMENT

Editor
Johann Angermann

DPH
DISCOVERY
PUBLISHING HOUSE

Published by:

DISCOVERY PUBLISHING HOUSE
4383/4B, Ansari Road, Darya Ganj
New Delhi-110 002 (India)
Phone : +91-11-23279245; 23253475; 43596065
Mobile : +91 9811179893 / +91 9871656464
E-mail : discoverybooksindia@gmail.com
orderdphbooks@gmail.com
namitwasan9@gmail.com
web : www.discoverypublishinggroup.com

Community Organizing and Social Movement
Edited by: **Johann Angermann**

International Standard Book Number: **978-93-6224-162-7** (Hardback)

Printed at:
Infinity Imaging Systems
Delhi (INDIA)

PREFACE

For over half a century, sociologists, psychologists, political scientists, and other social scientists have devoted extensive research to understanding social movements. Their investigations have explored the drivers of collective action and its profound impact on society. Many chapters in this book attest to the enduring relevance of their findings. Themes such as the mobilization of people and resources, resistance strategies, framing of issues, and identification of political opportunities have all played pivotal roles in analyzing the origins, operations, and outcomes of a wide spectrum of social movements. Both community organizing and social movements play critical roles in democratizing societies and amplifying the voices of marginalized groups. They empower individuals to participate actively in shaping their futures and challenging established norms and policies. By mobilizing resources, fostering solidarity, and promoting civic engagement, these efforts contribute to building more inclusive and responsive societies that strive for equity, justice, and meaningful social change.

Within this expansive body of research, the concept of organization holds a distinctive position. A significant breakthrough came with the realization that collective action and protests are not spontaneous, chaotic outbursts by marginalized individuals seeking to voice grievances. Rather, they are purposefully organized efforts. The resource mobilization perspective, notably championed by Zald and McCarthy (1987), elevated the role of organizing to the forefront of social movement analysis. However, this emphasis on organization primarily focused attention on formal social movement organizations (SMOs). These are often portrayed as complex entities characterized by bureaucratic structures—such as rigorous record-keeping, formal decision-making processes, and division of labor (Staggenborg, 2013).

This perspective sparked ongoing and often contentious debates about whether organizing within movements ultimately strengthens or weakens their ability to effect social change. Scholars like Piven and Cloward (1979; 2013) debated whether mass-membership SMOs are beneficial or detrimental in achieving societal transformation. However, it became clear that not all forms of organizing within movements conform to the traditional model of SMOs. Many movements engage in various forms of organization that may not fit the mold of complex, formal organizations with structured memberships.

This book *Community Organizing and Social Movement* aims to comprehensively cover the dynamics, strategies, and impacts of grassroots activism and collective action within contemporary society. It is crafted to appeal to a diverse audience, including scholars, researchers, students, practitioners, and activists interested in understanding and contributing to social change. The book deals with various facets of community organizing, exploring how local residents mobilize around shared concerns to address social injustices, advocate for policy changes, and empower marginalized groups. It provides detailed analyses of effective organizing strategies, the formation of alliances and networks, and the utilization of media and technology in modern activism.

Moreover, the book explores the broader implications of social movements, examining their roles in challenging existing power structures, influencing public discourse, and fostering civic engagement. It emphasizes the transformative potential of grassroots initiatives in shaping inclusive societies and advancing principles of equity, justice, and human rights.

With its interdisciplinary approach, the book draws insights from sociology, political science, communication studies, and organizational theory. It synthesizes theoretical frameworks with practical case studies and empirical research, offering both theoretical depth and practical relevance to those interested in exploring and promoting effective community organizing and social movement strategies.

I would like to express my sincere gratitude to the numerous individuals and organizations whose contributions have enriched the content of this book. This work would not have been possible without the valuable information sourced from widely regarded references.

I extend my heartfelt thanks to the editors, researchers, and experts whose pioneering work has laid the foundation for the topics covered in this book. Their dedication to advancing knowledge in their respective fields has been instrumental in shaping the content presented here.

Editor

CONTENTS

CHAPTER

1

THE ART OF COMMUNITY

INTRODUCTION

A community is a social unit (a group of living things) with commonality such as norms, religion, values, customs, or identity. Communities may share a sense of place situated in a given geographical area (e.g. a country, village, town, or neighborhood) or in virtual space through communication platforms.

A common definition of community emerged as a group of people with diverse characteristics who are linked by social ties, share common perspectives, and engage in joint action in geographical locations or settings. The participants differed in the emphasis they placed on particular elements of the definition. Community was defined similarly but experienced differently by people with diverse backgrounds.

Community is a broad topic within sociology, the social sciences generally, and indeed even in the natural and physical sciences. First, a community is a group of people who interact with one another, for example, as friends or neighbors. Second, this interaction is typically viewed as occurring within a bounded geographic territory, such as a neighborhood or city. Third, the community's members often share common values, beliefs, or behaviors.

UNDERSTANDING THE COMMUNITY

In sociology, community as a group who follow a social structure within a society (culture, norms, values, status). They may work together to organize social life within a particular place, or they may be bound by a sense of belonging sustained across time and space.

Community is a vague term often used in sociology, social sciences in general and even natural and physical sciences. While there is no commonly agreed definition of community, various sociologist have tried to define it in the following way based on certain common features. Talcott Parsons stated that community can be defined as a "collectivity, the members of which share a common territorial area as their base of operation".

Ferdinand Tonnies defined community as "an organic, natural kind of social group whose members are bound together by a sense of belonging created out of everyday contacts covering the whole range of human activities".

For Karl Mannheim, the German sociologist considered the founding father of classical sociology, "community is any circle of people who live together and belong together in a way that they do not share this or that particular interest but a whole set of interests".

However, there is a common group of features which sociologist recognize should be present for a group of people to be called a community. These common features are-

- It is a group of people who interact with each other.
- The interaction is happening within a bounded geographical territory. All daily activities (work and non-work) occur within a geographical area which is self-contained.
- The community's members share common values, beliefs and behaviors.
- The community has a particular social structure. There are also collections of people who might not be termed communities because of a lack of social structure.
- The members have a sense of belonging.

The community is a territorial group which shares a common soil and common way of life. People living within a certain area tend to cluster together and share a sense of belongingness. Thus different areas develop different ways of life, different cultures and from different communities. During urban planning, planners demarcate cities into different sectors and localities creating different communities. However, during the redevelopment of a city, it gets difficult to reorganize it into different divisions which are not similar to the earlier divisions because of this sense of territorial belongingness.

The community is not just about living together but developing the 'we feeling'. Living together creates common memories, cultures and traditions. The individual starts identifying his interest with a larger social group. Every individual has a certain social standing and the expectation of his contribution towards the community is based on this social standing and status. However, the community sentiment keeps changing. Communities do not have fixed boundaries to demarcate who belongs to which community. So instead of belonging to one all-encompassing community, all of us belong to multiple varying communities which might sometimes overlap. However modern transportation and the internet have made the world a very connected place and lessened the coherence and intensity of community sentiment.

Structural Formation of Community

Whatever the form of community organization, the primary fact of Jewish communal life today is its voluntary character. While there are some differences from country to country in the degree of actual freedom to be Jewish or not, the virtual disappearance of the remaining legal and even social and cultural barriers to individual free choice in all but a handful of countries has made free association the dominant characteristic of Jewish life in the "postmodern" era. Consequently, the first task of each Jewish community is to learn to deal with the particular local manifestation of this freedom.

Country	
Aden	Entire community emigrated before Aden received its independence.
Afghanistan	Majority of the Jews emigrated leaving a small oppressed community behind.
Algeria	Virtually all the Jews fled the country in wake of the French evacuation, moving to France and Israel during the 1960s and essentially ending Jewish communal life.
Egypt	Successive oppressions and migrations to Israel after 1948 virtually ended the community's existence.
Iran	Community was reduced in size by emigration to Israel but continues to function as in the past with minor adjustment.
Iraq	Mass migration to Israel in the early 1950s reduced the community to a tiny oppressed minority which lived under severe government restrictions until the U.S. invasion of Iraq (2003).
Lebanon	With the help of a fairly sympathetic government, the community weathered the Arab-Israel conflicts but in 2005 was at the end of the process of self-liquidation through emigration, mostly to Latin America and Europe.
Libya	Migration to Israel accelerated after each Arab-Israel crisis and after the 1967 war the community finally ceased to exist as an entity. Very few Jews remain there.
Morocco	The community's slow decline through emigration to France and Israel after 1948 accelerated after Morocco received independence and picked up momentum after 1967 and 1979 wars.
Pakistan	Most of the small community emigrated, leaving a very small group to carry on minimal communal life in some cities.
Syria	Oppression after 1948 led to migration of a majority to Israel and Lebanon; government pressure increased against the remnant after the 1967 war. Practically all Jews emigrated, leaving no organized community life.
Tunisia	Despite official attempts to convince the Jews to stay, most migrated to Israel in successive waves after Tunisia's independence.
Turkey	Almost half of the 100,000 Jewish population left for Israel after 1948. The remainder were effectively reconstituted as a religious community with limited powers and under governmental supervision. Most of the Jews (nearly 20,000) live in Istanbul and a minority in Izmir (about 1,500) – the only two regularly organized communities.
Yemen	All but a tiny handful left for Israel immediately after the establishment of the state. The few remaining Jews mostly emigrated during the 1960s.

Australia	The postwar influx of refugees substantially enhanced Jewish life and necessitated changes in its communal structure, both locally and countrywide, to encompass the widened scope of Jewish activity and the more intensely "Jewish" Jews. These have continued into the 21st century, giving Australian Jewry comparatively favorable intermarriage statistics and continuing strong support for Zionism. Unlike the United States, a majority of Australia's Jews probably belonged to Orthodox synagogues.
Canada	Pressures of "Americanization," suburbanization and the general homogenization of Canadian society led to a weakening of traditional Canadian communal structure and the introduction of American-style "religious pluralism." But, characterized by a relatively strong sense of Diaspora identity, the Canadian Jewish community continued to grow, in large part through immigration. The community's center of gravity also continued to shift toward Toronto, now home to almost half of all Canadian Jews in the early 21st century. As in the United States, all of the denominations of Judaism are well represented in Canada, with the Orthodox stream very strong.
Ireland	Little significant constitutional change even though a native-born generation came to the fore. Some immigration from the former Soviet Union and elsewhere improved a declining situation.
New Zealand	Prior to about 1980, the continued emigration of the younger generation decreased the Jewish population and weakened the community structure. Subsequently, significant numbers arrived from the former Soviet Union and South Africa but emigration and assimilation continued.
Rhodesia (Zimbabwe)	The concentration of Jews from other countries of black Africa increased the size and importance of the Rhodesian community while the separation of Zambia and the Rhodesian secession increased its self-contained character. But with civil war and black independence the Jewish community began to shrink, leaving just a few Jews in the early 21st century.
South Africa	Changes in the regime and the rise of a native-born generation within the community shifted the emphasis of the communal institutions and the dominant mode of Jewish identification, weakening what had become the traditional structure. In the post-Apartheid era the tendency has been toward greater coordination and unity within the community.
United Kingdom	The rise to power of the last wave of immigrants and a native-born generation challenged the communal status quo from both left and right, weakening traditional institutions and strengthening new ones that reflected the community's greater diversity. The number of Jews in Britain has probably declined since its peak in the 1950s, with especially sharp declines in cities outside of London. On the other hand, in many respects Jewish consciousness has increased among Anglo-Jewry.

United States	The destruction of European Jewry transferred world Jewish leadership decisively to the American Jewish community. This plus the rise of a new generation and the disappearance of immigrant ideologies led to significant organizational changes to meet demands while also enabling American Jewry to become more rooted in the "religious pluralism" of the general society. Subsequently the traditional institutions, other than the synagogue became less significant as Jewishness tended more to find subjective expression.

This task is a major factor in determining the direction of the reconstitution of Jewish life in this generation. The new voluntarism extends itself into the internal life of the Jewish community as well, generating pluralism even in previously free but relatively homogeneous or monolithic community structures. This pluralism is exacerbated by the breakdown of the traditional reasons for being Jewish and the rise of new incentives for Jewish association. At the same time, the possibilities for organizing a pluralistic Jewish community have also been enhanced by these new incentives and the "postmodern" breakdown of the rigid ideologies that divided Jews in the latter third of the modern era. Certainly the creation of the State of Israel has given the Jewish people a new and compelling focus that enhances the Jewish attachments of virtually all Jews. The state's crucial role as a generator of Jewish ties, regardless of other differences, was decisively demonstrated at the time of the *Six-Day War (1967).

In each case, the Jewish community adapts itself to the environment of the host country so that its own structure reflects local conditions while facilitating (as far as possible) the achievement of the main purposes of corporate Jewish life. In virtually every case, the structure that emerges from the adaptation is based on federal principles and uses federal forms.

The pluralistic federalism of the voluntaristic community substantially eliminates the neat pattern of communal organization usually displayed as the model by those who concern themselves with rationalizing Jewish community life. Though smaller communities in different cultural settings are not likely to conform completely, more and more the seemingly anarchistic American pattern is revealed as the paradigm of their development, if not the vision of their future. Certainly the model of a hierarchic organizational structure does not offer an accurate picture of the distribution of powers and responsibilities in any Jewish community today. Even in the more formally structured communities of Central Europe and Latin America, the institution that appears to be at the top of the pyramid is really dependent upon and often manipulated by the institutions and organizations that would be placed farther down on the structure.

The local community that "should" be on the bottom is, in fact, often the real center of power. For communities like the United States, even the modified model is useless. Nor is there a central governing agent in most communities that serves as the point at which authority, responsibility, and power converge. Even in the communities ostensibly dominated by a consistory, the erstwhile central body has been shunted aside to become just another specialized institution in an oligopoly of such institutions.

The structure of contemporary Jewish communities is best understood as a multidimensional matrix (or mosaic) that takes the form of a communications network; a set of interacting institutions which, while preserving their own structural integrity and roles, are informed by shared patterns of culture, activated by a shared system of organizations, and governed by shared leadership cadres. The character of the matrix and its communications network varies from community to community, with particularly sharp variations separating the six basic types. In some cases, the network is connected through a common center, which serves as the major (but rarely, if ever, the exclusive) channel for communication. In others, the network forms a matrix without any real center, with the lines of communication crisscrossing in all directions. In all cases, the boundaries of the community are revealed only when the pattern of the network is uncovered. The pattern itself is perceptible only when both of its components are revealed, namely its institutions and organizations with their respective roles and the way in which communications are passed between them.

The pattern itself is inevitably a dynamic one; that is to say, there is rarely a fixed division of authority and influence but, rather, one that varies from time to time and usually from issue to issue, with different elements in the matrix taking on different "loads" at different times and relative to different issues. Since the community is a voluntary one, persuasion rather than compulsion, influence rather than power are the only tools available for making and executing policies.

1. Communities entrenching, adjusting, and moving toward greater internal unity:	
Argentina	Guatemala
Brazil	Mexico
Chile	Panama
Costa Rica	Uruguay
El Salvador	Venezuela
2. Communities of emigration and decline:	
Bolivia	Haiti
Columbia	Honduras
Cuba	Nicaragua
Dominican Republic	Paraguay
Ecuador	Surinam
3. Communities undergoing "Americanization" through expansion of American business and leisure interests in the Caribbean:	
Barbados	Jamaica
Curacao	Trinidad and Tobago

This also works to strengthen its character as a communications network since the character, quality, and relevance of what is communicated and the way in which it is communicated frequently determine the extent of the authority and influence of the parties on the communication.

Elements of Community

Some of the important characteristics or elements of community are as follows:

Meaning of community can be better understood if we analyze its characteristics or elements. These characteristics decide whether a group is a community or not. However, community has the following characteristics or elements:

(1) A group of people: A group of people is the most fundamental or essential characteristic or element of community. This group may be small or large but community always refers to a group of people. Because without a group of people we can't think of a community, when a group of people live together and share a common life and binded by a strong sense of community consciousness at that moment a community is formed. Hence a group of people is the first pre-requisites of community.

(2) A definite locality: It is the next important characteristic of a community. Because community is a territorial group. A group of people alone can't form a community. A group of people forms a community only when they reside in a definite territory. The territory need not be fixed forever. A group of people like nomadic people may change their habitations. But majority community are settled and a strong bond of unity and solidarity is derived from their living in a definite locality.

(3) Community Sentiment: It is another important characteristic or element of community. Because without community sentiment a community can't be formed only with a group of people and a definite locality. Community sentiment refers to a strong sense of awe feeling among the members or a feeling of belonging together. It refers to a sentiment of common living that exists among the members of a locality. Because of common living within an area for a long time a sentiment of common living is created among the members of that area. With this the members emotionally identify themselves. This emotional identification of the members distinguishes them from the members of other community.

(4) Neutrality: Communities are naturally organized. It is neither a product of human will nor created by an act of government. It grows spontaneously. Individuals became the member by birth.

(5) Permanence: Community is always a permanent group. It refers to a permanent living of individuals within a definite territory. It is not temporary like that of a crowd or association.

(6) Similarity: The members of a community are similar in a number of ways. As they live within a definite locality they lead a common life and share some common ends. Among the members similarity in language, culture, customs, and traditions and in many other things is observed. Similarities in these respects are responsible for the development of community sentiment.

(7) Wider Ends: A community has wider ends. Members of a community associate not for the fulfillment of a particular end but for a variety of ends. These are natural for a community.

(8) Total organized social life: A community is marked by total organized

social life. It means a community includes all aspects of social life. Hence a community is a society in miniature.

(9) A Particular Name: Every community has a particular name by which it is known to the world. Members of a community are also identified by that name. For example people living in Odisha is known as odia.

(10) No Legal Status: A community has no legal status because it is not a legal person. It has no rights and duties in the eyes of law. It is not created by the law of the land.

(11) Size of Community: A community is classified on the basis of it's size. It may be big or small. Village is an example of a small community whereas a nation or even the world is an example of a big community. Both the type of community are essential for human life.

(12) Concrete Nature: A community is concrete in nature. As it refers to a group of people living in a particular locality we can see its existence. Hence it is concrete.

(13) A community exists within society and possesses distinguishable structure which distinguishes it from others.

Changing theory of Community

The stable, solidary and intimate primary group type of 'perfect community' is fast disappearing as a result of industrialization, urbanization, modern means of communication and information technology. The local unit is increasingly absorbed into the larger economic and political society. Individuals no longer live wholly or even largely within the primary group but are oriented with reference to the larger social world outside.

Individual interests, transcending the locality, are integrated on a national or international level. As contacts have become more varied and extensive, they have also become more formal and external. The person is fractionalized, participating in each of his several or many groupings with only a limited aspect of his total self As a concrete, total personality, he is commanded by no one group, not even by his family. Intimacy has given way to acquaintanceship or to anonymity on the basis of above ideas some sociologists have put forth a thesis known as "loss of community".

Old characteristics of community, i.e., locality and community sentiment or 'we-feeling' are being eroded by the forces of modernity. These forces have fractured the myth of 'homogeneous community'.

The 'Muslim community", the 'Hindu community', the 'Black community' or the 'women's community' are now fractured into feminists versus conservatives or liberals versus conservatives or various other strands (leftist versus tightest) of opinions.

At many times, it is seen that women do not necessarily side with women just because they are women or belong to women community. In the end, we may conclude that the concept of community has become uncommonly elastic when we hear about the newly developed concepts like 'global village' or 'global community. Thus, this concept is now no more limited to a single or limited geographical area.

Imperative Basis of Community

In common parlance, the word 'community' is used for a collection of people who do related kinds of work, such as the "teacher's community" or the "doctors community". It is also used to denote a collection of people who share something in common as the "Hindu community", the "Parsi community", or the "Christian community" without necessarily living in a particular area. Sometimes, it is used to describe a supposedly coherent group, such as 'international community. Such loose use of the word 'community is always misleading and indicate just too amorphous mass.

1. The term 'community' is employed to describe a fixed locality (a given geographic area) as a basis of social organization. Thus, from this point of view, a traditional rural village is a community where people are born, live and die.
2. Community is used to refer to a local social system or set of relationships that center upon a given locality. From sociological point of view, it is the concentration of relationships, rather than the geographical factor that matters.
3. The term 'community' is also used to describe a quality of relationship which produces a strong sense of shared identity. This usage does not give any importance to the spatial or geographical aspect of the community. It does not depend on physical whereabouts or even on people having met each other.

For the last few years, this third sense of community is gaining ground and has been widely used. The old territorial character of the community (closed boundary) has relatively little to do and more or less given up in favor of quality of relationships (a sense of belonging and shared identity).

MacIver and Page (1949) have listed two important bases of community:

(1) Locality: A community always occupies a territorial area. Almost all sociologists (e.g., A. Green, K. Davis, Lundberg, Bogardus etc.) have mentioned it as a basic condition in their definitions of community. The strong bond of solidarity that we find in the members of a community is derived from the conditions of locality—living in a definite geographical area. This bond is weakening today due to the development of modem means of communications. But, the extension of communication has in some other way helped in territorial bond.

Now, the territorial area of the modern communities is expanding far and wide. Common place of residence does not automatically yield a community. "A community of like-minded men" and "the world-wide community of scholars" are such expressions which deny sharing a specific and delimited area of residence.

(2) Community sentiment: Locality, though a necessary condition, is not enough to create a community. There must be the common living with its awareness of sharing a common way of life. Local areas, which lack the social coherence, cannot be termed as community.

According to Alex Inkeles, the following three elements are relevant as a basis of a community.

A community exists:

(1) When a set of households is relatively concentrated in delimited geographical area;

(2) Their residents exhibit a substantial degree of integrated social interaction; and

(3) They have a sense of common membership, of belonging together, which is not based exclusively on ties of consanguinity.

Thus, the essence of community is a sense of common bond, the sharing of an identity, membership in a group, holding some things physical or spiritual, in common esteem, coupled with the acknowledgement of rights and obligations with reference to all others so identified.

The natural small community of permanent residents such as a village, a town, or a neighborhood combines all these elements. F. Tonnies (1887), L. Wirth (1938) and many other sociologists contend that as community grows in size, the nature of relationships between its member's changes accordingly.

Wirth noted that the size of the community prevents residents from getting to know most of the people in the community. It also facilitates spatial (or physical) separation, based on race, ethnicity, social class and lifestyles. Physical proximity, though an important element of community, does not itself make a community. Direct face-to-face interaction can be replaced to some degree by symbolic interaction fostered by the media of communication.

Communities may be large as much as a vast nation or they may be very small like a primitive tribe, a horde, a nomadic group, or neighborhood. A village, a town or a metropolis are other examples of a community. Community exists within greater communities—the town within a state, the state within a nation and the nation within the world community.

There are certain human groupings for which there is no clear-cut answer about their community character. Such groups may be termed as borderline cases such as a monastery, a convent, an immigrant group or a prison. MacIver and Page have accepted these groups as a community

COMMUNITIES: TYPES AND CHARACTERISTICS

Instead, a community is recognized as a distinctive social system that impacts and informs an individual's life through various influences and organizational factors. It is as much an environment as it is a set of relationships or even a feeling.

Apart from being locational, a community can also be relational, meaning that members share a deep sense of community that does not depend on their whereabouts (i.e. churches, fans of a particular sports team, or the military).

Because traditional psychology examines people on a fairly individual level, community psychology seeks to understand them within the context of their communities.

Often times, community psychologists will view their subjects with varying levels of analysis, the majority of which reference different types of communities.

Below are five levels of analysis used for research in community psychology and the corresponding types of communities that may be associated with each?

- **Individuals**. As you may have guessed already, an individual is not a community but rather its subject and agent. In terms of its focus, this is the narrowest level for analysis. The main consideration for this level is examining how an individual interacts with his or her community and vice versa.
- **Microsystems**. Just beyond the level of the individual are microsystems. Microsystems are the most intimate groups with which an individual participates, engages, and grows.

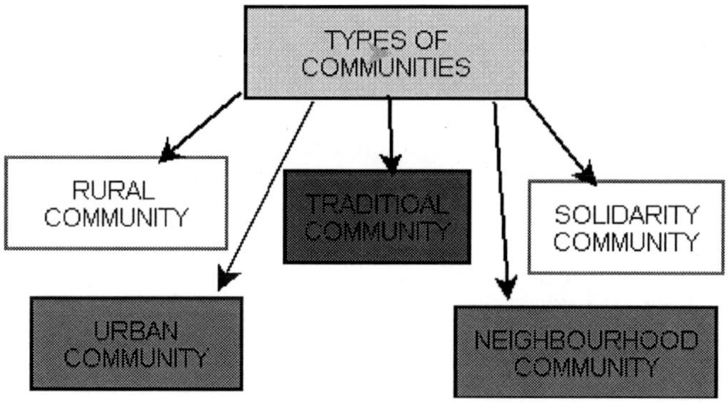

Figure 1. Community types and level.

Source: https://wikieducator.org/images/7/73/TYPES_OFCOM.png

These groups may consist of the following:

- Families
- Friends
- Classmates and teachers
- Coworkers
- Activity or team members

As you can see, most microsystems refer to the places and people an individual visits and interacts with on a regular basis.

- **Organizations**. Beyond the level of microsystems is organizations. This level is comprised of the institutions that often contain an individual's microsystems. These institutions can, depending on their own processes, influence either microsystems or the individual through various linkages. Examples of these types of communities may include the following:
  - Schools
  - Workplaces
  - Neighborhood associations
  - Religious centers
- **Localities**. For many of us, where we live is foundational to our sense of community. Locality, meaning the numerous spaces in which an individual resides, orients identity through the cultural, political, and economic events and activities that occur within them. Localities can be as small as neighborhood blocks or as large as entire towns, cities, and regions.
- **Macrosystems**. Of all these levels of analysis, macrosystems are the

broadest and, to a degree, the most intangible. Macrosystems encompass a wide range of behaviors and ideas characterizing community systems that are more universal in their scope, such as:

- Cultures
- Societies
- Governments
- Belief systems
- Social movements

Community psychologists must consider multiple levels of analysis when conducting research.

By understanding these five levels and their corresponding types of communities, a community psychologist can successfully discern how to serve their communities in the best possible ways.

Urban Community

Urban communities have a higher level of demographic complexity. The bonds that connect urban community members are weaker, and so are those between communities and the areas they live. This is because people living in urban communities often come from many different places, do not have long-established connections, and often do not know one another or have a strong understanding of the history of natural disasters in their neighborhoods.

Difficulties in engaging participation due to differences in income level, standard of living, and lifestyle of urban compared to rural population. Unlike in rural areas, people living in cities often have to travel longer distances to work, and are more strictly controlled by working hours, whether they are administrative employees or workers.

Lack of tools to assess impacts of local institutions, including laws, regulations, social rules, level of decentralization, and access to information.

Difficulties in mobilizing local government support: urban local governments are under more pressure and have more priorities, including socioeconomic development priorities. Local government leaders might not agree with adaptive measures suggested because they do not consider them their top priorities.

Different impacts of erosion on different households.

It is difficult to verify information provided and to identify groups because the selection and classification of groups are not the same as for rural areas.

Urban people have busier lives and work schedules, which might create time pressures and can cause assessment to be hasty and ineffective.

Urban community is something which an individual thought as, an area with high density of population, an area with the availability of basic requirements, an area of good resources, the area has lots of opportunity of employment and such an area which can be considered as life-giving for luxurious desires of human or individual. The word urban community has many meanings, the term 'community', only, denotes two conditions:

- **Physical condition**
- **Social condition**

Generally, by an urban area, we mean an area with a high density of population.

Density is not the only a term which may be considered as a definite term to confer a name of "urban city" to the particular village, area, land, city, town etc. two main factors must be kept in mind while declaring a community as urban, i.e.

- **Absolute population**: – it is an accurate numerical value with which the population of a society can be estimated or known.
- **Absolute area**: – Refers to a specific, fixed point on the earth's surface expressed by a coordinate system.

Other standards which are considered by different countries are: – presence of local authority; base of density of population and quality of population

The social condition of people in life is expressed as the fashionable living of people, the acquaintance of peoples with luxury and the fashionable life of people.

Urban lifestyle is such a style which has the effect of the act, done by an individual, on the other member of the same society; but is it true or is it not a full truth that only those, who are members of society does get affected? Or the other part of society also does get affected? Or the other societies have the effect of the particular activity? Or the rural areas are also experiencing the effects of vibes of the act of an individual?

Rural areas may get converted into urban areas. A government, taking into account the need of development, may change a society living in a rural area to such a society which is developed and educated.

Dentition of urban is not completely explainable and not much clear, but the difference between the word "rural" and "urban" is clear from the above explanation.

Rural areas differ from urban areas. In many ways, such as population density, quality and educated population, institution, requirements and the availability of sources.

The areas where resources are available to get converted into a appoint of attraction and the area around the resource become an area of settlement of people and crowd. A crowd, with it, brings many needs, desires; thus, to complete the task of completing wishes and demands of an individual opportunity of employment are provided. Thus, this opportunity attracts more people.

For example – the area near gang, London, Mumbai or Calcutta; any city which is developed today, has its past like an area, considered as a rural area, shall have. Urban area's population may possibly or with a very small probability shall have the fee schedule, which decreases their social interaction.

Characteristics of Urban Community

A sociological analysis of urban community contains several salient features. They are as follows:

1. Size: As a rule, in the same country and at the same period, the size of an urban community is much larger than that of a rural community. In other words, urbanity and size of a community are positively correlated.
2. Density of population: Density of population in urban areas is greater than in rural communities. Urbanity and density are positively correlated.
3. Family: So far as urban community is concerned, greater importance is attached to the individual than to the family. Nuclear families are more popular in urban areas.

4. Marriage: In case of urban community there is a preponderance of love marriages and inter-caste marriages. One also comes across a greater number of divorces. Sons and daughters enjoy considerable freedom in choosing their life partners.
5. Occupation: In the urban areas, the major occupations are industrial, administrative and professional in nature. Divisions of labor and occupational specialization are very much common in towns/cities/ metropolises.
6. Class extremes: In the words of Bogardus, "Class extremes characterize the city." A town and a city house the richest as well as the poorest of people. In a city, the slums of the poor exist alongside the palatial bungalows of the rich, amidst the apartments of the middle class members. The most civilized modes of behavior as well as the worst racketeering are found in the cities.
7. Social heterogeneity: If villages are the symbol of cultural homogeneity, the cities symbolize cultural heterogeneity. The cities are characterized by diverse peoples, races and cultures. There is great variety in regard to the food habits, dress habits, living conditions, religious beliefs, cultural outlook, customs and traditions of the urbanites.
8. Social distance: Social distance is the result of anonymity and heterogeneity. Most of one's routine social contacts in a town or city are impersonal and segmentary in character. In the urban community social responses are incomplete and halfhearted. There is utter lack of personal involvement in the affairs of others.
9. System of interaction: Georg Simmel held that the social structure of urban communities is based on interest groups. The circles of social contact are wider in the city than in the country. There is a wider area of interaction system per man and per aggregate. This makes city life more complex and varied. The city life is characterized by the predominance of secondary contacts, impersonal, casual and short-lived relations. Man, at any rate, the man in the street, virtually loses his identity being treated as a "number" having a certain "address".
10. Mobility: The most important feature of urban community is its social mobility. In urban areas the social status of an individual is determined not by heredity or birth but by his merit, intelligence and perseverance. Urbanity and mobility are positively correlated.
11. Materialism: In the urban community the social existence of man revolves round wealth and material possessions. The worth of an urbanite today is being judged not by what he is but by what he has. Status symbols in the form of financial assets, salaries, costly home appliances count a lot for the urbanites.
12. Individualism: The urbanites attach supreme importance to their own welfare and happiness. They hesitate to think or act for the good of others.
13. Rationality: In urban community there is emphasis on rationality. People are inclined to reason and argue. Their relationship with others

is governed, for the most part, by the consideration of gain or loss. Relationship takes place on a contractual basis. Once the contract is over, human relationship automatically comes to a close.

14. Anonymity: As Bogardus observes, the "Urban groups have a reputation for namelessness." By virtue of its size and population, the urban community cannot be a primary group. Here nobody knows anybody and nobody cares for anybody. The urbanites do not care for their neighbors and have nothing to do with their miseries or pleasures.
15. Norm and social role conflict: The urban community is characterized by norm and social role conflict. Factors such as the size, density and heterogeneity of the population, extreme occupational specialization and the class structure prevalent in the urban context lead to such a state of affairs.

In the absence of uniform and fixed social norms, individuals or groups often seek divergent ends. This has a considerable share in causing social disorganization.

16. Rapid social and cultural change: Rapid social and cultural change characterize urban life. The importance attached to traditional or sacred elements has been relegated to the background. The benefits of urban life have effected changes in respect of norms, ideologies and behavior patterns.
17. Voluntary associations: The urban community is characterized by impersonal, mechanical and formal social contacts occurring among the people. Naturally they have a strong desire for developing genuine social relationships to satisfy their hunger for emotional warmth and sense of security. They form associations, clubs, societies and other secondary groups.
18. Formal social control: Social control in urban community is essentially formal in nature. Individual's behavior is regulated by such agencies as police, jails, law courts etc.
19. Secularization of outlook: In cities ritual and kinship obligations are diluted. Caste and community considerations yield to economic logic. This results in secularization of outlook.
20. Urban areas provide impulses for modernization in society as a whole.

Suburban Community

Suburban communities have experienced a radical transformation in the past century. Many people live in suburbs. Suburbs usually have homes and small businesses. The population of suburbs are growing. People have more space in suburban areas than in urban areas. Homes in suburbs are usually large. Groups of homes in suburbs form neighborhoods. Many suburban homes have yards. Most do not have as much land as rural areas though.

Shops and other businesses are located in suburbs. Some of the people who live in suburbs work in these businesses. Other people commute to work in nearby cities. Many people enjoy living in suburbs. It is quieter and people have more space than in cities. Living in suburbs can also be challenging. There may not be as many businesses or things to do as in cities. People that commute may spend a lot of time driving or on trains.

Suburbanization as a social-spatial process is not a recent trend. It has been common among the higher social classes since the 17th century to have a second home outside the city. The attraction of living in a healthy and spacious environment in small, rural and peaceful environments as opposed to living in overcrowded and often unsanitary conditions in modern cities became a popular ideal in the 19th century. Through the Garden City movement this romantic ideal of living in the countryside was transferred to the lower middle and working class. Suburbanization became a mass movement from the 1950s in America and some 10 years later also in Europe. From a sociological point of view, the move to the suburbs is described—at least partly—as the result of the social process of growing domesticity, influenced by a variety of modern developments: the increase in wealth and technology which allowed people to do more things at home, individualization and the growing importance of the nuclear family. Because of these facts and because society became more and more complex, home developed a new meaning in the postwar period, from just a place to sleep, into a refuge, a place where people can relax, be with their family and have autonomy and control. The new ideas towards housing also brought about a demand for more living space in and around the house, which was provided in the new suburban estates. And because of increased mobility opportunities and affluence, suburban living became accessible to broad social categories. As a part of modernization, the suburb presents an element of the social sphere that Castells called the 'spaces of flows'.

From a geographical point of view, residents moved out of the city as a sign of social mobility, searching for detached single-family housing with a garden. People preferred the suburb for its absence of urban characteristics such as high-density building, small-stacked houses, heavy traffic, air pollution and litter, but also to escape from social attributes such as crime, poverty and ethnic minorities. Suburbanization was also primarily considered to be a positive development from a professional point of view. The first American suburbs, built by big private investment companies such as Levitt, were initially seen as social experiments, celebrating the best of the urban and rural way of life. However, they soon began to be perceived as a threatening social process and critics started to contrast negatively the new suburban areas with cities and villages. The way the suburban debate developed from that time onwards resembles—in our view—what Wellman has called the 'community question'. From the different views on local social life and social ties in suburbs, we see the same 'Lost', 'Saved' and 'Transformed' argument emerging both in academic debate and public opinion

Lost

In general, the 'Lost' concept of the community question refers to the negative and frequently permanent consequences ascribed to the changes in social ties, the move to rationality and efficiency and 'contracts' between individuals. This analysis received support by many critics in America, many also from an academic background. From the 1950s on, scholars have stated that the suburban way of life, largely privatized and devoid of any form of place attachment, has contributed to the current American 'drive-in culture'. The mass-produced, monotonous surroundings are believed to put down all natural creativity, individuality, sense of quality, beauty and being in touch with nature. According to Jackson, cities may have social problems, yet overall cohesion is strong because urbanites are still active and outgoing. This, according to Putman, contrasts with the suburbs. Suburbanites are almost constantly commuting between their home, workplace and shopping mall. This creates a 'civic penalty' leading to the loss of community.

In many countries, critics followed this argument, talking about 'new town blues'. However, their comments rarely became subject to real academic scrutiny. In recent times, critics who expressed a 'suburban Lost' view did not so much stress the social and cultural characteristics, but merely the spatial and geographical assets of suburbanization. These include urban sprawl, the division of functions, the segregation of social groups and the residential mobility of suburbanites. According to both American and European scholars, modernity and town planning in the past 50 years have created places without identity—non-places. They state that bad human habitats have come out of new suburban residential areas, being without history and tradition. The representation of suburbs by this lost approach as an abscess paralyzing society has become deeply rooted in public opinion, the media, cultural representations and even the academic world. The suburban lost view has also had profound effects on policy and town planning. This is illustrated by the rise of the 'new urbanism' movement which strives for the creation of more valuable communities in the form of traditional neighborhoods and has much influence on both sides of the Atlantic. However, reviews of suburban development today show that lost views are based on myths.

Saved

As in the general 'community question', the suburban Saved view states that communal solidarity still persists in contemporary society. Some suburban community studies put emphasis on the original idea of suburban living as an ideal lifestyle for the lower middle class. It is pictured as an improvement of both the urban and rural way of life. Bell's description of suburbanites having chosen 'familism' as an important feature of their lifestyle versus urbanites placing more value on careerism, has contributed substantially to the suburban Saved argument.

According to Gans, suburbanites have similar characteristics to many people living in cities—in terms of age, life stage, social background and work situation, for example. It is the fact that it is predominantly young and middle-class families that have chosen a suburban life that has created a relatively suburban homogeneity. The facilities and social characteristics of their residential surroundings are of secondary importance, but according to Gans this does not mean that suburbs lack social cohesion. People do relate to their neighbours and there is a considerable amount of mutual trust and aid among them. He also states that suburbanites develop a sense of community in terms of loyalty for the place and identification with the local organizations and sports teams. In addition to Gans, several researchers in both North America and Europe found suburbanites actively engaged in local social contacts, sometimes even more so than in the old city. A Dutch study concluded that suburbanites were able to maintain their relations with family and friends outside their place of residence, while important new local contacts were also made.

Transformed

The Lost and Saved arguments present contrasting views of the outcome of modernization processes, in this case suburbanization. However, both approaches encounter the 'community question' as preoccupied with small groups and the local, and with normative views about the value of social cohesion. Since the 1970s, several scholars have come to the conclusion that the suburban Lost and Saved views are in fact both based on myths, putting too much focus on suburbs as supposed to Gemeinschafts. This more critical community argument, the liberated or Transformed view, focuses on privatization, control and social mobility as general characteristics of suburban life. It is stated that the suburban dream does set the picture of a cozy, almost rural, lifestyle of the old days, but the choices people make in housing are—in the first place—based on individualistic and functional needs and demands. Suburbanites seek a good way to live with their family, not their neighbors. Several studies point to the fact that suburbs, like urban areas, are actually communities of limited liability.

The fact that everything and everyone is new creates common problems and issues. This highly stimulates mutual contact. But the intense local contacts of the early periods ease over time, showing their strong functional aspects.

As adherents of the Transformed approach state, the collective organization of individuality is a function of the suburban dream itself. Many accounts of suburban living expressing the Transformed view, stress the fact that suburbanites are very keen on their privacy. The suburban definition of a good neighbor is someone who is there when needed, but not at your back all the time. This does not differ from the way most urbanites see their neighbors. The moral order Baumgartner (1988) found in studying a suburban community near New York is based on 'peace and quiet', being normal and acting inconspicuously. She sees suburbanites as having high standards concerning the look of their neighborhood, wanting it to appear nice and clean. Unknown elements, people or objects are often seen as offensive, deviant and potential threats. Many suburbanites have seen a steady growth of these nuisances over the years. As observed by many scholars, the classical suburbs and new towns have been expanding over recent decades, becoming more and more self-sufficient and also acquiring more urban characteristics. This 'urbanization of the suburbs' which has already been referred to in the discussion of the concept 'suburb', is especially true in a European context, where urban regions are more compact and suburbs tend to be much more tightly connected to the central cities compared with American suburbs. The changing geographical position of the suburbs has also altered their spatial and socioeconomic characteristics. Suburban settlements nowadays are less homogeneous in terms of residents and landscape as they are perceived by the lost approach.

Rural Community

Rural communities using the integrated system are appropriate examples of recycled societies that benefit from low-capital investments on a decentralized basis and such communities are attuned to the environment.

The ten essential characteristics of the rural community are as follows: a. Size of the Community b. Density of Population c. Agriculture is the Main Occupation d. Close Contact with Nature e. Homogeneity of Population f. Social Stratification g. Social Interaction h. Social Mobility i. Social Solidarity j. Joint Family.

a. Size of the Community: The village communities are smaller in area than the urban communities. As the village communities are small, the population is also low.

b. Density of Population: As the density of population is low, the people have intimate relationships and face-to-face contacts with each other. In a village, everyone knows everyone.

c. Agriculture is the Main Occupation: Agriculture is the fundamental occupation of the rural people and forms the basis of rural economy. A farmer has to perform various agricultural activities for which he needs the cooperation of other members. Usually, these members are from his family. Thus, the members of the entire family share agricultural activities.

d. Close Contact with Nature: The rural people are in close contact with nature as most of their daily activities revolve around the natural environment. This is the reason why a ruralite is more influenced by nature than an urbanite. The villagers consider land as their real mother as they depend on it for their food, clothing and shelter.

e. Homogeneity of Population: The village communities are homogenous in nature. Most of their inhabitants are connected with agriculture and its allied occupations, though there are people belonging to different castes, religions and classes.

f. Social Stratification: In rural society, social stratification is a traditional characteristic, based on caste. The rural society is divided into various strata on the basis of caste.

g. Social Interaction: The frequency of social interaction in rural areas is comparatively lower than in urban areas. However, the interaction level possesses more stability and continuity. The relationships and interactions in the primary groups are intimate. The family fulfills the needs of the members and exercises control over them.

It is the family, which introduces the members to the customs, traditions and culture of the society.

Due to limited contacts, they do not develop individuality and their viewpoint towards the outside world is very narrow, which makes them oppose any kind of violent change.

h. Social Mobility: In rural areas, mobility is rigid as all the occupations are based on caste. Shifting from one occupation to another is difficult as caste is determined by birth. Thus, caste hierarchy determines the social status of the rural people.

i. Social Solidarity: The degree of social solidarity is greater in villages as compared to urban areas. Common experience, purposes, customs and traditions form the basis of unity in the villages.

j. Joint Family: Another characteristic feature of the rural society is the joint family system. The family controls the behavior of the individuals. Generally, the father is the head of the family and is also responsible for maintaining the discipline among members. He manages the affairs of the family.

Traditional Features of Rural Communities

A rural community is marked primarily by a small, sparsely settled, relatively homogeneous population that engages primarily in agriculture (although there are exceptions to this rule, especially in industrial societies). The traditional rural community tended to be a folk society.

Kinship, its relationships and institutions, are the type of categories of experience and the familiar group is the unit of action. The sacred prevails over the secular; the economy is one of status rather than of the market." Today, however, traditional rural community is losing its folk society character and flavor as described above. It would be a mistake to fit all rural communities into one set of image because all rural communities are not alike. Yet certain features have been found common to nearly all kinds of rural communities.

These are:

1. Rural society was based predominantly on agriculture. Land was the basic means of subsistence. Nearly all rural population was involved in agricultural way of life directly or indirectly. A substantial part of their income was drawn from agriculture. All faced common problems, performed common tasks and shared common helplessness before the awesome natural calamities (floods, droughts etc.), which man cannot control.
2. The rural way of life used to be quite different from urban life. Thrift was an honored value and conspicuous consumption was seen as an urban vice. A farmer's status was measured by his lands, his herds, his crops and the inheritance he could pass on to his children.

Distrust of city people and disapproval of urban life was a predictable rural attitude. Rural people used to be suspicious of intelligentality and book learning. Their life used to be simple without any fun and fair in the modem sense of the term. They used to have deep faith in religion and duties.

3. The rural social system was marked with minimum of social differentiation and social stratification. It was mostly based on land and property relations. These relations determined the share of various socio-economic groups and the distribution of agricultural wealth among the various sections of the rural population.
4. There was predominance of primary groups. On one hand, these groups were important in the development of the personality (socialization) and ort the other hand they used to exercise primary control over the lives of the rural people.

DETERMINANT OF COMMUNITY ORGANIZATION

The community organizing process has been widely used in developed and developing countries to assist communities to recognize and address local health and social problems. In public health work, many disease prevention and health promotion goals can only be realized through the active involvement of community citizens, leaders, and organizations. Community organization is "a planned process to activate a community to use its own social structures and any available resources to accomplish community goals decided primarily by community representatives and generally consistent with local attitudes and values. Strategically planned interventions are organized by local groups or organizations to bring about intended social or health changes". It is sometimes referred to as community empowerment, capacity building, and partnership development.

An important outcome of this dynamic process is community ownership (i.e., by community leaders and institutions), which allows citizens to build skills and resources to effect community health change and to sustain such efforts over time. Experienced public health facilitators or community organizers often assist in this process, but control remains with local groups. The use of community organization strategies is not new in public health. In the early 1900s, for example, the National Citizens Committee on the Prevention of Tuberculosis worked closely with public health professionals and communities to control this infectious disease. In the twenty-first century, hundreds of community partnership groups are working locally to reduce the incidence of HIV/AIDS (human immunodeficiency virus/ acquired immunodeficiency syndrome), heart disease, child and spouse abuse, and other threats to community health. T. Lasater have described the use of church groups in mobilizing interventions for heart health. S. Verblen-Mortensen illustrated a multistage process of community organizing to empower citizens to enforce alcohol sale ordinances for minors in rural communities. Community participation requirements are often mandated by both public and private health-funding agencies.

Models of Practice in Community Organization

Should community organization be about collaboration among people sharing common interests or confrontation with those in power? This is a false dichotomy that ignores the context of the work. Several models of practice emerged in various contexts of community organization work (Rothman, 1995).

Social Planning: Social planning uses information and analysis to address substantive community issues such as education, child development, or environmental health. For example, planning councils or task forces engage (usually) professionals in setting goals and objectives, coordinating efforts, and reviewing goal attainment.

Social planning might occur in a context of either consensus or conflict about goals and means. For example, information about high rates of adolescent pregnancy, and factors that contribute to it, may help communities focus on the goal of preventing teen pregnancy, and even decisions about using controversial means such as sexuality education and enhanced access to contraceptives. Use of social planning helps build agreement on common results.

Social Action: Social action involves efforts to increase the power and resources of low-income or relatively powerless or marginalized people. For example, advocacy organizations, such as those for disability rights or tobacco control, often use social action approaches. They might arrange disruptive events -- including lawsuits, sit-ins, or boycotts -- to draw attention and focus to their concerns by those in power.

Organizers create events, such as a protest or strike, that those in positions of power (such as employers) can avoid or stop by coming to an agreement. For example, people with disabilities might stop picketing a business when it modifies policies that discriminate against people with disabilities. Or, a tobacco company might avoid a lawsuit by tobacco control advocates by eliminating advertising directed at minors. Social action tactics are used in lots of situations involving conflicting interests and imbalance in power; they usually take place when conventional negotiations aren't working.

Locality Development: Locality development is another way to get people to work together. It is the process of reaching group consensus about common concerns and collaborating in problem solving. For example, local residents in urban neighborhoods or rural communities may cooperate in defining local issues, such as access to job opportunities or better education, and in taking action to address the concerns.

Community Partnerships or Coalitions: There are many hybrid models that combine elements of the three approaches. For example, community partnerships or coalitions combine elements of social planning and locality development when people who share common concerns, such as child well -being or substance use, come together to address them. The goal of many coalitions is to change community conditions -- specific programs, policies, and practices -- that protect against or reduce risk for these concerns. These models, and their variations, may be implemented at local, state, regional, and even broader levels.

Organizational Change

One helpful way to think about effecting change at the community level is to consider the community as a dynamic system composed of several major sectors (business, government, schools, media). The people within each of these sectors interact with and influence each other, and when a change or alteration occurs in one sector it will have an impact on other sectors. A prohibition against secondhand smoke in public buildings, for example, may lead to a ban on smoking in restaurants. When health-oriented interventions are incorporated into many sectors of the community, the likelihood of a positive change increases. This focus on the total community system and its population is the hallmark of modern health-promotion programs. Mittelmark has summarized the results of diverse international community health-improvement programs and has found that community organization strategies are commonly utilized. Such techniques work regardless of whether the goal is behavioral in nature (e.g., to increase daily exercise among special groups) or whether the goal is to achieve health-policy changes (e.g., to eliminate tobacco billboard advertising near schools).

Useful Phases of Community Organization

In many community organization strategies, a five-stage process can be identified. What follows is a summary of the key factors and tasks in each stage. It should be noted that these stages are dynamic and overlapping. In addition, some tasks from an early stage may need to be repeated in later stages (e.g., updating a community resources inventory).

Conducting Community Analysis. A commitment to community participation in health campaigns requires above all else a knowledge of the assets, capacity, and history of a local community. This is accomplished by a careful "mapping" of the community to document its unique qualities, issues, and modes of decision making. This will provide the basis of an informed approach that realistically matches health goals with citizen readiness, expectations, and resources. Analysis is a critical first step in shaping the design of campaign interventions, and it is important to involve members of the community at this stage. The product of community analysis is an accurate profile that blends health and illness statistics with demographic, political, and sociocultural factors.

Design and Initiation of a Campaign. Following a community analysis and the identification of local priorities, the design aspects for a collaborative community campaign begin to emerge. A core group of citizens and professionals (with both public and private sectors represented) will usually begin the process of establishing a permanent organizational structure and making preliminary decisions about campaign objectives and interventions. This group may also write a mission statement and select a project coordinator. In organizing community partnerships, several structural forms (e.g., coalition, lead agency, citizen network) can be considered. B. Thompson (1999) provides a helpful discussion of the pros and cons of using various structures.

Campaign Implementation. Implementation turns theory and ideas into action, translating a mission into an effectively operating program. At this stage, organizations and citizens are mobilized and involved in the planning of a sequential set of activities aimed at accomplishing campaign objectives. Written plans with specific timelines have been shown to be a critical forerunner of success. Cost estimates should be included in the plan, along with monitoring and feedback strategies to measure progress. The key element in this stage is the careful determination and selection of priority intervention activities that can achieve maximum impact.

Program Refinement and Consolidation. During this stage both successes and problems in implementation are reviewed. Task forces of the local citizen organization need to determine any new directions or modifications for the program, including activities to maintain high levels of volunteer involvement. Efforts of organizers to have health program elements and interventions become more fully incorporated into the established structures of the community (e.g., exercise programs becoming a regular part of worksite culture) should continue in this phase as well.

Dissemination and Durability. In this last stage the strategic dissemination of information on project results and the finalization of plans for the durability of intervention efforts are the key considerations. Communities and citizens need to receive clear, succinct messages describing what has been accomplished and what continuing effort may be required. Such messages are reinforced when community leaders and local advocates are involved in their presentation. The local durability plan should include a vision for future health and social improvements and lay out a strategy to identify, recruit, and involve new people in current or future projects and community activities.

A common set of essential planning and organizing tasks has emerged from the many community mobilization and health promotion experiences of recent decades. These tasks include selecting broadly representative community participants and clearly identifying their decision-making authority, establishing an effective organizational structure, achieving mission clarity and realistic objectives, identifying community assets as well as resistance factors, establishing evaluation and tracking mechanisms early, managing and reinforcing volunteer involvement, conducting ongoing training for citizen intervention skills, recruiting a community organizer/facilitator with appropriate competencies and experience, and securing the necessary resources for the durability of program results.

Understanding (and Addressing) Opposition and Resistance

Societal problems sometime serve the interests of those in power. For example, a regulatory policy that permits environmental polluters to go unpunished serves the economic interests of businesses that pollute, and those elected and appointed officials who may benefit from campaign contributions or bribes. Similarly, the existence of drugs and violence may indirectly benefit elected officials since they often gain public support when they rant against perpetrators of drugs and violence. When those in authority oppose community action efforts (or ignore appeals for substantive intervention), there may be a disconnect between the public interest (common good) and the private interests of those with disproportionate influence.

Racial and ethnic tension and controversies have disrupted and destroyed many community organization efforts. Race and ethnic differences matter in this work. For instance, most African Americans share a common history of discrimination based on race, such as being followed more closely in a store or being ignored by cabs in a city. When you are part of an ethnic minority, people may assume they can think and speak for you, even if they have given no evidence that they care about you. Accordingly, understandable distrust of the "other" (the majority culture) may breed conflict that disrupts reciprocity and collaboration among people of different races and cultures.

Social action tactics, such as disruptive protest, have many detractors. Participating in (or supporting) protest can be dangerous, especially for those who remain in the community. For example, following a school boycott launched by residents of a low-income public housing project, it was my friend Myrtle Carter, a welfare mother and visible leader, who was subjected to police harassment. She was arrested and jailed for a minor parking violation while we outside organizers who were also part of the effort experienced only small inconveniences. Activists using protest tactics should expect those in power to retaliate, even by establishing criminal penalties for particularly effective disruptive actions such as strikes.

Less in-your-face social action approaches can produce a strong political base from which to make change. For example, the Industrial Areas Foundation (IAF) appeared to be relatively effective in attracting support (and avoiding opposition) for their causes. Consistent with the "I Ching" and other statements of Eastern philosophies, less direct or forceful actions may be less likely to beget opposition and adverse reaction.

Opposition and resistance may come in many forms. An analysis of the advocacy literature suggests different ways in which change efforts might be blunted. These include deflecting attention from the issue, delaying a response, denying the problem or request, discounting the problem or the group, deceiving the public, dividing and conquering the organization, appeasing leadership with short-term gains, discrediting group members, or destroying the group with slur campaigns through the media. Skilled practitioners can help group members recognize (and avoid or counteract) sources and modes of opposition.

Community organizations may respond to opposition with appropriate counteractions. Consider the case of local welfare officials (the opposition) who discount claims of a disability rights group that people with disabilities are being denied assistance unfairly. To counteract this opposition, disability advocates might document the number and kinds of cases denied, and use media advocacy about the consequences of denying eligibility to arouse public concern. Depending on the nature and form of opposition, appropriate counteractions may include reframing the issues, turning negatives into positives, going public with opponents' tactics, concentrating the organization's strength against the opponents' weakness, and knowing when to negotiate.

Opposition to change may be like an onion. Advocates should expect multiple layers of opposition and resistance to community and system change. For example, community organizations working for better schools may face resistance initially from school board officials; later, from local principals; and still later, from teachers. Peel off one layer, and another form of resistance or opposition may be there to protect vested interests.

Community and Governance: Organizational Dynamics

The Jewish polity as a whole, however, functions on several planes. The federal connections between local and countrywide communities and between Jewish communities around the world have also undergone important changes since World War ii, and the feedback has begun to have a significant effect on the countrywide and local communities involved.

Before the modern era, although there were no formal organizations that functioned on a worldwide basis to unite the various Jewish communities, the common allegiance to halakhic Judaism and reliance upon traditional Jewish law gave the Jewish people the constitutional unity it needed. During the modern era, this unity was shattered, and nothing comparable developed to replace it. By the end of the 19th century, all that there was in the way of an organized worldwide Jewish polity was an informal alliance and organizations of Jewish "aristocrats" in the Western world who had taken it upon themselves to try and defend Jewish interests and protect the rights of individual Jews, so as to aid in their emancipation. These inadequate arrangements effectively perished in World War i, when the world which encouraged that mode of community action came to an end.

Meanwhile, tentative steps in the direction of a reorganization more appropriate to the 20th century were beginning to be made. The World Zionist Organization and its member organizations, the *American Jewish Joint Distribution Committee, the B'nai B'rith, and later the *World Jewish Congress began to offer more routinized and less elitist means of tying Jews together on a worldwide basis. All together, they began to create an infrastructure for a new Jewish confederation in the making.

1. Communities founded or given new form:	
Hong Kong	Ryukyu Islands
India	Taiwan
Japan	Thailand
Philippines	
2. Communities abandoned or substantially reduced in size:	
Angola	Kenya
Burma	Malaysia
China	Singapore
Congo Republic	Uganda
Cyprus	Zambia
Indonesia	

After World War ii, the structure of the Jewish confederation underwent further adaptation. This strengthening of the organizational aspects of the worldwide Jewish polity was partly a consequence of the changes taking place in its constituent communities. The other crucial factor is the State of Israel. The trend has been clear: the concentration in Israel of the major decision-making organs of the Jewish confederation and the organizations that serve it and the routing of their decision-making procedures through Jerusalem, even as the structures, centered in Israel, have at the beginning of the new century been experiencing considerable strain. This trend has become particularly noticeable since the Six-Day War, after which the Israel government began to take very explicit steps to reorganize and strengthen the institutions and organizations of world Jewry by tying them closer to the state. Israel's greater ability, as an independent state, to deal with political matters and its great stake in strengthening the worldwide Jewish confederation has led it to assume this role.

Two major events – the Six-Day War in 1967 and the beginnings of the Soviet Jewry movement in 1963 – signaled that the American Jewish communal agenda would be more particularistic than it had been. Israel became the focal point of Jewish identification, the one Jewish phenomenon whose crucial importance is accepted by virtually all Jews and that has the ability to mobilize widespread public efforts in what is, after all, still a voluntary polity. Perhaps paradoxically, at the very moment that free individual choice in the matter of Jewish attachment has reached heights never previously attained, there has been a rediscovery of the Jewish polity, i.e., of the special political character of the Jewish community. In the first decade of the 21st century, however, new patterns in the American Jewish community – and especially in the consciousness of a younger cadre of Jews – had emerged. There was a diminution of the idea of a collective "community" as the meaning of Jewishness was increasingly defined in subjective individual constructs. American Jews found less meaning in formal Jewish organizations (except the local synagogue), political activity, philanthropic endeavors, and attachment to the state of Israel. The traditional institutions of community became less significant than they were to earlier generations of Jews in America. Because they feel that their identity as Jews is immutable, American Jews increasingly do not need the normative communal behaviors of the past in order to express their identity. This changing approach to "community" will have significant implications for the future of Jewish communal organizational structures, for communal fundraising, and for a range of communal involvements.

REFERENCES

1. Barton, D., & Tusting, K. (Eds.) (2005). Beyond communities of practice: Language power and social context. Learning in doing: social, cognitive and computational perspectives. New York: Cambridge University Press.
2. Bauman, Zygmunt. (2001). Community: Seeking Safety in an Insecure World. Cambridge, UK: Polity Press.
3. Hilde, Thomas C. (2004). "The Cosmopolitan Project: Does the Internet Have a Global Public Face?" In The Internet in Public Life, ed. Verna V. Gehring. Lanham, MD: Rowman and Littlefield.
4. Kim, J., & Kaplan, R. (2004). Physical and psychological factors in sense of community – new urbanist Kentlands and nearby orchard village. Environment and Behavior, 36(3), 313–340.
5. Longino, Helen E. (2002). The Fate of Knowledge. Princeton, NJ: Princeton University Press.
6. Paoli, L. (2003). Mafia brotherhoods: Organized crime, Italian style. Oxford: Oxford University Press.
7. Porter, C. E. (2006). A typology of virtual communities: A multi-disciplinary foundation for future research. Journal of Computer-Mediated Communication, 10(1), 631–5171.

CHAPTER 2

SOCIAL THOUGHT AND MOVEMENT

INTRODUCTION

Social thought is a philosophical and intellectual ideas of a person or persons regarding to a particular time, place and about the growth, development and decay of human societies. Social thought is a current social thinking about the structure and functions of a social system.

Order, purity, clarity: such were the Classical ideals. They had dominated traditional theology as represented by its last great master, Jacques-Bénigne Bossuet. Bossuet believed in the unity of knowledge as so many branches of Christian truth. His compelling logic and magisterial writing had a strong influence. When, however, the hypotheses were tested and found wanting, the very comprehensiveness of the system ensured that its collapse was complete. Bossuet had encouraged Richard Simon when he set out to refute Protestantism through historical study of the Bible but was shocked when he saw where it led. Inevitably, scholarship revealed inconsistencies and raised questions about the way that the Bible should be treated: if unreliable as history, then how sound was the basis for theology? Simon's works were banned in 1678, but Dutch printers ensured their circulation. No censorship could prevent the development of historical method, which was making a place for itself in the comprehensive search for truth. With Edward Gibbon (himself following the example of the 17th-century giants of church history), Jean Mabillon, and Louis Tillemont historians were to become more skilled and scrupulous in the use of evidence. The philosophes characteristically believed that history was becoming a science because it was subject to philosophical method. It also was subject to the prevailing materialist bias, which is why, scholarly though individual writers like David Hume might be, the Enlightenment was in some respects vulnerable to fresh insights about man—such as those of Étienne Bonnot de Condillac, who believed that human beings could be molded for their own good—and further research into the past—which, for Claude-Adrien Helvétius, was simply the worthless veneration of ancient laws and customs.

ESSENTIALS OF SOCIAL THOUGHT

Most social thought in the sense of group thought about social questions has contributed little to knowledge. Discussion-group thinking illustrates social thinking on its higher levels, but discussion-group thinking is not yet extensive. However, a great deal may be expected from it in the future. In fact in countries that preserve freedom of speech, it promises to become ultimately the main type of thought.

The thinking of persons about social life falls into three categories:

1. That involving the advancement of human groups as groups.
2. That referring to the manipulation of human beings to the gain of a special clique or group.
3. That which aims to analyze the underlying social processes and laws irrespective of the effects of such analyses or the uses to which they are put.

The history of Social thought rises out of the beginnings of human struggle on earth and with jagged edges extends along the full sweep of the changing historical horizon. It finds expression through some of the world's best minds. Our quest will bring us in contact with the most vital moments of the world's most valuable thinkers.

Social thought usually finds its initial expression during social crises. When "prosperity" reigns and people are – in general, satisfied, new social thought is at ebb tide. But when social conditions are marked by gross injustices or when social changes come rapidly due to inventions, wars or other basic disturbances, then thinking about social life and problems is highly stimulated and new ideas or systems of ideas that is ideologies are originated.

Social thought is that branch of thought which is primarily concerned with man's general social life and its problems as created, expressed and endured by human interrelations and interactions. E.S. Bogardus has defined social thought by saying that, "Social thought is thinking about social problems by one or few people here and there in human history or at present."

Social Thought in Social Interaction

Sociality or sociability has been the central problem in sociological discussions. "Why man depends on society?" is a pertinent question for which we have different and even contradictory explanations. Each aspect of man's social life must have been the result of at least some people's experiences, mutual adjustments, and experiments. People must have been directly or indirectly, and explicitly or implicitly thinking about the ways in which they could share their feelings and emotions, problems and challenges, miseries and maladies, etc., from the very beginning. They must have also tried on their own the ways of facing the problems and challenges of life, to secure some amount of stability for their social life and contentment for their individual mind. The thought that they have entertained in this regard, no matter how irrational and unscientific it is, could be referred to as "social thought."

Definition of the term "Social Thought"

In simple words, it can be said that "social thought" essentially refers to the thought concerning the social life and activities of man. Sociologists have given their own definitions of social thought among which the following may be cited.

*Bogardus:*Social thought is thinking about social problems by one or a few persons here and there in human history or at the present."

*Rollin Chambliss:*Social thought is concerned with human beings in their relations with their fellows."

*H.E. Jenson:*Social thought is "the totality of man's thought about his relationship and obligations to his fellowmen.

*William P. Scott:*Social thought refers to any relatively systematic attempt to theories about society and social life, whether it be classical or modern, scientific or unscientific."

Characteristics of Social Thought

Social Thought is Societal Thought:

Social thought is basically the thought regarding societal issues or matters. It is concerned with the ways in which people live together and face collectively their problems and challenges. These thoughts may themselves have solutions to these problems.

Social Thought is Not the Sum Total of the Thoughts of all the Members of Society

Social thought has evolved out of the capacity for critical and analytical thinking of a few scholars, rationalists, scientists and philosophers. People of average intelligence can hardly enrich the existing social thought.

Only a handful of people can delve deep into the social matters, events, and problems and form opinions and theories about them. Bogardus thus comments: "However, the developing and perfecting of new ideologies are usually the work of scholars, somewhat removed from the turmoil of the hour. Social thought thus is the product of social crisis and of scholarly analysis and synthesis.

Social Thought need not necessarily be Scientific Always

Social thought touches upon various aspects of our social life, experiences, conclusions, opinions, assessments, valuations, etc. All these cannot be put to scientific tests to assess their validity and dependability. In spite of this deficiency they have their own practical importance.

Social Thought is not the same everywhere

Social thought has been immensely influenced by factors such as time, place, environment and conditions. Social thought normally arises in part from the nature of the prevailing social conditions. To understand it properly the student must know the times which furnish the setting for it. "A thorough going knowledge of the culture and of the social, economic, political and religious standards of a people is a minimum essential for a social thought."

Every Human Community has given its Own Contribution to the Development of Social Thought

Social thought is not the monopoly of any particular community. At the same time all the nations or communities have not contributed equally to its enrichment. For example, the ancient Indian, Chinese, Egyptian, Babylonian, and Hebrew civilizations of the East and the ancient Greek and the Roman civilizations of the West, have given commendable contributions to the realm of social thought. The rural and the tribal people also have played their role in the enrichment of social thought.

Social Thought is Continuous in its Development

Social thought has been found to be consistent in its development. As Bogardus has pointed out, "the history of social thought rises out of the beginnings of human struggle on earth and with jogged edges extends along the full sweep of the changing historical horizons."

Social Crises or Hardships have always provided Motivation for the General Social Thought

Social thought usually finds its initial expression during social crises. When "prosperity" reigns and people are, in general, satisfied, new social thought is at ebb tide. But when social conditions are marked by gross injustices or when social changes come rapidly due to inventions, wars, or other basic disturbances, the thinking about social life and problems is highly stimulated and new ideas or systems of ideas, that is, ideologies, are originated.

Other Characteristics

(i) Social thought though continuous is very slow and gradual in its development. We do not find fast developments taking place in this field as in the realm of physical sciences.

(ii) Major portion of the social thought is not found to be preserved in the form of but in the unwritten forms such as folklores, folksongs, legends, myths, folktales and so on.

(iii) "Social thought is abstract" – says Bogardus. All thinking is abstract and social thought is no exception to this general rule.

(iv) Social thought has not always been utilitarian and beneficial to mankind. It has been, at times, abused by some people to subserve their own ends. Example:

(i) The theory of inborn superiority of the Aryan Race advocated by Nazis of Germany,

(ii) The ideologies such as Gandhianism, socialism, secularism, etc.

Development of Social Thought

Social thought is not something that emerges suddenly or abruptly. Its development is slow and gradual. Old thoughts form the basis for the new ones. New thoughts do not completely negate the old ones.

Many a times we find the combination of the old and the new. Social thought in its historical development can be stated to have undergone at least four important stages namely:

(1) Stage of folklore,

(2) Stage of Social Philosophy,
(3) Stage of Social Theory, and
(4) The Stage of Social Sciences.

The Stage of Folklore

Pre-literate people were also inquisitive. They thought about the dramatic phases of life, and they sought their own explanation. Their imagination worked out only supernatural explanations. They reasoned about the daily occurrences of life in concrete and personal terms.

Archaeological records indicate that the pre-literate people had a simple and crude awareness which had its own social implications. Early mythologies speak of the importance of social bonds which early people had developed among themselves.

The proverbs of the primitive people give us some idea about social property and social responsibility. Folktales, folksongs, etc., give us ideas about the primitive man's family, life, his religious beliefs, social organizations such as clans and so on.

There are enough proofs to say that primitive man's mind entertained social thinking. Communal property was the outcome of communal thinking. Group dances, feasts, festivals, building enterprises, celebrations, etc., denote a social spirit.

Warfare, which they engaged in, indicates tribal loyalty and group spirit. Folkways of these people mirror their notions of societal welfare. All these things reveal the beginnings of social thought. Though it appears premature today, it had its own prominence then.

The Stage of Social Philosophy

Just as human society proceeded from simplicity to complexity, human thinking also started becoming more complex. Early people started thinking in terms of facing the challenges in a better manner, and finding solutions to the social problems more efficiently. In their efforts to do so, their thinking style underwent a change. It got ascended from the stage of folklore to the stage of social philosophy.

In the stage of social philosophy, large number of poets, philosophers, moralists, spiritual leaders, metaphysical thinkers, social visionaries, social reformers and others expressed their views, and enriched human thought.

Their views influenced the ways of life then and also of the future generations. The views of Manu on Varnashrama system, the opinions of Kautilya on politics, the beliefs of Confucius on ideal family, and practical morals, etc., could be cited here as examples.

The Stage of Social Theory

In the stage of social theory, there is scope for discussion, logic, analysis, appreciation, acceptance, rejection and so on. The views or ideas expressed or advocated by a philosopher or scholar need not necessarily be accepted by all as though it is "divine", "unchangeable" and "ultimate." The views of Manu, Aristotle, Cicero, Confucius and others were taken for granted in the beginning. As years passed on, social theoreticians like John Locke, Thomas Hobbes, Rousseau, Karl Marx, Adam Smith, Ferguson, Machiavelli, Montesquieu, and a host of others established their own theories regarding human society and its dynamics.

Jeremy Betham's "Utilitarianism", Thomas More's "Utopianism", Spencer's "theory of social evolution", Marxian "theory of classless society", Huntington, Lombroso and other social geographer's "theory of geographic determinism" can be mentioned here as examples.

The Stage of Social Sciences

It is very difficult to say when exactly the stage of social sciences began, because different social sciences emerged at different times. Example: Political science and history are pretty old social sciences, whereas anthropology, psychology and sociology are quite new.

The success attained and the progress registered in the field of natural sciences also provided inspiration for the social thinkers to emulate the same in the field of social sciences.

The methods that helped the physical sciences to attain success were also borrowed to understand and analyses the social world in a scientific manner. This new approach added precision, credibility and dependability to the social sciences. Most of the social sciences have now obtained a stage in which they stand on their own, have their own field of study, and pursue their own approach.

SOCIOLOGY AND SOCIAL THOUGHT

Sociology and Social Thought – The terms such as "social thought", "sociology" or "sociological thought" or "social theory", "sociological theory" though are not one and the same, are closely interrelated. It is true that roots of sociology are to be found in social thought and social philosophy. Social thought itself provided the stimulus for the establishment of sociology.

Sociology and Social Thought: Difference in Meaning

Sociology is the science of society. Its main purpose is to study human life, activities and relations in a scientific way. It is an independent science by itself and applies scientific method to its studies.

Whereas social thought is nothing but societal-thought; it is the totality of man's thought about his relationships with his fellowmen. According to Bogardus, it is co-equal with social problems. As and when social problems cropped up, the social thought sprang up. Social thought is a kind of thought and it need not necessarily be classical or systematic in its nature.

Sociological Study is more scientific whereas Social Thought is more general in Nature

Sociology has become a relatively well established social science. It is able to make a scientific analysis of human society, its structure, function, organization, institutional network, changes, challenges, and problems and so on. Sociology is now recognized as an empirical and a rational science. It tries to be "value-free" in its approach and objective in its findings.

Social thought, on the contrary, is bound by the values, norms and the expectations of the people of a particular epoch. There is no insistence on it to be scientific. Plato's "idealism", Hindus' concept of "Rama Rajya", Marx's "Communism", Bentham's "Utilitarianism" or Gandhiji's "Sarvodaya", etc. for example, represent high thoughts, but they are not considered as scientific.

They are either regarded as value-based or imaginary or even ideological. Social thought is more based on logic, imagination, intuition, and capacity of creative thinking, whereas sociology is based on science, rationality, empiricism and reality.

Sociology has a Limited Range while Social Thought is More Pervasive

Sociological thoughts or theories have limited range. They are applicable to limited contexts. They contain issues or themes which are basically social in nature. On the contrary, the scope of social thought is wider. It is all-inclusive, because it may incorporate in itself knowledge that is not only social but also spiritual, moral, political, economic, psychological, philosophical, and so on.

Social Thought is Ancient Whereas Sociology is Modern

Social thought is old when compared with either sociology or sociological thought. The history of social thought is very ancient and it begins from pre-historic times, whereas the history of sociology and sociological thought is very short; it begins from the time of Auguste Comte.

Other Differences

(a) Social thought adopts no scientific criterion of validity whereas in the case of sociology or sociological thought there is definite validity criterion.

(b) Only the people with specialized skills and training can make contributions to the realm of sociology whereas, any knowledgeable person whether he is a scientist or an artist, a philosopher or a social reformer, a psychologist or an educationist, an uneducated man or an educated one, an ordinary man or a genius, can enrich the field of social thought.

(c) Thinkers who contributed to the realm of social thought were known as social reformers, social philosophers, social visionaries, social revolutionaries and so on, but not as sociologists. The era of sociology and sociologists began only in the middle of the 18th century.

Formation of Sociological Thought

Having grown up during the aftermath of the French Revolution, Auguste Comte was the first to use the term sociology as a way of studying the world in terms of society. Along with the industrial revolution in England during the 18th century and the rise of urbanization and mass social change, thinkers such as Comte, Durkheim and Marx began to realize the need to study society in all its dynamic nature. This period of history is often described as 'the great transformation', which led to the emergence of sociology. Around the late 18th century an intellectual period known as 'the Enlightenment' challenged many of the established orders of society from an analytical and scientific perspective. Following French revolution, the citizens of France were granted new legal rights, a broad centralized education system and a new system of inheritance. It could be argued that the intellectual revolution known as 'the Enlightenment' laid the foundation for the French revolution which created significant social change. It brought about an ideology which believed that scientific and historical study should be looked at and incorporated into a philosophical perspective. Enlightenment figures such as Charles Montesquieu, one of the pioneers of social science, saw humanity as something that develops from infancy to maturity with conflict in between the different stages. He also believed that the Enlightenment could be the beginning of a great period of human development, as science was being applied to humanity. This could be described as the birth of sociology and of social scientific thought.

The Enlightenment period coincided with the increase in knowledge in other scientific fields such as life sciences. Darwin's studies on evolution challenged the old established ideas of the church. The concept of 'Social Darwinism' was based on the ideology that society will gradually improve on the basis that the 'fittest' will be the most successful and therefore 'survive'. The period of the late 18th century and early 19th century contributed significantly to the emergence of sociology due to the significant revolutions that occurred during this time.

The Enlightenment was in many respects a renaissance of scientific thought and signalled the beginning of sociology as a discipline. It changed the way philosophers looked at the world by giving a scientific and analytical approach to their theories. This intellectual revolution made way for the French revolution, and is thought by some to be the most important political event of modern times. It granted citizens individual freedoms and removed old established orders such as the church and crown, and gave people a new perspective of the world and the society in which they live. The French revolution also led to the emergence of Nationalism which changed the way many people viewed the state as whole.

The industrial revolution saw massive changes in society by the destruction of the feudal system and the establishment of capitalism, which is a key area of discussion within sociology. Urbanisation and industrialisation led to the emergence of the working class as a large and powerful body, which led to the birth of Marxism, and gave people a new perspective and relationship with the society they lived in. Thus French revolution and Industrial revolution were events integral to the emergence of sociology and social sciences.

Social background of Sociology

Sociology emerged from enlightenment thought, shortly after the French Revolution, as a positivist science of society. Its genesis owed to various key movements in the philosophy of science and the philosophy of knowledge. Modern academic sociology emerged as a reaction to modernity, capitalism, urbanization, rationalization, and secularization. Within a relatively brief period the discipline greatly expanded and diverged, both topically and methodologically, particularly as a result of reactions against empiricism.

French Revolution

The French revolution challenged and overthrew the old order of society. It was a revolution that strengthened the state which aimed to represent the will of the people. It is important to recognise that the political and cultural climate that existed before the revolution was dominated by the church and the monarchy.

The French Revolution was a period of radical social and political upheaval in France that had a major impact on France and throughout the rest of Europe. The absolute monarchy that had ruled France for centuries collapsed in three years. French society underwent drastic transformation. Feudal, aristocratic and religious privileges were removed from the society. Old of monarchy, aristocracy, and religious authority were overthrown by new Enlightenment principles of equality and citizenship. The Ancien Régime, the aristocratic, social and political system established in France from approximately the 15th century to the 18th century was identified as one of the causes of the Revolution. Economic factors included hunger and malnutrition after several years of poor grain harvests. Bad harvests rising food prices, and an inadequate transportation system that hindered the shipment of bulk foods from rural areas to large population centers contributed greatly to the destabilization of French society in the years leading up to the Revolution. France's inefficient and antiquated financial system was unable to manage the national debt, which was both caused and aggravated by the burden of an inadequate system of taxation. Meanwhile, the royal court at Versailles was seen as being isolated from, and indifferent to, the hardships of the lower classes.

Many other factors involved resentments and aspirations given focus by the rise of Enlightenment ideals. These included resentment of royal absolutism, resentment by peasants, laborers and the bourgeoisie toward the traditional privileges possessed by the nobility, resentment of the Church's influence over public policy and institutions, aspirations for freedom of religion, resentment of aristocratic bishops by the poorer rural clergy; aspirations for social, political and economic equality, and republicanism.

The French Revolution began in 1789 with the convocation of the Estates-General in May. The first year of the Revolution saw members of the Third Estate proclaiming the Tennis Court Oath in June, the assault on the Bastille in July, the passage of the Declaration of the Rights of Man and of the Citizen in August, and an epic march on Versailles that forced the royal court back to Paris in October. The next few years were dominated by tensions between various liberal assemblies and a right-wing monarchy which tried to resist major reforms.

A republic was proclaimed in September 1792 and King Louis XVI was executed the next year. Internally, popular sentiments radicalized the Revolution significantly, culminating in the rise of Maximilien Robespierre and the Jacobins and virtual dictatorship by the Committee of Public

Safety during the Reign of Terror from 1793 until 1794 during which between 16,000 and 40,000 people were killed. After the fall of the Jacobins and the execution of Robespierre, the Directory assumed control of the French state in 1795 and held power until 1799, when it was replaced by the Consulate under Napoleon Bonaparte.

The modern era has unfolded in the shadow of the French Revolution. The growth of republics and liberal democracies, the spread of secularism, the development of modern ideologies, and the invention of total war originated during the Revolution. Subsequent events that can be traced to the Revolution include the Napoleonic Wars, two separate restorations of monarchy (Bourbon Restoration and July Monarchy), and two additional revolutions (1830 and 1848) as modern France took shape.

Decline of Estate System

French Society was divided into three classes or "estates". The first estate was the clergy, the second estate, nobility and the third estate, the commoners. Each estate was granted an equal voice in an advisory legislative group called the Estates General who would meet whenever there was a need to advise the king.

The estate system was division of three different groups. The first estate was made up of the clergy (Church). Although the clergy amounted to no more than a hundred thousand men, they owned about 1/10th of the land in France. The clergy enjoyed many privileges. The second estate was made up of nobles and kings. They lived rich lives and taxed peasants to avoid paying their taxes. The power of this class was based on the feudal seigniorial system. They served as councillors to the royalty, diplomats and governors. They enjoyed rights of local justice, village surveillance, and monopoly over hunting and the maintenance of wells and wine presses. The most important differentiation between the nobles and the non-nobles was that the former enjoyed immunity from direct taxation and various other taxes. The traditional nobility held political authority on the basis of landed wealth and got this as a reward to the military aid given to the king. The Third estate was everybody else. They were workers and farmers. The third estate was taxed heavily making the poor poorer and this helped the rich stay rich.

All three of these estates had influence on the French Revolution; without them, the revolution never would have existed. It was because of the oppression of the higher classes that the lower class rose up and stood up to them. The third estate was suppressed and delineated in society. The third estate reacted against this situation whereas, the other two acted as if things were perfect in their present state.

Emergence of Capitalism and Establishment of Democracy in Europe

Capitalism in Europe followed the stage of feudalism. Under feudalism, land was the main means of production. Land was owned by feudal lords, and a large number of peasants bound to the land worked in the farms. There were also a small number of artisans too. The surplus product of these peasants and artisans was extracted by the feudal lords. The basic conflict in feudal society, the conflict that propelled society forward, was between these direct producers and the landowning lords. In order to maintain their class power, the feudal lords tried to maximize the rent they extracted from the peasants. The peasants struggled in various ways to end this extraction of the surplus.

In the course of these struggles many peasants were able to relax the stranglehold of the lords, to keep some surplus for themselves, and to improve and extend their cultivation. Additionally some artisans and merchants became wealthy enough to buy land in their own right, breaking the lords' monopoly on land ownership. And so another process began: some producers improved their production faster than others, and were able to accumulate some capital and over time there developed a class of relatively prosperous farmers along with the poor peasants. This polarization helped lay the basis for the wage labor that would be needed under capitalism.

Over the centuries of feudal society, as the surplus grew to some extent, trade also grew. Around that trade grew towns where merchants enjoyed some political power. The money power of the towns, the relative political freedom of the towns, and the contact with ideas from distant lands helped to create changes in religious doctrines and philosophy, mathematics and science. The associated change in the world-view of the intelligentsia has been termed the Enlightenment. According to the new ideology, the force of human Reason replaced established authority, such as the Church and the King. The State itself was now no longer seen as God-given, but the product of Man, a 'social contract' among men for their benefit. That implied that if the State were not functioning for their benefit, it was justified to overthrow it and replace it with a new one.

Under feudalism, most household requirements were made at home. A limited number of goods were produced for the market by artisans/craftsmen employing, say, two or three men, working with their own tools and raw materials. But as trade grew, merchants, seeking to increase production, began supplying materials and purchasing the finished goods from the craftsmen; the latter largely lost their independence and were now working for the merchant. However, what definitively marked the emergence of capitalism was not simply production for the market, but the system in which all the means of production – the tools/machines, the raw materials, and the location – belonged to the capitalist, and the laborer had nothing to sell but his/her own labor power. Feudalism had needed the use of custom, law and force to extract the surplus from the producers, but under capitalism it was no longer necessary to rely on such non-economic methods. The worker had the choice of working for the capitalist or starving. Surplus extraction now was carried out by the impersonal laws of the market. The new capitalists demanded the abolition of monopolies and privileges in trade and industry on which merchant capital had fattened under feudalism, and thus established free competition at home.

Intellectual background of Sociology

The discipline of Sociology was heavily influenced by the enlightenment period. The Enlightenment was a period of intellectual development and change in philosophical thought beginning in the eighteenth century. Enlightenment thinkers sought to combine reason with empirical research on the model of Newtonian science. They tried to produce highly systematic bodies of thought that made rational sense and that could be derived from real-world observation. They were of the opinion that the social world could be controlled using reason and research. They also believed that traditional social values and institutions were irrational and inhibited human development. Their ideas conflicted with traditional religious bodies of feudalism. They placed their faith instead in the power of the individual's capacity to reason. Early sociology also maintained a faith in empiricism and rational inquiry

Scientific Revolution

The Scientific Revolution changed the way people saw the world. The movement helped shape the attitudes that made the scientific advances of the modern world possible. Many new ideas were developed about humanity's place in the universe and the universe itself. Throughout Europe many individuals began to critically analyse the validity of existing theories. The philosophers and intellectuals of this period had immense faith in the power of human reason. The Scientific Revolution was enormously impressed by Isaac Newton's theory of gravity. The scientists of this period tried to discover the laws underlying all of nature and society. A greater importance was placed on the discovery of truth through the observation of nature rather than through the study of religious sources.

The rise of the new science progressively undermined the ancient geocentric conception of the cosmos. The dramatic success of the new science in explaining the natural world promoted philosophy to an independent force with the power and authority to challenge the old and construct the new, in the realms both of theory and practice, on the basis of its own principles.

Freedom of thought

Freedom of thought is the freedom of an individual to hold a viewpoint, or thought, regardless of anyone else's view. The suppression of freedom of thought is a prominent characteristic of totalitarian and authoritarian regimes, while freedom of thought is one of the fundamental principles of most democracies. Freedom of thought helped in the development of revolutionary ideas and thought

The Enlightenment may be characterized as a catalyst for the development of particular styles of social thought. It does not represent a set of ideas which can be clearly demarcated, extracted and presented as a list of essential definitions, but represents a general shift in thought. These ideas, when fused with governmental practice, produced some core themes.

- A concept of freedom based upon an autonomous human subject who is capable of acting in a conscious manner.
- The pursuit of a universal and foundational 'truth' gained through a correspondence of ideas with social and physical reality.
- A belief in the natural sciences as the correct model for thinking about the social and natural world over, for example, theology and metaphysics.
- The accumulation of systematic knowledge within the progressive unfolding of history.

Collectively, these changes acted as catalysts for the scientific study of human societies.

Efforts to Interpret Social change

Sociology and other social sciences emerged from a common tradition of reflection of social phenomena. The development of sociology and its current contexts has to be understood in the contexts of the major changes of the modern world. Sociology originated in 18th century philosophy, political economy and cultural history The major conditions, societal changes and revolutions that gave rise to the emergence and development of sociology as an academic science include the Industrial Revolution , French Revolution, the Enlightenment and advances in natural sciences and technology. These revolutions had brought about significant societal changes and disturbances in the ways of society. Since sociology was born in the midst of the great socio- political and economic and technological changes of the western world, it is said to be the science of modern society. The pioneering sociologists were very much concerned about the great changes that were taking place and they felt that the existing sciences could not help understand, explain, analyses and interpret the fundamental laws that govern the social phenomena. Thus sociology was born out of these revolutionary contexts and events.

Need for a new Social Science

We need social science because social processes shape human destinies. If we are to take control of our future, we need to understand society as much as we need to understand the atmosphere, the earth, and other things. Social practices are creating new realities in society. Social science, concerned with this reality, has to be empirical. It tries to discover and describe the way things are in the world. The accuracy of its statements matters, its claims have to be testable and, ultimately, tested. The social sciences developed as a field of study during the nineteenth century. Social science helped people understand the consequences and application of the new technologies.

The precursor to Industrial revolution, French revolution and the American War of Independence was the period of 'Renaissance' which started in Italy in 15th century and later moved northwards sweeping all of Europe. The period of Renaissance changed the complete outlook of the society in the social, cultural, political and economic field. It brought about ideological changes in almost all the spheres. The 'New Scientific Method' led to various discoveries and innovation. It was the 'New Scientific Method' which ultimately gave rise to Industrial revolution. It was marked by change from 'Subsistence society' to 'Monetary society' or Capitalist society. Mass production of factory goods changed the complete social structure. But the social changes were so rapid that society was not able to catch up with the changes. The result was huge amount of unrest in society which threatened social stability. Peasants moving to urban areas, growth of cities, adoption of nuclear family etc. were all opposed to traditions existing prior to Industrial society. It lead to rising number of suicides and violence. Thus there was an urgent need to understand the cause of these social changes, and to provide some meaningful explanation for the increased problems. No other discipline was catering to the newly developed problems. These changed scenarios resulted in the rise of 'Science of Society'- Sociology.

Enlightenment

The Age of Enlightenment was a cultural movement of intellectuals whose purpose was to reform society and advance knowledge. It promoted science and intellectual interchange and opposed superstition. The intellectual movement called "The Enlightenment" is usually associated with the 18th century, but its roots in fact go back much further. They believed that human reason could be used to combat ignorance, superstition, and tyranny and to build a better world.

The Enlightenment is the period in the history of western thought and culture, stretching roughly from the mid-decades of the seventeenth century through the eighteenth century, characterized by dramatic revolutions in science, philosophy, society and politics. Enlightenment thought laid the foundation of the French Revolution, in which the traditional hierarchical political and social orders were replaced by a political and social order characterized by the Enlightenment ideals of freedom and equality for all. The Enlightenment begins with the scientific revolution of the sixteenth and seventeenth centuries.

The Enlightenment is associated with the French thinkers of the mid-decades of the eighteenth century who were known as "philosophes" included Voltaire, Diderot, Montesquieu, etc. The philosophes constitute an informal society of men of letters who collaborate on a loosely defined project of Enlightenment centered around the project of the Encyclopedia. The Enlightenment wasrelated to ideas about what the human mind was capable of, and what could be achieved through deliberate action and scientific methodology. Many of the new, enlightened ideas were political in nature. Intellectuals began to consider the possibility that freedom and democracy were the fundamental rights of all people. Egalitarianism became the dominant value and it meant fair treatment for all people, regardless of background.

In Europe, Voltaire and Jean-Jacques Rousseau were the torchbearers of Enlightenment literature and philosophy. Rousseau was a strong advocate for social reform of all kinds. Rousseau's work on behalf of social empowerment and democracy would remain influential long after his passing. Espousing similar political positions, Voltaire employed dry wit and sarcasm to make convincing arguments for reform. Together, Voltaire and Rousseau are the most well-known of a collective of European writers who propagated Enlightenment philosophy.

Contributions of Rousseau

Rousseau's most important work is The Social Contract, which outlines the basis for a legitimate political order within a framework of classical republicanism. The treatise begins with the dramatic opening lines, "Man is born free, and everywhere he is in chains. Those who think themselves the masters of others are indeed greater slaves than they."

Rousseau claimed that people were in the state of nature which was a primitive condition without law or morality. Human beings left the state of nature for the benefits and necessity of cooperation. As society developed, division of labor and private property required the human race to adopt institutions of law. Man is prone to be in frequent competition with his fellow men while also becoming increasingly dependent on them. This threatens both his survival and his freedom. According to Rousseau, by joining together into civil society through the social contract and abandoning their claims of natural right, individuals can both preserve themselves and remain free. This is because submission to the authority of the general will of the people as a whole guarantees individuals against being subordinated to the wills of others and also ensures that they obey themselves because they are, collectively, the authors of the law.

The stated aim of the Social Contract is to determine a legitimate political authority. In order to accomplish more and remove himself from the state of nature, man must enter into a Social Contract with others. In this social contract, everyone will be free because all individuals exercise the same amount of rights and same duties are imposed on all. Rousseau also argues that it is illogical for a man to surrender his freedom for slavery; and so, the participants must be free. Furthermore, although the contract imposes new laws, especially those safeguarding and regulating property, a person can exit it at any time and is again as free as when he was born. Rousseau says that any administration, whatever form it takes, should be divided into two parts. First, there must be the sovereign who represents the general will and is the legislative power within the state. The second division is that of the government, being distinct from the sovereign. Rousseau claims that the size of the territory to be governed often decides the nature of the government. Since a government is only as strong as the people, the larger the territory the more strength the government must be able to exert over the population. In his view, a monarchical government is able to wield the most power over the people since it has to devote less power to itself, while a democracy the least. In general, the larger the bureaucracy, the more power required for government discipline. When Rousseau uses the word democracy he refers to a direct democracy. Rousseau argues that small city-states are the form of nation in which freedom can best flourish. For any state large enough to require intermediaries between the people and the government, an elected aristocracy may be preferable, and in very large states a benevolent monarch; but even monarchical rule, to be legitimate, must be subordinate to the sovereign rule of law.

Contributions of Montesquieu

Montesquieu's Spirit of the Laws is one of the outstanding works of modern social thought. He constructed a naturalistic account of the various forms of government and of the causes that made them and that affected their development. He also explained how governments might be preserved from corruption. He saw despotism, in particular, as a standing danger for any government not already despotic, and argued that it could best be prevented by a system in which different bodies exercised legislative, executive, and judicial power, and in which all those bodies were bound by the rule of law.

Montesquieu's aim in The Spirit of the Laws is to explain human laws and social institutions. Unlike physical laws, which are, according to Montesquieu, instituted and sustained by God, positive laws and social institutions are created by fallible human beings who are "subject ... to ignorance and error, hurried away by a thousand impetuous passions" In his view, the key to understanding different laws and social systems is to recognize that they should be adapted to a variety of different factors, and cannot be properly understood unless one considers them in this light. Specifically, laws should be adapted "to the people for whom they are framed. When we consider legal and social systems in relation to various factors, Montesquieu believes that we will find that many laws and institutions that had seemed puzzling are in fact quite meaningful. Understanding our laws will also help us to see which aspects of them are genuinely in need of reform, and how these reforms might be accomplished. If lawmakers understand the relation between laws and conditions of their countries and the principles of their governments, they will be in a better position to carry out such reforms without undermining the governments they seek to improve.

Montesquieu says that there are three types of governments: republican governments, monarchies; and despotisms. The republican government can be either democratic or aristocratic. Each form of government has a principle and each can be corrupted if its principle is undermined or destroyed.

In a democracy, the people are sovereign. They may govern through ministers, or be advised by a senate, but they must have the power of choosing their ministers and senators for themselves. The principle of democracy is political virtue, by which Montesquieu means "the love of the laws and of our country" including its democratic constitution. The form of a democratic government makes the laws governing suffrage and voting fundamental. A democracy must educate its citizens to identify their interests with the interests of their country, and should have censors to preserve its mores. Its territory should be small, so that it is easy for citizens to identify with it, and make it difficult for private interests to emerge.

Democracies can be corrupted in two ways: by what Montesquieu calls "the spirit of inequality" and "the spirit of extreme equality". The spirit of inequality arises when citizens no longer identify their interests with the interests of their country, and therefore seek both to advance their own private interests at the expense of their fellow citizens, and to acquire political power over them. The spirit of extreme equality arises when the people are no longer content to be equal as citizens, but want to be equal in every respect. Eventually the government will cease to function, and democracy will be replaced by despotism.

In an aristocracy, one part of the people governs the rest. The principle of an aristocratic government is moderation, the virtue which leads those who govern in an aristocracy to restrain themselves both from oppressing the people and from trying to acquire excessive power over one another. In an aristocracy, the laws should be designed protect this spirit of moderation. To do so, they must do three things. First, the laws must prevent the nobility from abusing the people. Second, the laws should disguise as much as possible the difference between the nobility and the people, so that the people feel their lack of power as little as possible. Finally, the laws should try to ensure equality among the nobles themselves, and among noble families. When they fail to do so, the nobility will lose its spirit of moderation, and the government will be corrupted.

In a monarchy, one person governs "by fixed and established laws" According to Montesquieu, these laws "necessarily suppose the intermediate channels through which power flows. These 'intermediate channels' are such subordinate institutions as the nobility and an independent judiciary; and the laws of a monarchy should therefore be designed to preserve their power. The principle of monarchical government is honor. The chief task of the laws in a monarchy is to protect the subordinate institutions that distinguish monarchy from despotism. A monarchy is corrupted when the monarch either destroys the subordinate institutions that constrain his will, or decides to rule arbitrarily, without regard to the basic laws of his country, or debases the honors at which his citizens might aim. In a functioning monarchy, personal ambition and a sense of honor work together.

In despotic states "a single person directs everything by his own will. Without laws to check him, and with no need to attend to anyone who does not agree with him, a despot can do whatever he likes. The principle of despotism is fear situation of a despot's subjects is genuinely terrifying. Education is unnecessary in despotism. Because property is not secure in a despotic state, commerce will not flourish, and the state will be poor.

Contributions of Saint Simone

Another important Enlightenment philosopher was Claud Henry de Saint Simon, who fell in-between enlightenment and counter enlightenment ideas.

Through the study of western history he believed in rational progress through scientific thought, and a new society based on industrial production and scientific discovery. His ideas were highly influential during this emergence of sociological thought.

Saint-Simon had introduced the concept of "industrialization" and written of social development and differentiation. He analyzed how elites must adapt to social development. He wrote of the role of classes in history. He took up common values and their consequences for society. He distinguished between stable structures and those that have not yet crystallized. He foresaw that European nations would develop into parliamentary republics; he even believed in a European parliament.

The socialism he represents is usually termed ethical socialism, which is also known as "utopian" socialism when it sought to establish co-operative model societies. This movement emerged when Western Europe embarked on modernization. It belongs to the period when factories became the new predominant institution in certain expansive local communities. Household and workplace were then separated, and the towns and their slums became the everyday setting for people who earlier lived in village. Ethical socialism claimed that human beings enjoy natural rights over the political ones. Ethical socialism postulated everyone's right to a decent living standard and the right to human relations in the emerging urban and industrial society. Saint-Simon also formulated the welfare state's solution to the social question: "from each according to his abilities, to each according to his needs". His experience of the Revolution had confirmed his opposition to violence as a political method.

In opposition to the feudal and military system he advocated a form of state-technocratic socialism, an arrangement where industrialists would lead society and found a national community based upon cooperation and technological progress, which would be capable of eliminating poverty of the lower classes. In place of the church, he felt the direction of society science. Saint-Simon correctly foresaw the industrialization of the world, and he believed that science and technology would solve most of humanity's problems. Accordingly, in opposition to feudalism and militarism, he advocated an arrangement whereby businessmen and other industrial leaders would control society. What Saint-Simon desired, in other words, was an industrialized state directed by modern science, and one in which society would be organized for productive labour by the most capable men. The aim of society would be to produce things useful to life. Saint-Simon also proposed that the states of Europe form an association to suppress war. These ideas had a profound influence on the philosopher Auguste Comte, who worked with Saint-Simon

SOCIAL MOVEMENT

Social movement, a loosely organized but sustained campaign in support of a social goal, typically either the implementation or the prevention of a change in society's structure or values. Although social movements differ in size, they are all essentially collective. That is, they result from the more or less spontaneous coming together of people whose relationships are not defined by rules and procedures but who merely share a common outlook on society. Collective behaviour in crowds, panics, and elementary forms (milling, etc.) are of brief duration or episodic and are guided largely by impulse. When short-lived impulses give way to long-term aims, and when sustained association takes the place of situational groupings of people, the result is a social movement.

Characteristics of Social Movements

A movement is not merely a perpetuated crowd, since a crowd does not possess organizational and motivational mechanisms capable of sustaining membership through periods of inaction and waiting. Furthermore, crowd mechanisms cannot be used to achieve communication and coordination of activity over a wide area, such as a nation or continent. A movement is a mixture of organization and spontaneity. There is usually one or more organizations that give identity, leadership, and coordination to the movement, but the boundaries of the movement are never coterminous with the organizations. For example, although organizations such as California's Sierra Club are influential in the movement to preserve the natural environment, anyone who works for the cause and interacts with other workers for this purpose is a member of the conservationist movement. The famous John Brown was not a member of any major abolitionist organization, but his martyrdom made him a leader and symbol for the movement, even though organizational leaders were reluctant to recognize him.

Social movements and social change

All definitions of social movement reflect the notion that social movements are intrinsically related to social change. They do not encompass the activities of people as members of stable social groups with established, unquestioned structures, norms, and values. The behaviour of members of social movements does not reflect the assumption that the social order will continue essentially as it is. It reflects, instead, the faith that people collectively can bring about or prevent social change if they will dedicate themselves to the pursuit of a goal. Uncommitted observers may regard these goals as illusions, but to the members they are hopes that are quite capable of realization. Asked about their activities, members of a social movement would not reply, "I do this because it has always been done" or "It's just the custom." They are aware that their behaviour is influenced by the goal of the movement: to bring about a change in the way things have "always" been done or sometimes to prevent such a change from coming about.

The membership

The quixotic efforts of bold, imaginative individuals do not constitute social movements. A social movement is a collectivity or a collective enterprise. Individual members experience a sense of membership in an alliance of people who share their dissatisfaction with the present state of affairs and their vision of a better order. Like a group, a social movement is a collectivity with a common goal and shared values.

The sense of membership suggests that individuals are subject to some discipline. In addition to shared values, a social movement possesses norms. These norms prescribe behaviour that will symbolize the members' loyalty to the social movement, strengthen their commitment to it, and set them apart from nonmembers. The norms prohibit behaviour that may cause embarrassment to the movement or provide excuses for attacks by opponents. Commitment is strengthened by participation in group activities with other members and by engaging in actions, individual or collective, that publicly define the individuals as committed members.

A social movement also provides guidelines as to how members should think. Norms of this kind constitute something resembling a "party line"—a definition of the "correct" position for members to take with regard to specific issues. There is subtle pressure on individuals to espouse this position even in the absence of personal knowledge of the arguments for it. Not every member can be expected to study and think through the philosophy that justified the movement and its values. Ideology provides them with a ready-made, presumably authoritative set of arguments.

One of the defining characteristics of a social movement is that it is relatively long lasting; the activity of the membership is sustained over a period of weeks, months, or even years rather than flaring up for a few hours or a few days and then disappearing. A social movement is usually large, but, like duration, largeness is only relative. Some social movements, lasting many decades, may enlist hundreds of thousands of members. Some movements take place within the boundaries of a specific secondary group, such as a religious association or a local community, and may include only a few score or a few hundred members.

The exact size of a social movement is impossible to determine exactly, for membership is not formally defined. Indeed, one of the salient characteristics of a social movement is the semiformal character of its structure. It lacks the fully developed, formal structure of a stable association, such as a club, a corporation, or a political party. The leaders do not possess authority in the sense of legitimatized power, and members are not formally inducted. The informal, noncontractual quality of membership and the absence of formal decision-making procedures place a premium on faith and loyalty on the part of members. While not all members display these traits, ideal members give their total, unselfish loyalty to the movement. Since no legal obligation is assumed on becoming a member, either to conform to the movement's norms or to remain a member, commitment to the movement and its values becomes one of the most important sources of control. Deeply committed members, accepting without question the decisions and orders conveyed by the leaders, sacrificing self, family, and friends if required to do so, are likely to be regarded by outsiders as fanatics. Some students of social movements, particularly those whose analysis has a psychoanalytic orientation, have suggested that the fanaticism of dedicated members results from individual psychopathological states. An alternative explanation is that the social movement becomes a reference group that provides dedicated members with a new and deviant view of social reality. Their basic assumptions about the nature of the social order become so divergent from those of "normal" members of society that their logic and conclusions are incomprehensible to them.

Types of Social Movements

There is no single, standard typology of social movements. As various scholars focus on different aspects of movements, different schemes of classification emerge. Hence any social movement may be described in terms of several dimensions.

Many attempts at categorization direct attention to the objective of the movement. The social institution in or through which social change is to be brought about provides one basis for categorizing social movements as political, religious, economic, educational, and the like. It may be argued that all movements tend to be either political or religious in character, depending upon whether their strategy aims at changing political structures or the moral values of individuals.

A commonly used but highly subjective distinction is that between "reform" and "revolutionary" movements. Such a distinction implies that a reform movement advocates a change that will preserve the existing values but will provide improved means of implementing them. The revolutionary movement, on the other hand, is regarded as advocating replacement of existing values. Almost invariably, however, the members of a so-called revolutionary movement insist that it is they who cherish the true values of the society and that it is the opponents who define the movement as revolutionary and subversive of basic, traditional values.

Some attempts to characterize movements involve the direction and the rate of change advocated. Adjectives such as radical, reactionary, moderate, liberal, and conservative are often used for such purposes. In this context the designations "revolutionary" and "reform" are often employed in a somewhat different sense than that described above, with the implication that a revolutionary movement advocates rapid, precipitous change while a reform movement works for slow, evolutionary change.

The American sociologist Lewis M. Killian advanced still another typology based on the direction of the change advocated or opposed. A reactionary movement advocates the restoration of a previous state of social affairs, while a progressive movement argues for a new social arrangement. A conservative movement opposes the changes proposed by other movements, or those seeming to develop through cultural drift, and advocates preservation of existing values and norms.

Killian and the American psychologist Ralph H. Turner argued that it is useful at times to categorize social movements on the basis of their public definition, the character of the opposition evoked, and the means of action available to the movement. This scheme is designed to eliminate the subjective evaluation of goals inherent in such categories as reformist and revolutionary. A movement that does not appear to threaten the values or interests of any significant segment of society is publicly defined as respectable. If there is no competing movement advocating the same objective, it is also nonfactional. The respectable nonfactional movement must contend primarily with the problems of disinterest and token support, but it has access to legitimate means of promoting its values. A respectable factional movement must contend with competing movements advocating the same general objective but also has access to legitimate means of extending its influence.

A movement that appears to threaten the values of powerful and significant interest groups within the society is publicly defined as revolutionary and encounters violent suppression. As a result, it is denied access to legitimate means of promoting its program. Another type of movement is defined as neither respectable nor dangerous but as peculiar; this type, seen as odd but harmless, encounters ridicule and has limited access to legitimate means.

Social movements may also be categorized on the basis of the general character of their strategy and tactics; for instance, whether they are legitimate or underground. The popular distinction between radical and moderate movements reflects this sort of categorization. An obvious difference between types of movements depends upon their reliance on violent or nonviolent tactics. But a nonviolent movement may also be defined as revolutionary or radical because it accepts civil disobedience, rather than legal or parliamentary maneuvering, as a major feature of its strategy. It should be added that the distinction between violent and nonviolent movements is a relative one because a movement may shift rapidly from one to the other as it develops.

The Dynamics of Social Movements

As an enduring, sustained collectivity a social movement undergoes significant changes during its existence. This characteristic has led some scholars to formulate a theory of a "life cycle" or "natural history" common to all social movements. Other scholars question the value of the life-cycle approach to social movements, arguing that empirical studies of numerous movements fail to support the notion of invariant stages of development. The American sociologist Neil Smelser suggested as an alternative a value-added theory, which postulates that while a number of determinants are necessary for the occurrence of a social movement, they need not occur in any particular order.

Some may be present for some time without effect only to be activated later by the addition of another determinant. At most it can be said that the idea of the life cycle permits the discovery of conditions that must be present if any movement is to proceed from one stage to another. It may also help identify the conditions that cause a movement to change direction. Still, it can be said that a social movement has a career; for as it endures it always undergoes changes in many of its characteristics, though the sequence of these changes may vary from movement to movement.

Progressive changes in leadership and membership

One of the most apparent changes is a shift in leadership. In its earliest stages the strongest influence on a movement is likely to be the charismatic leader who personally symbolizes its values. At some point intellectuals play a leadership role by contributing to the developing ideology of the movement. And if a movement endures and grows for any length of time, administrative leaders arise who are concerned with the practical matters of organization and strategy. Influence in the movement may shift between these types.

Usually the membership of a movement grows during its career, which introduces an element of greater heterogeneity. In the early stages the followers typically are deeply committed with an almost fanatical dedication to the movement's values. If the movement gains a measure of respectability in some segment of society, members may be acquired who are not deeply committed. They are likely to have significant reservations about the movement, and their participation is sporadic. This heterogeneity also can be the basis for internal conflict in a movement. On the other hand, if a movement is publicly defined as revolutionary and subjected to harsh oppression, the membership is likely to be reduced mainly to deeply committed converts or to fanatics who derive some satisfaction from the feeling of being persecuted.

Progressive changes in goals and strategies

The goals rarely remain unchanged. As the movement endures and grows, they are likely to become broader and vaguer than they were at the beginning. Proposals for limited, specific reforms become embedded within programs of general social reform. As the leaders and members begin to acquire a sense of power through early victories, the power orientations of the movement may increase. Acquisition of greater power by the population segment that the movement purportedly represents, rather than the implementation of the values of the movement, then becomes a goal. At the same time, the statement of the movement's aim in acquiring power becomes vaguer and more utopian.

Changes also occur in strategy, which may tend in either of two general directions. It may emphasize personal transformation, bringing about social change by converting a majority of society to implement the values by their actions. Or it may emphasize a strategy of societal manipulation, changing social institutions so that the program may be implemented without regard to the number of people favouring the new order. Failure of a movement to gain a large number of converts, combined with indications that it has at its disposal effective means of coercion, leads to a shift to this type of strategy.

Strategy and changes in strategy are strongly influenced by the relationship of the social movement to the larger society and to other social movements. The social structure and the prevailing belief system may suggest either that change can be brought about by changing the hearts and minds of the individual members or that individuals have little effect on the social order. A public definition of the movement as dangerous and subversive may force it to rely increasingly on a strategy of societal manipulation, including violent tactics. The opposition posed by a countermovement may have the same effect, making attempts at persuasion difficult and dangerous and causing a nonviolent, noncoercive movement to use force.

Relations between Structural Elements

As a collectivity, a social movement is characterized by an emergent social structure and a culture. The social structure is reflected in the relationship between leaders and followers, the culture in the values and norms.

Unlike an association, a social movement does not possess legitimate leaders in the sense of being endowed with authority through some formal process. Leaders must constantly substantiate their claims to leadership by demonstrating the effectiveness of their influence on the followers. There is a relationship of reciprocal influence. The followers, for their part, lack institutionalized means of making their influence felt, such as referenda, legislatures, or periodic elections of leaders. It falls to the leaders, therefore, to formulate policies and decisions that will strike a responsive note in their following. Having advanced such proposals, they must rely on either persuasion or coercion to create the illusion that these are collective decisions made by the entire movement. Propaganda thus becomes an important tool of leadership.

Propaganda is also important for maintaining morale and unity. A social movement lacks both the intimacy of a primary group and the formal boundaries of an association. The speeches and writings of leaders serve, in part, to assure the followers of the size, the strength, and the potential for success of the movement—matters difficult for the followers to observe directly. Movements do utilize interpersonal relations to enhance their unity, encouraging small groups of members to meet frequently in circumstances in which they can form personal ties. Mass meetings and parades, with the accompanying ritual, reduce the feelings of isolation that scattered members may experience. Of extraordinary value to a movement is the example of martyrs whose fate arouses indignation in the members, symbolizes unreserved commitment, and lightens the burden of sacrifices. The culture of a movement encompasses norms and values. Norms are standardized expectations of behaviour developed by members. Values include the program and the ideology. The program is the scheme of change, the new social order that the movement proposes to bring about. The ideology is a body of ideas justifying the program and the strategy of the movement. It usually includes a reinterpretation of history, a projection of the utopia that the success of the movement will introduce, a projection of the disastrous consequences of failure, and a reevaluation of the relationship between population segments and the movement.

The Causes of Social Movements

Both individual psychological states and the characteristics of a society at a particular time may be considered as causes of social movements.

Psychological factors

Individual factors are psychological states that either convince people to join a movement or so weaken their commitment to conventional groups that they are willing to risk the groups' disapproval because of their belief in an unpopular cause. Failure to achieve a satisfying status and identity within normal membership groups may be such a factor. The prestige and sense of belonging, which such people may gain as members of a social movement, may be even more important to them than the values of the movement. Alienation, feelings of powerlessness, hopelessness, and estrangement from society may predispose individuals to participation. Some scholars argue, however, that there are different kinds of alienation. One type leads merely to apathy and resignation. Political alienation, however, reflects a loss of faith in the political community and predisposes the individual to join a movement that challenges it.

Deprivation, discontent, and frustration are frequently assumed to be sufficient causes for initiating or joining a social movement. The relationship is not a simple one, however. There is little evidence that the most deprived segments of a population are the most likely to participate in social movements. The concept of relative deprivation has been used to explain the fact that persons who could be much worse off than they are but still feel deprived in comparison with even more fortunate groups often play a prominent part in social movements.

Social factors

An important task of the student of social movements is to identify those conditions under which social movements are most likely to arise. While the existence of widespread poverty and suffering might seem sufficient to give rise to efforts at reform, it must be emphasized again that some basis for hope must also exist to stir people to make the effort. Paradoxically, partial alleviation of conditions of deprivation may provide such a basis, serving as the impetus for the formation of a social movement just as things seem to be getting better. The success of other people similarly situated, such as victorious revolutionaries in a neighbouring nation, may be another source of hope.

More general theories of the origin of social movements, such as those of Smelser, Turner, and Killian, suggest that social change may result in strains or conflicts in one or more crucial aspects of the social order. Normative strain arises when changing conditions create a situation in which the established norms no longer lead to the attainment of important, accepted values. Strain in values arises when the values themselves seem to interfere with the satisfaction of important needs of a segment of the society. This sort of strain often arises when different groups, such as immigrants, minorities, or the younger generation, develop values that conflict with those of more established groups. Even with little change in norms and values, changes in social structure reflected in the failure of important functionaries to play their roles adequately may lead to discontent.

The general nature of the belief system existing in the culture of a society affects the likelihood that social movements will arise and defines the type that will occur. For example, a system that is essentially fatalistic is less conducive to social movements, particularly those with a strategy of societal manipulation, than one that emphasizes the perfectibility of human beings and their control over their own fate.

Other theories

Since the early 1970s two new strands of theory and empirical research have arisen, one in the United States and one in western Europe. The first, called resource mobilization theory, takes as its starting point a critique of those theories that explain social movements as arising from conditions of social disorganization and strain and as finding their recruits among the isolated and alienated in society. By contrast, research mobilization theorists argue that the success of social movements rests mainly on the resources that are available to it; this means forming coalitions with already-existing organizations, securing financial support, and mounting effective and organized campaigns of political pressure. As a result of this emphasis, resource mobilization theorists downplay the factor of ideology—and irrational factors generally—in the study of social movements.

The second theory is the new social movement theory. It derives from an intellectual dissatisfaction with the predominantly Marxist view that treats social movements as reflecting a fundamental struggle among classes organized around economic production. That theory, it is argued, has become less relevant as these classes have been drawn into collective bargaining, the welfare system, and other social advancements within the state. The "new social movements" that have arisen in their place are interpreted as struggles against the social inequalities, the dominance of the mass media, and other features of postindustrial capitalism and the welfare state. These include youth, feminist, peace, ecological, civil rights, and racial justice movements. Jürgen Habermas, a German sociologist, interpreted such movements as protests against the excessive size and rationality of the state and its bureaucracies and their intrusion into the private worlds of individuals.

The Consequences of Social Movements

It has been suggested that committed participants in a social movement undergo a psychological reorganization. It is clear that their new sense of security and importance is acquired at the sacrifice of autonomy. As loyal members they tend to let the leaders do their thinking for them, suppressing doubts as to the validity of the ideology and the wisdom of the leaders' decisions. They repeat their arguments in a dogmatic fashion; persons who are not in the movement find it difficult to debate with them since they start from different premises. Their perception is selective in a different way from the perceptions of persons outside the movement. The ideology, for example, may lead them to view all governmental authorities as villains, while ordinary citizens view them as legitimate leaders, some good, some bad. The end product of this surrender of autonomy may be an altered worldview. Some things taken for granted before becoming part of the movement will never seem the same again, even after leaving the discipline of the movement. The end products of social movements as collectivities attempting to change the social order cannot be analyzed simply in terms of success or failure. Failure may come as a result of ruthless suppression of the movement or through widespread apathy. A movement may wither away because too few take it seriously and it does not develop enough power to force its program on society. Sometimes the remnants may linger for a long time as a cult, oriented inward toward the gratifications that the members obtain from participation but making no serious effort to change the social order.

Success is most apparent when a movement manages to have its power legitimized as authority. In a successful revolution the social movement becomes the new source of authority and respectability, and opposition to its values is defined as counterrevolutionary. In other instances, the movement achieves power through secession. Failing to compel acceptance of its values in the larger group or society, the members withdraw into a new social system in which they can attempt to implement the values separately from a hostile or indifferent society.

A less obvious form of success is the institutionalization of the values or some part of them. Accepting the legitimacy of the movement's values, the traditional associations in the society incorporate them into their own values and implement them without a transfer of authority to the movement. Thus the Socialist Party of America (1901–72) saw many of its proposals adopted by the two major political parties and the government without winning a major election or overthrowing the government. Sometimes the social movement itself is institutionalized by being accorded authority as the legitimate custodian of the new values. The movement is then transformed into a bureaucratic association, as happened with the American labour movement of the early 20th century and the Congress Party of India after British rule ended.

REFERENCES

1. http://archive.mu.ac.in/myweb_test/TYBA%20study%20material/Social%20Theory%20-%20IV.pdf

2. http://www.shareyouressays.com/essays/essay-meaning-and-nature-of-social-thought/86761

3. http://www.shareyouressays.com/essays/essay-on-development-of-social-thought/87739

4. http://www.shareyouressays.com/essays/essay-on-sociology-and-social-thought/86940

5. http://www.shareyouressays.com/essays/essay-on-the-importance-of-study-of-social-thought/86799

6. http://www.shareyouressays.com/essays/essay-on-the-importance-of-study-of-social-thought/86799

7. https://www.britannica.com/topic/social-movement/The-consequences-of-social-movements

8. Canda, E. R. (2013). Filial piety and care for elders: A contested Confucian virtue re-examined. Journal of Ethnic & Cultural Diversity in Social Work, 22:3-4, 213-2234, doi: 10.1080/15313204.2013.843134 (Special Issue: Culturally Informed Social Work Interventions, Program, Practice & Policy).

9. Witkin, S. L. (2011). Social construction and social work practice: Interpretations and innovations. New York, NY: Columbia University Press.

10. Balarajan, Yarlini, S. Selvaraj and S. Subramanian, (2011): Health Care and Equity in India, Lancet, New Delhi.

11. Baru, Rama and Others (2010): "Inequalities in Access to Health Care India: Caste, Class and Region", Economic and Political Weekly, Vol. XLV 38, September 18.

12. Banerjee, M. M. &Canda, E. R. (2009). Spirituality as a strength of African American women responding to welfare reform. Journal of Religion and Spirituality in Social Work: Social Thought

13. Canda, E. R. (2007). Foreword. In N. Pewewardy, Challenging white privilege: Critical discourse for social work education. Alexandria, VA: Council on Social Work Education.

14. Witkin, S. L. &Saleebey, D. (2007). Social work dialogues: Transforming the canon in inquiry, practice, and education. Alexandria, VA: Council on Social Work Education Press.

15. Canda, E. R. (2002). Wisdom from the Confucian classics for spiritually sensitive social welfare (link); (pdf). Currents: New Scholarship for the Human Services, 1(1), 1-14.

16. Wineburg, B. (2001). A limited partnership: The politics of religion, welfare and social service. New York, NY: Columbia University Press.

17. Fletcher Ronald, 2000, The Making of Sociology – A Study of Sociological Theory Beginnings and Foundations, New Delhi, Rawat Publications.

18. Fletcher, R. 2000, The Making of Sociology Vol. I Jaipur and Delhi, Rawat Publications.

CHAPTER 3

SOCIAL MOVEMENTS ORGANIZATIONS

INTRODUCTION

A social movement organization is an organized component of a social movement (SM). SMO usually is only part of a particular social movement; in other words, a specific social movement is usually composed of many social movement organizations – formal organizations that share movement's goals. Social movement organizations usually have coordinating roles in social movements, but do not actually employ or direct most of the participants, who are part of a wider social movement community. Social movement organizations carry out the tasks that are necessary for any social movement to survive and to be successful.

Social movements have long been identified with loosely structured collective conflict, in which "hundreds of groups and organizations – many of them short-lived, spatially scattered, and lacking direct communication, a single organization, and a common leadership – episodically take part in many different kinds of local collective action". Far from being a unique case, Bristol provides an excellent example of both the role of organizations in promoting and sustaining collective action, and of the different organizational logics that one can locate within social movements. Even though social movements do not equate with the organizations active in them, organizations often play very important roles within them. Like any kind of organization, organizations active in social movements fulfill – if to varying degrees and in varying combinations – a number of functions: inducing participants to offer their services; defining organizational aims; managing and coordinating contributions; collecting resources from their environment; selecting, training, and replacing members. Social movement organizations must mobilize resources from the surrounding environment, whether directly in the form of money or through voluntary work by their adherents; they must neutralize opponents and increase support from both the general public and the elite. Organizations are also important because they act as powerful sources of identity for a movement's own constituency, its opponents, and bystander publics. No matter how aware people may be of the complexity and heterogeneity of any movement, its public perception is likely to be associated with its most conspicuous characters. These need not necessarily be organizations, as the role of people like Martin Luther King in the US civil rights movement of the 1960s, or of Vandana Shiva or Jose Bove in the global justice movement, reminds us. Nevertheless, it is often organized groups that are associated with a movement, for better or worse: for instance, Greenpeace or WWF with environmentalism, Amnesty International with human rights activism, Attac or the so-called "Black Block" with the global justice movement.

For people committed to a certain cause, organizations are an important source of continuity, not only in terms of identity, but also in terms of action. At times of collective effervescence, when enthusiasm is high and the will to participate is strong, it is easier to mobilize people and resources even informally as individuals. But when opportunities for action are more modest and it gets more difficult to attract people spontaneously "to the streets," then organizations can secure continuity to collective action precisely because of their tendency to self perpetuation. Of course not all organizations survive the end of protest waves of particular intensity, yet without organizations collective action would be subject to extreme levels of variability, and challengers' political weight would be far more limited than it actually is. The role of organizations as sources of identity and as actors securing continuity to collective action also results in them playing representation and, to some extent, leadership roles on behalf of a movement. One of the reasons why political actors have trouble dealing with social movements, and media actors struggle to represent them in their accounts, is the lack of recognized movement representatives. With variable levels of acceptance from movements' grassroots, organizations often end up playing such a role simply by virtue of their greater visibility and greater ease of access.

At the same time, organizations perform their tasks by taking up very diverse forms. Following Scott's classic treatment, we can look at organizations as rational, natural, and open systems. The first approach sees organizations mainly as collectivities oriented to relatively specific goals, with a relatively formalized social structure; the second approach maintains that organizations are collectivities whose members/participants are little influenced by formal structures or official goals, but share an interest in the survival of the system and engage in activities, coordinated informally, to secure such survival; the third approach conceives of organizations mainly as unstable coalitions of interest groups that determine goals through a negotiation process: the structure of the coalition, its activities, and its outcomes are strongly affected by environmental factors.

It needs to be made very clear that these are analytical models and not empirical descriptions of specific types of organizations; in other words, we may also apply the three different logics to the same organization in order to identify different aspects of its way of operating and address different problems. For example, it may make eminent sense to look at Greenpeace by focusing on their explicitly stated goals and structure (adopting, in other words, a rational system perspective); by looking at the informal practices through which the people operating within Greenpeace ensure the reproduction of the organization (i.e., taking a natural system perspective); or by looking at how Greenpeace may be the result of tensions and struggles between different actors within it, and howsuch struggles may also be affected by the social, economic, and political environment in which the organization operates (thus following an open system model).

From our point of view, however, it is also legitimate and useful to recognize that each model best suits one of the organizational forms we have just identified. More specifically, in the Bristol global justice movement, as well as in any other movement, we can either focus on the characteristics of the groups and organizations who are mobilized within it, or on the organization of the movement as a whole, i.e., on the way that the different groups, organizations, and even individual activists interested in globalization issues relate to each other. If we take the first line of inquiry, we are likely to look first and foremost for varying combinations of rational and natural systems approaches. In general, a rational system approach makes more sense for heavily bureaucratic organizations with relatively specific goals such as firms or hospitals, than for organizations advocating broader and often vaguely defined social changes, like many of those involved in social movements. However, it can also provide useful insights in relation to the most formalized organizations active in movements (in our example, the likes of Oxfam and Greenpeace).

The more we refer to loose organizational forms, like those reflected in informal networks of radical activists, the more the natural systems perspective seems useful. The aspirations to radical change held by those activists are unlikely to be fulfilled; accordingly, for the reproduction of activism over time, internal solidarity and identity – and hence the informal links between the people involved – are of paramount importance. Finally, if our interest lies in the organizational structure of a movement taken as a whole, then the open system approach is likely to generate very useful insights. Again, it is all too obvious that negotiations about goals, instability of the coalitions, and strong exposure to environmental effects may shape any specific organization; however, these dynamics are probably most visible when we are talking about a broad range of different organizations, such as those making up social movements.

ORGANIZATIONAL DILEMMAS IN SOCIAL MOVEMENTS

In social movement analysis, the acronym SMO (standing for "social movement organization") has proved one of the most popular. But it has also proved very ambiguous, as it has taken very different meanings among different authors. Its original proponents defined the social movement organization as a "complex, or formal, organization which identifies its goals with the preferences of a social movement or countermovement and attempts to implement those goals", a conception that only fits highly structured and formal organizations. Conversely, another definition sees SMOs as "associations of persons making idealistic and moralistic claims about how human personal or group life ought be organized that, at the time of their claims making, are marginal to or excluded from mainstream society", but that hardly seems applicable to strong organizations such as Greenpeace, Amnesty International, or the like. Still others distinguish social movements (and thus SMOs) from parties and interest groups because of their main source of power and legitimacy (protest-mobilizing capacity as opposed to votes and influence respectively), but this does not necessarily imply distinct organizational forms.

Although most researchers in the field would not go as far as suggesting getting rid of the SMO label altogether, it is definitely important to be aware of the heterogeneity of organizational forms adopted by social movement activists. In a systematic analysis of such forms, drawing on the experience of the west European new social movements of the 1980s, Internal structuration as deriving from: (1) formalization, with the introduction of formal membership criteria, written rules, fixed procedures, formal leadership, and a fixed structure of offices; (2) professionalization, understood as the presence of paid staff who pursue a career inside the organization; (3) internal differentiation, involving a functional division of labor and the creation of territorial units; and (4) integration, through mechanisms of horizontal and/or vertical coordination.1 The degree to which specific SMOs meet those criteria reflects some basic organizational dilemmas, that are not peculiar to social movements only, but are certainly very important to our understanding of movement dynamics. Let us focus on threeof them, without claiming to provide an all-encompassing review.

Mobilizing People or Resources

Political organizations – in our case, specifically SMOs – may try to mobilize the largest possible support from the general public, and therefore the resources which are essential to the maintenance of a semi- or quasi-professional group. Available strategies range from calling upon broadly supported sets of values to the provision of selective incentives to prospective members/subscribers in the form of services, leisure-time activities, discount packages, etc. But this is not the only option: SMOs may also try to mobilize smaller but more carefully selected groups of committed activists. These are essential for the more demanding tasks of movement participation, including persistent organizational commitment and the promotion of costly forms of collective action

Putting it differently, there is a basic alternative between the mobilization of people's "money" or "time". These options are not easily compatible. Emotional messages, which provide a clear-cut definition of a movement's identity and opponents, are essential to mobilize core activists. Yet, their sharpness may alienate sectors of sympathizers and prospective supporters with less clear-cut orientations and motivations. It may also discourage potential supporters among established actors, not only public agencies but also "concerned" private sponsors, whose contribution will be easier to attract the larger the size of public support for a given movement. The choice of whether to mobilize time or money has important implications for SMOs: the two options require different "mobilization technologies" and therefore different organizational models.

SMOs differ in the opportunities available for their grassroots members' participation. Many of them emphasize participation and direct democracy, oppose delegation of power, and privilege consensual decision-making. This applies to contemporary Social Forums as well as to virtually all social movements who have followed each other from the 1960s. A participatory structure also favors internal solidarity. Having only limited access to material resources, social movement organizations may substitute for this with symbolic resources. Accordingly, many

SMOs give particular importance to internal relations, transforming the very costs of collective action into benefits through the intrinsic rewards of participation itself. As well as formal organizations, small groups held together by personal relations survive during periods of latency, providing important bases for the revival of movement activities. In particular, a small group of activists "uses naturally occurring social relationships and meets a variety of organizational and individual needs for emotional support, integration, sharing of sacrifice, and expression of shared identities". Within cohesive groups the conditions for the development of alternative value systems are constituted and "communal associations become free spaces, breeding grounds for democratic change". In these "free spaces," a "sense of a common good" develops alongside the construction of "direct, face-to-face, and egalitarian relationships". Thus, an all-embracing participation tends to permeate every aspect of activists' everyday lives. "In the climate of the late 1960s," Whalen and Flacks note with reference to the US student movement, "commitment to revolution had implications for carrying out virtually every detail of daily life: to be a revolutionary was to dress, eat, make love, and speak in certain ways and not others". Where politics "marks every moment of the day," fellow militants become a "family," as it is sometimes put on the extreme left in Italy. So much so that, in their value system and lifestyle, "those who participated in the youth revolt continue to be affected by it".

Hierarchical or Horizontal Structures

The distribution of power within an organization also needs to be considered. Power can be more or less centralized, as the literature on political parties in particular has revealed. National structures can have greater or less weight; there can be greater or lesser participation in decisions concerning resource allocation, goal definition, candidacies, or disciplinary procedures; and there can be greater or lesser centralization of leadership. Social movement organizations have different styles of leadership. Many organizations from religious sects to student movements, via revolutionary parties like the Bolsheviks or the Nazis, have displayed charismatic forms of leadership whose legitimacy was dependent above all on leaders' ability to manipulate ideological resources and to embody the movement as a whole, contributing to the creation of its collective identity. Overall, however, several different leadership styles have been noted in the literature: agitator, prophet, administrator, or statesman; charismatic, administrator, or intellectual; charismatic, ideological, or pragmatic; instrumental or affective.

Given their participatory nature and – frequently – democratic orientation, social movement organizations have always faced the dilemma of how to reconcile leadership roles with the requirements of grassroots democracy. They often reject authority and hierarchy on principle, but this does not necessarily eliminate the need for leadership functions, such as coordination and public representation. If we think of social movement leadership in relational terms, then "leadership roles need not entail control over a unified organization, or explicit recognition of charisma from followers. They may also, far less obtrusively, result from certain actors' location at the center of exchanges of practical and symbolic resources among movement organizations. This will not generate domination, if by that we mean actors' capacity to impose sanctions over others in order to control their behavior, but rather varying degrees of influence". From this perspective, rather than with charisma or authority, "leadership" may be associated with actors' ability to promote coalition work among movement organizations, or to establish connections to the media and political institutions, which in turn lead to operating de facto as movement "representatives". The plurality of functions important for social movement mobilization also means that playing influential, "leadership" roles depends on possession of constantly changing resources. Recently, for example, experts have often replaced ideologues as social movement leaders. Involved as they are in technological issues, contemporary movements assign a very important role to natural scientists and engineers: "challenging sophisticated technologies... such organized protests are dependent on recognized experts to interpret the issues and achieve public credibility". As a result of these multiple roles and requirements, leadership in social movements is often ad hoc, short lived, relates to specific objectives, and is concentrated in a limited area of the movements themselves.

Challengers or "Service Providers"

Not all social movement organizations are directly concerned with external challenges, oriented on political powerholders. Organizations may also act mainly with reference to the needs of social movement constituencies, and/or to support cultural and symbolic challenges or the practice of new lifestyles. Kriesi (1996) called these organizations movement associations, but other terms have also become popular (e.g. halfway houses or abeyance structures). Communes, therapy groups, and rape crisis centers were formed through the feminist movement, for example. Within student movements, used-bookstalls and advice centers of various kinds offered logistical support to sympathizers, allowing protest action in favor of the right to education to be combined with concrete activity aimed at "putting the goal into practice," while at the same time they helped widen support. Movement associations, too, are diverse in terms of levels of organization, internal power distribution, and degree of participation. Self-help groups, for example, tend to be informal, decentralized, and are frequently totalizing, while associations offering services to a wider public may adopt a more formal structure, and a hierarchical distribution of power, and fuse symbolic and instrumental incentives.

Besides groups involved in political mobilization and movement associations, both predominantly inward-looking, supportive organizations are also part of the social movement organizational structure. These consist of service organizations such as newspapers, recreation centers, educational institutions, or publishing presses, which contribute to a movement's aims but at the same time work on the open market. The film clubs, theaters, publishing houses created within several movements in order to further collective mobilization increasingly became market-oriented commercial enterprises with audited accounts, salaried staff, and a competitive market ethos. The same applied to natural food and health shops, originally set up by sympathizers if not activists of environmental movements.

The spread of this kind of structure contributes to the creation of movement countercultures in which political engagement permeates the whole of life.3 The Italian social centers that originated from the autonomist and anarchist movement sectors of the late 1970s, have over time evolved from inwardlooking countercultural communities towards an organizational model which is closest to that of supportive organizations. The fair-trade businesses and ethical banks that have developed in parallel with the global justice movement also fall under this heading. So does a network of alternative media operators linked together through various websites, like Indy media. Several neoreligious organizations over the last decades have also adopted organizational models combining elements from the movement associations and the supportive organizations types. For example, Hank Johnston (1980) characterized the Transcendental Meditation group as a "marketed social movement." While referring to a "marketed social movement organization" might have been more accurate, Johnston's analysis nonetheless captured important aspects of the role played by organizations providing specific services to "clients" longing for personal and social change.

TYPES OF SOCIAL MOVEMENT ORGANIZATIONS

Different responses to the dilemmas illustrated above generate different organizational models. Here we introduce some of them, without any aspiration to generate systematic typologies.

Professional Movement Organizations

A professional social movement organization is characterized by "(1) a leadership that devotes full time to the movement, with a large proportion of resources originating outside the aggrieved group that the movement claims to represent; (2) a very small or non-existent membership base or a paper membership (membership implies little more than allowing a name to be used upon membership rolls); (3) attempts to impart the image of 'speaking for a constituency,' and (4) attempts to influence policy toward that same constituency". Ordinary members have little power and "have no serious role in organizational policymaking short of withholding membership dues. The professional staff largely determines the positions the organization takes upon issues".

However, professional SMOs do not necessarily address themselves to their "natural" constituents, i.e., those groups (whether dispossessed like the unemployed or the homeless, or fairly well-off like in many new middle-class mobilizations) whose interests they promote, the way a normal pressure group would. Rather, they have a "conscience constituency" composed of those who believe in the cause they support. Their leaders are entrepreneurs whose "impact results from their skills at manipulating images of relevance and support through the communication media". They rely more on their reputation for technical expertise on specific matters than on mass mobilization.

There are recognizable advantages associated with professional organizations. Back in the 1970s, in his comparative analysis of American social movements, Gamson found that challengers are more likely to win when they possess a well-structured organization. Formal organizations would appear better placed to mobilize "because they facilitate mass participation, tactical innovations, and rapid decision-making". Structured organizations are also more likely to survive beyond a wave of protest to favor mobilization in succeeding waves. Professional organizers often spread mass defiance rather than dampening it, and "professionalization ofleadership and the formalization of movement organizations are not necessarily incompatible with grass-roots protest". Moreover, long-term survival is favored by the presence of motives for and methods of action which are already legitimated.

However, there are also problems. While professional organizations can generate a constant flow of funding they are bound by the wishes of their benefactors. "The growth and maintenance of organizations whose formal goals are aimed at helping one population but who depend on a different population for funding are ultimately more dependent upon the latter than the former". Patrons provide important resources, but they are usually available only for groups with low-level claims and consensual legitimacy – the disabled rather than the unemployed, for example.

Similar consequences may result from growing collaboration with authorities: "The establishment of a working relation with the authorities also has ambivalent implications for the development of the SMO: On the one hand, public recognition, access to decision-making procedures and public subsidies may provide crucial resources and represent important successes for the SMO; on the other hand, the integration into the established system of interest intermediation may impose limits on the mobilization capacity of the SMO and alienate important parts of its constituency, with the consequence of weakening it in the long run".

Echoing Robert Michels' analysis of the bureaucratization of socialist parties, Piven and Cloward (1977) have been most explicit in considering the development of formal organizations as hampering goal attainment in protest movements of the poor. Investment in building a permanent mass organization was seen as a waste of scarce resources. Moreover, such organizations tended to reduce the only resource available to the poor: mass defiance. It is certainly true that even professional bureaucratic organizations may promote radical challenges and defiance, and engage in various forms of vicarious activism on behalf of a fee-paying passive membership. But organizations focused entirely on fund-raising and the attraction of financial resources are likely sooner or later to face problems with their capacity to mobilize people. All in all, according to critics, professionalization might lead to defeat by taming protest.

The same dilemmas characterize an organizational type that has recently gained increasing attention, the "transnational social movement organization" (TSMOs). Jackie Smith defines TSMOs as "international nongovernmental organizations engaged in explicit attempts to [change] some elements of the social structure and/or reward distribution of society". Theirgrowth has exceeded that of international nongovernmental organizations at large. TSMOs comprise a small number (sometimes referred to as "the Big Ten") of organizations with numerous national chapters, membership in the millions, and strong levels of bureaucratization. These include the likes of Amnesty International, Greenpeace (between 2 and 3 million), Friends of the Earth (a federation of 61 national associations that coordinates about 5,000 local groups and a million members), WWF (5 million), or Oxfam (a confederation of 12 organizations). These organizations display many traits of the professional organization, even though participation is encouraged – if largely in the form of voluntary work and contributions to specific projects, rather than in decision-making processes, and with low levels of investment in the building of internal solidarity. However, TSMOs also include organizations with a distinctive profile but much smaller in terms of resources, and less neatly fitting the professional model. Well-known examples include ATTAC, an organization that campaigns against the deregulation of financial markets, founded in 1997 in France though it has made significant inroads in other Western countries; ACT UP, active since the 1980s in challenging the consequences of AIDS; or conservation organizations such as Conservation International or the Environmental Defense Fund.

Participatory Movement Organizations

We use the plural deliberately, to refer to different organizational types that can be grouped under this broader model. In particular we differentiate between mass protest organizations and grassroots groups.

Mass Protest Organizations

This model combines attention to participatory democracy with certain levels of formalization of the organizational structure. In the social movements of the 1970s, many political organizations like the communist K-Gruppen in Germany, the New Left parties in Italy, the Trotskysts in France, had adopted fairly rigid and hierarchical organizational structures, close to the model of the Leninist party. Gradually, however, this model fell out of favor for its excessive emphasis on the professional revolutionary role, and its indifference to grassroots democracy. With the crisis of the 1970s protest movements, alternative forms of organization developed, as exemplified by theemergence of green parties. These were formed for the most part during the 1980s campaigns on environmental issues, and nuclear energy in particular, although they have never been the official political representatives of the environmental movement. In seeking to defend nature, these parties also sought to apply the "think globally, act locally" principle to their organizations. The greens rejected, initially at least, any structured organizational power, just as they rejected centralizing technologies. They developed a ritual of direct democracy by introducing consensual decision-making, rotation of chair roles, and so on.

The model of open assemblies and always revocable delegates did not survive long, however. Participatory democracy may often reduce the decision-making efficiency of assemblies and lead to very long periods of confusion and incertitude. Particularly after they entered first regional and then national parliaments, the greens began to develop stable organizational structures, with membership cards, representative rather than direct democracy within the party, and a stable leadership. Public funding of the parties created a constant and generous flow of finance which was used to develop a professional political class, set up newspapers and supportive associations. The green parties' structure thus became formal and centralized. Participation moved towards excluding membership of other organizations, and ideological incentives began to predominate. Recently, however, grassroots democratic practices have been revitalized in the context of the growth of global justice mobilizations, and also extended to nontraditional unions such as the Cobas in Italy or Sud in France.

It is not difficult to identify the processes behind these recurrent switches. They not only have to do with the oligarchic tendencies to be found in any sort of organization, but also with problems associated with the model of participatory organizational democracy. In fairness, the concrete realization of the organizational principles of grassroots democracy has never been a simple matter. Many activists have complained of the de facto oligarchies which tend to form and impose their will when collective decision-making becomes difficult. An organized minority can win out in an assembly by wearing down the majority, and forcing them to give up and leave after hours of strenuous discussion. In a few extreme cases physical force has been used by some groups to occupy important decision-making positions such as the chair of meetings. Even without reaching those excesses, the risks of a "tyranny of emotions," whereby the most committed activists profit from the lack of formal procedures and secure control of decision-making processes, have been pointed out in reference to several movements of the recent and not-so-recent past. They have also been restated in reference to the global justice movement.

Grassroots organizations

In contrast to the mass protest model, the grassroots model combines strong participatory orientations with low levels of formal structuration. The existence of organizations of this kind depends on their members' willingness to participate in their activities. Such participation may be encouraged through different combinations of ideological and solidaristic incentives. Oftentimes this is related to locality. For example, the local groups that opposed road building in many corners of Britain in the 1990s could not rely on a strong ideological profile given the heterogeneity of their participants, and instead emphasized shared concerns in specific issues; so do the singleissue citizens' committees that characterize so much political activity in contemporary democracies or the residents' associations promoting environmental justice collective action in deprived urban areas. Other times, shared critical attitudes play a stronger and more explicit role in motivating participation, as in the semiformal direct action groups that have developed in the context of growing opposition to neoliberal globalization, or in the local independent women's groups that marked the spread of feminist movements in the 1970s and 1980s.

Despite their lack of resources, there are innumerable examples of grassroots organizations that have been successful in the pursuit of their goals, both in countries lacking a vibrant civil society and in Western countries. For example, grassroots environmental mobilizations have proved a constant feature of Western democracies, stopping threatening projects on innumerable occasions. At the same time, depending so heavily on their members' voluntary participation, grassroots organizations' capacity to act with continuity over time is obviously limited. Many of them actually see an alternation of phases of activism and latency, comparable to those identified by Melucci and his associates for social movements as a whole. They operate as "intermittent structures," i.e., "organizations or organizational units which are deployed and then "folded up" until their period of activity arrives again". "Intermittent social movement organizations", that resurface each time their issues of concern become salient political topics again, remind us that permanent stable structures are not necessarily a requirement for success.

Grassroots organizations may also face problems if they rely too heavily on ideology to secure their members' cohesion and commitment. Ideological incentives are an important surrogate for the lack of material resources, but their useincreases the rigidity of the organizational model because transformations have to be incorporated into the normative order of the group. Moreover, organizations employing symbolic incentives will run a greater risk of internal conflict. Especially for grassroots groups with very critical views of mainstream society, closure to the external world helps the formation of identity but also reduces the capacity to handle reality and identify reasons for failure.

How Do Social Movement Organizations Change?

Patterns of change

Just as the organizational characteristics of social movements vary, there is no single model accounting for organizational changes. A Weberian approach, focusing primarily on bureaucratization, initially dominated in the sociology of social movements as in other areas. Michels' "iron law of oligarchy," which states that in order to survive as an organization a political party increasingly pays attention to adapting to its environment rather than to its original goals of social change, was also held valid for social movements. Institutionalization used to be considered a natural evolution for social movement organizations. Recurrent lifecycles were identified in the histories of a number of movements. Herbert Blumer (1951: 203), for example, distinguished four stages in the typical social movement lifecycle. The first, or "social ferment," stage would be characterized by unorganized, unfocused agitation during which great attention is paid to the propaganda of "agitators." In the second phase, of "popular excitement," the underlying causes of discontent and the objectives of action are more clearly defined. In the third phase, of "formalization," disciplined participation and coordination of strategies for achieving the movement's aims are arrived at by creating a formal organization. Finally, in the "institutionalization" stage the movement becomes an organic part of society and crystallizes into a professional structure.

Others have questioned the "necessity" of such an evolution, however. Even organizational sociologists point out that adaptation is only one evolutionary possibility among many. In fact, an organization need not react by moderating its aims when conflict with the surrounding environment arises. It can also become more radical, hoping that a small but powerful nucleus of dissent will form in this way. Moreover, rather than adapt to external demands it may simply reduce contacts with the outside world. Although he referred to the Michelsian hypothesis (and emphasized that "there are organizational characteristics that dictate organization maintenance over every other possible goal"), Noted that "the phenomenon has little to do with goal displacement. Rather, the goals of an organization have become outwon with the need of maintaining the organization."

In fact, SMOs rarely get institutionalized. In the first place, few of them actually survive for a significant time spell. Some dissolve because their aims have been achieved. Organizations formed to coordinate specific campaigns, for example, tend to disappear as soon as that campaign is over. Leadership splits during downturns in mobilization, and the resultant processes of disintegration and realignment cause others to disappear. In the case of SMOs, whose life expectancy is short and whose aims are limited, an interest in the organization's continuing existence may not even develop. In other words, their members' first loyalty continues to be to the movement and the organization is simply seen as a temporary instrument for intervention.

Moderation of an organization's aims is not, of course, the only possible development even for those organizations that actually do survive in the long term. Other social movement organizations become more radical. Their aims become more ambitious, the forms of action adopted less conventional, and they become increasingly isolated from the outside world. One outcome of 1968, although certainly not the only one, nor the most important, was the formation of clandestine organizations which grew out of the student movement in Italy and Germany and adopted increasingly radical forms of action, including in some cases murdering political opponents. They are a tragic and extreme example of how reacting to a hostile environment can bring about an increasing closure of channels of communication with the outside world. In less extreme cases, spontaneous groups such as the German Spontis and the IndianiMetropolitani (literally, "metropolitan indians") in Italy, illegitimate offspring of the student movement in decline, increased rather than diminished their use of symbolic incentives, primarily in order to reinforce internal solidarity.

The direction taken by a social movement, therefore, may be that of moderation, but equally that of radicalization; of greater formalization, but also of progressive destructuration; of greater contact with the surrounding environment, or of sectarian "implosion." One must not forget that changes in specific organizations do not necessarily all take the same direction: the institutionalization of one organization can go along with the radicalization of another, and the overall profile of a social movement sector may remain relatively stable over time as a result. For example, in their analysis of changes in environmental organizations in the 1990s, Diani and Donati (1999) showed that trends towards institutionalization and professionalization went along with the emergence of new grassroots radical actors, and that established organizations had played a key role inenvironmental movements since the rise of environmental mobilization in the late 1980s.

Mapping all the possible factors behind changes in social movements' organizational forms exceeds the scope of this volume. Here we shall focus on three determinants of change that have attracted a lot of attention recently. Let us look first at the role of institutional factors.

Institutional Factors and Organizational Change

The availability of public or semipublic resources may facilitate the creation of powerful lobbies with links to social movements. Research on the civil rights movement in the United States, for example, has shown that funds from federal and local government agencies and programs such as the Community Action Programs or Volunteers in Service to America stimulated the creation of movement organizations at the same time as the Peace Corps and alternative military service provided paid positions for activists. The conditions governing access to public and private funding, tax exemptions, or advantageous postage rates influence the organizational structure of groups who wish to benefit from these possibilities. Thus the terms "funded" or "registered social movement organizations" have been used.

In many countries, organizations wishing access to a series of material resources must respect a long list of laws and regulations, first and foremost in their organizational structure. In the US these include "federal tax laws and policies and their enforcement by the Internal Revenue Service, the actions of formal coalitions of fundraising groups, United States Postal Service Regulations and their consequences for access to the mails, the rules and actions of private organizations monitoring groups, the dynamics of combined charity appeals, and state and local level fundraising regulations and their enforcement". In particular, "not-for-profit" or "nonpartisan" organization status, usually necessary for access to the above-mentioned resources, involves adherence to models considered legitimate for such organizations, such as the presence of a governing body and an annual audit. From this point of view certainly, increased availability of institutional resources accentuates the presence of formal, centralized organizations, as American public interest groups (such as Common Cause), with thousands of contributors and hundreds of local branches, demonstrate.

The openness of other institutional structures may also favor the development of formal organizations. In Europe, in contrast to the US, parties originating from social movements have often obtained remarkable results thanks partly to the rules regulating challengers' access to decision-making procedures. Proportional representation, for example, can promote the formation of movement parties, as happened when the various organizations of the new left in Italy fielded candidates at administrative and political elections in the 1970s,9 or when green parties enjoyed success in countries like Belgium, Germany, or Italy in the 1980s.

At the same time, however, formal organizations with a clear structure are not necessarily the outcome of an open, inclusive political environment. Often, formal, hierarchical structures have been established to better fight a hostile state apparatus. A repressive, centralized state may well produce well-organized movements, with solid alliances between different organizations and movements, sometimes with radical repertoires of action. For example, the Italian student movement of the 1970s found itself involved in an extremely polarized political conflict. The political system's closure and frequent physical clashes with neofascists and police favored the development of the centralized and bureaucratic organizations of the new left.

However, 30 years later, the events in Genoa 2001, and the violent behavior of police even towards peaceful demonstrators, did not result in a growing militarization of the global justice movement and in the adoption of organizational forms suited to conducting violent clashes with police. Conversely, an open, decentralized political system may also facilitate similar trends towards decentralization and informality among movement organizations. In Germany, again in the 1970s, and in contrast to Italy, institutional openness (particularly when Social Democrat Willy Brandt was chancellor) apparently favored the proliferation of decentralized movement organizations, such as the Bürgerinitiativen.

Similar considerations have also been suggested in relation to the American social movement sector, in contrast to the hypothesis that the American institutional system should be conducive only to formal, bureaucratic organizations. To sum up, rather than positing a rigid relationship between the form that social movement activists give to their organizations, and the traits of the institutional system in which they operate, it is wiser to recognize that multiple organizational forms may be accommodated within the same system.

Organizational cultures and organizational change

Although social movement actors have margins of choice when they are trying to adapt creatively to their environment, such margins are subject to limitations.

Just as we may speak of repertoires of forms of protest, we may do so for organizational forms. In any given country and at any given time, the repertoire of organizational forms is restricted. It can be expanded by borrowing from other countries or domains, but such transformations are slow. A particular organizational model is more likely to be adopted, "to the extent that the proposed model of organization is believed to work, involves practices and organizational relations that are already familiar, and is consonant with the organization of the rest of those individuals' social worlds".

Thus, the organizational resources already present within the social movement sector tend to influence the evolution of single organizations and, more generally, the forms of protest adopted. The dominant organizations in any given phase tend to contribute organizational resources to later mobilizations, thus contributing also to the definition of their strategies. Adopting the terminology of the resource mobilization approach, the SMOs created during a particular phase of mobilization "manufacture" resources for succeeding phases, influencing, or at least attempting to influence, their character.

Organizational choices, therefore, are influenced by the preexisting structures within which movements form, inheriting ideas, constraints, and facilities as well as allies and opponents. Thus earlier historical movements or "early riser" movements help produce their "spin-offs." During periods of mobilization new insurgents assimilate inputs from existing movements. The student movement provided the organizational resources for the formation of groups with objectives as diverse as defending the rights of the poor and those of animals. Similarly, the women's movement, formed within its student predecessor, would later transmit ideological frameworks, tactical innovations, organizational structures, and leadership to the peace movement. Today, global justice movement organizations also draw, if often critically, on the experiences of the organizations that in the recent and not-so-recent past have mobilized transnationally on issues such as the environment, human rights, or Thirld World development. Over time, then, a sort of collective memory on organizational possibilities is passed down from one generation of militants to the next or from one movement to another: "one movement can influence subsequent movements both from outside and from within: by altering political and cultural conditions it confronts in the external environments, and by changing the individuals, groups and norms within the movement itself". For this reason, it can be very difficult to change certain initial organizational traits, as they come to form a kind of genetic patrimony for movement organizations.

Modernization, Technological Innovation, and Organizational Change

One should also consider the relationship between modernization and organizational change. In general terms, economic progress may have a beneficial effect on the organizing capacity of social movements, since "as the amount of discretionary resources of mass and elite publics increases, the absolute and relative amount of resources available to the SMS [Social Movement Sector] increases". These resources include time and money, but also political freedom, means of communication, transportation, etc. As they grow, the amount of resources available for new organizations and movements is also likely to increase. Economic development, and the economic and time resources it creates, should lead to a growth in professionalized, formal groupings: "The larger the income flow to an SMO, the more likely that cadre and staff are professional and the larger these groups are".

However, technological change has attracted most attention of late, as it has influenced the organizational structure of social movements as well as their tactics. The expansion of both printed and electronic means of communication has permitted an "externalization" of certain costs. If organizations were previously required to be highly structured to get a message across, today a lightweight one may be adequate, provided it can gain media attention. The impact of the internet on social movement organizing is beautifully illustrated by a authoritative, nonacademic source like the Canadian Security Intelligence Service: "The internet will continue a large role in the success or failure of antiglobalization protests and demonstrations. Groups will use the internet to identify and publicize targets, solicit and encourage support, organize and communicate information and instructions, recruit, raise funds, and as a means of promoting their various individual and collective aims".

Websites operate with information, mobilization, or community-oriented functions. In the case of antiglobalization sites, they provide an easy way for information to circulate not only through email lists but through links between websites. It seems reasonable to suggest that the major no-global initiatives of the late 1990s and early 2000s have been made possible by the internet, even though, as Seattle demonstrates, it is combination of local grassroots organizing and web-based information diffusion that has done the trick.

In some cases, computer-mediated communication simply expands the capacity to act of already solid organizations such as Greenpeace or Oxfam; in other cases, however, it brings together networks of activists with very informal organizational structures, if any. Two examples are the Cokespotlight or McSpotlight websites, which expose Coca Cola's environmental record or McDonald's indifference to workers' rights and food quality; another example is the independent information network Indymedia, the first site of which was born during the 1999 Seattle campaign, and then spread to form other networks, including the European Counter Network that connects anarchists and autonomists and centrisociali. In still other cases, specific organizations are created that would not exist without the internet: e.g., Subversive Enterprises International, which is actually little more than a website that connects likeminded people interested in mobilizing support for the anticapitalist movement, with no hierarchical structure of any kind.

It has been suggested that changes in both technology and conceptions of political activity will result in the disappearance of traditional organizational forms. Some have stressed the role of media as independent sources of organizational resources. For example, Walgrave and Massens (2000) showed how the media played a major autonomous role in the success of the White march that took place in Brussels in 1996 to voice people's anger at the authorities' handling of the Dutroux pedophilia case. The opportunities for the formation of affinity groups, consisting of people who share a broad vision of political and social engagement, and come together on specific issues of interest and short-term campaigns, have also been greatly enhanced by new communication technologies. For example, mobile phone communications between private citizens have been credited with the success of the demonstrations that in January 2001 forced Philippine president Joseph Estrada to resign. For some radical critics of the role of traditional political organizations, "affinity groups" (i.e., selforganized and self-governing groups based on a commonality of values and interests) represent a major organizing principle behind the global justice movement, which denies any space to organizational identity and to organizations themselves. Skeptics would counter, however, that affinity groups' attempts to solve the problem of maintaining members' loyalty in a nonbureaucratic way lead to difficult decision-making and ultimately ineffective performance.

MOVEMENT ORGANIZATIONS TO SOCIAL MOVEMENT NETWORKS

The network nature of social movements has long been highlighted. In a few seminal contributions, Luther Gerlach pointed out that social movements are:

	Cooperation	Lack of cooperation
Competition for similar constituency	Competitive cooperation	Factionalism
Lack of competition	Noncompetitive cooperation	Neutrality

- segmented, with numerous different groups or cells in continual rise and decline;
- polycephalous, having many leaders each commanding only a limited following; and
- reticular, with multiple links between autonomous cells forming an indistinctly bounded network. Recently he qualified his argument by stressing the undirected, acephalous, rather than polycephalous, nature of such networks.

Movements so frequently take network forms because political organizations rarely manage to monopolize the representation of a certain complex of interests and values. When this happens, that usually spells the end of a social movement process and its replacement with organizational processes. Normally, a multiplicity of organizations operates on the same issues and on behalf of similar, if not identical, political and ethical projects. Exploring the nature of the relationships between them is crucial for our understanding of social movements.

Even though alliance-building seems a generally sensible and desirable option, in practice, however, interorganizational relationships can vary markedly in both content and intensity. One way to capture those differences is by asking whether organizations are in competition for the acknowledgment and support of the same social base; whether, that is, they are trying to acquire essential resources for action by tapping the same (limited) mobilization potential. By combining the presence or absence of cooperation and presence or absence of competition we can elaborate a typology of forms of interorganizational relationships.

We have first of all to recognize that many citizens' organizations, despite broadly dealing with similar problems, are basically involved in a relation of neutrality (or indifference) to each other, whereby an absence of cooperation corresponds to lack of competition. Such situations occur when organizations' definitions of issues make cooperation difficult, but at the same time they do not have to compete for members and support, because they appeal to diverse sectors of public opinion. The environmental movement of the 1970s in Italy was closeto this model. Its conservation and political ecology components were ideologically far enough apart to make it difficult for them to cooperate with each other. This did not lead to conflict, however, as both sectors were somewhat eccentric in relation to the principal, class-based conflicts in that period. Similar remarks may apply to environmentalism in a country with a far lower salience of the left–right divide like Britain. There, a political-ecology sector hardly developed at all in the 1970s, as new left groups were focusing strictly on traditional class issues while paying little attention to environmental problems.

High levels of competition and low levels of cooperation among movement organizations are instead likely to produce factional relationships. In such cases, the struggle to represent the same constituency leads to fragmentation and sectarian divisions. Cooperation among movement organizations is thus hindered, despite the proximity of their cultural models and styles of action. Donatella dellaPorta (1990) and Sidney Tarrow (1989a) have shown how the competitive dynamics within Italian movements eventually produced outcomes of this type at the end of the 1970s. The Italian situation was characterized at that time by transition from models which were predominantly cooperative, although also competitive, to models where cooperation was absent. The reduction of the potential to mobilize played a crucial role in this context, as it brought various organizations into open competition with each other, emphasizing their ideological differences. As a result, the potential for conflict within movement areas grew.

Intense exchanges between organizations with different natural constituencies produce noncompetitive cooperation. Movement organizations are not appealing to the same political market but have, at the same time, sufficient interests and motives for convergence to activate joint mobilizations. Cooperation is, moreover, limited, to the extent that it neither presupposes nor requires the development of a homogeneous perspective or of a "strong" and (semi)exclusive notion of collective identity. Relationships between central organizations with diverse concerns in the Italian environmentalist field in the 1980s were close to this model: political ecology groups such as Legambiente cooperated with conservationist groups such as Italia Nostra without coming into competition, inasmuch as their potential sources of support differed substantially.

Where collaboration develops between organizations competing for the same base of support, situations which we will define as competitive cooperation occur.

In such cases, two (or more) movement organizations concerned with the same issues are keen to develop joint initiatives, based on compatible definitions of the issues and some degree of identity; but at the same time they find themselves facing stiff mutual competition for the same support base, and for similarsectors of public opinion whose interests they wish to represent. The resulting model of interaction may be characterized by a degree of interorganizational polemic, but that does not lead to a breakdown of resource exchanges and communication. The new left groups which in the 1970s competed for control of radical youth movements in Italy adequately illustrate this model; so do the relationships between women's organizations supporting abortion rights in the USA. When collaboration between organizations takes place, ties may be largely instrumental, restricted to the exchange of resources for practical purposes, or may involve mutual obligation and a shared identity. This provides the foundation for the distinction between coalitional and social movement processes. Both coalitional and social movement processes generate extended networks of interaction between distinct social actors.

Social movement action on a large scale has always been organized in network forms. Examples may be found throughout the history of modern contention, from nineteenth-century working class and women's organizations, to antiwar or antipoverty coalitions, to environmental or women's movements, to mention just a few. Recently, however, the spread of global justice mobilizations has made the role of networks particularly visible. Increasingly, we see examples of coalitions that involve both transnational actors and networks and local actors on issues such as environmental protection, deprivation, or human rights, thus expanding the range of forms of transnational contention.

In many cases, network dynamics remain purely informal. Often, however, a hybrid model of "network organization" develops, combining elements of formality with those proper to a loose network structure. In contrast to classic formal organizations, which are based on the vertical integration of multiple units, the "network organization" model in organization theory points at another way of coordinating activities, based on the independence of the single components, horizontal integration, flexibility in goals and strategies, and multiple levels of interaction with the possibility of communitarian elements. Most frequently associated with the novel forms of production introduced by firms like Benetton or IBM, the "network organization" model, when it is applied to a social movement as a whole, also allows a greater degree of specificity and a more specific definition of goals than the network metaphor does.

Network organizational models are useful to coordinate efforts around specific campaigns or policy issues, in which many different activists and organizations have a stake. They do so while being neither dependent on the organizations that originally set them up, nor able to exert a leadership role beyond the boundaries of their specific domain. Many network organizations are inherently temporary – they do not survive the specific mobilization or campaign they are supposed to coordinate; however, some of them may convert into fullfledged organizations, increasingly independent from their original founders, and with a distinct identity. For example, in the environmental justice movement of the 1990s, many grassroots groups preferred to coordinate through an informal networking strategy, rather than relying on the intermediation of the rigid environmental bureaucracies who had so far secured "ownership" of those issues. Many organizations mobilizing on a transnational scale also have a network form. Recent examples include the Rainforest Action Network, that campaigns to protect the rainforest and targets financial actors backing destructive projects; the People's Global Action network, that connects hundreds of grassroots organizations worldwide; or the Alliance for Sustainable Jobs and the Environment, that played a visible public role in the 1999 Seattle anti-WTO demonstrations in bringing together environmentalists, working-class activists, and local community organizers. The most visible example of network organization, however, is probably the Social Forum model. Inspired by the experience of the World Social Forum in Porto Alegre, this model has then been extended to coordinate in a flexible and negotiated way the multiplicity of actors involved in global justice campaigns at the continental, national, and local levels.

Just to make the difference clear: we speak of "network organizations" in reference to relatively bounded organizational forms such as the European Counter Network or the Climate Action Network, defined by the interest in specific issues or by a distinct cultural perspective; but we also speak of networks in reference to whole movements, like the global justice movement or the environmental movement. Either way, many have long regarded flexible and decentralized network forms of organizing as particularly effective in achieving the aims of protestors. The ability to coordinate action and promote joint campaigns facilitates the diffusion of protest, and increases the relevance of certain themes on the political agenda and the opportunities to disseminate new interpretations of political and social conflict. The existence of a significant number of allies increases the chances of success for groups promoting protest. Network links also make movement organizations better equipped to deal with emergencies and threats coming from their environment. In particular, such structures should avert the danger of suppression by opponents (so much easier when the leadership is concentrated in afew people), maximize adaptability, allow the escalation of action by distributing the effects of one group's activities to all of them, promote innovation, and reduce the negative effect of failures. A network organization also allows some kind of mediation between the participatory ethos behind grassroots organizing and the coordination guaranteed by formal structures.

Groups and Organizations

Groups are prevalent in our social lives and provide a significant way to understand and define ourselves—both through groups we feel a connection to and those we do not. Groups also play an important role in society. As enduring social units, they help foster shared value systems and are key to the structure of society as we know it. There are four primary sociological perspectives for studying groups: functionalist, critical, feminist, and symbolic interactionist. We can look at the Occupy movement through the lenses of these methods to better understand the roles and challenges that groups offer.

The functionalist perspective is a big-picture, macro-level view that looks at how different aspects of society are intertwined. This perspective is based on the idea that society is a well-balanced system with all parts necessary to the whole. It studies the functions these parts play in the reproduction of the whole. In the case of the Occupy movement, a functionalist might look at what macro-level needs the movement serves. Structural functionalism recognizes that there are tensions or conflicts between different structural elements of the system. The huge inequalities generated by the economic system might function positively as part of the incentive needed for people to commit themselves to risky economic ventures, but they conflict with the normative structure of the political decision-making system based on equality and democratic principles. The Occupy movement forces both haves and have-nots to pay attention to the imbalances between the economic and political systems. Occupy emerges as an expression of the disjunction between these two systems and functions as a means of initiating a resolution of the issues.

The critical perspective is another macroanalytical view, one that focuses on the genesis and growth of inequality. A critical theorist studying the Occupy movement might look at how business interests have manipulated the system to reduce financial regulations and corporate taxes over the last 30 years. In particular, they would be interested in how these led to the financial crisis of 2008 and the increasing inequality we see today. The slogan, "We are the 99%," emblematic of the Occupy movement, refers to the massive redistribution of wealth from the middle class to the upper class. Even when the mismanagement of the corporate elite (i.e., the "1%") had threatened the stability of people's livelihoods and the entire global economy in the financial meltdown of 2008, and even when their corporations and financial institutions were receiving bailouts from the American and Canadian governments, their personal income, bonuses, and overall share of social wealth increased.

Feminist analysis of the Occupy movement would be interested in the connection between contemporary capitalism and patriarchy. Why are women the poorest of the poor? They would also be interested in the type of organizational models used by the Occupy movement to understand and address the resulting issues of power structure and economic injustice. The consciousness-raising techniques and non-hierarchical decision-making processes developed by feminists in the 1960s and 1970s were, in fact, incorporated into the daily political activities of the Occupy movement in order to extend the critique of corporate greed and financial institutions to largely invisible issues of privilege and daily, personal struggle. Occupy Montreal adopted the concept of stepping back or "progressive stack" in their meetings. Men and other dominant movement figures were encouraged to step back from monopolizing the conversation so that a diversity of opinions and experiences could be heard. "We are not here to reproduce the same monopolization of voice and power as the '1%,' we are here to diversify spaces for radical inclusion".

A fourth perspective is the symbolic interactionist perspective. This method of analyzing groups takes a micro-level view. Instead of studying the big picture, these researchers look at the day-to-day interactions of groups. Studying these details, the interactionist looks at issues like leadership style, communicative interactions, and group dynamics. In the case of the Occupy movement, interactionists might ask, "How does a non-hierarchical organization work?"; "How is the social order of a diverse group maintained when there are no formal regulations in place?"; "What are the implicit or tacit rules such groups rely on?"; "How do members come to share a common set of meanings concerning what the movement is about?

At one point during the occupation of Wall Street, speakers like Slovenian social critic and philosopher SlavojZizek were obliged to abandon the use of microphones and amplification to comply with noise bylaws. They gave their speeches one line at a time and the people within earshot repeated the lines so that those further away could hear. The symbolic interactionist would be interested in examining how this communicational format, despite its cumbersome nature, could come to be an expression of group solidarity.

Types of Groups

Most of us feel comfortable using the word "group" without giving it much thought. But what does it mean to be part of a group? The concept of a group is central to much of how we think about society and human interaction. As GeorgSimmel (1858–1915) put it, "society exists where a number of individuals enter into interaction" (1908). Society exists in groups. For Simmel, society did not exist otherwise. What fascinated him was the way in which people mutually attune to one another to create relatively enduring forms. In a group, individuals behave differently than they would if they were alone. They conform, they resist, they forge alliances, they cooperate, they betray, they organize, they defer gratification, they show respect, they expect obedience, they share, they manipulate, etc. Being in a group changes their behaviour and their abilities. This is one of the founding insights of sociology: the whole is greater than the sum of its parts. The group has properties over and above the properties of its individual members. It has a reality *sui generis*, of its own kind. But how exactly does the whole come to be greater?

Sociologist Charles Horton Cooley (1864–1929) suggested that groups can broadly be divided into two categories: primary groups and secondary groups. According to Cooley, primary groups play the most critical role in our lives. The primary group is usually fairly small and is made up of individuals who generally engage face-to-face in long-term, emotional ways. This group serves emotional needs: expressive functions rather than pragmatic ones. The primary group is usually made up of significant others—those individuals who have the most impact on our socialization. The best example of a primary group is the family.

Secondary groups are often larger and impersonal. They may also be task focused and time limited. These groups serve an instrumental function rather than an expressive one, meaning that their role is more goal or task oriented than emotional. A classroom or office can be an example of a secondary group. Neither primary nor secondary groups are bound by strict definitions or set limits. In fact, people can move from one group to another. A graduate seminar, for example, can start as a secondary group focused on the class at hand, but as the students work together throughout their program, they may find common interests and strong ties that transform them into a primary group.

Peter Marsden (1987) refers to one's group of close social contacts as a core discussion group. These are individuals with whom you can discuss important personal matters or with whom you choose to spend your free time. Christakis and Fowler (2009) found that the average North American had four close personal contacts. However, 12 percent of their sample had no close personal contacts of this sort, while 5 percent had more than eight close personal contacts. Half of the people listed in the core discussion group were characterized as friends, as might be expected, but the other half included family members, spouses, children, colleagues, and professional consultants of various sorts. Marsden's original research from the 1980s showed that the size of the core discussion group decreases as one ages, there was no difference in size between men and women, and those with a post-secondary degree had core discussion groups almost twice the size of those who had not completed high school.

In-Groups and Out-Groups

One of the ways that groups can be powerful is through inclusion, and its inverse, exclusion. In-groups and out-groups are subcategories of primary and secondary groups that help identify this dynamic. Primary groups consist of both in-groups and out-groups, as do secondary groups. The feeling that one belongs in an elite or select group is a heady one, while the feeling of not being allowed in, or of being in competition with a group, can be motivating in a different way. Sociologist William Sumner (1840–1910) developed the concepts of in-group and out-group to explain this phenomenon. In short, an in-group is the group that an individual feels he or she belongs to, and believes it to be an integral part of who he or she is. An out-group, conversely, is a group someone doesn't belong to; often there may be a feeling of disdain or competition in relation to an out-group. Sports teams, unions, and secret societies are examples of in-groups and out-groups; people may belong to, or be an outsider to, any of these.

While these affiliations can be neutral or even positive, such as the case of a team-sport competition, the concept of in-groups and out-groups can also explain some negative human behaviour, such as white supremacist movements like the Ku Klux Klan, or the bullying of gay or lesbian students. By defining others as "not like us" and inferior, in-groups can end up practicing ethnocentrism, racism, sexism, ageism, and heterosexism—manners of judging others negatively based on their culture, race, sex, age, or sexuality. Often, in-groups can form within a secondary group. For instance, a workplace can have cliques of people, from senior executives who play golf together, to engineers who write code together, to young singles who socialize after hours. While these in-groups might show favouritism and affinity for other in-group members, the overall organization may be unable or unwilling to acknowledge it. Therefore, it pays to be wary of the politics of in-groups, since members may exclude others as a form of gaining status within the group.

Reference Groups

A reference group is a group that people compare themselves to—it provides a standard of measurement. In Canadian society, peer groups are common reference groups. Children, teens, and adults pay attention to what their peers wear, what music they like, what they do with their free time—and they compare themselves to what they see. Most people have more than one reference group, so a middle-school boy might look not only at his classmates but also at his older brother's friends and see a different set of norms. And he might observe the antics of his favourite athletes for yet another set of behaviours. Some other examples of reference groups can be one's church, synagogue, or mosque; one's cultural centre, workplace, or family gathering; and even one's parents. Often, reference groups convey competing messages. For instance, on television and in movies, young adults often have wonderful apartments, cars, and lively social lives despite not holding a job. In music videos, young women might dance and sing in a sexually aggressive way that suggests experience beyond their years. At all ages, we use reference groups to help guide our behaviour and show us social norms. So how important is it to surround yourself with positive reference groups? You may never meet or know a reference group, but it still impacts and influences how you act. Identifying reference groups can help you understand the source of the social identities you aspire to or want to distance yourself from.

Groups and Networks

Dyads, Triads, and Social Networks

A small group is typically one where the collection of people is small enough that all members of the group know each other and share simultaneous interaction, such as a nuclear family, a dyad, or a triad. Georg Simmel wrote extensively about the difference between a dyad, or two-member group, and a triad, a three-member group. No matter what the content of the groups is—business, friendship, family, teamwork, etc.—the dynamic or formal qualities of the groups differ simply by virtue of the number of individuals involved. In a dyad, if one person withdraws, the group can no longer exist. Examples include a divorce, which effectively ends the "group" of the married couple, or two best friends never speaking again. Neither of the two members can hide what he or she has done behind the group, nor hold the group responsible for what he or she has failed to do.

In a triad, however, the dynamic is quite different. If one person withdraws, the group lives on. A triad has a different set of relationships. If there are three in the group, two-against-one dynamics can develop and the potential exists for a majority opinion on any issue. At the same time, the relationships in a triad cannot be as close as in a dyad because a third person always intrudes. Where a group of two is both closer and more unstable than a group of three, because it rests on the immediate, ongoing reciprocity of the two members, a group of three is able to attain a sense of super-personal life, independent of the members.

The difference between a dyad and a triad is an example of network analysis. A social network is a collection of people tied together by a specific configuration of connections. They can be characterized by the number of people involved, as in the dyad and triad, but also in terms of their *structures* (who is connected to whom) and *functions* (what flows across ties). The particular configurations of the connections determine how networks are able to do more things and different things than individuals acting on their own could. Networks have this effect, regardless of the content of the connections or persons involved.

For example, if one person phones 50 people one after the other to see who could come out to play ball hockey on Wednesday night, it would take a long time to work through the phone list. The *structure* of the network would be one in which the telephone caller has an individual connection with each of the 50 players, but the players themselves do not necessarily have any connections with each other. There is only one node in the network. On the other hand, if the telephone caller phones five key (or nodal) individuals, who would then call five individuals, and so on, then the telephone calling would be accomplished much more quickly. A telephone tree like this has a different network structure than the single telephone caller model does and can therefore accomplish the task much more efficiently and quickly. Of course the responsibility is also shared so there are more opportunities for the communication network to break down.

Network analysis is interesting because much of social life can be understood as operating outside of either formal organizations or traditional group structures. Social media like Twitter or Facebook connect people through networks. One's posts are seen by friends, but also by friends of friends. The revolution in Tunisia in 2010–2011 was aided by social media networks, which were able to disseminate an accurate, or alternate, account of the events as they unfolded, even while the official media characterized the unrest as vandalism and terrorism. On the other hand, military counterinsurgency strategies trace cell phone connections to model the networks of insurgents in asymmetrical or guerilla warfare. Increased network densities indicate the ability of insurgents to mount coordinated attacks. The amorphous nature of global capital and the formation of a global capitalist class consciousness can also be analyzed by mapping interlocking directorates; namely, the way institutionalized social networks are established between banks and corporations in different parts of the world through shared board members.

Christakis and Fowler (2009) argue that social networks are influential in a wide range of social aspects of life including political opinions, weight gain, and happiness. They develop Stanley Milgram's claim that there is only six degrees of separation between any two individuals on Earth by adding that in a network, it can be demonstrated that there are also three degrees of influence. That is, one is not only influenced by one's immediate friends and social contacts, but by their friends, and their friends' friends. For example, an individual's chance of becoming obese increases 57 percent if a friend becomes obese; it increases by 20 percent if it is a friend's friend who becomes obese; and it increases 10 percent if it is a friend's friend's friend who becomes obese. Beyond the third degree of separation, there is no measurable influence.

Large Groups

It is difficult to define exactly when a small group becomes a large group. One step might be when there are too many people to join in a simultaneous discussion. Another might be when a group joins with other groups as part of a movement that unites them. These larger groups may share a geographic space, such as Occupy Montreal or the People's Assembly of Victoria, or they might be spread out around the globe. The larger the group, the more attention it can garner, and the more pressure members can put toward whatever goal they wish to achieve. At the same time, the larger the group becomes, the more the risk grows for division and lack of cohesion.

Group Leadership

Often, larger groups require some kind of leadership. In small, primary groups, leadership tends to be informal. After all, most families don't take a vote on who will rule the group, nor do most groups of friends. This is not to say that de facto leaders don't emerge, but formal leadership is rare. In secondary groups, leadership is usually more overt. There are often clearly outlined roles and responsibilities, with a chain of command to follow. Some secondary groups, like the army, have highly structured and clearly understood chains of command, and many lives depend on those. After all, how well could soldiers function in a battle if they had no idea whom to listen to or if different people were calling out orders? Other secondary groups, like a workplace or a classroom, also have formal leaders, but the styles and functions of leadership can vary significantly.

Leadership function refers to the main focus or goal of the leader. An instrumental leader is one who is goal oriented and largely concerned with accomplishing set tasks. An army general or a Fortune 500 CEO would be an instrumental leader. In contrast, expressive leaders are more concerned with promoting emotional strength and health, and ensuring that people feel supported. Social and religious leaders—rabbis, priests, imams, and directors of youth homes and social service programs—are often perceived as expressive leaders. There is a longstanding stereotype that men are more instrumental leaders and women are more expressive leaders. Although gender roles have changed, even today many women and men who exhibit the opposite-gender manner can be seen as deviants and can encounter resistance.

Former U.S. Secretary of State and presidential candidate Hillary Clinton provides an example of how society reacts to a high-profile woman who is an instrumental leader. Despite the stereotype, Boatwright and Forrest (2000) have found that both men and women prefer leaders who use a combination of expressive and instrumental leadership.

In addition to these leadership functions, there are three different leadership styles. Democratic leaders encourage group participation in all decision making. These leaders work hard to build consensus before choosing a course of action and moving forward. This type of leader is particularly common, for example, in a club where the members vote on which activities or projects to pursue. These leaders can be well liked, but there is often a challenge that the work will proceed slowly since consensus building is time-consuming. A further risk is that group members might pick sides and entrench themselves into opposing factions rather than reaching a solution. In contrast, a laissez-faire leader (French for "leave it alone") is hands-off, allowing group members to self-manage and make their own decisions. An example of this kind of leader might be an art teacher who opens the art cupboard, leaves materials on the shelves, and tells students to help themselves and make some art. While this style can work well with highly motivated and mature participants who have clear goals and guidelines, it risks group dissolution and a lack of progress. As the name suggests, authoritarian leaders issue orders and assigns tasks. These leaders are clear instrumental leaders with a strong focus on meeting goals. Often, entrepreneurs fall into this mould, like Facebook founder Mark Zuckerberg. Not surprisingly, this type of leader risks alienating the workers. There are times, however, when this style of leadership can be required. In different circumstances, each of these leadership styles can be effective and successful. Consider what leadership style you prefer. Why? Do you like the same style in different areas of your life, such as a classroom, a workplace, and a sports team?

Conformity

We all like to fit in to some degree. Likewise, when we want to stand out, we want to choose how we stand out and for what reasons. For example, a woman who loves cutting-edge fashion and wants to dress in thought-provoking new styles likely wants to be noticed within a framework of high fashion. She would not want people to think she was too poor to find proper clothes. Conformity is the extent to which an individual complies with group norms or expectations. As you might recall, we use reference groups to assess and understand how we should act, dress, and behave. Not surprisingly, young people are particularly aware of who conforms and who does not. A high school boy whose mother makes him wear ironed button-down shirts might protest that he will look stupid—that everyone else wears T-shirts. Another high school boy might like wearing those shirts as a way of standing out. Recall Georg Simmel's analysis of the contradictory dynamics of fashion: it represents both the need to conform and the need to stand out. How much do you enjoy being noticed? Do you consciously prefer to conform to group norms so as not to be singled out? Are there people in your class or peer group who immediately come to mind when you think about those who do, and do not, want to conform?

A number of famous experiments in the 1950s, 60s, and 70s tested the propensity of individuals to conform to authority. Within days of beginning the simulated prison experiment the random sample of university students proved themselves capable of conforming to the roles of prison guards and prisoners to an extreme degree, even though the conditions were highly artificial.

Stanley Milgram conducted experiments in the 1960s on how structures of authority rendered individuals obedient. This was shortly after the Adolf Eichmann war crime trial in which Eichmann claimed that he was just a bureaucrat following orders when he helped to organize the Holocaust. Milgram had experimental subjects administer what they were led to believe were electric shocks to a subject when the subject gave a wrong answer to a question. Each time a wrong answer was given, the experimental subject was told to increase the intensity of the shock. The experiment was supposed to be testing the relationship between punishment and learning, but the subject receiving the shocks was an actor. As the experimental subjects increased the amount of voltage, the actor began to show distress, eventually begging to be released. When the subjects became reluctant to administer more shocks, Milgram (wearing a white lab coat to underline his authority as a scientist) assured them that the actor would be fine and that the results of the experiment would be compromised if the subject did not continue. Seventy-one percent of the experimental subjects were willing to continue administering shocks even beyond 285 volts even though the actor was clearly in pain and the voltage dial was labelled with warnings like "Danger: Severe shock."

Formal Organizations

A complaint of modern life is that society is dominated by large and impersonal secondary organizations. From schools to businesses to health care to government, these organizations are referred to as formal organizations. A formal organization is a large secondary group deliberately organized to achieve its goals efficiently. Typically, formal organizations are highly bureaucratized. The term bureaucracy refers to what Max Weber termed "an ideal type" of formal organization (1922). In its sociological usage, "ideal" does not mean "best"; it refers to a general model that describes a collection of characteristics, or a type that could describe most examples of the item under discussion. For example, if your professor were to tell the class to picture a car in their minds, most students will picture a car that shares a set of characteristics: four wheels, a windshield, and so on. Everyone's car will be somewhat different, however. Some might picture a two-door sports car while others might picture an SUV. It is possible for a car to have three wheels instead of four. However, the general idea of the car that everyone shares is the ideal type. Bureaucracies are similar. While each bureaucracy has its own idiosyncratic features, the way each is deliberately organized to achieve its goals efficiently shares a certain consistency. We will discuss bureaucracies as an ideal type of organization.

Types of Formal Organizations

Sociologist AmitaiEtzioni (1975) posited that formal organizations fall into three categories. Normative organizations, also called voluntary organizations, are based on shared interests. As the name suggests, joining them is voluntary and typically done because people find membership rewarding in an intangible way. Compliance to the group is maintained through moral control. The Audubon Society or a ski club are examples of normative organizations. Coercive organizations are groups that one must be coerced, or pushed, to join. These may include prison, the military, or a rehabilitation centre. Compliance is maintained through force and coercion. Goffman (1961) states that most coercive organizations are total institutions. A total institution is one in which inmates live a controlled life apart from the rest of society and in which total resocialization takes place. The third type are utilitarian organizations, which, as the name suggests, are joined because of the need for a specific material reward. High school or a workplace would fall into this category—one joined in pursuit of a diploma, the other in order to make money. Compliance is maintained through remuneration and rewards.

	Normative or Voluntary	**Coercive**	**Utilitarian**
Benefit of Membership	Non-material benefit	Corrective or disciplinary benefit	Material benefit
Type of Membership	Volunteer basis	Obligatory basis	Contractual basis
Feeling of Connectedness	Shared affinity	Coerced affinity	Pragmatic affinity

Bureaucracies

Bureaucracies are an ideal type of formal organization. Pioneer sociologist Max Weber (1922) popularly characterized a bureaucracy as having a hierarchy of authority, a clear division of labour, explicit rules, and impersonality. Bureaucracies were the basic structure of rational efficient organization, yet people often complain about bureaucracies, declaring them slow, rule-bound, difficult to navigate, and unfriendly. Let us take a look at terms that define bureaucracy as an ideal type of formal organization to understand what they mean.

Hierarchy of authority refers to the aspect of bureaucracy that places one individual or office in charge of another, who in turn must answer to her own superiors. For example, if you are an employee at Walmart, your shift manager assigns you tasks. Your shift manager answers to the store manager, who must answer to the regional manager, and so on in a chain of command up to the CEO who must answer to the board members, who in turn answer to the stockholders. There is a clear chain of authority that enables the organization to make and comply with decisions.

A clear division of labour refers to the fact that within a bureaucracy, each individual has a specialized task to perform. For example, psychology professors teach psychology, but they do not attempt to provide students with financial aid forms. In this case, it is a clear and commonsensical division. But what about in a restaurant where food is backed up in the kitchen and a hostess is standing nearby texting on her phone? Her job is to seat customers, not to deliver food. Is this a smart division of labour?

The existence of explicit rules refers to the way in which rules are outlined, written down, and standardized. There is a continuous organization of official functions bound by rules. For example, at your college or university, student guidelines are contained within the student handbook. As technology changes and campuses encounter new concerns like cyberbullying, identity theft, and other issues, organizations are scrambling to ensure their explicit rules cover these emerging topics.

Bureaucracies are also characterized by impersonality, which takes personal feelings out of professional situations. Each office or position exists independently of its incumbent, and clients and workers receive equal treatment. This characteristic grew, to some extent, out of a desire to eliminate the potential for nepotism, backroom deals, and other types of "irrational" favouritism, simultaneously protecting customers and others served by the organization. Impersonality is an attempt by large formal organizations to protect their members. However, the result is often that personal experience is disregarded. For example, you may be late for work because your car broke down, but the manager at Pizza Hut doesn't care why you are late, only that you are late.

Finally, bureaucracies are, in theory at least, meritocracies, meaning that hiring and promotion are based on proven and documented skills, rather than on nepotism or random choice. In order to get into graduate school, you need to have an impressive transcript.

In order to become a lawyer and represent clients, you must graduate from law school and pass the provincial bar exam. Of course, there is a popular image of bureaucracies that they reward conformity and sycophancy rather than skill or merit. How well do you think established meritocracies identify talent? Wealthy families hire tutors, interview coaches, test-prep services, and consultants to help their children get into the best schools. This starts as early as kindergarten in New York City, where competition for the most highly regarded schools is especially fierce. Are these schools, many of which have copious scholarship funds that are intended to make the school more democratic, really offering all applicants a fair shake?

There are several positive aspects of bureaucracies. They are intended to improve efficiency, ensure equal opportunities, and increase efficiency. And there are times when rigid hierarchies are needed. However, there is a clear component of irrationality within the rational organization of bureaucracies. Firstly, bureaucracies create conditions of bureaucratic alienation in which workers cannot find meaning in the repetitive, standardized nature of the tasks they are obliged to perform. As Max Weber put it, the "individual bureaucrat cannot squirm out of the apparatus in which he is harnessed... He is only a single cog in an ever-moving mechanism which prescribes to him an essentially fixed route of march" (1922). Secondly, bureaucracies can lead to bureaucratic inefficiency and ritualism (red tape). They can focus on rules and regulations to the point of undermining the organization's goals and purpose. Thirdly, bureaucracies have a tendency toward inertia. You may have heard the expression "trying to turn a tanker around mid-ocean," which refers to the difficulties of changing direction with something large and set in its ways. Inertia means bureaucracies focus on perpetuating themselves rather than effectively accomplishing or re-evaluating the tasks they were designed to achieve. Finally, as Robert Michels (1911) suggested, bureaucracies are characterized by the iron law of oligarchy in which the organization is ruled by a few elites. The organization serves to promote the self-interest of oligarchs and insulate them from the needs of the public or clients.

Remember that many of our bureaucracies grew large at the same time that our school model was developed—during the Industrial Revolution. Young workers were trained and organizations were built for mass production, assembly-line work, and factory jobs. In these scenarios, a clear chain of command was critical. Now, in the information age, this kind of rigid training and adherence to protocol can actually decrease both productivity and efficiency. Today's workplace requires a faster pace, more problem solving, and a flexible approach to work. Too much adherence to explicit rules and a division of labour can leave an organization behind. Unfortunately, once established, bureaucracies can take on a life of their own. As Max Weber said, "Once it is established, bureaucracy is among those social structures which are the hardest to destroy" (1922).

The McDonaldization of Society

The McDonaldization of society refers to the increasing presence of the fast-food business model in common social institutions. This business model includes efficiency (the division of labour), predictability, calculability, and control (monitoring). For example, in your average chain grocery store, people at the cash register check out customers while stockers keep the shelves full of goods, and deli workers slice meats and cheese to order (efficiency). Whenever you enter a store within that grocery chain, you receive the same type of goods, see the same store organization, and find the same brands at the same prices (predictability). You will find that goods are sold by the kilogram, so that you can weigh your fruit and vegetable purchases rather than simply guessing at the price for that bag of onions, while the employees use a time card to calculate their hours and receive overtime pay (calculability). Finally, you will notice that all store employees are wearing a uniform (and usually a name tag) so that they can be easily identified. There are security cameras to monitor the store, and some parts of the store, such as the stockroom, are generally considered off-limits to customers (control).

While McDonaldization has resulted in improved profits and an increased availability of various goods and services to more people worldwide, it has also reduced the variety of goods available in the marketplace while rendering available products uniform, generic, and bland. Think of the difference between a mass-produced shoe and one made by a local cobbler, between a chicken from a family-owned farm versus a corporate grower, or a cup of coffee from the local roaster instead of one from a coffee-shop chain. Ritzer also notes that the rational systems, as efficient as they are, are irrational in that they become more important than the people working within them, or the clients being served by them. "Most specifically, irrationality means that rational systems are unreasonable systems. By that I mean that they deny the basic humanity, the human reason, of the people who work within or are served by them."

REFERENCES

1. Allemang, John. 2009. "Elizabeth May is not only Losing Confidence – she agrees with Conrad Black." The Globe and Mail. Toronto. April 18: F.3.
2. Boatwright, K.J. and L. Forrest. 2000. "Leadership Preferences: The Influence of Gender and Needs for Connection on Workers' Ideal Preferences for Leadership Behaviors." *The Journal of Leadership Studies* 7(2): 18–34.
3. Boler, Megan. 2012. "Occupy feminism: Start of a fourth wave?" Rabble.ca. May 29. Retrieved February 25, 2014, from http://rabble.ca/news/2012/05/occupy-feminism-start-fourth-wave
4. Cabrel, Javier. 2011. "NOFX – Occupy LA." LAWeekly.com, November 28. Retrieved February 10, 2012 (http://blogs.laweekly.com/westcoastsound/2011/11/nofx_-_occupy_la_-_11-28-2011.php).
5. Carroll, William. 2010. *The Making of a Transnational Capitalist Class: Corporate Power in the 21st Century*. London: Zed Books.
6. Christakis, N., & J. Fowler. 2009. Connected: The surprising power of our social networks and how they change our lives New York: Little Brown and Co.
7. Christakis, Nicholas and James Fowler. 2009. *Connected: The Surprising Power of Our Social Networks and How They Shape Our Lives*. NY: Little, Brown and Company
8. Department of the Army. 2006. *Counterinsurgency*. Marine Corps Warfighting Publication No. 3-33.5. Retrieved February 28, 2014, from http://www.fas.org/irp/doddir/army/fm3-24.pdf
9. Dowd, Maureen. 2008. "Can Hillary Cry Her Way Back to the White House?" *New York Times*, January 9. Retrieved February 10, 2012 (http://www.nytimes.com/2008/01/09/opinion/08dowd.html?pagewanted=all).
10. Foot, Richard. 2008 "May changes debate rules." *Edmonton Journal* October 13: A.3.
11. McInturff, Kate. 2013. Closing Canada's Gender Gap: Year 2240 Here We Come! *Canadian Centre for Policy Alternatives*. Ottawa. Retrieved February 28, 2014, from http://www.policyalternatives.ca/sites/default/files/uploads/publications/National Office/2013/04/Closing_Canadas_Gender_Gap_0.pdf

CHAPTER 4

COMMUNITY SOCIAL PROGRAM AND SERVICES

INTRODUCTION

Community programs and services encompass a broad array of initiatives designed to meet the diverse needs of local populations. These programs are typically developed and implemented by governmental agencies, non-profit organizations, community groups, and sometimes private entities, aiming to enhance the well-being and quality of life within a specific community or region.

At their core, community programs and services are geared towards addressing various social, economic, health, educational, and environmental issues that impact residents. They often focus on improving access to essential resources such as healthcare, education, housing, and employment opportunities. For instance, healthcare programs may include clinics offering medical services, health education workshops, or initiatives promoting healthy lifestyles and disease prevention. Education-focused programs strive to support learners of all ages by providing tutoring, after-school programs, vocational training, and scholarships. These initiatives aim to enhance educational outcomes and promote lifelong learning among community members. Similarly, housing programs may involve subsidized housing options, homelessness prevention efforts, or housing counseling services to ensure safe and affordable living conditions for residents.

Social services within community programs encompass a range of support systems, including food assistance programs, counseling services, youth development programs, and senior citizen services. These services aim to strengthen social ties, promote mental and emotional well-being, and provide a safety net for vulnerable individuals and families facing crises or challenges.

Environmental programs focus on sustainability practices, conservation efforts, and community beautification projects. They aim to foster environmental stewardship among residents, improve local ecosystems, and mitigate environmental risks and hazards.

COMMUNITY SOCIAL PROGRAMS

Community social programs cover a wide range of programs or activities intended to help seniors beyond those provided by the market or for-profit institutions. Social programs for seniors may be sponsored by federal or state governments with branches or offices at the local community level, or they may be local programs run by cities or towns themselves. In some cases religious, fraternal, or service organizations like the Lions Clubs or Knights of Columbus organize programs to benefit seniors; the Lions Clubs in particular are known for their work in hearing and vision care programs and assistance to the blind. Community social programs for seniors usually fit under one of the following categories.

Understanding Community Context

High profile commissions and reports create conditions for experimentation and optimism about public problem solving. For example, during the 1960s, the U.S. President's Commission on Juvenile Delinquency helped spawn innovative efforts such as those of Mobilization for Youth in New York City. Similarly, in the early 1990s, a national level task force on infant mortality helped launch a multi-site demonstration program known as Healthy Start. High-profile studies such as this help set the public agenda by highlighting what should be addressed and how. Prominent reports frame the dominant explanations for societal problems. For example, a report could focus attention on poverty as a "root cause" of many societal problems or infant mortality as a pressing issue. It might also feature a promising alternative solution, such as equal access to health care or legal assistance, as an innovative way to address social problems.

You might need to use more than one model of community organization practice to fit the variety of contexts in which community work is done. For example, social planning or locality development strategies may fit a context of consensus about common purpose such as working together to reduce violence. By contrast, the strategy of social action, with its disruptive activity and related conflict, may be more appropriate in a context of conflicting interests, such as organizing for decent wages or safe conditions in the workplace.

Crosscutting issues are good contexts for community organization practice. Some community issues, for example, neighborhood safety or substance use, affect the majority of people who share a common place. They also offer a solid basis around which a critical mass of local people can work together. When community organization efforts involve people from diverse backgrounds of income and power -- such as educational or public health improvements that affect people across social class -- substantive change is a lot more likely to happen.

Community organization can't always be separated from politics or controversy. Consider the case of people coming together in a rural community to address issues of toxic waste and environmental pollution. Public debate may focus on both the economic interests of affected businesses, and the health concerns of local residents. It's typical that when two parties are on opposite sides of an issue, neither will get everything they want. Inevitably, a resolution is going to involve politics: the art of reconciling or balancing competing interests.

Poor people can make substantial gains (or losses) during periods of tumultuous change, and related realignment of political parties. Would there have been a Civil

Rights Act of 1964 without rioting and a realignment of the Democratic Party? Political parties want to avoid mass protest or any unorganized behavior if it's at all possible, by changing (or appearing to change) policies, programs, and practices related to voiced concerns. Since mass protest is something those in power try to avoid, it's an important means by which poor people -- with otherwise limited resources -- can achieve power and influence.

Strategies used in community organization should match the times. In times of turmoil, organizing protests and strikes by the people affected by the issues can yield maximum gains. By contrast, in the long times between periods of disruptive actions, community organization might use less conflict-oriented approaches, such as locality development or collaborative partnerships, to define and pursue common purposes.

Mass protest and grassroots community organization can work together. When public protests and other forms of disruption increase, so do the grassroots organizations that address prevailing issues. For example, protests regarding pro-life (anti-abortion) interests were associated with increases in local organizations supporting this and other related causes. When public concern declines, so does organizing at the grassroots. Although protest nourishes organization, the reverse does not hold. Organization doesn't produce protest -- it may even retard it (as when agencies may avoid controversy to protect their funding).

Community organizations form when people are ready to be organized. Although organizations may exist to promote interest in an issue, such as child hunger, little will happen until a significant number of people care about the issue and feel that their actions can make a difference. A big challenge is figuring out when your issue matters to enough people who share a common place or experience, so they can be organized around the issue.

Institutions that want to avoid conflict and controversy may be a difficult base for community organization work. Consider the case of a school-community initiative to prevent adolescent pregnancy or HIV/AIDS. Although schools are well positioned to deliver information and health services to youth, school officials often oppose providing sexuality education or enhanced access to contraceptives for those who choose to be sexually active. So, human service agencies and educational institutions that rely on public funding may be bad choices for lead agencies in community organization efforts that are likely to draw opposition.

Hands-on Assistance with Activities of Daily Living

Social programs of this type are intended to help seniors who need some assistance with food preparation, transportation, or household chores maintain their independence. Meals on Wheels is an example of this type of community social program, as are chore services offered by local nonprofit groups. Chore service programs are often staffed by volunteers who do snow shoveling and other small repair jobs for the elderly, such as putting up storm windows or installing grab bars in the shower. The senior may be asked to pay for any materials needed, but the labor is often free or charged according to a sliding scale.

Transportation services—usually small vans or buses—are another type of community program offered in many cities. In many cases the vans are wheelchair-accessible.

Information and Referral Services

These types of community services help seniors with financial, legal, or health care system issues. As the health care system and government institutions become more complex and hard to navigate, many seniors need help with such tasks as filing taxes, making wills, arranging for household help, or finding their way through the maze of regulations involving Social Security and Veterans Administration benefits. Information and referral services also help seniors locate resources in the local community, such as the transportation, food, and chore services described above. These services may be located in senior centers, public libraries, town halls, or other municipal office buildings.

Some of these services help with job networking, referring seniors who are in good health and looking for part-time employment to potential employers. Others, such as the Experience Works program, go a step further and offer job training and help with resumé writing to low-income seniors who want to continue working and break through the barriers to employment that may have held them back when they were younger. Experience Works is one of 13 national organizations that together operate the Senior Community Service Employment Program (SCSEP), a federal program that provides employment and service opportunities to 100,000 seniors across the United States as of 2008.

Community Planning

Societal and community problems are evidence that institutions are not functioning for people. Much of the framing of societal problems in the 1980s and 1990s focused on the personal attributes of those immediately affected. For example, stated "causes" of high rates of youth crime may highlight the values and behavior of youth and their families such as "poor anger control" or "bad parenting." Such analyses rarely emphasize the contribution of broader environmental conditions, such as availability of jobs or chronic stresses associated with low income, and the institutions responsible for them. In addition to individual responsibility, public institutions -- such as schools, business, religious organizations, and government -- should be held accountable for widespread problems in living.

It's essential to set realistic goals for community organization efforts. Community-based initiatives often overpromise, particularly with grantmakers. Setting unrealistic objectives -- for example, to reduce academic (school) failure by 50 percent in the next two years -- sets the group up for perceived failure. Organizations should carefully assess the feasibility of their proposed aims.

If we set only modest goals, we will probably achieve less. Although goals ought to be achievable, they should also be challenging. Objectives can be overly modest. For example, an overly modest goal might be to reduce rates of school failure (now at 80 percent) by 10 percent within three years. Insufficiently challenging objectives may not bring forth the necessary effort, resources, and degree of change needed to address the community's concern.

Social planning can engage experts (and local people) in helping address societal problems, particularly when there is consensus on the issue. We can advance locally valued purposes by engaging technical experts and local people in defining problems and solutions. Outside experts, such as university-based researchers or public officials, can assist local people in obtaining and interpreting data, facilitating the process of setting priorities, and identifying promising alternatives. But planning can go beyond the traditional roles of facilitating coordination and communication among agencies to identifying environmental conditions to be changed.

Locality development or self-help efforts can also assist in addressing community issues. Local people have the experiential knowledge to come together to define local issues, such as neighborhood safety or jobs, and take action in addressing them. Such self -help efforts have their roots in the settlement house movement in urban neighborhoods. They are guided by respect for the autonomy of local people to decide (and act on) what matters to them.

Local control can hinder collaboration at broader levels of planning. Planning at higher levels than the neighborhood, city, or town may be necessary to address the broader conditions that affect community organization efforts. For example, the growing concentration of poverty in the urban core, a result of regional planning decisions and other broader policies, is a structural issue that affects community development efforts within inner-city neighborhoods. Although it's desirable for community building, strong local control may hinder the broader planning and coordination necessary to address local issues.

Companionship and Fellowship

Many communities and local churches or synagogues sponsor senior centers where older adults can gather for companionship as well as physical exercise and other activities. Although senior centers in the 1960s and 1970s were primarily social clubs, the aging of the baby boomer generation has led to a wider range of activities offered. Many senior centers have grown into large free-standing buildings offering everything from educational courses, language classes, field trips, game nights, and book discussion clubs to adult day care , yoga and t'ai chi classes, medical screening, nutritional information, and vocational counseling.

There are also many volunteer organizations related to religious institutions or local schools and colleges that recruit and train members to visit homebound seniors and relieve their loneliness. In some cases these visitation programs lead to the formation of long-term friendships between the senior and his or her visitor.

Active Volunteering

There are a growing number of organizations that offer seniors opportunities to serve others. The wisdom and life experience that many seniors have acquired is a valuable resource to the larger society. A national organization that offers volunteer opportunities to seniors 55 years of age and older is the Senior Corps, authorized under the Domestic Volunteer Service Act of 1973. The Senior Corps is the umbrella organization for three programs, the Foster Grandparents Program, which began in 1965; the Senior Companions Program, which began in 1968, and RSVP, which is a more varied program in which senior volunteers can do everything from helping small businesses get started to assisting with disaster relief to planting community gardens. All three programs provide orientation and on-the-job training; the Foster Grandparents program provides insurance coverage and a modest stipend to volunteers caring for or tutoring neglected or educationally disadvantaged children.

Viewpoints

There is little debate about the many benefits that community social programs offer, not only in providing hands-on help to seniors in need, but also in keeping seniors involved in the life of their local community and less vulnerable to social isolation . The many gifts and talents that older adults have to offer are a resource for children and younger adults, many of whom need mentoring and companionship too. In a period of history in which American society seems to be increasingly divided into racial, gender, or socioeconomic groupings, community programs that help to break down age-related barriers may soften the other divisions as well.

Community Action and Mobilization

*Each individual has the capacity for self-determination, self-help, and improvement.*A basic assumption of community organization is that people most affected by local concerns, including those labeled as "clients" of agency services, can do something about them. This "strengths" perspective highlights people's assets and abilities, not their deficits and limitations. While it acknowledges personal and community competence, it also recognizes the importance of environmental supports and barriers that affect engagement in community life. For self-determination efforts to be successful, we must create opportunities for working together, and increase the positive consequences of community action.

You can't do it by yourself. Addressing what matters to local people -- good health, education, and jobs, for example -- is beyond any one of us. The idea of "ecology" -- interactions among organisms and the environment -- helps us see community action as occurring within a web of relationships. Community life is enhanced when individual strengths are joined in common purpose -- an expression of the principle of interdependence. We are interconnected: each of us has a responsibility to make this a world good for all of us.

Strong leaders are present in even the most economically deprived communities. Authentic leaders -- those who enable constituents to see higher possibilities, and pursue them together -- are among us. Yet, they may not always be acknowledged by those in authority. When doing community organizing in low-income public housing, I found that a simple question helped in "discovering" local leaders: "Who do children go to when they are hurt and an adult isn't home?" Such questions help us discover the "servant leaders" among us: those who "lead" by addressing the interests of their "followers."

Community practitioners should never get used to the terrible conditions they see in their community work. Those doing community work, particularly in low-income communities, are exposed to horrible things: children in uncaring and unhealthy environments; adults without adequate food, clothing, and shelter; and other conditions essential for a decent life. Practitioners should avoid becoming desensitized about how they feel about what they see and hear. Disclosing experiences and feelings to colleagues is one way to help support each other. Community activists must also decide how to use those feelings -- such as anger about conditions in which some people live -- to energize and sustain their work.

People's beliefs and values enable them to stay committed. To make a difference, those doing community work must be in it for the long haul. People's values, such as fairness or respect for the dignity of others, help sustain their efforts. For instance, a personal or family history of discrimination -- a common experience for many racial and ethnic minorities -- may incline us to embrace the value of social justice and to work for equality of opportunity.

The work of community organization is like that of a "secular church." Faith communities and religious institutions help shape our beliefs about what is right and good, such as our responsibility to care for others. Community-based organizations, such as a homeless coalition or tenants-rights organization, call us to serve the common good -- things beyond ourselves. As such, they enable us to devote our lives to higher purposes, while working in this world.

Community practitioners have few opportunities to reflect on the work. Those doing the work of community building are often consumed by its demands. For example, leaders and staff of community-based organizations rarely take time to consider the lessons learned about community action, barriers and resources, or other features of their work. Personal reflection journals and periodic group retreats help leaders and groups to reflect on and review the initial purposes and recent directions of their organizations. As such, they promote "praxis" -- the joining of understanding (theory) and action (practice).

Responding to events and opportunities to build community often takes us beyond what we know. Community practice is largely an art form. Effective intervention is shaped more by trial and error than by tested general statements about the conditions under which specified interventions (the independent variable) effect desired behavior and outcome (the dependent variables). Yet, attention to the conditions that matter to local people -- crime, drug use, and poverty, for example -- cannot wait for the findings of research trials. We must be decisive in the face of uncertainty, even when the scientific evidence for a chosen course of action is inadequate.

COMMUNITY EDUCATION

In numerous polls and surveys, Americans identify education as one of the leading domestic challenges of the twenty-first century. Specifically, the challenge is not just to reform public schools but also to achieve the goal of academic success for all students. Many educational experts agree that reaching that goal will require increased cooperation among the schools themselves and a new kind of collaboration with the families and communities served by the schools.

Community education offers a structured, effective way to respond to the challenge to improve public education because it expands the school's traditional role and creates a mutually interdependent relationship among home, school, and community. Community education has three basic components–lifelong learning opportunities, community involvement in schools, and efficient use of resources–and is based on a set of ten broad principles:

- *Lifelong learning.* Education is a birth-to-death process, and everyone in the community shares in the responsibility of educating all members of the community. Formal and informal learning opportunities should be available to residents of all ages in a wide variety of community settings.
- *Self-determination.* Community residents have a right and a responsibility to be involved in assessing community needs and identifying community resources that can be used to address those needs.

- *Self-help.* People are best served by their leaders when their capacity to help themselves is acknowledged and developed. When people assume responsibility for their own well-being, they achieve some degree of independence.
- *Leadership development.* Training local leaders in problem solving, decision-making, and group-process skills is essential to community improvement efforts.
- *Institutional responsiveness.* Because public institutions exist to serve the public, they are obligated to develop programs and services that address constantly changing public needs and interests.
- *Integrated delivery of services.* Organizations and agencies that operate for the public good can best use their limited resources, meet their own goals, and serve the public by collaborating with organizations and agencies with similar goals and purposes.
- *Localization.* Community services, programs, and volunteer opportunities close to people's homes have the greatest potential for high levels of public participation.
- *Maximum use of resources.* The physical, financial, and human resources of every community should be fully available and rationally interconnected if the diverse needs and interests of the community are to be met.
- *Inclusiveness.* Community programs, activities, and services should involve the broadest possible cross-section of community residents without segregation by age, income, sex, race, ethnicity, religion, or other characteristics.
- *Access to public information.* Public information should be shared across agency and organization lines because an effective community not only has "the facts," but it also knows what those facts mean in the lives of the diverse people who make up the community.

A Comprehensive Plan

The current lack of confidence in public education has been more pervasive and prolonged than the crisis in confidence that followed the launch of *Sputnik* in 1957 by the Soviet Union. Community education has become the approach of choice of many educators who are determined to improve the public confidence in schools and to build partnerships in support of public education.

Community education is a way of looking at public education as a total community enterprise. A community education program is a comprehensive and coordinated plan for providing educational, recreational, social, and cultural services for all people in the community. The following strategies provide a framework for developing such a program. The strategies have overlapping characteristics and functions, but taken together, they outline a comprehensive action plan.

Encourage increased use of community resources and volunteers to augment the basic educational program. Every community has human, physical, and financial resources that can be used to enrich and expand traditional education programs. Community resources and volunteers have been used to expand curricular options, conduct field and study trips, offer various kinds of tutoring, sponsor student-based enterprises, and support experiential learning.

Develop educational partnerships between schools and public and private service providers, business and industry, and civic and social service organizations. Complex, often interrelated, social and economic problems create a broad array of service needs in many communities, and meeting them effectively is likely to require more resources than any single agency or organization can provide. The development of partnerships for cooperative use of available resources will help prevent unnecessary duplication in the delivery of such services as child care, after-school programs, drug education and treatment, literacy and remedial programs, internships and work-study programs, and career awareness activities.

Use public education facilities as community service centers for meeting the educational, social, health, cultural, and recreational needs of all ages and sectors of the community. Since community attitudes and support affect the schools' ability to carry out their mission to educate all children, educators must consider the needs and concerns of nonparents in the community. This strategy encourages keeping school buildings open on a planned, organized basis at hours beyond the regular school day. It takes advantage of the strong support community centers generally receive, as well as the economic benefits to the community of more efficient use of public facilities.

Develop an environment that fosters lifelong learning. This strategy acknowledges learning as a lifelong process. It recognizes that learning takes place, both inside and outside the school setting, without formal instruction. It encourages the development of education programs to meet learning needs that change over a lifetime, including the need for new skills and knowledge. Lifelong learning programs and activities may include early childhood education, extended-day and enrichment programs for school-age children, adult education, vocational training and retraining programs, leisure activities, and intergenerational programs.

Establish a process for involving the community in educational planning and decision-making. The total community has a stake in the mission of educating community members. Individual community members, therefore, have a right and a responsibility to participate in determining community needs, setting priorities, and allocating resources. The cyclical process of planning, evaluating, and changing takes advantage of a basic fact of human behavior: Those who participate in planning and decision-making develop feelings of ownership. Encouraging the broadest possible involvement capitalizes on another fact: The greater the number and diversity of people involved, the greater the likelihood that diverse needs will be met. Involvement opportunities should range from participation in ongoing advisory councils to membership on ad hoc task forces and committees.

Provide a responsive, community based system for collective action by all educational and community agencies to address community issues. Many community problems are so complex that resolving them requires cooperative use of a broad range of resources. Seeking the involvement of non-school agencies can help schools address such social, health, and economic issues as substance abuse, housing, child abuse, mental illness, violence, crime, vandalism, teen pregnancy, and various kinds of discrimination.

Develop a system that facilitates home-school-community communication. Research shows that schools that involve all their publics and keep them well informed have community support, and that those that fail to reach beyond the parents of current students do not. Effective home-school-community communication goes beyond news releases, speeches, newsletters, and open houses; it includes use of the media, home visitations by teachers and administrators, school displays throughout the community, and special community outreach programs conducted both in the schools and at other sites in the community.

Community School

The term community school designates a school site where the concept of community education is put into practice. Community education may also be implemented in community agencies and organizations, but the most common site is a public school.

A community school departs from a traditional public school's schedule and curriculum. A community school is open year-round, eighteen hours or more a day, often seven days a week. The school thus becomes not just a place to teach children but a community learning center with multiple uses.

In a community school, the concept of public education is extended beyond the traditional K–12 program to include the provision of learning opportunities for the entire community. The traditional schedule is expanded through extended day programs (including before- and after-school activities and care), and recreational, social, and educational programs for community residents of all ages. Activities and programs may not be limited to the school building, itself, as the school extends itself into the community, turning agencies, factories, businesses, and the surrounding environment into learning laboratories.

By organizing programs and activities that serve all ages and populations, a community school encourages disparate elements of the community to come together to work toward common goals. It provides a physical setting as well as an organizational structure for school-community collaboration.

Impact on Education and Communities

Because many community problems ultimately affect a community's ability to educate all children, educators in some communities are taking a leadership role in the search for solutions to community problems. From a problem-solving point of view, a community school can be a support center for a network of agencies and institutions committed to addressing broad community needs. Using schools as community centers is a cost-effective, practical way to use one of the community's largest investments–its school buildings. The community school reaches out to the community and works as a cooperative partner to address community needs, including educational needs. The possible benefits to schools and communities from a well-designed and carefully implemented community education program have been described in a variety of studies, including the U.S. Department of Education's Strong Families, Strong Schools (1994) and Safe and Smart, from the U.S. Departments of Education and Justice (1998). Documented improvements include a better school learning climate, reduced violence and vandalism, more efficient energy use, increased family involvement, and broadened community-wide educational opportunities. Other studies show improved institutional responsiveness to the needs of parents and community members and increased public support for schools and other public agencies.

Community Education in Action

Community education takes advantage of local resources and capabilities and responds to an individual community's particular needs and wishes. Just as no two communities have exactly the same program, no community retains exactly the same program over a period of years. As a community matures, its institutions, population, assets, and problems change, and its community education program must be modified to reflect those changes if it is to remain successful.

Because every community education program is designed to reflect the current needs of a specific community and the resources available to meet those needs, there are literally hundreds of models of programs. The website of the National Center for Community Education has descriptions of exemplary models and case studies of community education programs in three model settings–school, district, or agency. The website of the Coalition for Community Schools profiles nine community schools (four elementary, two middle, two high schools, and one preschool).

COMMUNITY SERVICE

Community service is work done by a person or group of people that benefits others. It is often done near the area where you live, so your own community reaps the benefits of your work. You do not get paid to perform community service, but volunteer your time.

Community service can help many different groups of people: children, senior citizens, and people with disabilities, even animals and the environment. Community service is often organized through a local group, such as a place of worship, school, or non-profit organization, but you can also start your own community service projects.

Many people participate in community service because they enjoy helping others and improving their community. Some students are required to do community service in order to graduate high school or to receive certain honors. Some adults are also ordered by a judge to complete a certain number of community service hours.

When someone performs an action which benefits his or her community, it is known as community service. Some people associate community service with punishment, since it is often offered to small-time offenders as an alternative to fines or jail time. However, community service can also be altruistic, and it is a vital part of many small communities. Getting involved in your community makes it healthier and livelier, and numerous organizations around the world support community service activities.

Things which could be considered community service include tutoring children, building homes in low income areas with Habitat for Humanity, assisting the elderly, socializing animals at animal shelters, being a museum docent, performing habitat restoration, contributing to the operations of volunteer fire departments and emergency services, or helping with civic beautification. In all cases, community service work is performed by volunteers who are not paid for their time. In some instances, the work would not be accomplished without the work of such volunteers, and many small organizations rely on people with community spirit to survive.

For people who are given community service as a punishment or sentence, it can be an opportunity to atone for a crime. Others engage in community service out of a spirit of altruism, or a desire to connect with their communities by helping out. For people who are new to a community, community service can be a great way to learn more about the place in which they live and the people they live with. Community service may also be required for things like high school graduation or membership in an organization, in which case the school or organization often helps to organize community service opportunities.

For people who are not affiliated with an organization, finding community service opportunities is easy. In many cases, an organization which needs the assistance of volunteers has a volunteer coordinator. Contact the organization you are interested in to ask about volunteers, or check bulletin boards around town for organized community service activities. You may find anything from a group of birdwatchers performing habitat restoration in a local wetlands to an association of businesses sponsoring graffiti cleanup.

Many people engage in community service because they believe that it carries rewards beyond the obvious and tangible. Clearly, engaging in things like environmental restoration and civic beautification will make your life enjoyable by making the world around you more pleasant. But community service can also help to ensure that important services like meals for the elderly and volunteer fire departments continue to run. It also helps to build a rich and supportive community of people who know each other and lend each other a hand when it is needed.

Types of Community Service

The term community service refers to any act that is performed for the benefit of the community at large. Acts can range from a one-time effort to collect canned goods for the local food pantry to a weekly commitment to serve meals to the homeless. People do not receive financial compensation for their services, although a number of award programs exist to recognize the contributions of volunteers.

In many cases, community service is performed as part of a person's membership in a social organization. Boy Scouts or Girl Scouts may volunteer to read to the elderly residents at a local nursing home or collect toys to distribute to needy children in the community. Members of a church fellowship may take a weekend trip to help build houses for Habitat for Humanity. A professional association for accountants may organize an effort to provide low-income people with tax preparation assistance.

A person does not have to be a member of a specific organization to participate in community service activities, however. Many people choose to volunteer as a way to meet other people with similar interests, much like how one might socialize at a nightclub or a sporting event. Volunteering can be a great way for retirees to remain active in their community. Stay at home parents often use volunteer work to keep their professional skills sharp during their break from the workforce.

Community service, while ideally a voluntary act, is sometimes required by schools as a condition for high school graduation. In addition to enhancing a student's college application, studies have shown that teenagers who volunteer typically show improved academic performance. Under mandatory service arrangements, teenagers must complete a specified number of hours of supervised community service per semester. However, they are usually allowed to choose activities that best fit their own personal interests, such as singing in the church choir or helping to organize library books.

Community service may also be ordered as punishment for a crime. In the case of nonviolent offenders, such as people convicted of drunk driving, it may be ordered instead of jail time. For incarcerated inmates, community service is sometimes required as part of the prison's rehabilitation program. Cleaning up trash, removing graffiti, planting trees, or building playground equipment while under the supervision of prison guards are common tasks performed under this type of arrangement.

Illustrations of Community Service

Community service is work done by a person or group of people that benefits others. It is often done near the area where you live, so your own community reaps the benefits of your work. You do not get paid to perform community service, though sometimes food and small gifts, like a t-shirt, are given to volunteers.

Community service can help any group of people in need: children, senior citizens, people with disabilities, English language learners, and more. It can also help animals, such as those at a shelter, and it can be used to improve places, such as a local park, historic building, or scenic area as well. Community service is often organized through a local group, such as a place of worship, school, or non-profit organization. You can also start your own community service projects.

Some students are required to complete community service as part of a class requirement in order to graduate high school or become a member of certain organizations, such as the National Honor Society. Adults can also participate in community service as a way to help others or if they are ordered to do so by a judge.

There are hundreds of ways to participate in community service, depending on your skills and interests. Some common community service examples include:

- **Working with schoolchildren:** Tutoring children after school, collecting school supplies to donate, planting a school garden.
- **Working with senior citizens:** Visiting residents of a retirement center, delivering meals to senior citizens, driving them to appointments.
- **Improving the environment:** Holding a recycling contest, planting trees, creating a new trail at a nature center.
- **Helping low-income people:** Passing out food at a soup kitchen, collecting used clothes to be donated, making first aid kits for homeless shelters.

Role of Community Development Worker

A community development worker is a professional who seeks to improve a community through the creation, management, and operation of community assistance and outreach programs. There are many different job categories for a person in this position; the tasks of the job vary based on the region, type of organization, and available programs. Working in community development is a possible career path for anyone who wants to use communication skills and an organized mind to help benefit local people. The educational background of a community development worker may vary. Some have bachelor's degrees in social work, business, political science, or communications. In some cases, development workers may have a master's degree or PhD in a related field. Community development workers may also have specialty licenses that allow them to provide unique services to an organization, such as lawyers, doctors, and accountants. Jobs with higher salaries and more responsibilities may require greater education, but some less-educated development workers may rise to high positions through talent and tenacity alone.

The day-to-day tasks of a community development worker will depend largely on where he or she is employed. Community service organizations may be governmental, non-profit, religious, or even based out of educational institutions. Different organizations offer very different services, with everything from low-cost meals for disabled and elderly citizens to free legal advice for people facing eviction. The goal that most community development organizations have in common is to make noticeable changes that benefit all citizens, but the means to achieving that goal can be very unique to each organization.

Some tasks that a community development worker might have include working directly with clients of the organizations, writing grant proposals and working on fund raising, compiling and analyzing research on community issues so as to create targeted programs, and hiring or managing volunteers. Development workers may also need to liaise with other organizations and local governments, so that resources can be pooled and applied in the most effective way possible. The multitude of possible job opportunities means that the field is wide open to those with a passion for helping the local community.

People who go into the field of community development often have a passion for social justice, politics, and helping others. Skills that may be useful in this field include the ability to work in teams, excellent communication, strong leadership qualities, and belief in the organization's mission. Armed with these skills, a community development worker can be a powerful force for change in their work.

Community Service Importance

Community service is unpaid work performed by a person or group of people for the benefit and betterment of their community without any form of compensation. Community service can be distinct from volunteering, since it is not always performed on a voluntary basis and may be compulsory per situation. Although personal benefits may be realized, it may be performed for a variety of reasons including citizenship requirements, a substitution of criminal justice sanctions, requirements of a school or class, and requisites for the receipt of certain benefits.

Most importantly, students learn that the work they do can make a real impact in the world. By getting involved in community service at a young age, children also:

1. **Develop a Richer Perspective of the World They Live In.** Volunteering is an essential part of preparing students to "take responsibility as open minded, principled citizens in a global community." While performing community service, children have the opportunity to see first-hand just how much their work can have an impact on the world. Many of our

students at volunteer locally at food shelves, animal shelters, in retirement communities, and even at orphanages abroad. They get to interact with people who have vastly different backgrounds, and learn patience and empathy as they develop a global perspective.

For example, Grade 5 students recently partnered with students in Grades 1 and 2 to host a "Green" (used) Book Fair. Through the sales of donated books, the children were able to donate money to help other children at Chester Addison Community Center in Stamford.

2. **Connect What They Learn in School to the Real World.** Community service gives students an opportunity to explore academic interests through a real world lenses. If a child is intrigued when he or she learns about recycling in school, for example, they can pick up recyclables from local businesses and take them to a local recycling center to see the impact firsthand. Volunteering during an election can help them learn more about how the government functions, or cleaning up the Long Island Sound can help them learn more about environmental issues firsthand.

We've found that when students connect what they're learning in school to issues that actually matters in real life, they throw themselves into learning. Research also back this up. Studies show that students who give back to the community perform better in school, particularly in subjects such as math, reading, and history. Furthermore, students who participate in community service are also more likely to graduate from high school.

3. **Get Ahead in the College Admissions Process.** As admission to elite colleges and universities has become more competitive, volunteer experience can prove an advantage in the college admissions process. For that reason, many students start doing community service projects as they advance through high school. Students who begin earlier, however, have a distinct advantage because their breadth of experience allows them to quickly step up to leadership positions within organizations.

Family Involvement in Community Service

It's easy to feel disconnected, as many parents juggle work, school, kids, and activity after activity. But some simple things can bring a family closer — playing a game, going for a hike, or cooking a meal together.

One of the most satisfying, fun, and productive ways to unite is volunteering for community service projects. Volunteerism also sets a good example for your kids and helps the community.

Reasons to Get Involved

Why should your family lend a helping hand?

- **It feels good.** The satisfaction and pride that come from helping others are important reasons to volunteer. When you commit your time and effort to an organization or a cause you feel strongly about, the feeling of fulfillment can be endless.
- **It strengthens your community.** Organizations and agencies that use volunteers are providing important services at low or no cost to those who

need them. When a community is doing well as a whole, its individuals are better off, too.

- **It can strengthen your family.** Volunteering is a great way for families to have fun and feel closer. But it can be hard to find the time to volunteer. So try rethinking some of your free time as a family. You could select just one or two projects a year and make them a family tradition (for example, making and donating gift baskets to care facilities for the elderly around the holidays).

What Kids Can Learn From Volunteering

If volunteering begins at an early age, it can become part of kids' lives — something they might just expect and want to do.

It can teach them:

- **A sense of responsibility.** Kids and teens learn what it means to make and keep a commitment. They learn how to be on time for a job, do their best, and be proud of the results. But they also learn that, ultimately, we're all responsible for the well-being of our communities.
- **That one person can make a difference.** A wonderful, empowering message for kids is that they're important enough to have an impact on someone or something else.
- **The benefit of sacrifice.** By giving up a toy to a less fortunate child, a child learns that sometimes it's good to sacrifice and that there are important things besides ourselves and our immediate needs.
- **Tolerance.** Working in community service can bring kids and teens in touch with people of different backgrounds, abilities, ethnicities, ages, and education and income levels. They'll learn that even the most diverse individuals can be united by common values.
- **Job skills.** Community service can help young people decide on their future careers. Are they interested in the medical field? Hospitals and clinics often have teenage volunteer programs. Do they love politics? Kids can work on the real campaigns of local political candidates. Learning to work as a team member, taking on leadership roles, setting project goals — these are all skills that can be gained by volunteering and will serve kids well in any future career.
- **How to fill idle time wisely.** If kids aren't involved in traditional after-school activities, community service can be a wonderful alternative.

Getting Your Family Involved

The Internet offers lots of sites with information about volunteer opportunities. You can also call a favorite charity, hospital, or church directly to see if they have any needs. Or contact a local volunteer clearinghouse, which matches up volunteers and community organizations and can help you find openings at nonprofit organizations in your area.

When looking for a volunteer position, remember that it may be difficult to find the perfect volunteer slot. Be flexible, and keep looking if the agency you were referred to doesn't meet your needs. It may take a while to find a perfect fit, but once you do, it will be worth it.

Good Volunteer Jobs for Families and Kids

Families can do many volunteer jobs. Even the smallest child (with adult supervision) can pick up garbage at the park, playground, or beach. You don't even have to be part of a big effort to do this. Get your family together, find some garbage bags, and head out.

Or become involved in repair and renovation efforts for low-income residents. Younger kids might not be able to do the big jobs, but helping out by fetching a paintbrush or holding the nails involves them just the same.

Work at a community food bank or soup kitchen as a family. Find an organization that serves the elderly. Take food to people who are homebound and visit with them. Your kids can brighten a lonely senior's day instantly. Offer your family's help at the local animal shelter. Help plant flowers or trees. The possibilities are endless. Whatever you choose to do, volunteering and community service can benefit both the community and your family. Get involved today!

Intervention and Maintenance of Efforts

The strategy of community organization should fit the situation.

The broad and specific means of intervention should match the ends, and the context. For example, social planning -- using technical information often with the guidance of outside experts -- may assist in defining goals when people share common interests. Similarly, locality development -- featuring self-help efforts of local people -- may be appropriate for reducing a particular problem, such as substance use or neighborhood safety, around which there is widespread agreement. In contrast, social action -- with its disruptive tactics and related conflict -- may be needed in contexts of opposing interests such as in reducing discrimination or disparities in income or power.

Using multiple strategies usually has an advantage over any single strategy.

Some initiatives -- for instance, a campaign for school reform -- get stuck using one preferred means of action, such as collaborative planning or disruptive tactics, even when the goals or conditions shift. By invoking only one strategy, the organization's actions may be easier to ignore and the benefits of complementary approaches may go untapped. For example, the threat of disruptive tactics (social action) may make support for self-help efforts (locality development) more likely. Flexibility in strategy, and use of multiple means, may enhance community efforts and outcomes.

Being in two cultures promotes creativity.

Some community practitioners operate in more than one system of influence. For example, those who combine research and practice must respect the influences of both academic disciplines and members of community-based organizations. Being open to different audiences helps integrate disparate ideas, discover novel solutions, and transform practice.

The work of community organization takes time, and follow-through.

Mobilizing people for action requires substantial time and effort. Making the calls and personal contacts to bring about a change in school policy, for example, cannot be done solely by volunteers. The stimulation and coordination of community work, like any other valued work, should be paid for. Without salaries for community mobilizers or organizers, follow-through on planned actions is rare.

External support may be both a necessity and a trap for community organizations.

Community organization efforts seldom are maintained without external resources.Yet, financial support usually has strings attached. For example, accepting money from foundations or the government may restrict advocacy efforts. Although often a necessity, outside resources may come at the price of compromising the group's goals or available means of action.

Community organizations often fade away.

When the issue that a community organization was formed around begins to fade, so may the organization. For example, a taxpayer rights organization may dissolve when its goal of blocking a particular public expenditure, such as a school bond issue, is resolved. Organizations that endure after the issue subsides may lose members unless they reinvent themselves to address other emerging issues.

Organizations need small wins.

"Small wins" are shorter-term, controllable opportunities that can make a tangible difference. For example, a good neighborhood organizer might work for improved trash pickup or more streetlights to provide (literally) visible benefits of group action. Without the small victories, community organizations won't retain current members -- or attract new ones.

Promoting Community Change

The central ideal of community organization practice is service.

Practitioners' interests should always be lower on the list than the interests of those of the people served. Yet, when disciplines, such as social welfare or public health, market training for "professionals" in the work of community organization, they risk creating professions in which the practitioners benefit more than the clients. Professions that certify people -- and not promising practices or demonstrably effective methods -- may emphasize the interests of professionals (or guild interests), and not those experiencing the problems.

Community organization must go beyond the process of bringing people together.

For some practitioners, dialogue among representatives of different groups is a sufficient "outcome" of community development efforts. Yet, local people who come together to address what matters to them are usually interested in going beyond talk, and on to action and achieving results. Community organization efforts should bring about tangible benefits such as community change, problem solving, and furthering social justice.

The primary need is not for individuals to adjust to their world, but for environments to change so people can attain their goals.

Much framing of societal problems focuses on the deficits of those most affected. For example, prominent labels for causes of academic failure might include "poor motivation" (of youth) or "poor monitoring" (by parents). Alternatively, analyses of academic failure might address such environmental conditions as "few opportunities to do academic work" (in schools) and "limited opportunities for employment" (following school). Community health and well being are private and public matters, calling for both individual and social responsibility.

Community-based organizations can function as catalysts for change.

Effective community organizations transform the environment: they alter programs, policies, and practices related to the group's mission. For example, a disability rights organization might modify policies regarding employment discrimination against people with disabilities or establish new job training programs that accommodate people with different impairments. In their role as catalysts for change, community organizations convene others, broker relationships, and leverage resources for shared purposes.

Influencing Systems (Or Broader) Change

The level(s) of intervention should reflect the multiple levels that contribute to the problem.

Consider the typical interventions for most societal problems. For example, job training to address unemployment or drug awareness programs to counter substance use, is typical of initiatives trying to change the behavior of those with limited power who are closest to the "problem," for instance, low-income adults (unemployment) or youth (substance use).

When used alone, service programs and targeted interventions, such as for so-called "at risk" adults or youth, may deflect attention away from more root causes, such as poverty and the conditions of opportunity that affect behavior at a variety of levels. Resolution of many societal issues, such as crime or unemployment, requires changes in decisions made by corporate and political decisionmakers at levels higher than the local community.

Systems change does not occur simply by reporting felt needs to appointed or elected officials.

For those with higher economic or political status, simply expressing a concern may have influence on decisions that affect them. A variety of traditional means is available to such groups as a way of exerting influence; they include petitioning, lobbying, influencing the media, supporting political candidates, and voting in large numbers. These means are largely unavailable to those most affected by many societal problems, however, such as children and the poor. Marginalized groups lack the resources to exert influence in conventional ways.

The great power of social movements is in communicating a different vision of the world.

Marginalized groups use the drama of protest -- and the conflict it provokes -- to display realities not widely regarded as important. For example, the media may cover a strike and related protests by farm workers or coal miners, and the violence it often evokes from owners, the police, or others in power. Media coverage helps convey the story of the conditions faced by the protesters, and the unfairness of the action (or inaction) of businesses or institutions that are targeted. The dramatic nature of protest and related conflict can help politicize voters who, through enhanced public support of the positions of marginalized groups, can exert influence on those in power.

Community organizations should seek changes within their power to manage.

Since ignoring is likely and retaliation is possible, small organizations with limited power should avoid seeking fundamental changes in the system. For example, a single grassroots organization in a low-income neighborhood may not be positioned to effect systems changes such as altering the priorities of grantmakers who support work in the community. But, small and scrappy organizations may succeed in bringing about community change when their bulkier counterparts do not.

Community and broader systems change can be brought about through collaboration.

Collaboration involves alliances among groups that share risks, resources, and responsibilities to achieve their common interests. For example, local community-based organizations interested in the well being of children can link with each other to create local programs (e.g., mentoring), policies (e.g., flextime to be with children after school) and practices (e.g., adults caring for children not their own).

Additionally, broader partnerships with grantmakers, government agencies, and business councils can affect the conditions in which change occurs at the community level. An example is altering grantmaking programs to support collaborative work or promoting child-friendly business policies through industrial revenue bonds or new corporate policies. Collaborative partnerships help bring about community and system change when they link local people to resources and institutions at the multiple levels in which change should occur to address common interests.

Achieving Community-Level Improvements

Societal problems often reoccur. Consider the problem of gang violence that occurred after World War II and reoccurred in the 1990s. Broad social conditions -- wide disparity of income, weak social ties, and related mistrust of others -- appear to affect the likelihood of societal problems such as increased death rates, infant mortality, and perhaps youth violence. Improvements achieved in one era may need to be reestablished by future generations that must again transform the environmental conditions that support the reoccurrence of societal problems.

Most community efforts "chip" away at the problem. The majority of community interventions do not match the scale of the problem. For example, a community effort may prepare 10 unemployed people to compete for only one available job, or may create 100 jobs in a community with thousands of unemployed. We often make small changes in a context that remains unchanged.

Real change is rare. Significant improvements in community-level outcomes are highly unusual -- such as cases of reducing rates of adolescent pregnancy or academic failure by 50 percent or more. Yet, in requests for grants, community-based organizations often promise (and grantmakers expect) statements of objectives that indicate significant improvements as a result of only modest investments over a short time. We should not perpetuate myths about what most interventions can actually accomplish.

Development of community leadership may be a positive byproduct of even a "failed" community effort. Although an initiative may not produce statistically significant changes in community benchmarks or indicators, it may develop new leaders or build capacity to address new issues in the future. For instance, a public health initiative that produces only modest reductions in rates of adolescent pregnancy may develop the capacity to produce changes that matter, such as four years later when the group switches its efforts from adolescent pregnancy to child well-being.

Community documentation and evaluation must help us see what is actually achieved by community initiatives, including evidence of intermediate outcomes (e.g., community and system change) and other indicators of success or "failure" (i.e., community capacity over time and across issues).

Optimal health and development for all people may be beyond the capacity of what communities can achieve, but not beyond what they should seek. Most community-based efforts, such as those to create healthy environments for all our children, will fall short of their objectives. Yet, justice requires that we create conditions in which all people can make the most of their inherently unequal endowments. Support for community initiatives should be guided by what we must do for current and future generations, not by what limited gains we have made in the past.

BENEFITS OF COMMUNITY SERVICE

There are many benefits of participating in community service, and some of the most important ones are listed below.

Have the opportunity to help others: This is often the most important benefit of community service. Participating in it gives you the opportunity to know that you are improving someone's life and making your community better, and you get to see the direct impact of your work.

Gain hands-on experience: You can learn a lot of skills while performing community service such as construction, painting, customer service, and medical skills. You can also include your community service work on your resume.

Learn about different careers: Sometimes you can focus your community service in a field you may want to work in down the road. Some examples of this include volunteering at an animal shelter if you are thinking about becoming a veterinarian, working at a hospital if you want to be a doctor, or volunteering in a museum if you like history. The experience gained from community service can help you get an internship or job in the future, and it also gives you the opportunity to see how much you would really enjoy a particular career.

Personal growth: Doing community service has personal benefits as well. It often makes participants more organized, responsible, and compassionate, which are all good qualities to have, as well as qualities that both colleges and employers like to see in applicants.

Gain new friends: A final benefit is that you can meet a lot of great people while doing community service. Community service is often done in groups, so it's easy to make friends with the people you are working with. You may also become friends with the people you are helping, especially if you volunteer at the same place regularly.

Community service is when you work for free to help benefit the public or your community. Usually, students who choose to do community service do so as volunteers, meaning that they choose to help out because they want to do so. Community service can have a lot of positive effects on students, such as helping them to develop skills, making contacts, and allowing them to improve the quality of life of others.

You probably know some students in your school who choose to volunteer their free time through community service. There are many ways that you can do this, such as joining a non-profit organization, working with a church group, or you can choose a cause and create your own service project.

For some ideas of community service activities, see our list of volunteer ideas.

Volunteer work can range from the relatively simple, like helping coach the lacrosse team at your old junior high, to the much more complex, like starting a non-profit that helps settle new refugees in your area.

Health Benefits

Numerous studies over the past several years have shown that volunteering isn't just good for your mind and conscience; it's also good for your body. By focusing on others' problems instead of their own, students have reported reduced stress, and overall improvement in mood and health.

Researchers at the London School of Economics and Political Science found a link between self-reported levels of good health and happiness and formal volunteer work. Furthermore, a study by United Health Group says that 76% of people who have volunteered in the past twelve months say that volunteering has made them feel happier, and 94% of people report that it improves their mood. 78% of volunteers say that it has lowered their stress levels.

Volunteering can also help protect people from depression during challenging times, as it tends to help create a strong support system for participants. Volunteering also keeps people physically healthy by keeping them active. Certain activities, such as working to clean up a park or a beach, can be good exercise. Studies have shown that especially as people get older, volunteering in these kinds of projects can keep people healthy and can even lessen the symptoms of certain diseases.

Of course, not all the benefits of volunteering are limited to the volunteer. Another big way that people benefit is in their involvement with their community.

Community Benefits

Volunteering allows students to become directly involved in their communities. Some students don't realize how important volunteers are to the country and to many organizations. But try to imagine if no volunteers showed up to work tomorrow. Can you imagine what would change?

Volunteers are responsible for many things that we take for granted. When hurricanes hit the south coast or wildfires burn up California, volunteers are critical in helping victims get re-settled, fed, and back to their "normal" lives as quickly as possible. Without volunteers, many of our country's elderly would not be able to get food. Our parks and beaches would be much dirtier. Our children would struggle more without the help of volunteer tutors and mentors.

To get a real idea of how important volunteers are to keeping the country running, let's look at the numbers. The top activities performed included raising money for important causes; collecting, preparing, and giving out food to people who need it; providing labor and transportation; tutoring and mentoring youth; and lending professional expertise.

Furthermore, volunteers are almost twice as likely to donate to charities as non-volunteers. In all, just over 50% of Americans donated over $25 to charities in 2013, making at least $4 billion in donations.

The knowledge that they are making a real difference also affects student volunteers on a more personal level. When students know their work is helping someone, they show increased rates of self-esteem. Furthermore, students who volunteer are more likely to become actively involved citizens who take a strong interest in current events and local affairs, and are much more likely to vote.

Apart from helping out your community here and now, you'll also be helping out your future self.

School Benefits

You may be familiar with community service already because it is something that your school requires. In fact, many high schools throughout the United States require their students to help out the community in some way in order to graduate. Though it's often on the honor system to report what you've done, these high schools may require up to 200 hours of community service before they're willing to grant a degree.

This type of requirement can be especially common at religious schools, and in particular at Christian schools. Many Christian schools set requirements based on the Biblical idea that it is the Christian's duty to do community outreach with whatever "gift" they have been given by God. Because of this, many of these Christian schools will have branches of Christian non-profits, such as the Salvation Army or Habitat for Humanity, on campus or affiliated with the school, which make it much easier for students to donate their time.

Many other schools require service learning. This term describes an approach to education that aims to connect lessons learned in the classroom with real-life lessons learned through community service. It is a practice that has become increasingly common in both high schools and universities in the United States, because educators like that the learning process benefits both the students and the communities. It allows students to learn more about their personal motivations, practice academic material outside of the context of the classroom and testing, develop critical thinking skills while solving real-world problems, and to think about problems and social issues in new ways.

This kind of experiential learning, or applying what you have learned in the classroom to the real world, has a lot of positive benefits for students apart from meeting a requirement to graduate. These include a better understanding of the value of teamwork, decision-making skills, development of leadership abilities, and the gain of practical skills.

Working with a team, you would gain a better understanding of the importance of sharing information in a usable way. You might eventually expand your duties into other areas, such as managing the organization's social media accounts, which would further develop your writing skills.

Additionally, you would be gaining a new perspective on your community and on what life is like for a group of people that is often overlooked: the terminally ill. This could change how you see the world and your role in it. In fact, many students report that this kind of personal development is the most valuable part of a service learning projects.

College Benefits

Have you ever wondered if volunteering makes a big difference in college admissions?

The truth is that it's one of the most popular extracurricular activities that students list on their college applications. And while colleges don't necessarily expect students to have spent all their free time volunteering, schools (especially the more competitive ones) will usually notice a total lack of community service.

Colleges like seeing that students have done community service. Keep in mind that most universities want to admit students who are actively involved in activities that better themselves, and eventually, will better the world. Students who have been actively involved in community service in high school show colleges that they will be the type of student who will be actively involved in making the college community a better place to be. Eventually, that they will be the kind of people who care about changing the world.

On a more practical level, the personal benefits and development that you will get from volunteering can be great topic matter for a college application essay.

The people you work with on community service projects will be good people to turn to when the time comes for letters of recommendation. They'll be able to speak to your leadership abilities, passion, and character. Finally, doing this kind of work shows prospective schools that you can balance activities with your schoolwork and that you have good time management.

The good news doesn't end there, though. The benefits of volunteering will follow you out of school and into the workplace, as well.

Professional Benefits

Did you know that employers love volunteers? The results were very positive for those who have chosen to donate their time:

- 84% of employers agreed that volunteering is a good way for people to find work.
- 70% of employers said that volunteers have a better chance of getting a higher salary and a promotion.
- 80% of employers said that they like to see volunteer work on a resume.
- 23% of employers said that volunteering had helped their staff learn key skills, such as time management, communication skills, and leadership skills.

The study also showed that half of the employees surveyed thought that their volunteer experience had helped them land their job, and up to 20% of employees thought that their volunteer experience helped them gain key skills in communication, leadership, and time management that were important to their jobs.

As you can see, there are a lot of ways that your community service work will help you down the road once you start work, beginning with what you choose to do.

Volunteering is a great way to explore different interests. High school students who do community service can try different kinds of work and work environments that they otherwise would likely not be exposed to at such a young age. Most paying jobs that high school students are eligible for – such as working in fast food - are not the most interesting. But volunteering can give you a chance to try things that you will be interested in as a career, such as working in social media, organizing events, or working in a specific type of institution such as a hospital.

The experiences that you gain will also look great on your resume. Future employers will likely be much more interested in hearing about a fundraiser that you ran than they will be in hearing about your burger flipping skills. Why? A lot of the personal development benefits discussed above, such as leadership skills and the ability to collaborate with a team, are things that translate well to many jobs and workplaces.

Networking is another major benefit of volunteering. As a volunteer, you will be very likely to meet like-minded individuals who share your interests. In the future, these people can be important contacts for writing letters of recommendation and for putting you in touch with the right people for scholarships and jobs.

Now that you know that community service is an extracurricular that will help you out in your personal life, as well as in high school, college, and your professional life, what are you waiting for?

Personal Development Benefits

One of the big ways that students will benefit from volunteer work is through personal development.

This happens in a number of ways.

First of all, many students learn about their personal strengths and weaknesses. When you're working on campaigns and projects and getting to see real-life results, you'll get to know how your personal attributes and actions can make a difference. Many of these qualities are things that students can't get good feedback on in the classroom. For example, students may learn that they have excellent skills in coping with a crisis or other stressful situations, or may learn that they find taking charge of a team to be a struggle. This kind of exposure to different situations can then teach students how to further develop skills that they have, and how to work on areas they struggle in.

In particular, students find that they are able to develop skills in leadership, communication, working well with a team, and finding solutions for problems.

Many students also find that community service makes them more aware of and interested in issues of social justice.

For example, if you spend your days going to school, playing sports, and doing homework, you will likely not spend a lot of time thinking about the problems that homeless people encounter.

On the other hand, if you're working every day at a homeless shelter, you'll have a chance to dispel stereotypes about why people become homeless while also learning about the unique challenges that homeless people face in getting off the streets. Many homeless people face prejudice that makes returning to work and earning a self-supporting living more difficult than it is for non-homeless people.

Once people learn more about struggles and injustices that other groups of people face, they are statistically more likely to want to actively take part in making a change in the policies and social structures that keep certain groups from succeeding. This change can take many forms, such as active campaigning, voting in elections, and continuing to volunteer time to important causes.

Volunteering has also been shown to have one other, more tangible major personal benefit. Did you know that it's actually good for your health?

HELPING PROCESS IN COMMUNITY SERVICE

Community service is a non-paying job performed by one person or a group of people for the benefit of their community or its institutions. Community service is distinct from volunteering, since it is not always performed on a voluntary basis. It may be performed for a variety of reasons.

- It may be required by a government as a part of citizenship requirements, like the mandatory "Hand and hitch-up services" for some municipalities in Germany, or generally in lieu of military service or for civil conscription services.
- It may be required as a substitution of, or in addition to, other criminal justice sanctions – when performed for this reason it may also be referred to as community payback.
- It may be mandated by schools to meet the requirements of a class, such as in the case of service-learning or to meet the requirements of graduating as class valedictorian.
- In the UK, it has been made a condition of the receipt of certain benefits.
- In Sweden it is a suspended sentence called "samhällstjänst" ("society service").

Community service is a great way to help others and improve your community, and it can also help you gain skills and experience.

Below here listed over lots of community service ideas to get you started with brainstorming.

General Ideas

- Donate or raise money for your local Red Cross
- Organize a community blood drive
- Send cards to soldiers serving overseas
- For your next birthday, ask for charitable donations instead of gifts
- Hold a bake sale for your favorite charity
- Read books or letters to a person who is visually impaired
- Organize a wheelchair basketball team
- Participate in a charity race
- Organize an event or parade for Memorial Day
- Volunteer to help at a charity auction
- Participate in National Youth Service Day in April
- Contact a tree farm about donating Christmas trees to nursing homes, hospitals, or to families who can't afford to buy their own
- Collect unused makeup and perfume to donate to a center for abused women

- Help register people to vote
- Organize a car wash and donate the profits to charity
- Help deliver meals and gifts to patients at a local hospital
- Write articles / give speeches advocating financial literacy. First you should learn about the topics themselves, like calculating housing costs, or understanding personal loans, and then give presentations on these topics.

Helping Children and Schools

- Tutor children during or after school
- Donate stuffed animals to children in hospitals
- Organize games and activities for children in hospitals or who are visiting hospitalized relatives
- Knit or crochet baby blankets to be donated to hospitals or homeless shelters
- Collect baby clothes and supplies to donate to new parents
- Organize a Special Olympics event for children and teenagers
- Sponsor a bike-a-thon and give away bike safety gear, like helmets and knee pads, as prizes
- Collect used sports equipment to donate to families and after-school programs
- Volunteer at a summer camp for children who have lost a parent
- Sponsor a child living in a foreign country, either on your own or as part of a group
- Coach a youth sports team
- Put on performances for children in hospitals
- Give free music lessons to schoolchildren
- Become a volunteer teen crisis counselor
- Organize a summer reading program to encourage kids to read
- Organize an Easter egg hunt for neighborhood children
- Create a new game for children to play
- Organize events to help new students make friends
- Babysit children during a PTA meeting
- Organize a reading hour for children at a local school or library
- Donate used children's books to a school library
- Work with the local health department to set up an immunization day or clinic to immunize children against childhood diseases
- Volunteer to help with Vacation Bible School or other religious camps

Helping Senior Citizens

- Read to residents at a nursing home
- Deliver groceries and meals to elderly neighbors
- Teach computer skills to the elderly
- Drive seniors to doctor appointments
- Mow an elderly neighbor's lawn
- Host a bingo night for nursing home residents
- Host a holiday meal for senior citizens

- Make birthday cards for the elderly
- Donate and decorate a Christmas tree at a nursing home
- Organize a family day for residents of a retirement home and relatives to play games together
- Ask residents of a retirement home to tell you about their lives
- Pick up medicine for an elderly neighbor
- Perform a concert or play at a senior center
- Help elderly neighbors clean their homes and organize their belongings
- Rake leaves, shovel snow, or wash windows for a senior citizen
- Deliver cookies to a homebound senior citizen

Helping Animals and the Environment

- Take care of cats and dogs at an animal shelter
- Clean up a local park
- Raise money to provide a bulletproof vest for a police dog
- Plant a tree for Arbor Day
- Place a bird feeder and bird fountain in your backyard
- Start a butterfly garden in your community
- Sponsor a recycling contest
- Grow flowers in your backyard then give bouquets to hospital patients or people who are housebound
- Help create a new walking trail at a nature center or park
- Update the signs along a nature trail
- Adopt an acre of rainforest
- Help train service dogs
- Participate in the cleanup of a local river, pond, or lake
- Foster animals that shelters don't have space for
- Organize a spay and neuter your pet program
- Care for a neighbor's pet while they are away
- Sponsor an animal at your local zoo
- Train your pet to be a therapy animal and bring it to hospitals or nursing homes
- Build and set up a bird house
- Organize a carpool to reduce car emissions
- Campaign for more bike lanes in your town
- Volunteer at a nature camp and teach kids about the environment
- Test the water quality of a lake or river near you
- Plant native flowers or plants along highways

Helping the Hungry and/or Homeless

- Build a house with Habitat for Humanity
- Donate your old clothes
- Volunteer at a soup kitchen
- Donate old eyeglasses to an organization that collects that and distributes them to people in need
- Donate non-perishable food to a food bank
- Donate blankets to a homeless shelter

- Host a Thanksgiving dinner for people who may not be able to afford their own
- Offer to babysit or nanny for a family in need
- Make "care kits" with shampoo, toothbrushes, combs, etc. to donate to homeless shelters
- Prepare a home-cooked meal for the residents of a nearby homeless shelter
- Collect grocery coupons to give to a local food bank
- Help repair or paint a local homeless shelter
- Donate art supplies to kids in a homeless shelter
- Help organize and sort donations at a homeless shelter
- Babysit children while their parents look for jobs
- Become a Big Buddy for children at a homeless shelter
- Take homeless children on outings
- Bake a batch of cookies or loaf of bread and deliver it to a soup kitchen
- Build flower boxes for Habitat for Humanity houses
- Organize a winter clothes drive to collect coats, hats, scarves, and gloves to be donated
- Make first aid kits for homeless shelters

Reducing Crime and Promoting Safety

- Volunteer at a police station or firehouse
- Become a certified lifeguard and volunteer at a local pool or beach
- Paint over graffiti in your neighborhood
- Organize a self-defense workshop
- Organize a drug-free campaign
- Sponsor a drug-free post-prom event
- Start or join a neighborhood watch program
- Create and distribute a list of hotlines for people who might need help
- Teach a home-alone safety class for children
- Create a TV or radio public service announcement against drug and alcohol use
- Become CPR certified
- Volunteer as a crossing guard for an elementary school

Promoting Community Enhancement

- Paint park benches
- Donate used books to your local library
- Become a tour guide at your local museum
- Repaint community fences
- Plant flowers in bare public areas
- Organize a campaign to raise money to buy and install new playground equipment for a park
- Participate in or help organize a community parade
- Clean up vacant lot
- Produce a neighborhood newspaper
- Campaign for more lighting along poorly lit streets

- Create a newcomers group in your neighborhood to help welcome new families
- Petition your town leaders to build more drinking fountains and public restrooms
- Volunteer to clean up trash at a community event
- Adopt a local highway or road and clean up trash along it
- Help fix or raise funds to repair a run-down playground
- Clean up after a natural disaster

REFERENCES

1. Adler, M. (1981). *Six great ideas: truth, goodness, beauty, liberty, equality, justice: ideas we judge by, ideas we act on*. New York, NY: Macmillan.
2. Alinsky, S. (1969). *Reveille for radicals*. Chicago: University of Chicago Press.
3. Altman, D., Balcazar, F., Fawcett, S. B., Seekins, T., & Young, J. (1994). *Public health advocacy: Creating community change to improve health*. Palo Alto, CA: Stanford Center for Research in Disease Prevention.
4. Balcazar, F., Seekins, T., Fawcett, S., & Hopkins, B. (1990). *Empowering people with physical disabilities through advocacy skills train*. American Journal of Community Psychology, 18, 281-295.
5. Bracht, N. (Ed.) (1990). *Health promotion at the community level*. Newbury Park, CA: Sage Publications.
6. Brager, G. & Specht, H. (1973). *Community organizing*. New York, NY: Columbia University Press.
7. Branch, T. (1988). *Parting the waters: America in the King years* 1954-63. New York, NY: Simon and Schuster.
8. Brown, M. (2006). *Building powerful community organizations: A personal guide to creating groups that can solve problems and change the world*. Arlington, MA: Long Haul Press.
9. Cobb, R., & Elder, C. (1972). *Participation in American politics: The dynamics of agenda-building*. Baltimore: The Johns Hopkins University Press.
10. Cook, T. & Campbell, D. (1979). *Quasi-experimentation: Design and analysis issues for field settings*. Chicago: Rand McNally.
11. Cox, F., Erlich, J., Rothman, J., & Tropman, J. (1987). *Strategies of community organization: Macro practice*. (4th ed.). Itasca, IL: F. E. Peacock Publishers, Inc.
12. Cuoto, R. (1990). *Promoting health at the grass roots*. Health Affairs, 9, 145-151.
13. Dass, R. & Gorman, P. (1985). *How can I help? Stories and reflections on service*. New York, NY: Alfred A. Knopf.
14. Dunham, A. (1963). *Some principles of community development*. International Review of Community Development, 11, 141-151.
15. Fawcett, S. (1991). *Some values guiding community research and action*. Journal of Applied Behavior Analysis, 24, 621-636.
16. Fawcett, S., Lewis, R., Paine, A., Francisco, V., Richter, K., Williams, E., & Copple, B. *Evaluating community coalitions for the prevention of substance abuse: The case of Project Freedom*. Health Education and Behavior.
17. Fawcett, S., Paine, A., Francisco, V., Vliet, M. (1993). *Promoting health through community development. Promoting Health and Mental Health in Children, Youth, and Families* (pp. 233-255). D. S. Glenwick & L. A. Jason (Eds.). New York, NY: Springer Publishing Company.

CHAPTER 5

COMMUNITY DEVELOPMENT

INTRODUCTION

Community development is a practice-based profession and an academic discipline that promotes participative democracy, sustainable development, rights, equality, economic opportunity and social justice, through the organization, education and empowerment of people within their communities, whether these be of locality, identity or interest, in urban and rural settings.

Community development is a process where community members come together to take collective action and generate solutions to common problems. Community wellbeing (economic, social, environmental and cultural) often evolves from this type of collective action being taken at a grassroots level.

Community development is a process where people come together to take action on what's important to them. At its heart, community development is rooted in the belief that all people should have access to health, wellbeing, wealth, justice and opportunity. It recognizes that some people, some groups and some communities are excluded and oppressed by the way society and structures are organized. Community development seeks to challenge this and ensure fairness for all citizens.

In practice, community development:

- Supports communities, of place and identity, to use their own assets to improve the quality of community life.
- Helps communities and public agencies to work together to improve services and the way in which decisions are made.
- Community development is fundamentally based on the values of human rights, social justice, equality and respect for diversity.
- The principles which underpin its practice are:
- Self-determination - people and communities have the right to make their own choices and decisions.

- Empowerment - people should be able to control and use their own assets and means to influence.
- Collective action - coming together in groups or organizations strengthens peoples' voices.
- Working and learning together - collaboration and sharing experiences is vital to good community activity.

APPROACHES OF COMMUNITY DEVELOPMENT

Community development is a process where community members take collective action on issues that are important to them. This might be done with or without the support of a community development professional or agency. Community development is intended to empower community members and create stronger and more connected communities.

Community development is a holistic approach grounded in principles of empowerment, human rights, inclusion, social justice, self-determination and collective action. Community development considers community members to be experts in their lives and communities, and values community knowledge and wisdom.

Community development programs are led by community members at every stage – from deciding on issues to selecting and implementing actions, and evaluation. Community development has an explicit focus on the redistribution of power to address the causes of inequality and disadvantage.

Outcomes of Community Development

There are potential outcomes at both individual and community levels. Children and families directly involved in community development initiatives may benefit from an increase in skills, knowledge, empowerment and self-efficacy and experience enhanced social inclusion and community connectedness. As community members are empowered and develop as leaders, they can begin to challenge and improve conditions that are resulting in their disempowerment or negatively impacting their wellbeing.

At a community level, community development initiatives are likely to achieve long-term outcomes such as stronger and more cohesive communities, evidenced by changes in social capital, civic engagement, social cohesion, community safety and improved health.

Community development is not one-off events, consultation to inform goals or strategies, community advisory groups or committees, or leadership training. All these things could be part of a community development strategy but, by themselves, they are not community development.

Community-Based Work and Community Development Work

Community development can be undertaken independently by community members or groups, or with the support of a community development professional or agency. Community-based work that consults or involves community members is often confused with community development work. Table 1 outlines the difference between community-based work, which involves the community, and community development work, which is led by the community.

Table 1. Comparing community-based with community development work

Community-based work	Community development work
An issue or problem is defined by agencies and professionals who develop strategies to solve the problem and then involve community members in these strategies. Ongoing responsibility for the program may be handed over to community members and community groups. Characteristics: • Decision-making power rests with the agency. • The problem or issue is defined by the agency. • There are defined timelines. Outcomes are pre-specified, often changes in specific behaviours or knowledge levels.	Community groups identify important concerns and issues, and plan and implement strategies to mitigate their concerns and solve their issues. Characteristics: • Power relations between agency and community members are constantly negotiated. • The problem or issue is first named by the community, then defined in a way that advances the shared interests of the community and the agency. • Work is longer term in duration. • The desired outcome is an increase in the community members' capacities. • The desired long-term outcomes usually include change at the neighbourhood or community level.

When to use Community Development

Community development is not always a suitable approach to use. Community development may be particularly appropriate:

- **to address social and community issues** – community development is a good approach when you are trying to create change at a community or neighbourhood level. For example, if your goal is to improve community safety, increase community cohesion, reduce social isolation or create communities that are better for children.
- **for Aboriginal and Torres Strait Islander communities** – community development is a good approach to use with Aboriginal or Torres Strait Islander communities because it can enable self-determination and strengthen local First Nations organisations and grassroots community groups
- **for disadvantaged communities** – community development initiatives work well in disadvantaged communities where they can alleviate some of the impacts of disadvantage on children and families by building social

capital and social inclusion (Ife, 2016; McDonald, 2011; Price-Robertson, 2011 [AIFS]; Ortiz et al., 2020) and can empower community members to challenge inequitable conditions that are negatively impacting their wellbeing (Ife, 2016).

Community development may not be the best approach if:

- **You already know what you want to do** – If the outcomes you want to achieve and the activities that you will use are already decided then there is no space for the community to determine outcomes and activities. Similarly, if you don't have the authority or resources to implement the community's decisions, community development is not a suitable strategy.
- **You have limited time or short-term funding** – Community development is a long-term process. Engagement and planning can take a year or more, and it can take several years to implement projects and ensure sustainable results.
- **Your focus is improving specific individual skills** – If you are seeking to build individual skills in a specific area (e.g. parenting skills or literacy), a program that targets these directly may be more appropriate.

Who can do Community Development?

It is important to recognise that community development is a practice with a well-developed theoretical framework. Community development practitioners should be familiar, through training or experience, with the theory, practice and principles of community development work. In saying this, it is important that community development practitioners have effective and respectful relationships with the communities they are working with, and sometimes the ability to build these relationships with the community is a more important quality for a worker than having a community development qualification. In these instances, it is important that the worker is supported by someone who has a good understanding of community development theory and practice.

Role of a Community Development Practitioner

The key role of a community development practitioner is to resource and empower the community. This is done through a broad range of actions and activities, which change depending on the context. Community development practitioners support community members through the provision of information needed to identify issues and plan actions. This could include sharing information on local data, good practice around particular identified issues, and relevant programs and resources that are available. Community development practitioners also connect with and build local networks and leaders, undertake community engagement and plan, deliver and evaluate projects and programs. Community development practice has a focus on facilitation, education, capability building and resourcing skills.

Difference between Community Development and other Approaches

Asset-Based Community Development (ABCD): ABCD is a version of community development that begins the development process by identifying and building on a community's 'assets' rather than needs. Assets include physical spaces, skills, local knowledge, local groups and associations and networks as well as financial resources (Kretzmann & McKnight, 2005).

Strengths-based approach: A strengths-based approach seeks to build on an individual's strengths rather than deficits. This can be a good practice for a community development practitioner to use but by itself is not community development.

Collective impact: Both community development and collective impact are place-based initiatives (i.e. they are developed in – and are unique to – the area in which they are delivered). Collective impact aims to create community-wide change on a particular social issue, and practitioners seek to do this by working towards five 'conditions' that provide a framework for collaboration between stakeholders. A key difference between collective impact and community development is the role that community members play in leadership and decision making. While initial descriptions of collective impact did not centre community as decision makers, collective impact is an evolving practice and more recent conceptualisations include a greater role for community engagement and leadership. However, while some collective impact projects may be community-led, this is not universal. Community development is always driven by the community, with issues and actions determined by community members.

Principles in Community Development

Promote Community Leadership and Ownership. The most important principle is, through the community development process, to actively working with the community to increase leadership capacity, skills, confidence, and aspirations. Our work is to help community members understand the economic, social, political, environmental, and psychological impact of alternative solutions to the problem. The community has the primary responsibility for decision-making. This decision-making includes issue identification, planning, implementation, and resource mobilization to solve agreed-upon problems by emphasizing shared leadership and active citizen participation. Therefore, the community members are primarily responsible for initiating community change work and should own it.

Secure Human Rights. The community initiative should focus on human rights principles. The community and practitioners must adopt the Universal Declaration of Human Rights in their work. The first three articles of the Universal Declaration of Human Rights states that "All human beings are born free and equal in dignity and rights"; "Everyone has the right to life, liberty, and security of person," and "Everyone is entitled to all the rights and freedoms without distinction of any kind, such as race, colour, sex, language, religion, political or other opinion, national or social origin, property, birth or other status ". The Universal Declaration of Human Rights must shape our collective work with the community because this instrument allows community and Community Development workers to identify their challenges and barriers. This instrument (Universal Declaration of Human Rights) also provides community and Community Development workers provided legitimate/lawful grounds for addressing community issues, human development, and fighting against poverty, discrimination, and oppression. As a Community Development worker, you may practice various approaches such as the Human Rights-Based Approach, Anti Oppression Approach, and Anti-

Racism Approach in community development work. One common thing in these approaches is that 'people are at the heart of community development and workers collaborate with the community members to bring positive change'.

Enhance Quality of Living. The community development should focus on the well-being and quality of living. The initiative may focus on economic, physical, and/or social development. A multi-year initiative may focus on all these components. However, the community initiative is most successful when the community takes one step at a time.

Promote Social Justice. As transformative community workers, our work must be guided by social justice principles, especially equity and inclusion. Community workers work with the community and critically examine the root causes of poverty, marginalization, and exclusions. Therefore, community practitioners work with excluded community members and equip them with knowledge, skills, and resources for their empowerment.

Bottom-Up Approach: Community Participation and Engagement. Community workers continue to put their efforts into ensuring the active participation of community members in the community change process. Community group members who experience poverty, marginalization, violence, conflicts, or environmental disasters know their needs and what needs to be done. Community workers should engage community members in problem diagnosis so that those affected may adequately understand the causes of their situation (Michigan State University). Therefore, as community workers, we must strive to engage the community from 'the bottom-up' in every step of the project/program, from issue identification to project planning, implementation, and evaluation. The traditional top-down service delivery approach where community members are just recipients of services and not active participants is disempowering and further marginalizes community members. Without a bottom-up approach, community initiatives may cause harm to people.

Community Assets / Capital and Resource Mobilization. Community development initiatives should build upon and focus on community assets / capital. Both terms 'assets' and 'capital' are used interchangeably, and mean the same thing, which are the strengths of the community. Asset-based CD (ABCD) is a term used to each community relies on different forms of capital to maintain itself and grow stronger. Capital includes environmental, physical, economic, human, information, political, and social resources in the community. A community needs all these forms of capital. Among these, social capital is most important in community development. We create social capital when we become involved with one another in routine, often organized ways. High levels of social capital in a community promote coordination, communication, participation, cooperation, and engagement; thus, positive change is possible. Rather than seeing communities as "needy" and problem-based, communities should be seen in terms of assets, skills, and capacities. Exploring, identifying, and mobilizing local capital are the key responsibilities of community workers for sustainable community development. The sustainable development of communities requires mobilizing citizens and their governments to strengthen all forms of community capital.

Partnership and Collaboration. Community issues and problems are complex. These issues may arise due to individual, cultural and systemic oppression, colonialism, neoliberal policies, patriarchal system, and climate change. A community may not have all the necessary resources and capital to address its issues and problem. Therefore, community work highly depends on partnership and collaboration. A partnership may involve institutions, external philanthropists, and/or community advocates that can support the host community with technical, financial, and resources.

Sustainability. Community development initiatives must consider results for the present time and future. Sustainable development meets the needs of the present without compromising the ability of future generations to meet their own needs. Sustainable development requires a fundamental economic and social change to improve human well-being while protecting the environment. Therefore, community development should produce self-reliant, self-sustaining communities that mobilize resources for the benefit of all members. Community work must not compromise any environmental and socio-economic degradation; instead, it works with the community with a holistic plan and actions for the community members' well–being.

Respect Indigenous Worldviews and Local Culture. Indigenous communities see development holistically. Indigenous worldviews see the whole person (physical, emotional, spiritual, and intellectual) as interconnected to land and in relationship to others (family, communities, nations). Therefore, these holistic values should be adopted for socio-economic well-being and sustainable development in the community work practice. On the other hand, each community has a rich culture and heritage. Our community development work should respect local culture, norms, and practices. However, some community work may address harmful cultural norms and practices for fair living.

Resilience and Empowerment. Finally, the ultimate goal of community work is to make the community resilient and empowered so that community people should be able to control and use their assets and means to influence. The community development practice should promote self-determination so that people and communities have the right to make their own choices and decisions. Community development initiatives should promote active citizen participation so that community members can meaningfully influence decisions that affect their situation (Michigan State University). In other words, the community development should strengthen people's voices and allow them to take collective actions for their socio-economic, cultural, and environmental development and well-being.

Process in Community Development

Step 1: Defining the professional's role

Community worker may act as organizer, educator, coach, facilitator, advocate, negotiator, manager, researcher, and communicator

Step 2: Researching the Community

Community worker should learn the community by gathering information from secondary (statistics, Government and non-government agencies report etc.) and primary sources (interacting with community).

Step 3: Entering the Community

This step is important because community worker needs understand the community dynamics, their history, culture, social capitals, power relations, and gradually approach community. Sometimes, community worker need formal approval to work with a community. For example, I had to take formal permission from Village Head while entering into an Indigenous community.

Step 4: Consciousness-raising

At the initial phase, community workers engage with local residents and discuss socio-economic issues by asking questions. In this step, community worker may utilize adult education for encouraging dialogue and learning. This process build sense of belonging among the community members, help them to understand and challenge oppression.

Step 5: Assessment of Needs and Assets

It is a process where community worker collect information public forums, through survey, interviews, focus group discussion. Needs refers to gap between what exist and what should be in a community and assets are resources that can bridge the gap. This step helps community to develop a plan. A few tasks can be done at this stage:

- Identify community/affected people. This group/people will be the focus of community work
- Identify community issues, capacities and needs by engaging local community, agencies/institutions working/affiliated with the community.
- Identify stakeholders for the community project/initiative. Stakeholder means people or agency that are directly or indirectly related to the issue which may include local agencies, leaders, funders.

Step 6: Setting Goals

A goal is a short statement about "what a group wants to accomplish and should be based on reality" and example might be " to form a neighborhood youth council". A community worker can facilitate this process through a brainstorming session with community members and agency staff working locally.

Step 7: Organization Building

Community development work can be initiated by a group community people. It is helpful to establish an organization so that community and agency can raise funds. Most funders provide funding to non-profit and registered charities.

Step 8: Strategizing

A community worker can support agency to develop agencies strategic plan with vision, mission, objectives that reflects community proprieties.

- Objectives are statements of what to accomplish by when and they are concrete and action oriented. Here is an example SMART objective: For a youth initiative may be "to increase the employment rate for youth in Regent Park by 10 % over three years".
- Strategies describe "how the objectives will be accomplished".
- The action steps explain who will do what by when.

- Select appropriate resource mobilization strategy.
- Identify local in-kind and cash resources to link with other resources to implement a specific plan with the community.

Step 9: Taking Action

Taking action is the critical step in community work. The community imitative may face challenges and resistance from community. Some work can be done at this stage are:

- Implement the strategy/plan emphasizing on shared leadership and collaboration.
- Engage the community in the implementation and monitoring of the project/ initiative
- Gather ongoing feedback on the interventions from the community

Step 10: Evaluation

At this stage, following work can be done:

- Assess the program impacts on the target audience and others to determine if the stated goals and objectives are met.
- Community members and program participants are consulted using research methods such as interviews, focus group discussion, case study collection
- Celebrate project success and share lessons learned
- If not successful, engage with community to re-plan and implement revised plan

COMMUNITY DEVELOPMENT STRATEGY

Leaders in towns, cities, and villages all over the world know that their communities do not simply spring up overnight. The particular elements that make up a community need to be placed in the appropriate environment, under the appropriate circumstances, and they need to be cultivated into something that is both successful and cohesive as a whole. It takes time, effort, and a lot of patience to get results. Certainly, it isn't going to be an easy task for anyone to do.

Community development is a crucial aspect for any municipal area. Civic leaders dedicate resources and sections of their budgets toward community development because of the value it holds for their residents. It's a major part of urban planning, and the two frequently are tied together even when they are separated. As a result, it is incredibly important to have an understanding of what community development entails and what can be done to ensure its success.

Clearly defining community development and what its primary elements include allows for a better understanding of the more complex aspects. The value of community development, both domestically and internationally, and who in the community is involved in the process.

Many people mistake community development as another name for urban planning. It's often what people think of first when the concept is brought up. While the two are similar and can have a symbiotic relationship in a community, they are not the same. Community development is defined by the United Nations as a process where the conditions of social and economic progress are created through participation within the community and reliance on community initiatives. Different communities tend to use different means to achieve this, but it is generally a universal concept regardless.

Until recently, community development was imagined as a type of gentrification and renovation for poor, decrepit neighborhoods in desperate need of improvement. This has been the typical view of community development for many years and is still treated as such to some degree today. However, many communities use community development as a means of general improvement for the benefit of all. The goal(s) a community has will often focus on providing resources to residents of all socioeconomic levels in the neighborhood, and giving them the opportunities to use services they need when they need them.

It should be noted that when discussing community development, "community" isn't necessarily specific to a particular geographic area-although that will often be the case. The concept can be applied to communities of identity, interests, or culture and heritage. There's a central theme to each community, something that ties its members together in the first place. The actions taken for community development will often need to focus on that theme and the individual elements associated with it in order for a plan to be formulated and for things to be successful. In many instances, the involvement and participation of community members is necessary as they are each individual components that make up the whole. This also makes each community unique, so paying attention to the individual elements is very important.

So how is community development done? In many cases, it's through the implementation of different policies and practices by leaders and residents within the community. This may be done with the assistance or involvement of local, state, and/or federal government, but it is not always a necessity. There are resources available throughout multiple levels of government for communities to obtain a healthy, safe, and equal environment for their residents, but they are not the only options community leaders have. Whatever methods and means a community uses for community development will be dependent on aspects such as the community's goals, location, size, internal resources (e.g. budget and funding), and existing condition.

International and Domestic Value

Much of the value community development has is contingent on what it can do for a community when properly implemented and maintained. The process is applied because a community and its members have a particular set of goals that they want to achieve, thus the value lies in the process' success under those particular circumstances. There are going to be some communities who see a different kind of value from community development due to the variety of factors involved, aside from what it is that they sought to achieve.

Community development does over some value on a more general level, applicable regardless of the circumstances. This includes:

- **Improved Quality of Life-**One of the primary purposes of community development is to improve things for those in the community. The resources that are made available through the process are intended to improve the overall quality of life for the residents that use them. This can include anything from safety to health and well-being and then some.

Again, this will be subject to the existing circumstances *before* the process is implemented and what is done during the process. This is certainly the largest measure of community development's value, and it is often equal to or greater than the cost of achieving it in most cases.

- **Unity-**Community development prompts the residents and leadership of a community to come together to reach a collective goal. That collaboration generates a sense of unity throughout the community and brings home the idea that everyone has earned a place in it. Most people interpret that as meaning that they have value within their community, that they belong as an integral part of the whole. It can be both valuable and beneficial for the community to be united as it can help ensure the continued success of the process of community development, and everything that has been brought into the community through it.
- **Openness and Communication-**When people are able to successfully work together as a united group, they tend to have strong communication abilities. Nothing can really get done without effective communication, so it's both an important part and byproduct of community development. Studies that have looked into community development have found that communication are essential for communities to achieve their goals. It was also found that openness is an equally essential value, as it affords communities with some degree of flexibility and the ability to grow in different ways. Communities that have gone through the process of community development will often find that the communication and openness amongst residents and leaders has improved overall and aids in their continued progress.
- **Sustainability-**It does warrant some attention as part of the value of community development. The process of community development allows communities to be more autonomous and self-sustaining than they were before. The improvements made bring forth new resources and changes that empower the community to take action on its own. The promotion of self-sustainability is another key aspect of community development, and it certainly contributes to its value for those that apply it to their own communities. For many communities, sustainability is something that repeatedly pays off and has a higher value in the long run when compared to the cost of its original implementation.
- **Stability-**Community development itself can be a stabilizing force for communities to build upon and grow from. Many of the communities that have long used community development use it as a means of improving themselves on a large scale. Since it is often a long process, the stability it provides is crucial to its success. It very much lays the foundation that the community builds its improvements upon. Many of those communities lack that stability in the first place, so it is an incredibly valuable commodity that cannot necessarily be generated on its own.

Most of the above is applicable for both domestic and international communities. There is value that is applicable to international communities, whether that means communities throughout the world or domestic communities that are culturally diverse.

- **Education-**Whenever there is any kind of diversity present in a community-domestic or international-there is usually interaction between the different cultures and interests. When that happens, there is the opportunity for residents to learn about those that are different than them in their community. Education is something that is available through community development and can be used to implement some of the improvements the process brings about. It also provides the chance for new ideas and concepts found in different cultures to be introduced into the community and to cultures where they are not currently present. Depending on the circumstances, this can help boost the other values of community development.
- **Global Cohesion-**Communities are not merely small, individual groups that are isolated and independent from each other. In many cases, they intersect with other communities and are a part of larger ones. In terms of community development's value, this can build upon the unity that a community has by generating a global cohesion within a particular community and those it intersects with. This can help with the community's internal collaboration amongst residents and with the communities that it works with.
- **Economic Growth-**While economic growth is often a goal of a community going through the process of community development, it does give the process a lot of value on an international level. This is another byproduct of globalization, which often plays a role in economic growth in general. Internationally speaking, it fuels the community's global cohesion and developmental progress. Steady economic growth brings in new resources and maintains the connections with existing ones, fostering progress.

Who Is Involved In Community Development?

While it may be obvious that the community is involved in community development, the particular roles that different members play may not be. Involvement and participation are required to some degree, so it's important to identify the roles in play. Those who are involved are not necessarily going to be those directly impacted by community development, and may simply benefit when applied on a larger scale.

- **The Residents-**The residents of a community are the ones who are going to be intimately involved and impacted by community development. They are the ones who actually take action and put the effort into making improvements to their community using their particular knowledge and skillset. Residents often do this through their employment in the community or through volunteer efforts, although it can also be done through their normal activities.
- **The Local Government-**Most of the leadership in community development will be found through the local government. They are the ones who organize and plan things, identify goals, and possibly provide funding during the process. Members of the local government are going to be the ones that guide the rest of the community in their

efforts and make sure things stay on track. They may also be the ones who first initiate the process of community development and recognize that it needs to occur in the first place. In a sense, it's a supervisor or coordinator-like role that's paired with the worker role of the residents and other community members.

- **The State and Federal Government-** the government on the state and federal levels may play a role in community development through things like assistance programs and other similar resources. This isn't going to be universal for every community that goes through community development, but its common enough for the potential to be there. The involvement of state and/or federal governments are often going to need to be invited into the process by the community itself, usually through application for the programs they offer. No invitation, no involvement. However, upper levels of government may get involved without an invitation if the improvements made through community development intersect with other communities, such as roadwork and new construction.

The Process of Implementing Change with Community Development

Community development has been described as a process that is done to implement change. This suggests that there are a particular set of steps and requirements that a community needs to follow in order for their efforts to be successful. To some degree, this is true. There are certain things that need to be done in order for any actions to be taken within the community and for there to be any real results from them. However, the process isn't something that is completely set in stone due to the circumstances surrounding each community and social progressions that impact things. In a way, the community development process is more of a series of guidelines or a checklist that communities should consult as they make improvements. It can be adjusted as needed and still be successful, so long as the key principles are met.

Collect and Analyze Data

No improvements can be made through community development if you have not identified what needs to be improved. To some degree, this might require more work than any other stage in the process. The size of the community, and the issues present in it, may mean that there is a lot of information to gather and sort through before taking action. Depending on how many people are involved in the community development process at this point, it could take some time to do so.

So how does one go about collecting and analyzing data for community development? Some methods can include:

- **Learning-**Take a look at the community and learn as much about it as possible. Familiarize yourself with what the details about the community, including the issues, needs, and resources available there. Some of this information can be obtained through simple observation and participation in the community; attend a local event, for example. It may also be documented through things like newspaper articles, reports, and social media.

- **Get Feedback-**When there's a problem in the community, people are going to be vocal about it in the hopes that something is done. This feedback can be incredibly valuable because not all of the information you obtain about the community is going to come through formal channels. Surveys, open forums, and even talking with your peers in the community are all good methods of getting honest feedback. So long as the dialog between development organizers and the community members remains open, information should be able to flow.
- **Consider Motivations-**Why are YOU choosing to take action to improve the community? Why is anyone doing so and why are they choosing now to do it? The motivations of those who are leading the process in a community often can be sources of information as members of the community. Perhaps they were directly impacted by the issues in the community, or they witnessed the effects first hand. Such information may not be found elsewhere and can provide a different perspective on the issues already identified.
- **Compare and Contrast-**Take the information about the community and compare it to what is known about other communities that lack those issues. The differences can help identify what is missing and what needs to be done, which can be helpful later on in the processes when actions need to be taken. The data can also go through a SWOT analysis-Strengths, Weaknesses, Opportunities, and Threats-to identify pertinent information and discrepancies in the data.

Set Goals and Objectives

Using the information collected, determine what goals and objectives you seek to achieve through community development. These can be long-term, short-term, or whatever it is necessary to generate improvements. In the early stages of the process, it's best to set a few tentative goals for the community, as things can change as the process continues.

Some things to consider as you set goals:

- **Practicality-**It's admirable to set an ambitious goal, but it can backfire if it isn't practical. In many cases where community development fails, the goals are unrealistic and the leaders lack a real understanding of the situation. This may be a result of visibility issues or a lack of information, but it could also be due to a misinterpretation of the data.
- **Time-**Goals often have a deadline attached to them, which can provide some restrictions. There's only so much that can be done in a set amount of time and that will impact the fail/success rate for the community development process. Prioritize what needs to be done based on the demands of the community and any time constraints. It may be helpful to break up goals into stages that can be completed in batches over time, rather than one giant goal with a final deadline.
- **Resources-**The ability to meet goals on time will depend on what resources are needed to do so. This is one of the reasons why analysis of information is important, as it identifies what the community already has and what it needs. A goal can't be met if the community does not

have the necessary resources to achieve it, or if they don't know what resources they need in the first place.

- **Commitment-**Goals can't really be achieved if no one is actively working on them. Community development's success is dependent on people being committed to doing the work that is needed; nothing's going to get done if they quit half-way through. The goals need to be something that the community is willing to commit to or little will be accomplished.

Address Options

Basically, once you know what it is you're trying to achieve and why, you need to consider how you're going to do it. Every community is going to have different options for the actions it can take for community development. Some are going to be better than others, depending on the circumstances. Not every available option is going to work, either, so it's best to address and consider each one in regard to what it is that the community wants to accomplish. Again, this is another step that is going to require some information analysis and collection in order to find the solutions that are going to fit best.

Determining what options are at your disposal requires a bit of research and brainstorming; look at the details of the community's issues and goals, as well as your available and needed resources. Weigh each option carefully and consider the different factors that can impact a particular action's effectiveness. Some of the same factors that affect the goals in the previous step, such as practicality and time, can also affect what actions and methods can be used. If there are too many factors working against an option, then it will most likely have a high possibility of failing-and possibly even cause additional problems that can worsen the situation. It may be necessary to consider back-up options, just in case, in addition to the primary actions and methods being planned.

Make a Written Plan

Once the details have been nailed down and smoothed out, they need to be written out into a comprehensive plan. Putting it in writing creates a record of it that can be referenced throughout the process and accessible to participants. The process is a rather long one and can continue until well after the goals have been met. Having a detailed written plan can help ensure that everyone involved is literally and figuratively on the same page.

The written plan can also serve as the formal documentation and collection for all of the information that has gone into the process thus far. It solidifies the reasoning that went into the actions being taken, which can help later on if an action is questioned. Citing the written plan may also be required if there's a need for formal application for resources, like grants and other funding-it's information that helps the sources of those things determine if the recipient is truly deserving of those resources and if they are going to use them responsibly.

A formal written plan can be made by anyone involved in the process, but whomever does write it should have full access to all of the necessary information. If something changes during the earlier planning stages, then they need to know. For communities that are using professional services for their community development, keeping those that were hired in the loop can impact the overall costs of those services. Failing to inform such professionals can also lead to mistakes being included in the plan, leading to a ripple effect later on when action is actually taken.

Implementation

So you've decided upon what you're doing, why you're doing it, and how, and you have it formally laid out-it's time to take action! The implementation part of the community development process takes everything that has been done during planning and puts it into motion. It's a good idea to make sure that everything is ready to go *before* going ahead and acting. If there are elements missing-resources, funding, volunteers, etc.-then things are not going to go along as intended. This is why planning and preparation are key principles of community development and why they are so important to the process. Taking the time to make sure things are ready is going to help save time that may go to fixing mistakes once the implementation stage begins and is going to make it more effective for the community development process.

During the implementation stage, actions should be monitored to make sure that they are having the intended effect(s). If something doesn't work, then you want to make sure that you catch it before it impacts future actions. Evaluating as you go may take up some additional time, but it will help ensure that things are progressing as intended. Monitoring will also assist in making sure that the plan is being followed as it should. Unexpected delays due to screw-ups or failure to do what needs to be done can result in a waste of resources, funding, and time. This can be especially important when there's a deadline in place or some kind of restriction or limitation involved. One solution would be to use the written plan made in the previous stage as a checklist for each task that is needed to implement the improvements and keep things on track. Breaking things down into stages or phases can also help; until everything is done in one phase, the next phase cannot begin.

Continued Progression

The community development process doesn't end when all of the goals are met and the last part of the plan is complete. Even the best community development plan isn't going to be self-sustaining-at least not from the start. In most cases, some degree of maintenance is going to be needed. This may mean that the entire community development process-or certain parts of it-is going to need to be repeated to keep things going. In this way, the process is a cycle that doesn't really have a true end.

A cyclic community development plan isn't necessarily a bad thing. Being able to go back to an earlier stage means that there is always an option to fall back on when things go wrong. Circumstances change and new issues are bound to arise within the community that can lead to new problems. Society and the world are ever evolving and the communities that want to successfully exist in such a place need to have that flexibility if they want to survive.

FUTURE OF COMMUNITY DEVELOPMENT

Just as community development has changed over the course of its history, so will it continue to do so for years to come? There are enough changes that occur in society over a few years' time that it's likely to think that there will be an impact on community development's progression. If the community development process does not change as society and communities change, then it will lose its effectiveness and value. Change is, ultimately, an inevitability that everything and everyone must one day face. Not taking that idea seriously when trying to understand community development can impact the process' effectiveness in the future and the effect is has on communities.

For community leaders, paying attention to the ways in which community development can progress in the future can help them avoid issues further down the line. Changes in community development are definitely going to have an impact on the communities that use the process to improve themselves. Discrepancies between the practices and methods used in the development process verses the social norms present in a community can open up the path for things to stagnate. Trying to improve upon a situation or remedy a problem using means that are no longer relevant or effective won't have the desired effect-it can even generate more problems. Taking into consideration the impact that potential changes can have on communities and the community development process is a precaution that can pay off when those changes actually happen.

Community development's future is certainly going to be different from both its past and present. There are different issues that are already beginning to develop in communities and the process is becoming increasingly complicated as it tries to address them on multiple levels. The different factors and aspects of society are already changing at a rapid rate and impacting communities in a variety of ways-health care, food costs, energy usage, income, etc. Research groups, like some of the CDCs, are already testing new solutions that can handle the workload with better, more efficient results. Current solutions are not having the impact that they once did, and many of the issues that community development seeks to fix are continuing and returning despite best efforts. The only question is, what is the future going to hold for communities and what can be done to prepare for it?

Resources

One of the biggest areas that is going to be different in the future is the resources used in community development. The things that are going to be necessary in order for improvements to even work, let alone be properly implemented, are going to be different from what is used now. Different approaches towards community development are going to use different resources and supplies, that is a given. The onset of sustainable development in recent years is a prime example of that; it's new enough that many of the resources that are used during the process are not of the "normal" variety that is traditionally expected.

Where community development resources come from is also something that is expected to change in the future as much as *what* resources are used and *how*. More communities are attempting to become self-reliant when it comes to the resources they use, so they are trying to use what is locally available. Part of it is a cost issue-prices rise the farther a resource needs to travel in order to get to where it will be used-but it's also a popular trend that has proven to be beneficial when used. Dependence on outside forces is something that is being viewed, both in communities and in society, as something that doesn't help in the same way it once did. There's also an issue that some natural resources are being used faster than they can be replaced, which means that something's are likely to run out if usage rates don't slowdown.

New Roles

Currently, there are particular roles in community development that are being filled and carry their own value in the process. This is the same for the roles that are present in communities, and in society at large. However, not all of those roles are things that have existed throughout most of history; in some cases, they are more recent occurrences that have developed in response to changes. Likewise, roles that were present fifty, one hundred years ago or more are no longer there and no longer relevant to society, communities, the development process, etc. What exists now may not exist in the same capacity in the future, and may even have been replaced altogether.

The structures of community development and society are evolving at a steady rate, which is causing a shake-up in the available roles. As new roles are being created, old ones are fading away and dying out. They have ceased to serve a purpose that may not even exist anymore and are being pushed out to make room for ones that still have value. Even the roles that still exist may not function in the same way. The federal government's role in community development, for example, is slowly dwindling as communities lose faith in what government agencies and leaders can offer and begin excluding them where possible. They are no longer the instigators of development and change in communities; if anything, they're a last resort.

Growth

It's safe to say that there's quite a bit of growth occurring in the world. The global population alone has jumped from 2.5 billion people in 1950 to 7 billion today with steady increases expected in the years to come. Communities themselves are getting bigger in both population and physical size. The amount of things available are also increasing and some of them are also increasing in their size-homes, cars, and other products, for example. The value that people place on certain things like relationships and interests are also growing. The aspects of society are adapting to these increases-some slower than others-as they happen. For many, this growth translates as a sign of progress of any kind.

Unfortunately, not all growth is being viewed as a positive thing. Consumption of resources is increasing. There is growth in the amount of waste that communities generate. Debt-personal, business, and federal-is getting bigger. The cost of living is increasing, whether it's food, housing, shelter, transportation, or healthcare. There are greater gaps between different socioeconomic status and social classes that are still growing. The list goes on, and on, and on. Such negative instances of growth are more than likely going to generate serious problems for communities and their residents the longer they continue. Many of these issues will be the future targets of community development plans and tactics.

Cultural Shifts

Culture is one of the things in society that is constantly evolving with each new generation. What is valued in one area or by a certain demographic is not seen in the same way by another. These cultural shifts can happen gradually or suddenly-think about social trends that have sprung up and then quickly faded into obscurity. The circumstances influencing the culture of a community can easily lead them to change. What was once the case in a community may not be the same in a year's time? The things that were of value to the members of a community are certainly going to changes and morph as time passes, and the community development process is going to reflect that.

One of the most common and noticeable ways that culture has shifted in communities in recent years is in how things are valued and prioritized. For the longest time, the professional world placed a stronger focus on work that generated a high return on investment and profit. Now, there's more of a value being placed on the social impact of a person's professional work. Things that were once seen as unconventional or a non-issue are now being focused on as normal parts of society. Values are changing, all because of changes in culture that are occurring over time.

Economic State

Economic changes-good or bad-are always going to be a factor when discussing the future of community development. The status of the economy will often dictate what issues are present in a community and what options are going to be available to fix them. Even on its own, there is quite a bit of concern about what direction the economy will take next. Recessions and slow markets are issues that are typical in the current economy, with their occurrence being documented enough that they can be predicted and monitored by experts. However, just because the economy is in a certain state now that is considered acceptable doesn't mean that it will continue to stay that way.

The fluctuations in the economy mean that there are going to be times when communities take a beating. Currently rising issues surrounding income inequality suggest that such instances are going to be more frequent, especially if nothing is done to remedy them soon. There is enough evidence and expertise available to gauge what the effects will be on communities of all kinds. How community development will be used in those instances can be predicted-to a degree-using that information. The cyclic state that the community development process often takes can also be adjusted to address those economic changes as they occur, giving the community just a bit of an edge over the challenges that may be up ahead.

Policy Changes

Formal and informal policies on any level in the community are bound to change. New laws are passed and social rules are modified all the time. Society, in its constant state of change, is going to need some means of guidance in order to keep things from descending into chaos. Policy changes are going to happen and they need to happen, whether you like it or not.

So what does that mean for community development? Pretty much everything. Changes in policies can put forth new restrictions on what actions and improvements can be taken. Even the ways in which the process works can be hindered by changes in its own methodology, which is a kind of law system that governs it. Bureaucracies already generate a lot of red tape for communities *now*, so thinking about what they can do in the future is almost a nightmare waiting to happen. New policies can also help make it easier for communities to implement the process and solutions, not just impede them. Of course, the political landscape on all levels of leadership-which changes with every election cycle-and the details of these new policies are going to determine which way things go.

Technological Advancements

Technology is advancing quickly, much more than anyone outside of the tech industry realizes. The inclusion of different types of tech-like social media and the internet-have acted like the flood gates of change in community development. How something as simple as information is analyzed and collected is impacting how communities operate. The applications of technology in anything, not just community development, are seemingly limitless due to the advancements being made. Most of those advances are just in the last few years and are increasing in quantity and quality. Just imagine what could possibly be the case in the future and how it can impact lives!

In some cases, technological advancements can be used to literally help predict aspects about the future. The amount of factors that can contribute to the changes in community development are too numerous for any one person to calculate all of the potential outcomes that are possible. Analysis using tech can quickly and efficiently take the data and predict what can happen for any facet of community development. It can be continuously updated with new data and new tech in order to get a clearer picture.

PRINCIPLES OF COMMUNITY DEVELOPMENT

For every concept, theory, or method, there are certain basic fundamentals that determine its very nature. These facets are referred to as principles and they act as the key identifiers for a concept down to its simplest state. They are similar to the materials that are used in the construction of a building; the building blocks that individually play a role in the overall structure and function of the final product. Analysis of these principles can offer a person further insight into the concept they are trying to understand.

Understanding each piece will provide further understanding of the concept as a whole, as each one is necessary for the process to be successful. Those listed in this are the major principles that have the most significant purpose, although there may be smaller, less frequently applicable principles that are present when the process is used. In those cases, those additional principles will be pertinent to the specific situation and its circumstances instead.

Empowerment

From a psychological standpoint, people are more likely to do things that they are motivated to do so and feel like they have come level of control over their actions. Not only does this give them the sensation and satisfaction that what they are doing is of their own free will, but that their actions actually have some value in the long run. This empowerment acts as a motivator in society and it holds a great deal of importance in community development. Members of a community who are empowered to take action for improvements are going to have genuine cause to do so, rather than because they were told to by others.

As a key principle of community development, empowerment often is what prompts things to get done in the first place. There needs to be a reason for people to want to improve things in their community for themselves and others; it can't just be a facet of social or public duty. Parents, for example, typically want their children to be able to be safe as often as possible-regardless of if it's at home, at school, or just walking down the street to the local playground. If there is something within their surroundings that prevents or otherwise impedes upon their children's safety, the parents will make attempts to remedy the situation. Their own children do not necessarily have to directly be in danger, as even the possibility of a threat to their child's safety is enough to raise some parent's concerns in most cases. Those who see that something is missing or lacking in their surroundings, regardless of the degree that they are impacted by it, will often be empowered to do something about it.

Character and Appearance

While some may think that focusing on the physical appearance of something can be rather shallow, principles of character and appearance are actually important components of community development. Many communities and neighborhoods have a distinct appearance and sensory association that are clear identifiers for them. These features set the tone within the community and are a strong influence for the community's public reputation. Since many people who are active participants in community development have a clear visualization of what they want for their community, things like character and appearance are incredibly important.

The character-the overall sense of a place-of a community is typically set and introduced through the appearance of the community. It's an ingrained habit-or an instinct, in some instances-for people to judge or come to a conclusion about something based on a quick observation. A community will have a positive or a negative association attached to it based on what people perceive about it, and that can impact things like how residents and members view or care about it, the resources available, and what influences those resources to be there in the first place. Resources, like new businesses, are not going to make themselves available in communities that have a poor sense of character where they may not be able to sustain themselves long enough to have an impact.

Inclusion and Diversity

Many people have heard about inclusion and diversity in recent years as individual topics. Their growing involvement in society and their connection to each other make them necessary parts of successful community development. Diversity typically refers to the traits present in a group-gender, race, socioeconomic status, religion, political views, etc.-and it's a term that almost everyone is familiar with in some way. The world is a very diverse place, so it's not uncommon for a single community to have a fairly healthy level of diversity even when the group at large is built upon a specific focus or interest. Everything in a community needs to be addressed during the community development process, so it's important to pay attention to even the smallest degree of diversity in a community. Inclusion, however, is not a term that everyone is familiar with. From a social or community-based perspective, inclusion is best defined as actions taken to make sure that everyone is equally valued and has equal access to resources. It's basically a way to put everyone in a community on a level playing field, regardless of what it is that makes them different from their peers. One of the main points behind community development is to make improvements for those within the community; it doesn't make a lot of sense if those improvements only benefit certain people while putting others at a great disadvantage in the process. It would be like giving instructions to a crowd, but you're whispering instead of shouting or talking loudly. Those closest to you are probably going to pick up on what you're telling them to do, but those furthest away are going to have no idea what is going on.

Planning and Preparation

Since community development is a process that can get rather complicated based on the circumstances, planning and preparation are key principles necessary for it to work. The instigators of community development need to be able to take a look at what they want to do and how they want to do it. It's not an easy task to enact widespread changes, so careful consideration and preparation are required to make sure that all needs are being addressed and that there are legitimate reasons behind the actions being taken. The process is a long one, and there's often quite a bit that needs to be done in order to accomplish a single goal.

As one of the key principles, planning and preparation can be greatly beneficial to the community as it goes through the process of community development. The changes made are going to be significant, and there's a good chance that there may be some difficulty adjusting to them within the community. Planning things out gives those within the community a chance to acclimate to the new situation and offers opportunities for feedback to be given to those leading the changes before moving on to the next step. It can also allow a community to gather the necessary resources for changes to be made, especially if those resources have certain requirements for access (e.g. funding). Since there's little possibility that the process will be perfect, planning and preparation can help provide a community with a bit of a safety net against problems and errors.

Collaboration and Participation

Like its name suggests, community development isn't really something that is done on an individual level or by a single person. In order for it to actually accomplish something, the members of the community itself need to get involved and work together. As mentioned before, it can take a lot of work to implement the desired improvements through community development so it's best not to do it alone. Collaboration helps bring together people of different backgrounds who may have access to different resources that can be of benefit to the community. Each person also has a role that they play within the community, thus it is likely that they will each have a role to play in the process of community development. The interactions that occur through the collaborative efforts of community development can help bolster leaders and the skills they are using to guide the community through the process.

Participation, on its own, is a necessary component of community development in that it helps support the community members involved as they make decisions.

It's not just their peers and leaders that they're supporting during the process by participating, but their own decisions as a member of the community. Participation allows a person to exert any influence they have in that moment during the process-they're able to offer input and provide feedback on things that are going to directly impact them as a member of the community. This can tie together with empowerment as well, as the two principles will often feed into one another during the process.

Awareness

To be fair, it's hard to take action to improve upon something if you are unaware that something needs improvement in the first place. Awareness is a key principle of community development because it allows communities to identify things like resources and needs within their own space. A potential issue that's causing harm to a community and/or its members isn't going to have a giant sign saying "FIX THIS!" with an arrow pointing at it. Most likely, the problem(s) may not even be initially recognized as problematic until there's a significant enough impact on the community at large. Actively paying attention to things in the community and how they are affecting the community can help catch those issues early on and allow the community development process to handle them effectively. It allows the community to take ownership of their problems when they are aware of it, which can prompt them to take action on their own.

Awareness in the community development process can do more than just identify problems, it can also monitor the progress of the process and the improvements that are implemented. Just as you can't identify a problem if you're not paying attention, the same can be said for the solution to the problem. If the improvement or solution that has been put in place by the process isn't working as it should-it's causing more problems, it's not affecting the right people, etc.-then that can be caught before it causes further issue if the community is actively aware of it.

Transparency and Trust

For anything to work in a community of any type, there needs to be some level of trust and transparency between those involved. This applies to the leadership, those who are participating in the community development process, those who are being directly impacted by improvements, and anyone else in the community who may be indirectly affected. The process can result in major changes in a community, so there can be significant backlash if those implementing the changes are not completely honest about what is being done and why. People become comfortable and use to how things are when that's been the norm for so long; some resistance is going to be expected as people acclimate to the new circumstances, even if it's to their benefit.

As not everyone in the community is going to be able to fully participate or have their say in the community development process, there's going to be a degree of trust placed on those who are actively making decisions. Those in those leadership and decision making positions during the process will need to be transparent in their actions or risk losing that trust. Betraying that trust-especially if the actions taken are not universally beneficial for community members or if they are done in bad faith-can generate more problems in the community and make it difficult for future improvements to be made.

Involvement of Government in Community Development

Government role in the community development process is often an uncertainty as each community has its own opinion on the matter. The inclusion of government, on whatever level, is always a possibility with community development and it's a viable option for those going through the process.

Topics will also include government resources and programs that are available during community development and the role that politics plays. Also included will be the advantages and disadvantages communities are faced with when they involve the government in the community development process.

Government Involvement Necessary

Whether or not any level of government involvement is necessary in community development is going to depend on the community itself. Local governments prompt and manage community development in their own jurisdictions all the time; it's a part of their responsibilities to ensure a level of quality for residents. Many restrictions that exist in today's society are in place through laws created and enforced by the government. For some communities, this is the only involvement that government has in their community development process and it's not necessarily going to be a negative issue.

The factors present in a community will often dictate if government involvement is required. Serious issues with infrastructure, for example, can only be fixed with official approval from government officials-who are often the ones responsible for maintaining and monitoring aspects of infrastructure like roadways to begin with. The larger a community is geographically and structurally-which can make the process rather complicated-the more likely that some degree of government involvement will be needed during community development. More adventurous community development goals may also require some level of government involvement depending on the factors involved.

Seeking government involvement in the first place-whether it's for community development or something else-isn't always something that community members want to do. There has been quite a bit of aversion to government involvement in communities in recent years, especially higher levels like the federal government. Part of this is due to past failures or problems that have occurred when the government was involved, or cases where the government should have intervened and didn't. For years, there were expectations that government officials were instrumental in developing and improving different areas of society and they failed to live up to the hype. As a result, some communities will avoid including any levels of government in their community development plans unless it's absolutely necessary or they have no choice but to do so (e.g. permits).

On the other hand, some communities are more than comfortable with the government getting involved in their plans for community development for the resources they can provide. They recognize that it may be a necessity for their efforts and can offer benefits that they might not otherwise gain without it. The private sector, while it may have a lot to offer, isn't going to have everything a community needs to improve itself; government programs tend to be available to fill those gaps. Resources sponsored by government offices are going to appeal to communities that desperately need the programs and funding they provide in order to make improvements. Local government involvement is often welcomed the most because it can act as a support system for communities who may be dealing with less than stellar circumstances, even if it's just encouragement from officials. Again, it's all dependent on the situation and the factors present in a community during the community development process.

Advantages

A community might not want or require government involvement in their community development plans, but they may still consider it. There are certain advantages that come with seeking assistance from the local, state, and federal governments that might appeal to community leaders. Even if it's not a necessity needed to accomplish their objectives, government resources can still give them a boost and make the process easier. Some advantages to government involvement in community development include:

- **Funding-**Access to money and other resources are definitely going to make government involvement in the community development process look attractive. It's a huge motivator and for many communities it may be an obstacle that is keeping them from reaching their goals. There are a variety of programs on the federal and state level-more on that later-that communities can apply for. Things like tax breaks that can ease some of the financial burdens for communities, especially if they are using the services of a CBO or a non-profit in the process. There's also project funding and loan guarantees available to those that meet the necessary requirements.
- **Lower Risks-**When there is someone or something that has the knowledge and resources to do something, it's more likely that it's going to get done the way it should. Government involvement acts as both a guide and a buffer for community development, and can lower some of the risks that communities have when making improvements. The rules they put in place help keep things on track, which means it's a little harder to accidentally or intentionally skip steps. There are also contingencies attached to government programs and funding sources in the event of failure or issue; communities using those resources are not going to be at a complete disadvantage if something goes wrong.
- **Protections-**In addition to helping lower some of the risks that come with community development, government involvement can also provide economic and environmental protections. Protecting the things in their respective jurisdiction is a part of the government's job after all. Enforcement of the community's rights and regulations to prevent those rights from being abused or taken advantage off are going to be the most common protections. Community development actions cannot be carried out if they somehow harm the community as a result-repairs and improvements to public spaces need to follow government-induced safety protocols, for example.

- **Experience-**Community development and urban planning tend to be a part of the government's responsibilities, so officials often have some experience with the community development process. It's knowledge that can be a valuable resource, especially in young communities where leaders may not be entirely sure of their actions. Even some of the tasks that a community may need to complete in order to implement improvements may involve actions that members of the government do all the time in the course of their jobs.

Disadvantages

For every advantage that something offers, there's a disadvantage. Communities that are hesitant to involve any government assistance will usually cite the disadvantages as a reason to go through the development process on their own. Even when the benefits are all but guaranteed, **community leaders** still need to understand what potential drawbacks may arise by seeking government assistance.

Some may include:

- **Restrictions-**The same laws and rules that can help a community with their improvements can also restrict their actions. There's a lot of politics and bureaucracy with government involvement and it can be more trouble than it's worth at times. Some communities will actually avoid or give up on certain goals because of the amount of restrictions in place that are making it difficult to achieve them. Even if the restrictions do not create such problems, they can still be incredibly frustrating to navigate through.
- **Loss of Control-**Possibly more of a fear than an actually, government involvement can result in a loss of the community's control over the situation. Intervention is viewed as a means of taking or restricting personal freedom, and community members are not able to make the same decisions as easily without it. Such an imbalance of power can lead to other issues and even impede the community development process' success. For some, this is why government intervention is viewed more as a hostile takeover than a benevolent assistance.
- **Corruption-**Government officials or leaders of any kind may have agendas that are counteractive to the goals and objectives of the community, which may be viewed as corrupt. Lobbying has become such a major part of government that many people are concerned about the intentions behind their government leader's actions. What motivations are there and where are they coming from? Who's actually going to benefit from this relationship and who's going to end up with the short end of the stick? Many of the communities who choose to go through the community development process are already at a disadvantage in society, which can make them a prime target of abuse from anywhere-including corrupt members of the government.

The Role of Politics

When discussing government involvement in anything, politics are sure to be a factor. Everything as of late seems to have a political side to it so it's not surprising that politics plays a role in community development. Politics tend to be tied to people's motivations and actions, so many of the goals a community has for improvement may have or be influenced by a political agenda. This can include what is being done, how it's being done, why it's being done, and who is involved. As a result, there is often a question regarding the involvement of government officials and leaders in the community-are they doing things out of a genuine desire to help or to further their own agenda? The drive and enthusiasm for community development around the world in recent years has often been cited as a byproduct of political agendas, especially when it reflects positively on certain groups. Those who enact improvements and lead the community development process usually obtain some degree of power and recognition for themselves within the community. It can help them personally and it can help whatever cause they are a part of; public support is going to go towards what or who has proven that they are a beneficial force.

The role of politics in community development can also be problematic when the government is involved. The community itself will have its own politics, and there's always the potential that they can clash with the politics of those helping them. Leaders in the process could reject any offers of assistance or resources from the government if their political beliefs counter one another. The refusal of any government assistance in and of itself can be political for communities that view federal or even state-level involvement is an overstepping of boundaries.

Available Government Programs

On a federal level, the Department of Housing and Urban Development (HUD) is going to be the main sources of government-sponsored community development programs. They can come in the form of assistance for housing, health services, financial aid, disaster relief, and finances like loans. HUD also manages the Community Development Block Grant program or CDBG, which includes financial and educational resources for communities in the community development process. The department also oversees similar community development programs on the state levels and manages the regulations and procedures that those programs need to adhere to.

Additional federal programs include:

- **Community Economic Development (CED)**, a grant program offered through the U.S. Department of Health and Human Services' Office of Community Services.
- **TIGER or the Transportation Investment Generating Economic Recovery,** which is specific to development projects related to transportation. It's offered through the U.S. Department of Transportation (DOT) as part of the Recovery Act.
- **The Sustainable Communities Partnership**, which is a collaborative effort between HUD, the DOT, and the Environmental Protection Agency (EPA). The partnership maintains an active list of federally offered grants, programs, and assistance for communities.

Non-federal government programs are going to be different for each state, county, and city in the country. Determining what's available in your area for community development and what the application process entails will require a bit of research. Most of that information will be publically available in places like government offices and websites. There may be local equivalents to government-sponsored programs that are higher up in the hierarchy, like the CDBG program. You can also contact your local representatives and government officials for more information.

REFERENCES

1. Brown, J., & Hannis D. (2012). *Community Development* in *Canada (2nd ed.). Toronto,* CA: *Pearson*
2. Isiolo, T. (2019). *Susan and the seeds of hope: Once a casual labourer, now a supplier at the local market. ActionAid Kenya. Retrieved on June 25, 2022 from* https://kenya.actionaid.org/stories/2019/susan-and-seeds-hope-once-casual-labourer-now-supplier-local-market
3. Michigan State University, (n.d.). *Principles of Community Development- Center for Community Economic Development.* Retrieved June 23, 2022, from https://ced.msu.edu/about-cced/principles-of-community-development
4. Parada, H., Barnoff, L, Moffatt, K., & Homan, M. S. (2012). *Promoting community change: Making it happen in the real world.* (2nd Canadian ed.). Toronto: Nelson Education Ltd
5. Roseland, M. (2012). *Toward Sustainable Communities* (4th ed.). Canada. New Society Publisher.
6. Scotish Community Development Center, (n.d). *What is community development?* Retrieved June 23, 2022, from https://www.scdc.org.uk/who/what-is-community-development
7. Smart, J. (2017). *What is community development?* Australian Institute of Family Studies, CFCA Resource Sheet, January 2017. Retrieved June23, 2022 from https://aifs.gov.au/cfca/expert-panel-project/what-community-development

CHAPTER

6

SOCIAL RIGHT AND IDENTITY

INTRODUCTION

A right is described as an entitlement or justified claim to a certain kind of positive and negative treatment from others, to support from others or non-interference from others. In other words, a right is something to which every individual in the community is morally permitted, and for which that community is entitled to disrespect or compulsorily remove anything that stands in the way of even a single individual getting it. Rights belong to individuals, and no organization has any rights not directly derived from those of its members as individuals; and, just as an individual's rights cannot extend to where they will intrude on another individual's rights, similarly the rights of any organization whatever must yield to those of a single individual, whether inside or outside the organization. Rights are those important conditions of social life without which no person can generally realize his best self. These are the essential conditions for health of both the individual and his society. It is only when people get and enjoy rights that they can develop their personalities and contributes their best services to the society.

Identity theory, in philosophy, one view of modern Materialism that asserts that mind and matter, however capable of being logically distinguished, are in actuality but different expressions of a single reality that is material. Strong emphasis is placed upon the empirical verification of such statements as: "Thought is reducible to motion in the brain."

The double-aspect theory is similar to this, with one notable exception: reality is not material; it is either mental or neutral. The latter case is illustrated by an undulating line that is both concave and convex at the same time; each aspect is an integral, but only a partial, expression of the total reality.

RIGHTS AND PEOPLE

Rights and people are intrinsically linked, as rights define the freedoms and protections individuals possess in a society. These rights, enshrined in legal frameworks and moral principles, are fundamental to human dignity and the functioning of a just and equitable society.

Human rights are universal and inalienable, meaning they apply to all individuals regardless of nationality, ethnicity, gender, religion, or any other status. These rights are often categorized into civil, political, economic, social, and cultural rights. Civil and political rights include the right to life, freedom of speech, freedom of assembly, and the right to a fair trial. These rights protect individuals from abuses by the state and ensure participation in the political process.

Economic, social, and cultural rights, on the other hand, focus on the conditions necessary for individuals to live with dignity. This includes the right to work, the right to education, the right to health, and the right to an adequate standard of living. These rights emphasize the state's responsibility to provide the means for individuals to achieve a decent quality of life.

The recognition and protection of these rights are vital for personal freedom and societal harmony. When people's rights are respected, they are more likely to contribute positively to their communities, fostering a stable and prosperous society. Conversely, the violation of rights can lead to social unrest, conflict, and a breakdown of trust in institutions.

Legal systems around the world, including international agreements like the Universal Declaration of Human Rights, aim to protect and promote human rights. However, the realization of these rights varies significantly across different countries and regions. Factors such as political will, economic development, and social norms influence the extent to which rights are respected and upheld.

Moreover, the advocacy and activism of individuals and groups play a critical role in advancing rights. Grassroots movements, non-governmental organizations, and international bodies work tirelessly to highlight abuses, campaign for changes, and support victims of rights violations. This collective action is essential in holding governments and institutions accountable and pushing for reforms.

Evaluation

Commenting on the Marxist theory of rights Norman Barry observes: the Marxists are hostile of natural rights. It is due to the fact that rights cannot be separated from the economic relations of society. The apologists of the theory of natural rights have endeavored to trace the origin of natural rights to something outside the materials or economic basis of society.

But the Marxist view of right suffers from ambivalence. Marx and his followers have advised common and oppressed people to wage a revolutionary struggle against colonialism and the purpose of the struggle would be to establish political and economic rights propagated by liberal philosophers. Even these rights include natural rights which they cannot support. Barry has discovered another lacuna in Marxist theory of right. In On the Jewish Question "Marx saw the rise of human rights in historical content. The liberation of man from the oppressive and restrictive feudal economic and social structure was a stupendous achievement which realized the major aims of natural rights thinkers.

However, he was insistent that the so-called rights of man are nothing but the rights of the member of civil society i.e. egoistic man". Egoistic man is self-centered. In civil society and alienation automatically develops between the property-owners and wage-earners. In Marxist concept of rights there is no place of universal theory of rights.

In Marx's classless society there will be no individual rights which will limit the freedom of others. It is presumably because the sources of production will be socialized and economic relations will be on cooperative basis. But the success of such a conception of rights depends on to what extent human nature has undergone changes.

There is no guarantee or scientific evidence that with the change of economic structure of society people have thrown away their previous motives, outlooks and mentality. Marxian materialism is quite silent on this. So how can we conclude that a cooperative society based on Marxian principle will create an Eden for people's perfect and ideal rights system? Marx castigated the human rights as simply the expressions of bourgeois capitalism. But his portrayal of a future society is out and out a Utopia. "But if the coercion-less cooperative society fails to materialize and the legal system which could, in principle, embody positive expressions of human rights is abolished, there is little prospect that the individual will be protected against the invasions of the state".

Though Marx recommended the abolition of bourgeois legal system, in practice it is not possible. There must be an organ or agency where the people can lodge their complaints against authority for violation of rights. We do not argue that the capitalist legal system which is authorized to safeguard individuals' rights is impartial and efficient. But we argue in the same breath that the socialist system is not suspicion. The collapse of the Soviet system is a proof of its inefficiency to protect people's rights.

Marxists have squarely objected to the capitalist system of rights. But it is an irony that the erstwhile Soviet constitution and the present Chinese constitution embodied all the human rights propagated by bourgeois theoreticians. The only difference is that while the bourgeois thinkers have stressed the political rights the Marxists have given greatest importance to economic rights. But this is a different issue. Marx would perhaps be horrified by the deplorable condition of rights, in various forms, in the socialist countries.

If Marx and Engels were alive today they would have amended their views about rights in bourgeois society. Today, the workers and common people have, through their protracted struggle and agitation, forced the bourgeois authority to make concession regarding basic rights and privileges.

This is really a great success of the workers. Common people of the present capitalist society are enjoying more rights than their counterparts enjoyed in the past. This is a great achievement which Marx and Engels failed to foresee. However, the common people of capitalist systems are deprived of many rights and for this they will have to fight against the capitalists and their henchmen.

Correct Picture of rights

Neither liberal theory nor Marxist theory of rights depicts the correct picture of rights.

Defects of the liberal views are:

(a) Too much emphasis on individuals' freedom and his ability to look after his own interests,

(b) Guarantee of political rights can cure all the evils, and

(c) Negligence of economic rights.

These shortcomings of liberal theory of rights have ultimately deprived a majority of people to enjoy rights. Rights have become the privileged opportunities of the property owners and have not been utilized for the development of the best qualities of all men which is the chief objective of rights.

On the contrary, the Marxists have seen rights from economic perspectives. To them these are to be economic first-and then political and by declaring this the Marxists have relegated political rights to absolute insignificance. But both political and economic rights, any sensible man will admit, are essential for the overall flourish of individual's good qualities. How to effect a balance between political and economic rights is perhaps the most vexed problem of political science.

Elimination of exploitation and injustice in economic field should be declared the leitmotif of any government determined to achieve welfare objectives Mere declaration; it is to be noted here, is not enough. Through its sincere activities the government must prove its good intention. Government's control over means of production and property-owners has been suggested as a powerful weapon of eliminating injustice and exploitation from the surface of society. Laski has argued that there shall be special provision for awarding additional privileges to deserving persons. But this can be granted on two conditions.

One is, before doing that, all the persons in society are provided with minimum privileges and the other condition is the granting of special privileges will augment the general interests or welfare of the society. The materialization of basic rights of all citizens irrespective of race, sex, caste and religion is the urgent task of any government embedded with welfare objectives.

What are the basic rights? There is a difference of opinion on this question. But we should not ponder over the various aspects of the matter. Food, drink, health, home—these are basic necessities.

Along with these, citizens will have the right to express their own views and will be allowed to lead a social and peaceful life. If we just look at these wants or requirements we shall find that these include both political and economic rights. Cultural rights are also included.

It is wrong to assume that the liberal theory of rights has argued against the fulfilment of these basic wants. So far as the philosophy of this theory is concerned we have nothing to say against it. But its attempt to incapacitate a state fails to receive any acclaim from the ordinary people seeking redress from wants.

The state has a positive role to play. It must come to the aid and advice of the millions. Its apparatus is not for few property-owners and elites who are sufficiently equipped with weapons to fight against the odds. The majority people have not that weapon and it is the primary duty of the state to supply that. Laski in his Introduction to Politics has said that if the state fails to satisfy the effective demand of citizens they are not legally and ethically bound to show obligation to it and these demands can be met by creating an environment in which every individual will get the opportunity of developing qualities. Hence the declaration of rights and the efforts for their implementation is the basic task of the state. If we think over the matter seriously we shall find that this approach is neither liberal nor socialist, but combines the elements of both. It is absolutely humanitarian. Progress of civilization is of prime necessity and this is possible if maximum human progress is achieved. Rights are indispensable for the progress of civilization and man and the state has something to do.

A Synthesis: Rights and Responsibilities

Responsive communitarianism may be considered a synthesis of both liberal and academic-communitarian concerns. Sandel and Taylor in effect held that many forms of philosophical liberalism, especially libertarianism, overemphasize autonomy and rights at the expense of the common good. However, in doing so, they were less than clear about the standing of individual rights, including human rights. Indeed, Alasdair MacIntyre asserted that rights were merely figments of the imagination, like unicorns. Responsive communitarians attempted to bridge this divide. In their platform and in their academic works, they posited that all societies must heed the moral claims of two core values, the common good and autonomy and rights. They also held that, because actual societies tend to tilt toward one core value or the other, they need to be pulled back toward the centre. Thus Japan, in their view, was strongly dedicated to the common good but insufficiently committed to the rights of women, ethnic minorities, and the disabled, while the United States during the presidential administration of Ronald Reagan (1981–89) and the United Kingdom during the prime ministership of Margaret Thatcher (1979–90) attached undue importance to individual rights. The early prime ministership of Tony Blair demonstrated a concern for the common good through its policies of devolution and the "stakeholder society" (the idea that businesses should be responsive to workers, consumers, and other groups whose interests they affect), as did the early administration of George W. Bush through its dedication to "compassionate conservatism." After the 2001 September 11 attacks, however, the common good in the United States was increasingly identified with national security, and some individual rights (e.g., the right to habeas corpus) were curtailed.

In the same vein, responsive communitarians also warned against excessively expansive definitions of rights and championed modern communities in which people find both a rich web of social relations and considerable degrees of freedom. In the early 21st century, responsive communitarians believed that the Scandinavian countries had achieved the best balance, though even there some individual rights were being curtailed for security reasons and in response to anti-immigrant sentiment.

Government and the Extension of Rights

We shall now briefly discuss how an expansion of state activity extends the rights of the individuals. We hold the view that a state can easily play an expanded role— particularly in economic sphere—and this helps the individuals to have more rights.

For example, if right to personal security is extended individuals will get a number of rights. There are various forms of security such as security from hunger, security from unemployment, security from hazards of life, security from drudgery of monotonous life.

Many countries of the West have introduced social insurance schemes and these have considerably extended the rights of citizens. Britain is the pioneer in this field. In 1942, Sir William Beverage produced the Report on the Social Insurance and Allied Services and it is call Beverage Report. This Report calls upon the government to adopt a comprehensive policy to attack Want, Disease, Ignorance, Squalor and Idleness.

The Report also stresses that the; state should provide security to all its citizens. The change in outlook has impelled the government to take a number of measures which have extended various rights of the individuals. The individuals of today's world enjoy the rights to be protected from unemployment and age. Many countries have introduced unemployment allowances.

Restrictions on the right of factory owners to retrench workers have been imposed. There is a system of old age pension in many countries of the world. This is a right to live comfortably in old age. Laws have been enacted to save the workers from the hazards of job.

The state, factories and other organizations provide medical benefits to its citizens and these have alleviated the risks of sickness. This is the right against diseases or the right to protect himself. Workers' rights to protection have been broadened by a new method called Joint Venture. A fund is built up with the contributions of employers and workers. This is compulsory and strengthens the social security of the employee.

The recreation is also an essential part of employee's life and we find several states to open recreation centers which are also called social service centers. This enables employees the right to enjoy. The right to form or join organization has been recognized by state. The trade union right is also a very important right which is found in every state.

The employees or workers have got right to freedom of speech and also to bargain with the employer. Thus, it is both a political and economic right. The general result is the expansion of various rights and this has been possible because of the increased role of the state.

It is now universally believed that the state is the most powerful, effective as well as the proper institution (the state is sometimes so called) to guarantee and protect rights and all the individuals irrespective of their cast, creed, religion, language and sex lay faith on the state. The issue of the protection of rights is too important to be left to the private person or agencies.

If we want a comprehensive system of rights and its realization, it is argued, the responsibility shall be vested in the state. It is a fact that the role of the state is not suspicion and criticism but on this account it should not be debarred from playing its role.

Types of Rights

Natural Rights

They stated that people inherit several rights from nature. Before they came to live in society and state, they used to live in a state of nature. In it, they appreciated certain natural rights, like the right to life, right to liberty and right to property. Natural rights are parts of human nature and reason. Political theory maintains that an individual enters into society with certain basic rights and that no government can deny these rights.

In classical political philosophy "natural right" denotes to the objective rightness of the right things, whether the virtue of a soul, the correctness of an action, or the excellence of a regime. Aristotle stated in Politics (1323a29-33) that no one would call a man happy who was completely lacking in courage, temperance, justice, or wisdom. A man who was easily terrified, unable to restrain any impulse toward food or drink, willing to ruin his friends for a trifle, and generally senseless could not possibly lead a good life. Even though chance may occasionally prevent good actions from having their normal consequences, so that sometimes cowards fare better than brave men, courage is still objectively better than cowardice. The virtues and actions that contribute to the good life, and the activities intrinsic to the good life, are naturally right.

The modern idea of natural rights grew out of the ancient and medieval doctrines of natural law, but for other scholars, the concept of natural rights is unreal. Rights are the products of social living. These can be used only in a society. Rights have behind them the recognition of society as common claims for development, and that is why the state protects these rights. John Locke (1632–1704), the most influential political philosophers of the modern period, argued that people have rights, such as the right to life, liberty, and property that have a foundation independent of the laws of any particular society. Locke claimed that men are naturally free and equal as part of the justification for understanding legitimate political government as the result of a social contract where people in the state of nature conditionally transfer some of their rights to the government in order to better ensure the stable, comfortable enjoyment of their lives, liberty, and property. Since governments exist by the consent of the people in order to protect the rights of the people and promote the public good, governments that fail to do so can be resisted and replaced with new governments.

Moral Rights

Moral Rights are based on human consciousness. They are supported by moral force of human mind. These are based on human sense of goodness and justice. These are not assisted by the force of law. Sense of goodness and public opinion are the sanctions behind moral rights.

If any person disrupts any moral right, no legal action can be taken against him. The state does not enforce these rights. Its courts do not recognize these rights. Moral Rights include rules of good conduct, courtesy and of moral behavior. These stand for moral perfection of the people.

Moral rights were first acknowledged in France and Germany, before they were included in the Berne Convention for the Protection of Literary and Artistic Works in 1928. Canada recognized moral rights in its Copyright Act. The United States became a signatory to the convention in 1989, and incorporated a version of moral rights under its copyright law under Title 17 of the U.S. Code. There are two major moral rights under the U.S. Copyright Act. These are the right of attribution, also called the right of paternity and the right of integrity.

Legal Rights:

Legal rights are those rights which are accepted and enforced by the state. Any defilement of any legal right is punished by law. Law courts of the state enforce legal rights. These rights can be enforced against individuals and also against the government. In this way, legal rights are different from moral rights. Legal rights are equally available to all the citizens. All citizens follow legal rights without any discrimination. They can go to the courts for getting their legal rights enforced.

Legal Rights are of three types

Civil Rights: Civil rights are those rights which provide opportunity to each person to lead a civilized social life. These fulfil basic needs of human life in society. Right to life, liberty and equality are civil rights. Civil rights are protected by the state.

- Political Rights: Political rights are those rights by virtue of which inhabitants get a share in the political process. These allow them to take an active part in the political process. These rights include right to vote, right to get elected, right to hold public office and right to criticize and oppose the government. Political rights are really available to the people in a democratic state.
- Economic Rights: Economic rights are those rights which provide economic security to the people. These empower all citizens to make proper use of their civil and political rights. The basic needs of every person are related to his food, clothing, shelter, and medical treatment. Without the fulfilment of these no person can really enjoy his civil and political rights. It is therefore essential, that every person must get the right to work, right to adequate wages, right to leisure and rest, and right to social security in case of illness, physical disability and old age.

Human and Legal Rights

There is some difference between moral or human rights and legal rights. Legal rights require for their justification an existing system of law. Legal rights are, roughly, what the law says they are, at least insofar as the law is enforced. Legal rights gain their force first of all through legislation or decree by a legally authorized authority. Those who support adoption of laws establishing legal rights often appeal to a notion of human rights. Laws against theft might appeal to notions of a moral right to own property. But human or moral rights must gain their validity through some other source other than legal rights, since people can appeal to human or moral rights to criticize the law or advocate changes in the law (or legal rights), and people could not do this if moral rights were based upon the law.

Contractual Rights

Contractual rights originated from the practice of promise-keeping. They apply to particular individuals to whom contractual promises have been made. Contractual rights ascend from specific acts of contract making. They normally come into being when the contract is made, and they reflect the contractual duty that another party has acquired at the same time. As a result of a contract, party

A has a contractual duty, say, to deliver some good or service to party B, who has a contractual right to the good or service. Contractual rights may be upheld by the law, and in that sense can rest upon legal rights, but it is possible to conceive of contracts made outside of a legal framework and to rest purely upon moral principles. However, such contracts are less secure than contracts made within a legal framework, for obvious reasons. There are numerous examples of contractual rights such as:

- -Rights to purchase a particular product or service
- -Rights to be sell a product or service
- -Rights to be the only seller or buyer
- -Rights to delivery and timely payment
- -Rights to refunds or repairs
- -Various rights according to the specific intentions of each party

Human Rights

Human rights are those moral rights that are morally important and basic, and that are held by every human being because they are possessed in virtue of the universal moral status of human beings. Human rights are one of the significant aspects of human political reality. It is the moral rights of highest order. Human Rights are evolved out of self-respect. It is intrinsic to all humans without any discrimination of race, sex, nationality, ethnicity, language, religion and color etc. It received new shape when human beings began to think themselves. Each and every human beings are entitled to these rights without any discrimination. Human rights comprise of civil and political rights, such as the right to life, liberty and freedom of expression; and social, cultural and economic rights including the right to participate in culture, the right to food, and the right to work and receive an education.

Human rights are protected and supported by international and national laws and treaties. The UDHR was the first international document that spelled out the "basic civil, political, economic, social and cultural rights that all human beings should enjoy." The declaration was ratified without opposition by the UN General Assembly on December 10, 1948. Under human rights treaties, governments have the prime responsibility for proto shield and promote human rights. However, governments are not solely responsible for ensuring human rights. The UDHR states:

"Every individual and every organ of society shall strive by teaching and education to promote respect for these rights and freedoms and by progressive measures, national and international, to secure their universal and effective recognition and observance."

In theoretical review, many theorists expressed their views about human rights. S. Kim construed that human rights are "claims and demands essential to the protection of human life and the enhancement of human dignity, and should therefore enjoy full social and political sanctions". According to Subhash C Kashyap, human rights are those "fundamental rights to which every man inhabiting any part of the world should be deemed entitled by virtue of having been born a human being". Milne opined that "human rights are simply what every human beings owes to every other human being and as such represent universal moral obligation". According to Nickel, human rights are norms which are definite, high priority universal and existing and valid independently of recognition or implementation in the customs or legal system of particular country.

The Protection of Human Rights Act 1993 describes" Human Rights mean rights relating to life liberty, equality and dignity of the individuals guaranteed by the constitution or embodied in the International Covenants and enforceable.

The United Nation Centre of Human Rights defines Human Rights as "those rights which are inherent in our nature and without which we cannot live as human beings"

The Universal Declaration of Human Rights which adopted on 1948, states human rights as "rights derived from the inherent dignity of human person"

Historical origin of human rights: Records indicated that Though modern historians traced "Magna Carta" of 1521 as the historical beginning of human rights, but its real origin goes back to 539 B.C. when Cyrus, the great (king of ancient Persia) conquered the city of Babylon, he freed all slaves to return home and declared people to choose their own religion and even maintained racial equality. The idea of human rights quickly spread from Babylon to many nations especially, Greece and eventually Rome where the concept of natural law arose in observation of the fact that people tended to follow certain unwritten laws in due course of life. There the concept of "natural law" arose, in observation of the fact that people tended to follow certain unwritten laws in the course of life, and Roman law was based on rational ideas derived from the nature of things.

Documents asserting individual rights, such as the Magna Carta, the Petition of Right, the US Constitution, the French Declaration of the Rights of Man and of the Citizen, and the US Bill of Rights are the written precursors to many of today's human rights documents.

The Magna Carta, or "Great Charter," was debatably the most important early influence on the extensive historical process that led to the rule of constitutional law today in the English-speaking world. In 1215, after King John of England violated a number of ancient laws and customs by which England had been governed, his subjects forced him to sign the Magna Carta, which enumerates what later came to be thought of as human rights. Among them was the right of the church to be free from governmental interference, the rights of all free citizens to own and inherit property and to be protected from excessive taxes. It established the right of widows who owned property to choose not to remarry, and established principles of due process and equality before the law. It also contained provisions forbidding bribery and official misconduct. The Magna Carta was a crucial defining moment in the fight to establish freedom.

Another breakthrough in the development of human rights was the Petition of Right, produced in 1628 by the English Parliament and sent to Charles I as a statement of civil liberties. Rejection by Parliament to finance the king's unpopular foreign policy had caused his government to exact forced loans and to quarter troops in subjects' houses as an economy measure. Arbitrary arrest and imprisonment for opposing these policies had produced in Parliament a violent hostility to Charles and to George Villiers, the Duke of Buckingham. The Petition of Right, introduced by Sir Edward Coke, was based upon earlier statutes and charters and asserted four principles:

- No taxes may be levied without consent of Parliament.
- No subject may be imprisoned without cause shown (reaffirmation of the right of habeas corpus).
- No soldiers may be quartered upon the citizenry.
- Martial law may not be used in time of peace.

In 1789, the people of France brought about the abolishment of the absolute kingdom and set the stage for the establishment of the first French Republic. Sometime later, the storming of the Bastille, and barely three weeks after the abolition of feudalism, the Declaration of the Rights of Man and of the Citizen was espoused by the National Constituent Assembly as the first step toward writing a constitution for the Republic of France.

The Declaration decrees that all inhabitants are to be guaranteed the rights of "liberty, property, security, and resistance to oppression." It discusses that the need for law derives from the fact that "the exercise of the natural rights of each man has only those borders which assure other members of the society the enjoyment of these same rights." Therefore, the Declaration sees law as an "expression of the general will", intended to promote this equality of rights and to forbid "only actions harmful to the society."

In 1864, sixteen European countries and several American states attended a conference in Geneva, at the invitation of the Swiss Federal Council, on the initiative of the Geneva Committee. The diplomatic conference was held to adopt a convention for the treatment of wounded soldiers in combat. The main ideologies laid down in the Convention and maintained by the later Geneva Conventions provided for the obligation to extend care without discrimination to wounded and sick military personnel and respect for and marking of medical personnel transports and equipment with the distinctive sign of the red cross on a white background.

By 1948, the United Nation's new Human Rights Commission had attracted global attention. Under the dynamic headship of Eleanor Roosevelt, President Franklin Roosevelt's widow, a human rights winner in her own right and the United States delegate to the UN, the Commission set out to draft the document that became the Universal Declaration of Human Rights. Roosevelt, credited with its motivation, referred to the Declaration as the international Magna Carta for all mankind. It was accepted by the United Nations on December 10, 1948. The Declaration unequivocally proclaims the inherent rights of all human beings: "Disregard and contempt for human rights have resulted in barbarous acts which have outraged the conscience of mankind, and the advent of a world in which human beings shall enjoy freedom of speech and belief and freedom from fear and want has been proclaimed as the highest aspiration of the common people. All human beings are born free and equal in dignity and rights."

The Member States of the United Nations promised to work together to encourage the thirty of human rights that, for the first time in history, had been assembled and codified into a single document. As a result, many of these rights, in various forms, are part of the constitutional laws of democratic nations in present situation.

In nut shell, The written inventor to the modern human rights documents are the English Bill of Rights (1689), the American Declaration of Independence

(1776), the French Declaration of the Rights of Man and Citizen (1789), the first Ten Amendments of the Constitution of the United States (Bill of Rights 1791) and the Universal Declaration of Human Rights of UN (1948).

Human rights is the basic rights and freedom of all human, it include the right to life, liberty, freedom of thought, expression and equality before the law. It is unified, interdependent and indivisible.

Rights agree to duties in three ways:

- Individual duties of forbearance (non-interference)
- Institutional duties of assistance
- Individual duties of assistance

If we consider the right to property, conceived primarily as the right not to have one's personal property taken without one's consent. This implies that

- Other individuals have a duty to forbear from taking a person's possessions without his or her consent.
- Institutions, such as governments, should establish and enforce laws against theft and should do so in all neighborhoods where theft is a possibility.
- Officials in the government have an individual duty, as officials, to support such laws and or enforce them.

The individual duties of assistance are performed in several ways: If the government were lax in this area, citizens might have a positive duty to pressure government to pass an appropriate law if one were missing or to enforce already existing laws.

Beyond that, individual citizens who are aware of persons with sticky fingers, as it were, have an obligation, where it could be done at reasonable cost to themselves, to thwart acts of theft.

Many theories have been developed to explain human rights. According to Dr. Justice Durga Das Basu, "Human rights are those minimal rights, which every individual must have against the State, or other public authority, by virtue of his being a 'member of human family' irrespective of any consideration. The philosopher John Finnis argues that human rights are reasonable on the grounds of their instrumental value in creating the necessary conditions for human well-being.

The Universal Declaration of Human Rights (UDHR), 1948, stated that human rights as "rights derived from the inherent dignity of the human person." Human rights when they are guaranteed by a written constitution are known as "Fundamental Rights" because a written constitution is the fundamental law of the state.

Characteristics of human rights

- Human Rights are Inalienable: Human rights are deliberated on an individual due to the very nature of his existence. They are innate in all individuals irrespective of their caste, creed, religion, sex and nationality. Human rights are conferred to an individual even after his death. The different rituals in different religions bear testimony to this fact.
- Human Rights are essential and necessary: Human rights are needed to maintain the moral, physical, social and spiritual welfare of an individual.

Human rights are also essential as they provide suitable conditions for material and moral upliftment of the people.

- Human Rights are associated with human dignity: To treat another individual with dignity regardless of the fact that the person is a male or female, rich or poor is concerned with human dignity.
- Human Rights are Irrevocable: Human rights are irrevocable as they cannot be taken away by any power or authority because these rights originate with the social nature of man in the society of human beings and they belong to a person simply because he is a human being. As such human rights have similarities to moral rights.
- Human Rights are essential for the fulfilment of purpose of life: Human life has a purpose. The phrase "human right" is applied to those conditions which are essential for the fulfilment of this purpose. No government has the power to curtail or take away the rights which are sacrosanct, inviolable and immutable.
- Human Rights are Universal: Human rights are not a domination of any privileged class of people. Human rights are universal in nature, without consideration and without exception. The values such as divinity, dignity and equality which form the basis of these rights are inherent in human nature.
- Human Rights are never absolute: Man is a social animal and he lives in a civic society, which always put certain limitations on the enjoyment of his rights and freedoms. Human rights as such are those limited powers or claims, which are contributory to the common good and which are recognized and guaranteed by the State, through its laws to the individuals. As such each right has certain limitations.
- Human Rights are Dynamic: Human rights are not stationary, they are dynamic. Human rights go on expanding with socio-eco-cultural and political developments within the State. Judges have to construe laws in such ways as are in tune with the changed social values.
- Rights as limits to state power: Human rights infer that every individual has legitimate claims upon his or her society for certain freedom and benefits. So human rights limit the state's power. These may be in the form of negative restrictions, on the powers of the State, from violating the inalienable freedoms of the individuals, or in the nature of demands on the State, i.e. positive obligations of the State.

THEORY OF RIGHTS

Rights are those essential conditions of social life without which no person can generally realize his best self. These are the essential conditions for health of both the individual and his society. It is only when people get and enjoy rights that they can develop their personalities and contributes their best services to the society.

Laski's Theory of Rights

Several inferences can be drawn from this short and oft-quoted definition. Laski calls rights as conditions of social life. A stranger of outside world or a denizen of a solitary island cannot claim right. Rights are, in fact, social concept and deeply connected with social life. The essentiality of rights is established by the fact that individuals claim them for the development of their best self.

He places rights, individuals and state on the same plank in the sense that they cannot be separated from each other and there is no antagonism between them. Laski endorses the long-cherished .view that the state has a very important role to play in the realization and, before that, recognition of human rights.

The point which he stresses here is that it is the primary duty of the state to help the individual in his efforts to achieve his best self and, if that be the case, the state has a very big responsibility in the field of realization of rights.

Laski on Legal Theory of Rights

Laski analyses the legal theory of state. The central theme of the legal theory of rights is that they completely depend upon the institutions and recognition of state. An individual cannot claim rights if those are not recognized by the state. Mere recognition, moreover, is not sufficient for the exercise of rights. The state must, through law and institutions, implement the rights.

If these two conditions, the legal theory asserts, are not fulfilled the individuals will have hardly any opportunity to enjoy rights. This legal theory of rights was propounded by many—chief among them are Hobbes and Bentham. Legal theory further states that the law, in fact, determines the character and implementation of rights. Prof. Laski says that the legal theory is attractive. Various institutions, along with the individuals themselves, always take active interest in the matters of rights. But though attractive, this theory, according to Laski, is highly questionable.

He writes: "But so purely legalistic a view has nothing to contribute to an adequate political philosophy. A legal theory of rights will tell us what in fact the character of a state is; it will not tell us whether the rights there recognised are the rights which need recognition".

The point to which Laski wants to draw our attention is that the legal theory of rights does not constitute everything of rights.

Laski raises his objection against the legal theory of rights on many grounds. First of all, it does not throw sufficient light on the idea of political philosophy. What does he mean? He has not explained it properly. As a citizen every individual has a claim for right, but the question is whether he ought to have a right. Again, the purposes of rights are to be properly investigated.

It is to be assessed or analyzed in the background of social and political environment. Rights are to be viewed in economic terms also. These and many other questions need just treatment and when done so that will form the structure of political philosophy. Laski's categorical assertion is that the legal theory of rights is quite silent on the questions.

Legal theory, again, has committed a mistake by making rights upon the state. 'State recognizes rights' does not mean that it creates rights. Rights existed prior to state. The validity of rights is not derived from the recognition.

There are many rights which are not recognized by many states. Does it mean that these rights are devoid of validity? At a particular conjuncture a state recognizes certain rights or is forced to recognize them. It may be that people may place the demand for recognition of some rights, but these cannot be recognized because they ought not to be recognized.

Functional Theory of Rights

The most attractive part of Laski's theory is functional aspect of rights. It is attractive not because of its novelty but because of its emphasis on the relation between right and duty. He says, "Rights are correlative to functions".

He again comments: "He that will not perform functions cannot enjoy any more than he who will not work ought to enjoy bread". These two famous comments can be taken up for consideration. In his criticism of the legal theory of rights he has said that it does not offer an "adequate philosophy".

The functional theory of rights wants to stress that an individual is entitled to claim rights only when he performs duty Otherwise the claim or demand for right cannot be entertained. This definitely goes against the widely known theory of legal theory of rights. But today rights are recognized and protected mainly on political considerations.

Laski says that whether man will have rights and what or how many rights he will enjoy depends not upon the state but upon the person himself. Without doing any work a man cannot claim any bread.

Similarly, without doing any duty an individual cannot place any demand for right. Performance of duty automatically entitles a man to demand right and the state in that case is bound to grant right. Function is thus implicit in right. If an individual can contribute to the society that can be regarded as a ground for right.

But function is not enough. Any type of function cannot make one demand right His work or performance must be socially useful. That is, what he does that will enhance welfare of the society. A man has no right to do whatever he likes.

The work must relate to the general welfare of the state. Here Laski views the duty of individual and rights in the perspective of the whole society. The recognition of rights is not dependent upon the mercy of the state. If the individual performs functions which are undoubtedly socially useful and if the state recognizes that then the rights are to be recognized.

Hence, recognition of rights has a relation to the recognition of the services to the enrichment of state. If rights of certain individuals are not recognized by the state, in that case the general interests will be adversely affected and the state will do gross injustice not to the persons but to the public in general.

But to perform a duty which is socially necessary requires granting of some rights. A man cannot perform any duty if he has no right to do that considering this aspect of rights in their functional background he makes the following observation: "Rights, regardless of exact functions to which they relate, are at a minimum basis, identical. The state, at that level, must secure them for each of its citizens. Differentiation arises only when the elementary needs of each individual have been satisfied".

In his analysis of justice Rawls raises this issue. All men in a society cannot claim identical or equal rights because the needs of all men are not supposed to be identical. But for the sake of justice granting of unequal rights to different persons shall be admitted. This contention has been supported by many.

Right to Resist

Laski, in clear language, admits individual's right to resist that is, he has right against the state and in-this regard Laski does not agree with Green's views.

Before discussing his views, in order to be clear, we must add few words about Green's opinion. Green has said: a right against society as such, a right to act without reference to the needs or good of society, is an impossibility since every right depends on some social relation.

He has further observed that even if an authority adopts imperfect decisions, the individuals cannot resist them on the ground that he enjoys the right to resist. He can resist on the ground that his action aims at general welfare of the society. General welfare or common good, according to Green, is the supreme authority which none can violate.

Laski does not share fully the opinion of T. H. Green. He says that it is the responsibility of every citizen to consider the common good or the overall interests of all people. But that does not debar me from registering my objection against the performance of the state. Individual shall co-operate with the state in all matters, but where he finds that the function of the state is not in conformity with public interests he has right to resist.

"No claim of mine can be recognized by the state which involves the surrender by some other person of rights without which he cannot be his best self. The mutual claims of the state and of its citizens must be claims clearly justifiable by reference to a common good which includes the goods of all".

By recognising individual's right to resist Laski once again admits that liberal philosophy, though in amended form, is always active in his mind. The decision of the state cannot be accepted without any scrutiny. Every citizen has right to judge the function of the state in the light of its success. That is, to what extent it has been able to meet the requirements of the society as a whole. An argument in favor of the state shall be backed by its ability or success to meet people's demands. Laski, therefore, does not give unconditional power to state authority. Laski wants to see the state as a responsible and welfare institution. Individual to him is also responsible and reasonable. If both do their allotted duties, he is sure, no problem of obligation, implementation of rights and realization of general welfare will crop up. Viewing from this angle we can say that Laski's conception of rights is more balanced and to some extent pragmatic than that of Thomas Hill Green.

Barker's Theory of Right

Rights Defined and Nature Explained

So far as the theory of rights is concerned, Barker's view is not conceptually different from that of Laski. Both are liberal philosophers, but Barker has a clear bias to idealism. The ultimate purpose of every political organization called state is to see that the personality of the individual gets ample scope for development. It is the duty of the state to guarantee and secure the conditions essential for that objective.

These secured and guaranteed conditions are called rights. Individual's personality cannot develop automatically or under most adverse or antagonistic environment. Development of personality requires favorable conditions and these are to be guaranteed by the state through the enactment of law.

So we find that the state, rights and the individual all have purpose. The purpose of the former two is to help the individual in the attainment of his purpose.

It implies that the justification of the former two lies in how much they have been able to help the individual.

Barker endorses the views of Laski and Green when he says in his explanation of the nature of rights that the rights of an individual are embodied in him but these are parts of the whole system of rights and of justice.

The implication is that the rights of any particular individual are the parts of the rights which other persons exercise. Rights of one cannot be isolated from those of others. Attempts to segregate the rights of persons will lead to the nullification of rights to which other persons are entitled.

The development of self of all persons is a condition of the development of particular self. Naturally, rights are to be guaranteed to all persons and this task is to be done by the state through law. So law is a very important instrument for securing rights. This is the legal concept of rights, because if the state does not take initiative to secure rights through law individuals will be deprived of rights.

Here we find that Barker discusses the concept of right from the stand point of macro politics which means that the idea cannot be analysed treating individuals as separate from each other. Exercise of rights by each individual creates impact upon other individuals as well as on society as a whole. This must be remembered.

Barker also discusses the moral aspect of rights. He says, that law of the state helps me to secure rights. But rights are claims and the origin is the individual himself. The individual is a moral person and it is his determination that he will develop his moral personality through the rights. His purpose is not to inflict any harm upon the society. The implication of moral being is he releases his best efforts for the general welfare of society. There is another source of rights pointed out by Barker.

The state and its law are the sources of rights. This can be treated as a single source. The state recognizes rights and makes law for its implementation. "Ideally a right will always be derived simultaneously from two sources and will possess double quality: source of the individual personality and the source of the state and its laws".

Distribution of Rights

Mere declaration of rights is not enough for any society. Care is to be taken as to the distribution of them. Barker stresses the point that in distributing rights utmost importance is to be given to the idea of justice. Maintenance of justice shall be the ultimate goal of any state and distribution of rights must see that. He has suggested that the distribution of rights shall be based on three principles liberty, equality and fraternity.

The state will take measures for the distribution of rights remembering that all the individuals are free agents of the state and they have the abilities to develop their own personalities.

The freedom or liberty of the individual cannot be infringed. Taking this basic premise the state will proceed to distribute rights among the citizens. The implication, according to Barker, is the purpose of right will be to maximize liberty. Every citizen will have liberty to enjoy rights and he will allow others to follow him. The second procedural rule of the distribution of rights is the equality which means that in the eye of state authority all individuals are equal. The state cannot give more rights to some and less to others. So far as the state activity is concerned all are equal. Outside the state there is inequality in economic status, political power and cultural background.

But these inequalities are not supposed to disturb or affect the procedural principle or rule. Speaking about this procedural principle Barker writes: "It does not involve or mean equality in the social or extra-legal sphere: it is legal, and not social equality; it is equality in terms of capacity for the enjoyment and exercise of rights; but not in terms of capacity for the enjoyment and exercise of all the multitudinous forms of social activity".

The final procedural rule of the distribution of rights is fraternity. The principle of fraternity was first enunciated by the leaders of the French Revolution. Goodwill, co-operation and friendship should be the basis of human relations. It is the duty of the state to see that these eternal principles are encouraged and flourished through the distribution of rights or, to put it in other words, the state will not recognize rights in such manner as to exacerbate the relationship among people.

In order to do this the state must take an unbiased approach to all its citizens. The development of personality shall be the chief motive of the recognition and implementation of rights. If the principles of liberty, equality and fraternity are strictly and scrupulously adhered to in the distribution of rights then that will undoubtedly ensure the maximisation of justice.

Marxist Theory Rights

Marxist Analysis of Bourgeois Concept of Rights

Marx and Engle's have not allotted an exclusive place for the detailed analysis of rights, but they were quite conscious of the condition of various rights as it prevailed in bourgeois society. The liberal thinkers paid very little attention to the realization of economic rights. To them political rights were of prime importance and if citizens get the opportunity to enjoy all the political rights, absence of economic rights will not pose any problem on the way of political rights.

Moreover, non-realization of economic rights may finally result in the growing economic inequalities and according to liberal this theoreticians it is a good sign of freedom. But Marx and Engels denounced this approach to rights and they have stated in no uncertain terms that in the absence of economic rights there is practically no significance of political rights.

They have, of course, admitted that in a class society this is inevitable because economically powerful class will create an atmosphere in which the general public will not get any opportunity to have all sorts of rights.

The rights in bourgeois society are, therefore, partial in character, Partial in the sense that only a very limited number of persons get the freedom to have rights. The three organs of government are under the control of the powerful class and they work at its behest. Rights of the majority ate always suppressed the dominant class.

Marxists have admitted that in a bourgeois society attempts are always made to expand the number of rights and in reality this is done. But the rise in the number of rights does not come to the benefit of common people.

The powerful class, through its efficient machinery bole; all the rights for its enjoyment. The deprived of the population no benefit. Moreover, the separation between the two classes stands on the way of exercise of rights by the working class.

A recent analyst has offered the following comment: "Once citizens entered the factory gates their lives were fully determined by the dictates of the capital. The capitalist labor contract excludes the workers from formal rights over the control of the work place. This exclusion is not incidental to the capitalist state, but vital to it since the sphere of industry is specifically defined as being outside politics.

In substantial degree Marx was surely right". So we find that almost all the rights of any bourgeois society are meant for the powerful. These can be called bourgeois rights. Even few bourgeois theoreticians have admitted it. But some bourgeois thinkers have admitted that so far as the structure of capitalist society is concerned this situation is unavoidable and cannot be changed.

Rights, Citizenship and Obligation

Political scientists, in recent years, have investigated the relationship between rights on the one hand and citizenship and obligations on the other hand. Before entering into the details we shall see what is meant by citizenship. Citizenship may be regarded as a status conferred by law with the help of which (citizenship) an individual can make contribution to the welfare of the society.

It is now obvious from this definition that once an individual attains this status he can claim certain rights which will enable to contribute to the development of society. If the individual gets no rights his ability to contribute to society will stand on nothing. Again, once an individual has been awarded the status of citizenship he has legal claims to right. So we find that both citizenship and rights are closely linked.

There is another aspect of this issue. Citizenship implies the involvement of men in the affairs of the community. It's another implication is the title of citizenship entitles an individual to participate in the affairs of the community. Hence right citizenship and participation in the affairs of the community are all associated What about the obligation?

It is observed that if individuals (after having the status of citizenship) are not allowed to have rights and if they do not get the opportunities to participate in community affairs they can reasonably and logically withdraw their obligation to the authority or they may refuse to show obedience to the authority.

So, rights and citizenship are important concepts. The relationship may still be viewed from another context. To participate in the affairs of the state is an important political right and every citizen must have this right. Citizenship is generally defined as an ability to contribute to the progress of state. If the citizen is deprived of this right Ire is not supposed to show obligation to the state or authority.

Negative and Positive Rights

We shall now turn to a new concept of rights briefly stated by Andrew Heywood (Political Theory). He says that there are two forms of rights-negative and positive rights. Traditional rights mainly elaborated by Locke and Jefferson are called negative rights these rights are right to life, liberty, property and the pursuit of happiness.

It we scan these rights we shall find that they impose some restrictions upon the activities and power of the state authority. The state should not perform such acts or enact such laws as well prevent the individuals from exercising or enjoying the rights. These are also called forbearance rights. The implementation of rights requires the limitation upon the power of the state. Needless to say that both John Locke and Jefferson wanted this.

But in the twentieth century, especially after the Second World War, people demanded larger and comprehensive intervention in the affairs of society which means that the state must do something for the general welfare of the society and upliftment of the weaker of the community.

These activities of the state finally came to be regarded as rights which are called welfare rights, social and economic rights. These rights are known as positive rights. "These are positive rights in the sense that they demand not forbearance but active government intervention". The right to health care, right to education etc. fall in this category.

Equality before Law and Equal Rights

We shall now turn to what Marx and Engels have said about equality before law and equal rights. In liberal theory of rights large amount of space has been devoted to the utility of equality before law. All citizens, in liberal democratic countries, are equally treated. No sort of difference is counted.

The individuals claim it as their right and any authority or agency violating the right to equality before law will be subject to punishment. Scholars are of opinion that the concept of equality before law at first originated in the British political system and subsequently it found its place in many countries that followed, either partially or elaborately, Westminster model and today it is more or less found in all systems.

The Marxists challenge this right and their main ground is in a society where there are various sorts of inequalities such a right has no validity. The elites, bourgeois class and other powerful persons control the state administration and the judiciary interprets the constitution and laws always to safeguard the interests of these persons. Law is strict only where the poor people are involved.

Marx and his followers have asserted that for the proper implementation of equality before law there must be equality in the distribution of wealth. Gross economic inequalities are to be eradicated at first and then we shall think about equality before law. Unfortunately, the liberal philosophers have kept this issue outside their consideration. Their main concern is political rights, irrespective of economic problems.

Marx in his Critique of the Gotha Program has strongly criticized the bourgeois concept of equal rights. Two laborers cannot have equal physical strength and mental capability. The work or contribution of two laborers in this particular situation cannot be equal, differences are bound to arise. So, equal right idea is pernicious or meaningless.

This equal right is an unequal right for unequal labor. It recognizes no class differences, because everyone is only a worker like everyone else, but it tacitly recognizes unequal individual endowment and thus productive capacity as natural privileges. It is, therefore, a right of inequality, in its content, like every right".

Marx further maintains the equal right is still constantly stigmatized by a bourgeois limitation. "The right of the producers is proportional to the labor they supply, the equality consists in the fact that measurement is made with an equal standard of labor".

Marx wants to stress that while considering the concept of equal right or anything like that the class differences of society and the productive power all are to be properly considered. Mere announcement of equal right idea cannot absolve capitalists of responsibility.

THE PHENOMENA OF IDENTITY IN SOCIAL COMMUNITY

When members of a specific subgroup unite in order to affect political or social change, the result is often called identity politics. This phenomenon is not limited to the major racial or gender divisions of our time, but extends into sexual orientation, ethnicity, citizenship status and other instances where a specific group feels marginalized or oppressed.

The phenomenon sometimes derisively referred to as "identity politics" primarily appeared during the politically tumultuous years following the passage of the Civil Rights Act in 1965. While much of the attention was focused on the plight of disenfranchised African-Americans, other groups also sought recognition and acceptance through political activism and collective awareness raising.

The success of the desegregation efforts for marginalized African-Americans spurred other groups to take political action of their own. Under the concept of identity politics, women could unite in order to promote the passage of an Equal Rights Amendment. Homosexuals could organize political rallies or start grassroots campaigns to have stronger hate crime laws created or allow same-sex partners to qualify for marital benefits.

Other groups such as legal Hispanic immigrants or Native Americans were also empowered through identity politics. The idea was for marginalized or oppressed groups to be recognized for their differences, not in spite of them. By identifying himself or herself as an African-American or a homosexual or a feminist, a person could focus all of his or her energies on a specific political cause. This singularity of purpose appears to be the most positive aspect of this phenomenon.

There are those who see identity politics in a less positive light, however. By focusing so much energy on a specific political agenda, practitioners may appear to be just as closed minded or exclusionary as those they claim are oppressing or marginalizing their group. The idea that an outsider could not possibly understand the problems or needs of a specific group could create more problems in the political arena.

African-Americans who felt oppressed by a majority white government, for example, had to accept that passage of the Civil Rights Act required the votes of conservative white legislators. Under the focused umbrella of identity politics, such a compromise would have been much more difficult to achieve. This is why many organized minority political groups have largely abandoned this model for a more ecumenical approach to common goals.

Communitarianism

Communitarianism, social and political philosophy that emphasizes the importance of community in the functioning of political life, in the analysis and evaluation of political institutions, and in understanding human identity and well-being. It arose in the 1980s as a critique of two prominent philosophical schools: contemporary liberalism, which seeks to protect and enhance personal autonomyand individual rights in part through the activity of government, and libertarianism, a form of liberalism (sometimes called "classical liberalism") that aims to protect individual rights—especially the rights to liberty and property—through strict limits on governmental power.

There are strong communitarian elements in many modern and historical political and religious belief systems—e.g., in the Hebrew Bible(Old Testament) and the Christian New Testament; in the early Islamic concept of *shūrā*("consultation"); in Confucianism; in Roman Catholic social thought (the papal encyclicalRerumNovarum); in moderate conservatism ("To be attached to the subdivision, to love the little platoon we belong to in society, is the first principle...of public affections"—Edmund Burke); and in social democracy, especially Fabianism. Communitarian ideas have also played a significant role in public life through their incorporation into the electoral platforms and policies of Western political leaders of the late 20th and early 21st centuries, including British Prime Minister Tony Blair, Dutch Prime Minister Jan Peter Balkenende, and U.S. Presidents Bill Clinton and Barack Obama.

Varieties of Communitarianism

The term *communitarian* was coined in 1841 by John GoodwynBarmby, a leader of the British Chartist movement, who used it to refer to utopian socialists and others who experimented with unusual communal lifestyles. It was rarely used in the generations that followed.

It was not until the 1980s that the term gained currency through its association with the work of a small group of mostly American political philosophers who argued for the importance of the common good in opposition to contemporary liberals and libertarians, who emphasized the good for individuals, particularly including personal autonomy and individual rights. The Canadian philosopher Charles Taylor and the American political theorist Michael Sandel were among the most prominent scholars of this brand of communitarianism. Other political theorists and philosophers who were often cited as communitarians in this sense, or whose work exhibited elements of such communitarian thinking, included ShlomoAvineri, SeylaBenhabib, Avner de-Shalit, Jean BethkeElshtain, AmitaiEtzioni, William A. Galston, Alasdair MacIntyre, Philip Selznick, and Michael Walzer.

During the same period, students of East Asian politics and society used communitarianismto describe the social thinking within authoritarian societies such as China, Singapore, and Malaysia, which extolled social obligations and the importance of the common good and accorded much less weight to autonomy and rights. Indeed, these societies viewed individuals as more or less interchangeable cells who find meaning in their contribution to the social whole rather than as free agents. Scholars of this kind of communitarianism included the American political theorist Russell A. Fox and the Singaporean diplomat BilahariKausikan.

The Common Good versus Individual Rights

Whereas the classical liberalism of the Enlightenment can be viewed as a reaction to centuries of authoritarianism, oppressive government, overbearing communities, and rigid dogma, modern communitarianism can be considered a reaction to excessive individualism, understood by communitarians as an undue emphasis on individual rights, leading people to become selfish or egocentric. Excessive individualism was discussed in an oft-cited communitarian work, *Habits of the Heart: Individualism and Commitment in American Life*, by the American sociologist Robert NeellyBellah, who observed that by the early 1980s most Americans had become self-centred. Increasing prosperity from the 1950s, among other factors, had contributed to a decline in respect for traditional authority and institutions, such as marriage, and fostered a kind of materialistic hedonism, according to many communitarians. Earlier sociologists such as Ferdinand Tönniesand Émile Durkheim had discussed such antisocial tendencies in the context of modernization, which they viewed as a historical transition from oppressive but nurturing communities (*Gemeinschaft*) to liberating but impersonal societies (*Gesellschaft*). They warned of the dangers of anomie (normlessness) and alienation in modern societies composed of atomized individuals who had gained their liberty but lost their social moorings. Essentially the theses of Tönnies and Durkheim were supported with contemporary social-scientific data in Bowling Alone: The Collapse and Revival of American Community, by the American political scientist Robert Putnam.

The close relation between the individual and the community was discussed on a theoretical level by Sandel and Taylor, among other academic communitarians, in their criticisms of philosophical liberalism, including especially the work of the American liberal theorist Rowland that of the German Enlightenment philosopherImmanuel Kant. They argued that contemporary liberalism and libertarianism presuppose an incoherent notion of the individual as existing outside and apart from society rather than embedded within it. To the contrary, they argued, there are no generic individuals but rather only Germans or Russians, Berliners or Muscovites, or members of some other particularistic community. Because individual identity is partly constituted (or "constructed") by culture and social relations, there is no coherent way of formulating individual rights or interests in abstraction from social contexts. In particular, according to these communitarians, there is no point in attempting to found a theory of justice on principles that individuals would choose in a hypothetical state of ignorance of their social, economic, and historical circumstances (from behind a Rawlsian "veil of ignorance"), because such individuals cannot exist, even in principle.

Liberal scholars argued that this line of criticism is overstated or misconceived. Despite its emphasis on autonomy and rights, they contended, contemporary liberalism is not incompatible with the notion of a socially embedded self. Indeed, Rawls himself, in his foundational work *A Theory of Justice* (1971), recognized the importance of what he called "social unions" and asserted that "only in a social union is the individual complete." Thus, according to liberals, the communitarian critique does not rebut the core of liberal theory but merely serves as a corrective to "stronger" liberal doctrines such as libertarianism, which does embrace an atomized notion of individual identity. Academic communitarians also drew upon Aristotle and the German idealist philosopherGeorg Friedrich Wilhelm Hegelto argue that some conception of the good must be formulated on the social level and that the community cannot be a normative-neutral realm. Unless there is a social formulation of the good, there can be no normative foundation upon which to draw to settle conflicts of value between different individuals and groups. Such an overriding good (e.g., the national well-being) enables persons with different moral outlooks or ideological backgrounds to find principled (rather than merely prudential) common ground.

Liberals and libertarians responded by characterizing the communitarian position as akin to East Asian authoritarian communitarianism. They also argued that social formulations of the good—and the obligations they generate, which individuals must then discharge—can sometimes be oppressive. Some libertarians cited taxesand mandatory vaccinations as examples of such obligations.

A Synthesis: Rights and Responsibilities

Responsive communitarianism may be considered a synthesis of both liberal and academic-communitarian concerns. Sandel and Taylor in effect held that many forms of philosophical liberalism, especially libertarianism, overemphasize autonomy and rights at the expense of the common good. However, in doing so, they were less than clear about the standing of individual rights, including human rights. Indeed, Alasdair MacIntyre asserted that rights were merely figments of the imagination, like unicorns. Responsive communitarians attempted to bridge this divide. In their platform and in their academic works, they posited that all societies must heed the moral claims of two core values, the common good and autonomy and rights. They also held that, because actual societies tend to tilt toward one core value or the other, they need to be pulled back toward the centre. Thus Japan, in their view, was strongly dedicated to the common good but insufficiently committed to the rights of women, ethnic minorities, and the disabled, while the United States during the presidential administration of Ronald Reagan (1981–89) and the United Kingdom during the prime ministership of Margaret Thatcher (1979–90) attached undue importance to individual rights. The early prime ministership of Blair demonstrated a concern for the common good through its policies of devolution and the "stakeholder society" (the idea that businesses should be responsive to workers, consumers, and other groups whose interests they affect), as did the early administration of George W. Bushthrough its dedication to "compassionate conservatism." After the 2001 September 11 attacks, however, the common good in the United States was increasingly identified with national security, and some individual rights (e.g., the right to habeas corpus) were curtailed.

In the same vein, responsive communitarians also warned against excessively expansive definitions of rights and championed modern communities in which people find both a rich web of social relations and considerable degrees of freedom. In the early 21st century, responsive communitarians believed that the Scandinavian countries had achieved the best balance, though even there some individual rights were being curtailed for security reasons and in response to anti-immigrant sentiment.

Policy Implications

Responsive communitarianism developed criteria for the formulation of policies that would enable societies to cope with the potential conflicts between the common good and individual rights, including in areas such as public healthversus individual privacy and national security versus individual liberty. These criteria, which must be applied jointly, included the following:

1. No change is justified in governing public policies and norms unless society encounters serious challenges, because these kinds of changes exact considerable societal costs. (The September 11 attacks constituted such a challenge.)
2. Limitations on rights can be considered only if there are significant gains to the common good—what the U.S. courts refer to as a "compelling interest"—and if the intrusion is as limited as possible.
3. Adverse side effects that result from policy changes must be treated, all, by introducing stronger mechanisms of accountability and oversight.

An example of the application of these criteria can be seen in the debate in the United States concerning whether to improve public health by testing newborn babies for HIV. According to communitarians, such tests would be justified if:

(1) They saved lives (an infant infected with HIV has a strong chance of not developing AIDS if it is not breastfed and is treated with the drug AZT),

(2) The intrusion were limited to testing blood that would be collected anyway, and

(3) The adverse side effects could be limited by regulations that ban the disclosure of test results to nonmedical personnel.

Socially Constructed Preferences

The communitarian approach challenges the liberal view—reflected in many social sciences, especially neoclassical economics and the study of law—that the political and economic preferences of individuals should be respected and that their aggregation should guide the governance of the polity (through voting) and the economy (through the influence of consumer spending on the production and distribution of consumer goods). It is fully legitimate, for example, for public authorities to urge people to resist the appeals of political extremists or to encourage them to save more of their money. Communitarianism also challenges the libertarian position that it is paternalistic to interfere with individual choices based on personal preferences. In keeping with their view concerning the social constitution of individual identity, communitarians argue that personal preferences are to a significant extent not autonomous but rather a reflection of the larger culture, aspects of which can be heavily influenced by nonrational forces such as commercial advertising. Hence, public efforts to influence such preferences in beneficial ways, say in campaigns against smoking and obesity, do not undermine personal autonomy and are not a violation of human dignity.

The Third Sector

Communitarianism adds a major element to a centuries-old debate in the West over the proper roles of government on the one hand and the market on the other.

Communitarians argue that attention also must be paid to the role of civil society, including families, local and nonresidential communities, voluntary associations, schools, places of worship, foundations, and nonprofit corporations. It stresses that much of the behaviour that must be regulated in any society, as well as the factors that encourage people to discharge their social responsibilities (e.g., caring for children), are influenced by this third sector. Communitarians point to the importance of social norms and informal social controls in fostering pro-social conduct and in providing the moral foundations (e.g., trust) required for the successful operation of both governments and markets. The American political journalist Jonathan Rauch introduced the term "soft communitarianism" to refer to communitarianism that focuses on the role of civil society, in contrast to "hard," East Asian communitarianism, which views the state as the primary social agent.

Cultural Relativism and The Global Community

Because communitarians favour communal formulations of the good, which are necessarily particular to each community, they are vulnerable to the charge of ethical relativism, or to the claim that there is no absolute good but only different goods for different communities, cultures, or societies. Walzer adopted a clearly relativistic position, in which he asserted that the caste system is "good" by the standards of traditional Indian society. Critics argued, however, that his position was untenable. One simply needs to consider a community that champions honor killings, lynchings, or burnings to realize that communities should not be the ultimate arbiters of that which is good. While acknowledging that different communities may have different ultimate values, Taylor argued—as did Rawls—that an "overlapping consensus" on specific norms and policies is still possible, though different communities may have different reasons for believing that a given norm or policy is right. In the United States, for example, abortion-rights and antiabortion activists have worked together to make adoption easier and to improve the quality of day-care centers. According to a much more-contested argument, advanced by the American scholar of religion Don Browning, there are some substantive universal values, such as human rights and the integrity of the global climate that can provide a foundation for particularistic, communal ones.

Closely related to the question of the scope of morality is the question of the scope of community itself. Historically, communities have been local. However, as the reach of economic and technological forces extended, more-expansive communities became necessary in order to provide effective normative and political guidance to and control of these forces—hence the rise of national communities in Europe in the 17th century. Since the late 20th century there has been a growing recognition that the scope of even these communities is too limited, as many challenges that people now face, such as the threat of nuclear war and the reality of global environmental degradation, cannot be handled on a national basis. This has led to the quest for more-encompassing communities. The most advanced experiment in building a supranational community is the European Union(EU). However, so far the EU has not developed the kind of social integration and shared values that a strong community requires.

A similar issue arises with regard to the global community, currently more an ideal than a reality. Could such a community be constructed top-down, say, through some kind of enhanced United Nations (UN)? Or will it arise from the bottom up, through societal processes and institutions such as international nongovernmental organizations(NGOs), the transnational sharing of norms (e.g., for protecting the environment), a global second language (about one quarter of the world's population has at least a functional command of English), and other informal social networks? The question remains whether, ultimately, world governance can thrive without a worldwide community.

Multiculturalism

Multiculturalism, the view that cultures, races, and ethnicities, particularly those of minority groups, deserve special acknowledgement of their differences within a dominant political culture.

That acknowledgement can take the forms of recognition of contributions to the cultural life of the political community as a whole, a demand for special protection under the law for certain cultural groups, or autonomous rights of governance for certain cultures. Multiculturalism is both a response to the fact of cultural pluralism in modern democracies and a way of compensating cultural groups for past exclusion, discrimination, and oppression. Most modern democracies comprise members with diverse cultural viewpoints, practices, and contributions. Many minority cultural groups have experienced exclusion or the denigration of their contributions and identities in the past. Multiculturalism seeks the inclusion of the views and contributions of diverse members of society while maintaining respect for their differences and withholding the demand for their assimilation into the dominant culture.

Multiculturalism as a Challenge to Traditional Liberalism

Multiculturalism stands as a challenge to liberal democracy. In liberal democracies, all citizens should be treated equally under the law by abstracting the common identity of "citizen" from the real social, cultural, political, and economic positions and identities of real members of society. That leads to a tendency to homogenize the collective of citizens and assume a common **political culture** that all participate in. However, that abstract view ignores other politically salient features of the identities of political subjects that exceed the category of citizen, such as race, religion, class, and sex. Although claiming the formal equality of citizens, the liberal democratic view tends to underemphasize ways in which citizens are not in fact equal in society. Rather than embracing the traditional liberal image of the melting pot into which people of different cultures are assimilated into a unified national culture, multiculturalism generally holds the image of a tossed salad to be more appropriate. Although being an integral and recognizable part of the whole, diverse members of society can maintain their particular identities while residing in the collective.

Some more-radical multicultural theorists have claimed that some cultural groups need more than recognition to ensure the integrity and maintenance of their distinct identities and contributions. In addition to individual equal rights, some have advocated for special group rights and autonomous governance for certain cultural groups. Because the continued existence of protected minority cultures ultimately contributes to the good of all and the enrichment of the dominant culture, those theorists have argued that the preserving of cultures that cannot withstand the pressures to assimilate into a dominant culture can be given preference over the usual norm of equal rights for all.

Multiculturalism's Impact on Education

Some examples of how multiculturalism has affected the social and political spheres are found in revisions of curricula, particularly in Europe and North America, and the expansion of the Western literary and other canons that began during the last quarter of the 20th century. Curricula from the elementary to the university levels were revised and expanded to include the contributions of minority and neglected cultural groups. That revision was designed to correct what is perceived to be a falsely Eurocentric perspective that overemphasizes the contributions of white European colonial powers and underemphasizes the contributions made by indigenous people and people of colour. In addition to that correction, the contributions that cultural groups have made in a variety of fields have been added to curricula to give special recognition for contributions that were previously ignored. The establishment of African American History Month and National Hispanic Heritage Month in the United States is an example of the movement. The addition of works by members of minority cultural groups to the canons of literary, historical, philosophical, and artistic works further reflects the desire to recognize and include multicultural contributions to the broader culture as a whole.

Challenges to Multiculturalism

There are two primary objections to multiculturalism. One is that multiculturalism privileges the good of the certain groups over the common good, thereby potentially eroding the common good in favour of a minority interest. The second is that multiculturalism undermines the notion of equal individual rights, thereby weakening the political value of equal treatment.

Multiculturalism raises other questions. There is the question of which cultures will be recognized. Some theorists have worried that multiculturalism can lead to a competition between cultural groups all vying for recognition and that this will further reinforce the dominance of the dominant culture. Further, the focus on cultural group identity may reduce the capacity for coalitional political movements that might develop across differences. Some Marxist and feminist theorists have expressed worry about the dilution of other important differences shared by members of a society that do not necessarily entail a shared culture, such as class and sex.

Multicultural Politics

Multiculturalism is closely associated with identity politics, or political and social movements that have group identity as the basis of their formation and the focus of their political action. Those movements attempt to further the interests of their group members and force issues important to their group members into the public sphere. In contrast to multiculturalism, identity politics movements are based on the shared identities of participants rather than on a specifically shared culture. However, both identity politics and multiculturalism have in common the demand for recognition and a redress for past inequities.

Multiculturalism raises important questions for citizens, public administrators, and political leaders. By asking for recognition of and respect for cultural differences, multiculturalism provides one possible response to the question of how to increase the participation of previously oppressed groups.

REFERENCES

1. Alston, Philip, and Frederic Megret, eds. The United Nations and Human Rights: A Critical Appraisal. Second Edition. Oxford University Press, 2014.
2. Bassiouni, M. Cherif, and William A. Schabas, eds. New Challenges for the UN Human Rights Machinery: What Future for the UN Treaty Body System and the Human Rights Council Procedures? Intersentia, 2011.
3. Coomans, F., and Menno TjeerdKamminga. Extraterritorial Application of Human Rights Treaties. Intersentianv, 2004.
4. Crawford, James, and MarttiKoskenniemi, eds. The Cambridge Companion to International Law. Cambridge University Press, 2012.
5. Crawford, James. The Future of UN Human Rights Treaty Monitoring. Cambridge University Press, 2010.
6. Dembour, Marie-Bénédicte, and Tobias Kelly, eds. Paths to International Justice: Social and Legal Perspectives. 1st ed. Cambridge University Press, 2007.
7. Dembour, Marie-Bénédicte. Who Believes in Human Rights?: Reflections on the European Convention. 1st ed. Cambridge University Press, 2006.
8. Freeman, Marsha A., Christine Chinkin, and Beate Rudolf. The UN Convention on the Elimination of All
9. Higgins, Rosalyn. Themes and Theories: Selected Essays, Speeches and Writings in International Law. Oxford University Press, USA, 2009.
10. Hollis, Duncan B. The Oxford Guide to Treaties. Oxford University Press, USA, 2012.
11. Hopgood, Stephen. Keepers of the Flame: Understanding Amnesty International. annotated edition. Cornell University Press, 2006.
12. Joachim, Jutta M. Agenda Setting, the UN, and NGOs: Gender Violence and Reproductive Rights. Georgetown University Press, 2007.
13. Piccone, Ted. Catalysts for Change: How the U.N.'s Independent Experts Promote Human Rights. Brookings Institution Press, 2012.
14. Seibert-Fohr, Anjaed: Judicial Independence in Transition. Springer-lit, 2012.
15. Vandenhole, Wouter. The Procedures before the UN Human Rights Treaty Bodies: Divergence or Convergence? Intersentia, 2004.
16. Waldorf, Lars. "Anticipating the Past Transitional Justice and Socio-Economic Wrongs." Social & Legal Studies 21, no. 2 (June 1, 2012): 171–186.
17. Weller, Marc. Universal Minority Rights: A Commentary on the Jurisprudence of International Courts and Treaty Bodies. Oxford University Press, USA, 2008.
18. Young, Kirsten A. The Law and Process of the U.N. Human Rights Committee. Hotei Publishing, 2002.
19. Williams, Paul D., ed. Security Studies: An Introduction. 2nd ed. Routledge, 2012.
20. Bayefsky, Anne F. The UN Human Rights Treaty System in the 21st Century. Kluwer Law International, 2000.

CHAPTER

7

COMMUNITY LEARNING PARTNERSHIPS

INTRODUCTION

School and community learning partnerships have been part of school life for decades. Partnerships between school systems and community arts partners are effective ingredients of school improvement strategies. They increase community awareness of educational issues and mobilize community resources in the service of school improvement.

Partnerships are often a highly productive way of involving educators in effective curriculum development. Partnerships that build the arts into the curriculum as subjects in their own right and /or as learning integrated into other curricular areas invite imaginative thinking about curriculum design. The interactive nature of partnerships supports the creation of strong planning teams, professional development networks, and a legacy of curricular work and teaching methods that can be shared among classrooms, schools, and districts.

Partnerships forge a new relationship between community resources and schools, resulting in the professional development of all partners. Arts instruction enhances the teaching skills of teachers, helps community members better appreciate education, and prepares artists and other expert citizens to work productively in classrooms.

A superintendent of schools supports the partnership when he or she sees the measures of student success — student grades, test scores, attendance, and graduation rates — go up and community support for schools grow.

SCHOOL-COMMUNITY LEARNING PARTNERSHIPS

For the past decade the 21st Century Community Learning Centers initiative has asked schools to work in partnership with community- and faith-based organizations to support children's learning during the hours after school and during the summertime. Consequently, there has been tremendous growth across the nation in intentional efforts to forge meaningful partnerships between schools and afterschool and summer programs.

Increasingly, the field is recognizing that these partnerships are essential to efforts to expand when, where, how, and what students learn.

The Benefits of School-Community Partnerships

When schools and community organizations work together to support learning, everyone benefits. Partnerships can serve to strengthen, support, and even transform individual partners, resulting in improved program quality, more efficient use of resources, and better alignment of goals and curricula.

First and foremost, learning partnerships can support student outcomes.

In addition to supporting student learning directly, partnerships can have additional benefits to students and their families. They can

- provide continuity of services across the day and year, easing school transitions and promoting improved attendance in after school programs;
- facilitate access to a range of learning opportunities and developmental supports, providing opportunities for students and teachers alike to experiment with new approaches to teaching and learning;
- facilitate information sharing about specific students to best support individual learning; and
- provide family members with alternative entry points into the school day to support their student's learning.

Learning partnerships can also greatly benefit schools. They can

- complement the academic curriculum with a wider range of services and activities, particularly enrichment and arts activities that may not available during the school day;
- support transitions across the school years, particularly the critical middle to high school transition, which research indicates is a key predictor of high school graduation
- reinforce concepts taught in school without replicating the school day, often exposing classroom teachers working in the after school program to new pedagogies;
- improve school culture and community image through exhibitions and performances that help "shine the light" on students whose talents may not be apparent in the classroom; and
- gain access to mentors, afterschool staff, and other resources to support in-school learning and improve the teaching and learning in the classroom itself.

Finally, learning partnerships with schools can strengthen and support community partners. They can

- help gain access to and recruit groups of students most in need of support services;
- improve program quality and staff engagement, particularly when there is crossover between school and community organization staff;
- foster better alignment of programming to support a shared vision for learning, one which aligns curriculum to support state and local standards; and

- maximize resource use such as facilities, staff, data, and curriculum.

The Role of Partnerships in 21st Century Community Learning Centers

Partnerships are a critical component of 21st Century Community Learning Centers, and each year since 2006 the number of partners has continued to grow. By 2010, the 3,450 funded grantees engaged over 30,000 partners, with an average of almost 9 partners per grantee. Community-based organizations were the most common partners in 2010, almost three times higher than any other type of partner. For-profit corporations and school districts were the second and third most utilized partners, with colleges and universities also playing a main partnership role.

Partners perform a number of important roles: They offer programming, provide in-kind services, and provide paid and volunteer staffing (see Table 1). Further, Table 1 illustrates that more partners have steadily made more contributions to 21st Century Community Learning Centers over the past 5 years.

Table 1. Number of grants with a partner providing a given contribution type across 5 years of annual performance reporting.

Partner Contribution	2006	2007	2008	2009	2010
Programming	2,464	2,582	2,695	2,881	3,139
Paid Staffing	1,782	1,814	1,906	1,965	2,046
Volunteer Staffing	1,833	1,924	1,933	2,042	2,185
In-Kind Goods	2,113	2,246	2,351	2,477	2,698
Funding	813	872	968	915	929
Evaluation Services	1,043	1,076	1,049	1,078	1,160

Analysis of the financial support that partners contribute by providing the services listed above reveals that in 2010 alone, partners contributed over $230 million to the 3,450 initiative grantees. Over the past 5 years partners have contributed over $1 billion to support 21st Century Community Learning Centers programming.

Together, these data suggest that partners are an essential component of the 21st Century Community Learning Centers initiative and they have been growing significantly in all dimensions over the past 5 years. Partners provide vital in-kind services and supports, as well as real dollars, which add significant value to the work of 21st Century Community Learning Centers. As centers consider bringing on more partners it is important that project and site directors understand how to develop and cultivate effective partnerships.

Features of Effective School-Community Partnerships

There is emerging consensus on an inter-related set of features that help promote and sustain healthy school-community partnerships:

A shared vision for learning and developmental outcomes for students. This vision acknowledges the critical, complementary roles of schools, community partners, and families. A shared vision also helps partners avoid working against each other and instead pursue a common vision of student success. When school leaders embrace a vision for student success that considers students' physical, emotional, and social well-being in addition to academic outcomes, the partnership is more likely to be successful than when competing agendas operate during the expanded learning day.

A diverse set of partners with effective communications mechanisms and relationships among multiple staff at multiple levels. Strong and sustainable partnerships need relationships that are built at multiple levels (for example, at the district, school, and classroom levels) and among multiple school staff, including district and nonteaching staff. Working with partners at different levels helps the afterschool and summer programs become integral to the daily life and culture of the school at all levels, from the principal to the custodian. In addition, relationships at various levels can help mitigate the effects of staff turnover at other levels; for example, strong relationships with teachers can help sustain the partnership in the event of a change in principals.

Intentionally blended staffing with role clarity to promote understanding of how the work is relevant to all. For afterschool and summer programs, this means hiring staff who have legitimacy in the school building and who are skilled at building relationships with school staff. Some programs do this by hiring licensed teachers, people who "speak the same language" as school-day teachers, can substitute and consult in classrooms, and can participate in professional development activities. Hiring licensed teachers who also teach at a host school facilitates information sharing and forges connections with other teachers who might not otherwise make time for "outside" programs or services. Blended staffing may also mean a liaison who serves an important bridging function between the school and the afterschool or summer program.

Clear data-sharing processes and agreements. One feature of a strong collaboration is the ability of partners to access information and data from each other, including, if possible, student-level academic data (e.g., test scores and grades). Afterschool and summer programs can use these data both to track and strengthen student performance and to demonstrate the impact of their services. In addition to getting data from schools, some programs provide their own data to schools to promote reciprocal data sharing.

As efforts to expand learning opportunities and time continue to grow under a variety of approaches and models—whether afterschool, summer learning, expanded or extended learning day or year, or out-of-school time—it is important that all these efforts build on the strong base of effective partnerships already present among schools and afterschool and summer programs, capitalizing in particular on the rich history of partnerships advanced by 21st Century Community Learning Centers.

THE POWER OF COMMUNITY PARTNERSHIP IN THE PREPARATION OF TEACHERS

Teacher preparation programs in the United States within institutions of higher education (IHEs) have been beset by criticism from a diverse group of stakeholders. Such critiques have appeared in the scholarly literature as well as in various news media and public programming venues. The purpose of this editorial is not to add another critique to the existing collection or to comment on them. Rather, its purpose is to look at the response of institutions to the challenges associated with how they go about the complicated task of preparing future educators. Some of these institutions have responded to the pressure to justify themselves passively, by not responding or actively by defending their programmatic status quo; others have taken up the gauntlet and are examining the extent to which they offer a "value-added" experience through their programs to those who will be responsible for the education and well-being of their students.

The second of these groups is diverse in perspective and in action; they are, however, institutions where critical self-examination is taking place, particularly around the question of how well candidates are being prepared for the challenges they face in today's classrooms, schools, and communities to which they will hopefully contribute in significant ways. At some of these institutions, particular structural or philosophical elements are held constant, and changes in parts of existing programs are being made, while at others, a complete restructuring is taking shape. In this phase, argue that whatever changes are made must take account of three things about which those in the teacher education research community are contributing new and generative perspectives. These include (a) the beliefs which teacher candidates hold about their students' capacity for learning, (b) the kind of deep learning possible for youth in out-of school learning contexts, and (c) the power of partnership with community leader and community organizations in supporting the growth and impact of teachers.

Beliefs about Student Capacity

Numerous scholars have contributed to our knowledge of the understandings and beliefs that those with a desire to become teachers have about the capacity of children to learn. These beliefs are shaped in part by candidates' experiences in teacher preparation programs, but they are influenced even more by experiences they have accumulated over their many years as learners and with particular teachers they have had. These factors, in addition to the fact that most of the present teaching core is White and middle class, often result in teachers taking a deficit stance with regard to the perceived skills and needs of youth, particularly youth in high-poverty urban environments.

Practicing teachers as well as teacher candidates often do not appreciate the funds of knowledge that students bring with them into schools, nor the legitimacy of this knowledge and the language and cultural practices in which students engage, as contributors to student learning. These beliefs about students also are shaped in potent ways by contextual factors, including the nature of field placements.

Youth Learning in Community-Based Contexts

Work in this area has been quite varied with respect to the settings in which youth interact, which has included such spaces as museums, nature, and history centers; after-school programs and community based organizations; as well as the specific learning outcomes being investigated. Despite the diverse nature of such work, two related themes have emerged. The first of these is where and with whom important knowledge can be situated. The second is how problems that are of interest and importance to youth and the structures that permit them to own and express their developing understandings can be powerful agents of conceptual learning and of personal and social growth. Indeed, the dynamics that often develop among youth in identifying and addressing important problems, as described by researchers, resemble in many ways the processes that are in place in stable and productive teacher professional learning communities or communities of practice. The capacity of these kinds of spaces to generate such powerful knowledge and practices among students strongly suggests that those preparing to be teachers would benefit greatly by learning in, and from, these spaces and from the youth who inhabit them.

The Role of Community in Teacher Education

Educational stakeholders are many and diverse; traditionally, teacher preparation programs consider the most relevant places where learning to teach takes place as the IHE and schools, with an occasional "dip" into other contexts, in response, as often as not, to unique opportunities or individual commitments. But just as the power of "owning" knowledge by youth in out-of-school settings has been demonstrated in areas as diverse as science and literacy, the knowledge that exists within community settings, and the norms and practices which are valued by them, have the potential to inform programs and their participants in powerful and educative ways. The underlying reason is twofold: First, it is critical for those preparing to become teachers to understand what surrounds and drives the young people they will teach, and how and what they are outside of school offers valuable insights that can help them to become more effective educators. Second, those individuals who are deeply invested in community-based work are knowledgeable about the stressors that act on the lives and aspirations of the young people they serve, and these same individuals have the potential to offer teacher preparation programs knowledge and experiences that can enhance the power of these programs to support the development of teachers who know more about the contexts in which they are likely to be beginning their careers and to be more prepared to meet the challenges associated with these contexts.

In contrast, there has been little work done on the impact of such community-based experiences on specific subject matter-related teaching skills. A notable exception to this is Kate Brayko's work, which has demonstrated that teacher candidates show significant growth in their understanding of specific literacy strategies as a result of working with youth in CBOs. Clearly, more investigations with this kind of focus would be informative for the field.

A small but growing number of teacher education programs have made use of community-based experiences, in some cases, fairly early in the trajectory of candidates moving through their teacher preparation program, which allow them to learn with, and from, organizations and residents in the communities in which they will do their student teaching and possibly begin their careers. In addition to the work being done at the University of Washington is that being carried out at Illinois State University, under the auspices of their Chicago Teacher Education Pipeline? Alongside and integrated with its redesigned course experiences, this program features school- and community-based experiences, along with home stays with families who live in the neighborhoods where teacher candidates work the summer prior to their student teaching. Programs such as these are moving toward scalable models for teacher preparation in which both context and content are being reimagined and redesigned to be more responsive to the needs of children and more "democratic" in terms of who is considered expert and in the ownership and sharing of critical knowledge and practices.

FRAMEWORK FOR LEARNING THROUGH COMMUNITY SCHOOLS

In community schools around the country, school and community leaders are uniting to create results-focused, partnership-based learning opportunities to help all students thrive. Site-based coordinators are sitting down with principals, teachers, and other school leaders to determine how partnerships can help the school achieve its primary goal: improved student learning. This site-based leadership team is reviewing school- and student-level data and identifying student needs from health to tutoring to extra learning opportunities. The coordinator is mobilizing partners who can bring resources that can address these learning approaches.

The community schools use results-focused partnerships to support learning through three equally complementary areas (see Figure 1):

- Health and social supports and services,
- Family and community engagement, and
- An intentional focus on expanded learning opportunities.

Each of these categories relies on results-focused, school-community partnerships that make learning the shared responsibility of the school, its families, and its community before, during, and after the typical school day.

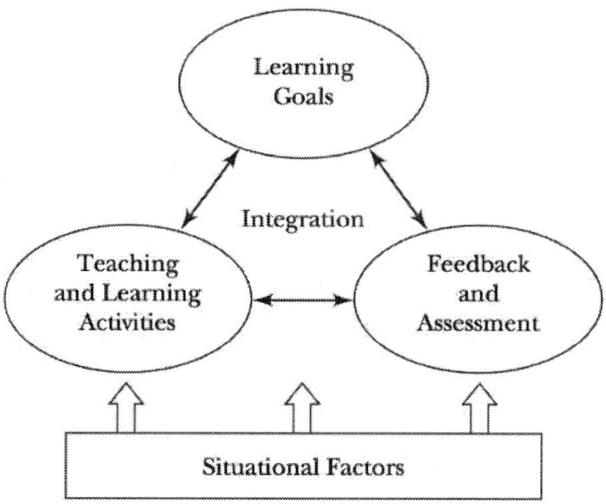

Figure 1. Framework for Better Learning through Results-Focused Partnerships.

Source: https://poorvucenter.yale.edu/sites/default/files/resize/images/Screen%20Shot%20 2017-09-14%20at%202_23_02%20PM-578x486.png

Results-Focused Partnerships

Community schools are planned and implemented with both system-level and school-based approaches that emphasize depth and breadth in the communities they serve, focusing on better learning through various partnerships across school, district, and community levels. Community schools highly value the local decision-making authority of both the schools and the community and the need to customize their approach in response to local needs and assets.

Results-focused partnerships are the foundation of the community schools framework for better learning. Local community school intermediaries establish networks of superintendents, principals, and community partners who are re-imagining the way schools and districts operate as a whole in order to remove barriers to learning, provide comprehensive supports for their students, and engage families and community members in student learning. Leaders form district and school based partnerships around a mutually agreed upon and shared vision for results and accountability. This vision drives the community school's activities. Formal agreements enable partners to hold each other accountable and help avoid miscommunication and disagreements about respective roles, scope, and resource sharing. Strong partnerships at the district level help ensure that community schools are aligned with the district's priorities and vision for better learning and student success.

At the school level, community school leaders, including principals, design practices that will best support students' healthy development. They provide engaging learning experiences connected to their local community context and resources, including civic and service-learning opportunities. Additionally, these experiences provide students with the diverse set of skills needed to succeed in college, their careers, and ultimately serve as productive citizens within their community.

The results schools and their community partners seek are where community schools start. How they achieve those results is the next question. Community school, results-focused partnerships work to provide health and social supports and services that remove barriers to learning. They work with families and communities to support a community where children can learn, and they provide more and better learning experiences during the typical school day and beyond. We turn to these three areas next.

Health and Social Supports & Services

Walk into a typical high-poverty urban or rural classroom and the teacher will quickly be able to identify the barriers to learning. Student hunger, homelessness, poor nutrition and sleeping habits, chronic absence, and mental health issues are just a few challenges that even excellent teachers face in their work. These schools often have fewer qualified and effective teachers, fewer financial resources, higher turnover, poor school climates, and high rates of chronic absence. A 2015 report demonstrated that over half of our public school students are poor. These factors are realities that teachers, principals, students, and families experience daily.

Research has shown that basic physical, social, and psychological needs influence a child's educational outcomes. These basic needs were described by Abraham Maslow in 1943 as a developmental triangle, built upon the most fundamental needs as building blocks for engaged learning.

The purpose of this partnership, barriers to learning refers to those student, school, and community elements that keep a child from learning to their full potential. At the student level, this may include health barriers, family factors, and access to social services. At the school level, this may include obstacles in opportunities to learn, such as time, quality of resources, and lack of access. At the community level, barriers may include the structural obstacles to providing a complete education.

Educational research shows a clear link between good health and better learning. To start, research is clear that nutritional deficiencies during childhood can negatively affect healthy brain development and have lifelong health consequences, including cognitive abilities. Specifically, nutrition has implications for students' academic performance. Undernourished children have been shown to have lower levels of school attendance, decreased attention span, and lower academic performance. They also experience more health problems compared to well-nourished children.

Physical activity also has been shown to have positive influences on concentration, memory, and classroom behavior, as well as a positive relationship with intellectual performance.

Recent literature reviews on physical activity or physical fitness and cognition have all reached the conclusion that physical activity (or aspects of physical fitness) favorably affects cognitive functioning. Further, research shows that sports help children and youth feel better connected to school, attend school regularly, and connect with a more positive peer network.

In a community school setting, the basic physical, mental, and emotional health needs of young people and their families are recognized and addressed as a core aspect of its work. The ultimate vision for community schools is to provide basic health and social services beyond what a school nurse can offer, including regular eye exams, mobile dental clinics, access to social workers and mental health professionals, and even co-located health clinics. Admittedly, some children learn despite these barriers.

However, upon visiting most high-poverty schools one quickly realizes that barriers to learning are not excuses; they are realities that need to be addressed so that all students may thrive.

While many education experts accept these basic conditions and barriers to be true, public schools do not have the infrastructure in place to address these barriers alone. Moreover, "silver bullet" approaches and education reform models that ignore these realities are unlikely to be sustained or effective. Community schools, in contrast, have the expertise and infrastructure to identify assets and deploy extensive resources and partnerships to target barriers to healthy development and learning that could otherwise prevent youth from participating and thriving in academic and enrichment activities. The services and programming that result help ensure that the necessary conditions for learning are in place to support healthy development and well-rounded, quality learning experiences.

Effectively addressing barriers to learning is possible. The Coalition has argued that community schools create the "conditions for learning," those elements that must be in place in order to holistically meet students' educational and developmental needs. Further, a recent review of research concluded that integrated student services that address barriers to learning shows promise in improving academic outcomes.

Family and Community Engagement

Family and community engagement is what separates community schools from reforms that focus solely on the classroom and those strategies that only provide wraparound services. Community schools recognize that learning happens not only inside school, but also in the home and in communities. Therefore, creating a community where learning can happen, where students feel safe and have the resources and supports they need, is essential to a community school learning strategy.

Strong family and community engagement increases the resources and relationships available to enable better learning. Community schools value the experiences of people from diverse backgrounds who are committed to the welfare of the community, and thus, work to identify and deploy numerous resources. These community assets include its residents and families, businesses and employees, faith-based institutions, institutions of higher education, and other local organizations. The community schools approach complements the framework developed by Johns Hopkins sociologist Joyce Epstein in recognizing the school, family, and community as three overlapping spheres of influence on student learning development. According to the framework, intentional partnership and coordination is required in order to create family and community-like schools and to achieve positive outcomes on a systematic basis.

Additionally, The Harvard Family Research Project (HFRP) researchers report community-school partnerships to be particularly beneficial in terms of out-of-school time for youth, with such partnerships facilitating year-long learning, shared and therefore expanded resources for educators, and family engagement. Statistics indicate that youth spend only 20% of waking time annually in classroom education; community-school partnerships can offer programming in the other 80% of the time, providing better engagement in out-of school time and beginning to close achievement gaps. Research also shows that partnering with families is just as important as schools creating partnerships with their community organizations. Ideally, there is a three-way dialogue that develops, opening up pathways that best support youths' learning. Finally, HFRP research also emphasizes the importance of reciprocity in school, family, and community partnerships, suggesting mutual benefits for schools, families, and community organizations as a key means toward sustainable partnerships.

Further, the National Education Association outlined 10 key strategies for effective partnerships, emphasizing the necessity of collaboration between schools and communities in connecting youth to their surroundings, creating high academic expectations, and targeting high-need students.

The ways that partners are leveraged and the services they provide vary from one community school to another, but the goal of all partnerships is to promote a school climate that is safe, supportive, respectful, and that connects students to a broader learning community. Once partnerships are formed and the community is engaged, community schools work to ensure that there is mutual respect and effective collaboration among parents, families, and school staff. Parents and guardians are a child's first teachers. Community schools and their partners work with parents to support them in creating a learning environment for their children.

Being a parent is hard, even more so when you are poor, working multiple jobs, or feel uncomfortable with the English language or your own educational level. Community schools work with parents to improve literacy experiences and opportunities in the home, work with early learning providers to bring families into schools, offer parenting classes on how to support child learning, and more.

Community schools are hubs of the community and offer parents multiple opportunities to come into the school through activities, such as adult education classes (e.g., GED), use of the computer lab, and financial management classes. Community schools also use their results-focused partnerships to engage the community in creating a learning-rich environment. They work with libraries and youth centers to align learning approaches. Community partners and residents are part of the school-site leadership team and align their strategies with the school's learning goals.

Increasingly, community members are organizing to start or expand community schools in their neighborhoods and cities. Parents and other members of the community, including teachers' unions, understand that schools require strong partnerships that provide the elements of the learning framework described above in order for children to thrive. Communities and families have organized at multiple levels for community schools as evidenced by the successful development of community schools. In a community school system, learning is everyone's responsibility.

Better Learning through Aligned Partnerships

Successful community schools make high-quality learning opportunities key aspects of their approach. As previously demonstrated, they work with partners to remove barriers to learning and engage families and the community. However, they also focus on ways to support learning during the typical school day and during times for expanded learning opportunities (e.g., afterschool and summer). In a community school, teachers and principals aren't alone in supporting a child's learning. If we value the ideal that our children are all of our responsibility, then that means community partners, residents, and family members all have important roles to play in educating our children. Community schools provide a vehicle for moving that belief to action. We highlight two areas of better learning through partnerships: quality instruction and engaged learning during the typical school day and expanded learning opportunities.

Quality Instruction and Engaged Learning during the Typical School Day

Community schools set high standards for all stakeholders to contribute to a high-quality core instructional program with qualified teachers, a challenging curriculum, professional development, and high expectations for students. In addition, community schools' partnerships bring strategies to enhance their emphasis on college, career, and citizenship through cognitive and non-cognitive skill-building, including a focus on academically based community service, civic education, **environmental education**, place based learning, service learning, and work-based learning opportunities.

Community schools use partnerships to create meaningful content that enables students to take ownership of their learning. These partnerships support teachers in their daily activities and are aligned with the school's improvement plan. Better learning and quality instruction are not only based on cognitive outcomes, but also require an intentional focus on the development of social-emotional, civic, and ethical competencies. For example, social-emotional learning is the process of acquiring attitudes, knowledge, and skills that are essential to success in school, career, and being a productive citizen. The Collaborative for Academic, Social, and Emotional Learning (CASEL) further defines social and emotional learning as "a set of interconnected competencies, including self-awareness, self-management, social awareness, relationship skills, and responsible decision making." As we increase our understanding of how young people learn and grow, the more important social-emotional learning seems. Without explicit attention to these core competencies, better learning is not as likely to occur.

Another example of the ways community school partnerships support learning is through the growing linked learning and career academy approaches. Linked learning high schools are part of a college and career ready strategy that originated with pilot programs in California in 2011 and are now gaining traction across the country. These high schools emphasize rigorous academics, personalized supports, and career-based learning. The academic model at linked learning high schools includes English, foreign languages, history, math, and science as core curricular subjects that are connected to challenging programs of study within supported career pathways. These include biomedical and health sciences; construction and building design; agriculture and renewable resources; arts, media, and entertainment, and engineering. Each pathway includes a structured instructional program that includes academic courses and electives, technical courses, integrated units, and support services. The pathways are also connected to work-based learning opportunities, including mentoring, job shadowing, internships, and virtual apprenticeships. Further, business partners in the community provide work-based learning opportunities that help inform the school's curriculum for each pathway.

Linked learning high schools also focus on student supports, providing personalized counseling, transportation, and supplemental instruction in core subjects to build skill mastery in academic and technical content. There is also a focus on supporting students' transition to postsecondary institutions or training after graduation, including two- and four-year degree institutions, apprenticeships, or formal employment training.

In order for schools to move from a typical design to the more innovative model of linked learning high schools, they must go through an intentional process of re-imagining and re-designing the use of time and resources. Because partnership development, planning, and community-based learning approaches are core to their work, community schools are an effective implementation vehicle for scaling linked learning strategies at the high school level.

Expanded Learning Opportunities

Community schools value opportunities for student engagement in expanded learning as a part of their efforts to diminish barriers between community and the classroom, and to better connect in-school and out-of-school learning experiences. In order to ensure the availability of learning opportunities and essential services to students and families, some community schools operate on a "7 a.m. – 7 p.m." schedule. This holistic approach meets the developmental needs of students and the scheduling needs of working parents. Expanded learning opportunities (ELO) often include a focus on ensuring that young people are becoming lifelong learners, productive contributors to the economy and civic life, and are connected with and invested in their communities.

In 2013, the Coalition developed a typology for ELOs, organizing them into four categories:

- ELO required for all students (i.e., expanded school day or year).
- ELO for some or all students to increase the number of school days (i.e., weekends, intersessions, school breaks, and summer).
- ELO for some/all students to increase time beyond the conventional school day (i.e., after school and before school).
- ELO for some/all students during the conventional school day

Each of these categories represents programs that are being used to varying degrees across the country. From the perspective, they each require partnerships and are best implemented when part of a broader and intentional results-focused community school strategy.

Research has shown positive outcomes of youth engagement in out-of-school time programming, with success outside the classroom as a key to student success inside the classroom. Specifically, participation in ELOs is correlated with better performance in school (as indicated by standardized test scores and grades), increased attendance, less disciplinary action, and better attitudes from students overall about school and the pursuit of higher education. After school programming has been shown to impact youth in terms of their social and emotional development as well as the avoidance of risky behaviors. Notably, it is not only participation in after school programming that matters in terms of youth outcomes, but higher-quality programs are associated with social competence, better academic performance and fewer youth participating in risky behaviors. Youth who participated in low-quality programming had similar outcomes as students who participated in no programming at all.

ACHIEVING RESULTS THROUGH COMMUNITY SCHOOL PARTNERSHIPS

A community school is a place and a set of partnerships connecting a school, the families of students, and the surrounding community. A community school is distinguished by an integrated focus on academics, youth development, family support, health and social services, and community development. Community schools extend the school day and week, reaching students, their families, and community residents in unique ways. Community schools are thus uniquely equipped to develop their students into educated citizens who are ready and able to give back to their communities.

The community school strategy is central to efforts to improve America's public schools. Community schools use partnerships to align school and community resources in order to produce successful students, strong families, and engaged communities. They combine quality education with enrichment opportunities, health and mental health services, family support and engagement, early childhood and adult education, and other supports

Research shows that low-income families regularly experience economic and material hardship. Missed rent, utility shutoffs, inadequate access to health care, unstable child care arrangements, and food insecurity are common experiences that inevitably affect students' readiness, attendance, performance, and completion rates at school.

By sharing resources, expertise, and accountability, community schools can address challenges related to economic hardship and create essential conditions for learning by concentrating on a single access point—public schools—to effectively target their efforts. Any type of public school can become a community school, including traditional, charter, alternative, magnet or others. The vision of a community school must be at the heart of emerging place-based initiatives, including Promise Neighborhoods, Choice Neighborhoods, cradle-to-career programs, and P-20 networks integrating educational opportunities from preschool through college.

It begins by describing the elements of a community school strategy, then draws on the experiences of several community school initiatives that use the following strategies to form and maintain key relationships:

- Ensure that all partners share a common vision. The entire community and all involved partners should agree on the same goals and expectations.
- Establish formal relationships and collaborative structures to engage stakeholders. Initiating and sustaining stakeholder participation often requires creating structured opportunities ranging from developing taskforces to creating formal agreements.
- Encourage open dialogue about challenges and solutions. To foster shared ownership, stakeholders must engage honestly and constructively with each other to solve problems and make midcourse corrections.
- Engage partners in the use of data. Sharing data enables all stakeholders to understand where things stand and hold each other accountable for making measurable progress.
- Create and empower central-office capacity at the district level to sustain community school work. Continued capacity can be created through establishing a high-level management position within a district's central office or through creating an office dedicated to supporting a community school agenda.
- Leverage community resources and braid funding streams. Community schools capitalize on the financial assets of community partners and funding streams to support programs and activities aligned with their common vision.

The importance of partnerships in a community school strategy

Every community school begins under a different set of circumstances and develops its own distinctive culture. What community schools have in common is a belief in the basic principles of collective impact: a commitment to partnerships, accountability for results, respect for diversity, belief in community strengths, and high expectations for all. Collective impact is created when two or more organizations realize that they can accomplish more by working together and sharing resources than they can by working alone.

A community school strategy recognizes that many public and private community institutions share responsibility for helping:

- Children develop socially, emotionally, physically, and academically
- Students become motivated and engaged in learning
- Families and schools work effectively together
- Communities become safer and more economically vibrant

Community schools establish "cradle to career" conditions for learning that make it possible for every child to succeed. This strategy works by creating a collaborative leadership structure, embedding a culture of partnership, and aligning resources. Partners set and achieve high standards of accountability across multiple outcomes. In a time of declining fiscal resources and greater demand for public services, districts with fewer dollars to spread around have learned that forming partnerships can also be fiscally prudent. A recent Coalition for Community Schools study finds that, on average, districts leverage three dollars from community partners for every dollar they allocate. Partners can contribute dollars or in-kind support in the form of access to family programs, health services, and more. The structures and functions associated with building a community schools strategy are built on a deepening foundation of collective trust. That trust is vital to achieving the collective impact that emerges when school and community partners share responsibility for the education of our children and youth.

While a wide range of community stakeholders across the country are engaged in developing systems of community schools. The seven communities described here were selected because they represent community school initiatives that have established robust partnership networks with districts, unions, local government agencies, and other organizations.

Organizing Collaborative Leadership Structures

The collective experience of these and other communities illuminates a basic strategy and set of institutional arrangements that can assist other localities to begin and expand community school initiatives.7 The ongoing work of a scaled-up community school initiative takes place through the Collaborative Leadership Structure. This is where shared ownership takes root and where the initiative's vision and results are set. Figure 2 identifies common participants, including school districts and unions, and shows how leadership is shared across key functions.

A communitywide leadership group develops a shared vision, builds a common policy framework, and aligns their resources. A similar entity at the school site, with strong parent and neighborhood participation, is responsible for planning, implementation, and continuous improvement. In most initiatives, a community school resource coordinator manages day-to-day community school activities. An intermediary entity provides planning, coordination, and management, and ensures communication between communitywide and school-site leaders.

Forming partnerships

Collaboration matters greatly in school reform. Successfully implementing a community school strategy is impossible without the active involvement of school districts and their local partners. Research shows a positive correlation between average student academic achievement and superintendents who engage all relevant stakeholders—including central-office staff, building-level administrators, and school board members—in creating goal-oriented districts focused on teaching and learning. School leaders involved in community schools recognize that "all relevant stakeholders" includes community partners.

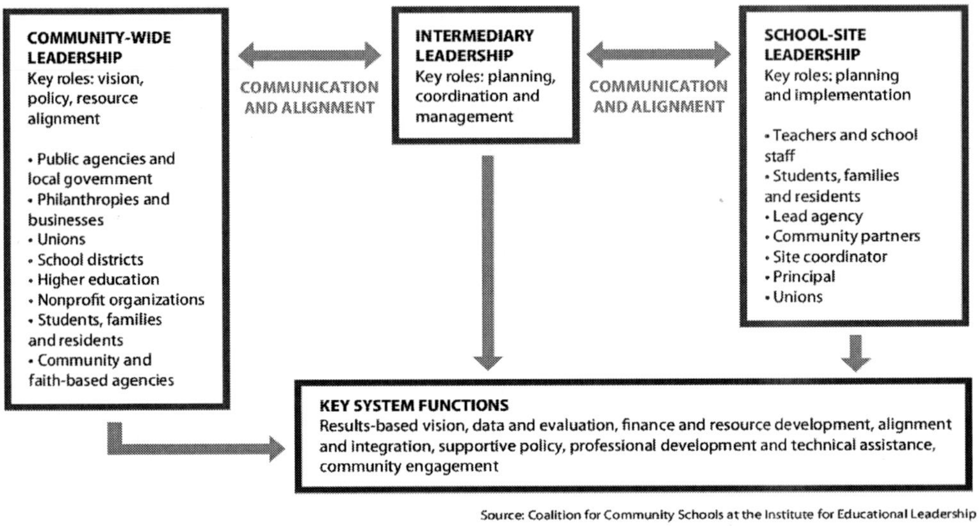

Figure 2. Collaborative leadership structure for community schools.

Source: https://www.semanticscholar.org/paper/Achieving-Results-through-Community-School-How-and-Blank-Jacobson/404ca19ef734137993793cdf3499c35e1ecc2c25

The experience of local community initiatives suggests that collaboration between school districts and community partners are initiated by districts or by partner organizations. Either way the ultimate goal is collaboration toward a common vision and shared results. Districts and their union partners play an essential role in planning and implementing a communitywide strategy. Together, they also have the ability to dramatically scale up the number of community schools and students being served. Indeed, collective impact results from the organization of key stakeholders into communitywide leadership groups that have a shared vision, build a common policy framework, and align their resources.

Strategies for building and maintaining successful partnerships

Collaborative leadership structures in community schools are designed to connect communitywide leaders—including union leaders, superintendents, and other local stakeholders—to school-site operations. But how can that be achieved? Individuals in the communities we interviewed shared six main strategies for building and continuing partnerships:

- Ensuring a common vision among all partners
- Establishing structured opportunities to engage stakeholders
- Encouraging open dialogue about challenges and solutions
- Engaging stakeholders in the use of data
- Creating central-office capacity to sustain community schools work

- Leveraging community resources and braiding funding streams

Ensure a common vision among all partners

Partners must be invested in a common vision and set of expectations for community schools. This will help to sustain partnerships in the long run, enhance community school efficacy, and encourage each stakeholder to clearly define its role in meeting specific goals. District leaders, including superintendents and school boards, must work to ensure the initiative's results-based vision is aligned and integrated with the district's overall school improvement plan and other core guidance documents. Community partners must adapt their mission to align with the community school vision. Since 2006 district leaders from both Tulsa and Union public schools have worked with other key stakeholders on a Management Team to ensure the TACSI strategy aligns well with their school districts' missions. These superintendents were visibly involved and encouraging of community school efforts, inviting their schools to become community schools as a vehicle for school reform. Significantly, in its 2010-2015 Strategic Plan, Tulsa Public Schools has included the expansion of community schools as a strategic objective to meet its core goal of improving student achievement. Evansville, Indiana, illustrates how school districts make community schools a part of their results-based vision. The district, after engaging the community in numerous listening sessions, developed a strategic plan around five core areas:

- Early childhood education
- Technology
- Professional development
- Innovative school models
- Family, school, and community partnerships

Leveraging community resources and braiding funding streams

Community schools garner financing and programmatic support from multiple sources. On average only about one-quarter of all resources in community school initiatives come from school districts. The remainder is leveraged from other sectors including local, state, and federal funding streams; foundations; and a mix of public agencies and community-based organizations—a 3-to-1 ratio in support of school success. School districts commonly provide space and cover maintenance and overhead costs at no cost to community partners, while community partners provide needed services, staff, and capacity through their own funding sources. Community schools and their partners also braid multiple funding streams to support their common vision. Title I funds as well as various private sources are often used to hire resource coordinators at individual school sites. Competitive grant funding from all levels of government provides important flexibility in meeting school site costs such as startup costs for a health clinic or expanding learning opportunities. Local foundations, local government, and others support the work of the intermediary and other community partners.

Community schools use these and other funding sources to focus on sustainability and growth. Evansville's early decision to install a community school leader as associate superintendent for Family, School, and Community Partnerships provided an opportunity to begin coordinating and strategically deploying a raft of school resources. Rather than looking for funds to support specific programs, Evansville demonstrates how partnering with the federal government can yield a variety of revenue streams that can be blended to advance a comprehensive community school strategy. The district was able to obtain formula and discretionary federal funds from the following sources:

- Title I
- School Improvement Grants
- 1003 G—School Improvement
- IDEA; Title II—Professional Development
- Title III—English Language Learner
- Title IV—Safe and Drug Free
- Even Start and Head Start
- Centers for Disease Control
- 21st Century Community Learning Centers
- Carol M. White Physical Education Grant
- Grant to Reduce Alcohol Abuse
- Safe School/Healthy Students
- McKinney Vento Homeless Grant
- Full-Service Community Schools Grant
- Other local, state, and philanthropic sources that support key partnerships.

Taking a different approach, organizations participating in partnership networks redirect existing resources to provide services at Community Learning Centers. Agencies and organizations in the partnership networks assume the responsibility for financial sustainability including third party billing where appropriate. For instance, a partnering organization that works on mental health issues can bill Medicaid for mental health services that students and families receive. The school district directly funds a Director of Community Schools to oversee district-wide implementation and uses Title 1 monies to underwrite the costs of resource coordinators at approximately 31 schools.

REFERENCES

1. Anderson, L. M., & Stillman, J. A. (2013). Student teaching's contribution to preservice teacher development a review of research focused on the preparation of teachers for urban and high-needs contexts. Review of Educational Research, 83(1), 3-69.
2. Bang, M., Warren, B., Rosebery, A. S., & Medin, D. (2013). Desettling expectations in science education. Human Development, 55(5-6), 302-318.
3. Barton, A. C., & Tan, E. (2010). We be burnin'! Agency, identity, and science learning. The Journal of the Learning Sciences, 19(2), 187-229.
4. Birmingham, D., & Calabrese Barton, A. (2014). Putting on a green carnival: Youth taking educated action on socioscientific issues. Journal of Research in Science Teaching, 51(3), 286-314.
5. Brayko, K. (2013). Community-based placements as contexts for disciplinary learning a study of literacy teacher education outside of school. Journal of Teacher Education, 64(1), 47-59.
6. Carter Andrews, D. J., & Castillo, B. (2016). Humanizing pedagogy for examinations of race and culture in teacher education. In F. Tuitt, C. Haynes, & S. Stewart (Eds.), Race, equity and higher education: The continued search for critical and inclusive pedagogies around the globe (pp. 112-130). Sterling, VA: Stylus Publishing.

7. Coffey, H. (2010). "They taught me": The benefits of early community-based field experiences in teacher education. Teaching and Teacher Education, 26(2), 335-342.

8. Davidsson, E., & Jakobsson, A. (Eds.). (2012). Understanding interactions at science centers and museums. Berlin, Germany: Springer Science & Business Media.

9. Harvard Family Research Project. (2010). Partnerships for learning: Promising practices in integrating school and out-of-school time program supports. Retrieved from http://www.hfrp.org/publications-resources/browse-our-publications/partn...

10. Little, P. (2011). Expanded learning opportunities in Washington state: Pathways to student success. Retrieved from http://www.schoolsoutwashington.org/UserFiles/File/ELO%20Policy%20Brief%...

11. Little, P., Wimer, C., & Weiss, H. (2008). Afterschool programs in the 21st century: Their potential and what it takes to achieve it (Issues and Opportunities in Out-of-School Time Evaluation No. 10). Retrieved from http://www.hfrp.org/content/download/2916/84011/file/OSTissuebrief10.pdf

12. Manhattan Strategy Group. (2011). High school promising practices project for the 21st Century Community Learning Centers program, Addendum 1. Washington, DC: U.S. Department of Education.

13. Miller, B. M. (2005). Pathways to success for youth: What counts in after-school. Retrieved from United Way of Massachusetts Bay and Merrimack Valley website: http://supportunitedway.org/

14. Neild, R. C., Balfanz, R., & Herzog, L. (2007). An early warning system. Educational Leadership, 65(2), 28–33.

CHAPTER 8

SCIENCE, SOCIETY, AND SOCIAL WORK

INTRODUCTION

Science, society, and social work research are interconnected fields that involve the application of scientific methods and principles to address social issues and improve the well-being of individuals, families, and communities. Let's explore each of these components and their relationship to social work research.

Science: Science refers to the systematic study of the natural and social world through observation, experimentation, and analysis. It encompasses various disciplines such as biology, psychology, sociology, and more. In social work research, scientific principles and methods are utilized to gather and analyze data, test hypotheses, and generate evidence-based knowledge to inform social work practice and policy.

Society: Society refers to the collective group of individuals who share common values, norms, and institutions within a specific geographic or cultural context. Social work research aims to examine and understand social issues and problems that impact individuals and communities within a society. This research explores topics such as poverty, inequality, mental health, substance abuse, family dynamics, and social justice, among others.

Social Work Research: Social work research is a specialized branch of research that focuses on studying social issues and applying scientific methods to develop effective interventions and policies. It encompasses both quantitative and qualitative research methods and aims to generate knowledge that can enhance social work practice, inform social policies, and contribute to social justice. Social work researchers investigate various aspects of human behavior, social systems, and societal structures to identify challenges, evaluate interventions, and propose solutions.

The relationship between science, society, and social work research is multi-faceted. Social work research draws upon scientific principles, theories, and methodologies to examine social problems and explore the impacts of social policies and interventions. The findings from social work research contribute to the scientific knowledge base and inform evidence-based social work practice, policy development, and advocacy efforts. Moreover, social work research often addresses societal concerns, seeks to improve the well-being of individuals and communities, and contributes to positive social change.

MENTAL HEALTH AND WELL-BEING

Mental health and well-being refer to the psychological and emotional state of individuals, characterized by their ability to cope with life's challenges, maintain positive relationships, and achieve a sense of overall satisfaction and fulfillment. It encompasses the overall state of one's mental and emotional well-being, including their thoughts, feelings, and behaviors.

At its core, mental health involves the absence of mental disorders and the presence of positive psychological functioning. It goes beyond the mere absence of illness and encompasses a state of flourishing and optimal functioning in various domains of life. Mental well-being encompasses aspects such as positive self-esteem, resilience, emotional regulation, and the ability to engage in meaningful relationships and activities.

Promoting mental health and well-being is essential for individuals, families, and communities. It contributes to overall quality of life, productivity, and social cohesion. Mental health plays a critical role in enabling individuals to reach their full potential, navigate life's challenges, and maintain healthy relationships.

Factors that influence mental health and well-being are diverse and include biological, psychological, and social determinants. Biological factors encompass genetic predispositions and neurochemical imbalances that can impact an individual's mental health. Psychological factors include cognitive processes, personality traits, and coping strategies that influence how individuals perceive and respond to stressors. Social determinants of mental health encompass the broader social and environmental factors that shape individuals' experiences, such as socioeconomic status, social support networks, discrimination, and access to resources and opportunities.

Mental health and well-being are influenced by a range of protective and risk factors. Protective factors, such as strong social support networks, positive relationships, healthy coping mechanisms, and access to healthcare and community resources, can promote mental well-being and resilience. On the other hand, risk factors, such as adverse childhood experiences, trauma, social isolation, poverty, and stigma, can negatively impact mental health and increase the likelihood of developing mental disorders.

Efforts to promote mental health and well-being involve a holistic approach that addresses prevention, early intervention, treatment, and recovery. Prevention efforts focus on promoting positive mental health through education, awareness campaigns, and interventions that target risk and protective factors. Early intervention involves identifying and addressing mental health concerns at an early stage, before they become more severe or chronic. Treatment encompasses a range of interventions, including psychotherapy, medication, and other evidence-based approaches tailored to the specific needs of individuals. Recovery emphasizes the process of regaining control, achieving stability, and living a fulfilling life, even in the presence of mental health challenges.

Addressing mental health and well-being is a shared responsibility involving multiple stakeholders, including individuals, families, communities, healthcare systems, and policy-makers. It requires creating supportive environments, reducing stigma and discrimination, promoting access to mental healthcare, and integrating mental health into various settings, such as schools, workplaces, and primary healthcare.

Mental health and well-being are fundamental to individuals' overall functioning, quality of life, and societal well-being. Promoting mental health and addressing mental health challenges require a comprehensive and multi-dimensional approach that considers biological, psychological, and social factors. By prioritizing mental health and well-being, societies can foster resilience, prevent mental disorders, and create environments that enable individuals to thrive and lead fulfilling lives.

The Impact of Adverse Childhood Experiences (ACEs) on Mental Health

The impact of adverse childhood experiences (ACEs) on mental health refers to the long-term psychological and emotional effects that traumatic events during childhood can have on individuals' mental well-being. ACEs encompass a wide range of negative experiences, including physical, emotional, or sexual abuse, neglect, household dysfunction, exposure to violence, and other forms of adversity. These experiences can profoundly influence individuals' mental health outcomes throughout their lives.

Research has demonstrated a strong association between ACEs and various mental health problems. Individuals who have experienced ACEs are at a higher risk of developing mental disorders such as depression, anxiety, post-traumatic stress disorder (PTSD), substance abuse, and suicidal ideation. The cumulative effect of multiple ACEs further exacerbates the risk, as each additional adverse experience increases the likelihood of poor mental health outcomes.

The impact of ACEs on mental health can be understood through several mechanisms. Firstly, ACEs can disrupt the healthy development of the brain and affect neurobiological processes. Adverse experiences during critical periods of brain development can alter the stress response system, impair emotional regulation, and increase vulnerability to mental health disorders.

Secondly, ACEs can shape individuals' cognitive and emotional patterns. Children who experience trauma may develop negative core beliefs about themselves, others, and the world, leading to distorted thinking patterns and maladaptive coping mechanisms. These cognitive and emotional patterns can persist into adulthood and contribute to the development and maintenance of mental health difficulties.

Furthermore, ACEs can have a profound impact on social and interpersonal relationships. Individuals who have experienced trauma may struggle with forming trusting relationships, establishing secure attachments, and maintaining social connections. The disruption of healthy social support systems can further increase the risk of mental health problems and hinder recovery. It is important to recognize that the effects of ACEs are not uniform. Factors such as the severity, duration, and timing of the adverse experiences, as well as the presence of protective factors such as supportive relationships or resilience, can influence the impact on mental health outcomes. Additionally, social and contextual factors, including socioeconomic status, access to resources, and community support, can mediate or exacerbate the effects of ACEs on mental health.

Understanding the impact of ACEs on mental health is crucial for developing effective prevention and intervention strategies. Early identification and intervention for children who have experienced ACEs can help mitigate the negative effects and promote resilience. Trauma-informed approaches, such as trauma-focused therapies and support services, can play a critical role in addressing the complex needs of individuals who have experienced ACEs.

Furthermore, addressing the underlying social determinants that contribute to ACEs, such as poverty, violence, and inadequate social support systems, is essential for preventing and reducing the occurrence of these adverse experiences. This requires a comprehensive approach involving collaboration among healthcare professionals, educators, policymakers, and communities to create safe and supportive environments for children and families.

Mental Health Stigma and Discrimination

Mental health stigma and discrimination refer to the negative attitudes, beliefs, and behaviors directed towards individuals experiencing mental health challenges or mental illnesses. It involves the societal devaluation and marginalization of people with mental health conditions, leading to prejudice, stereotypes, and discriminatory actions. Stigma and discrimination create barriers to seeking help, accessing adequate support, and integrating fully into society, exacerbating the challenges faced by individuals with mental health concerns.

Stigma surrounding mental health is deeply rooted in social and cultural perceptions that associate mental illness with weakness, incompetence, or dangerousness. These stereotypes perpetuate misconceptions and reinforce negative attitudes towards individuals with mental health conditions. Stigmatizing beliefs often lead to discrimination, such as social exclusion, employment discrimination, limited educational opportunities, and unequal access to healthcare services.

The consequences of mental health stigma and discrimination are wide-ranging and detrimental. Firstly, stigma discourages individuals from seeking help for mental health concerns. Fear of judgment, rejection, and labeling as "crazy" or "weak" may prevent individuals from disclosing their struggles, seeking professional assistance, or adhering to treatment plans. This delay in seeking help can exacerbate symptoms, hinder recovery, and contribute to the persistence of mental health conditions.

Secondly, stigma and discrimination can significantly impact individuals' self-esteem, self-worth, and quality of life. Internalizing societal attitudes may lead to self-stigma, where individuals with mental health challenges develop negative self-perceptions, feelings of shame, and a diminished sense of self. These internalized beliefs can further perpetuate social withdrawal, decreased self-confidence, and decreased motivation to pursue personal goals.

Moreover, stigma affects social interactions and relationships. Individuals with mental health conditions may face social rejection, isolation, and strained interpersonal connections due to stigmatizing attitudes and beliefs held by others. This isolation can amplify feelings of loneliness, contribute to decreased social support, and hinder the formation of meaningful connections, exacerbating mental health challenges.

Stigma and discrimination also have implications at the systemic level. Mental health services may be underfunded or inadequately resourced due to the prioritization of physical health, further exacerbating disparities in access to care. Mental health professionals may face challenges in combating stigma within healthcare settings, leading to disparities in the quality of care and contributing to the perception that mental health concerns are less deserving of attention and resources.

Efforts to address mental health stigma and discrimination require a multi-faceted approach. Education and awareness campaigns can play a crucial role in dispelling misconceptions, challenging stereotypes, and promoting empathy and understanding. Promoting positive portrayals of mental health in media and popular culture can help normalize discussions around mental health and reduce stigma.

Additionally, promoting contact and interaction between individuals with lived experiences of mental health challenges and the broader community can help challenge stereotypes and reduce prejudice. Peer support networks and advocacy organizations can provide platforms for individuals to share their stories, challenge stigma, and promote a sense of belonging and support.

Legislation and policies that protect the rights of individuals with mental health conditions are essential. Anti-discrimination laws can help prevent employment discrimination and ensure equal opportunities. Integration of mental health services into primary healthcare settings and comprehensive mental health policies can improve access to care and enhance the overall quality of mental health services.

Mental health stigma and discrimination contribute to the significant barriers faced by individuals with mental health challenges. Addressing stigma and discrimination is crucial for promoting mental health and well-being, ensuring equitable access to care, and creating inclusive communities. By challenging stereotypes, fostering understanding, and promoting social inclusion, society can work towards reducing the impact of stigma and discrimination and creating a more supportive and accepting environment for individuals with mental health conditions.

Resilience and Protective Factors in Mental Health

Resilience and protective factors in mental health refer to the personal and environmental characteristics that contribute to individuals' ability to adapt, cope, and recover in the face of adversity and mental health challenges. Resilience is not a fixed trait but rather a dynamic process influenced by various factors that promote positive mental health outcomes and mitigate the impact of stressors and risk factors.

Individual-level protective factors play a critical role in enhancing resilience. These include traits such as self-esteem, optimism, problem-solving skills, and emotional regulation abilities. Individuals with higher levels of self-esteem tend to have a stronger sense of self-worth and confidence, which enables them to navigate challenges more effectively. Optimism, characterized by a positive outlook and belief in one's ability to overcome difficulties, can foster resilience by promoting a proactive and hopeful mindset.

Problem-solving skills are another essential protective factor. Individuals who possess effective problem-solving abilities can identify and evaluate potential solutions, implement action plans, and adapt their strategies as needed. These skills enable individuals to approach challenges with a problem-solving mindset, enhancing their ability to cope and recover.

Emotional regulation, the ability to manage and regulate one's emotions in a healthy and adaptive manner, is crucial for resilience. Individuals who can recognize and understand their emotions, express them appropriately, and engage in coping strategies to regulate their emotional responses are better equipped to navigate stressful situations and maintain psychological well-being.

Social support is a significant protective factor at both the individual and environmental levels. Having access to supportive relationships, whether from family, friends, or other social networks, can provide emotional support, practical assistance, and a sense of belonging. Social support acts as a buffer against the negative impact of stressors and can help individuals better cope with and recover from mental health challenges.

Another important protective factor is the presence of safe and stable environments. Environmental factors, such as secure housing, access to education and healthcare, and supportive community resources, can significantly impact mental health resilience. Adequate resources and opportunities contribute to an individual's ability to meet their basic needs, pursue personal goals, and access necessary support systems.

Cultural and societal factors also influence resilience and protective factors. Cultural values that promote community cohesion, interdependence, and connectedness can strengthen social support networks and foster resilience. Societal factors, including equitable access to resources, social justice, and reduced stigma surrounding mental health, create environments that support mental well-being and enhance resilience. Understanding and promoting resilience and protective factors in mental health is essential for prevention and intervention efforts. Recognizing and fostering these factors can empower individuals to effectively navigate challenges, reduce the likelihood of developing mental health problems, and promote positive mental health outcomes.

Interventions and programs that aim to enhance resilience often focus on building individuals' skills and capacities. This includes providing opportunities for skill development, promoting self-efficacy, and teaching adaptive coping strategies. Psychoeducation programs that focus on emotional regulation, problem-solving, and building social support networks can empower individuals to develop and strengthen these protective factors.

Furthermore, creating supportive environments that foster resilience is crucial. This involves implementing policies and programs that address social determinants of mental health, such as poverty, inequality, and discrimination. Efforts to reduce stigma surrounding mental health and promote mental health literacy can also create a more supportive societal context.

Mental Health Promotion in Schools

Mental health promotion in schools refers to the intentional efforts and strategies aimed at enhancing the mental health and well-being of students within the school environment. It involves creating a supportive and nurturing atmosphere that fosters positive mental health, builds resilience, and equips students with the skills and knowledge to navigate challenges effectively. Mental health promotion in schools encompasses various components, including awareness, education, prevention, early intervention, and support.

One key aspect of mental health promotion in schools is raising awareness and reducing stigma surrounding mental health. Schools can implement campaigns and initiatives to educate students, teachers, and parents about mental health, common mental health challenges, and the importance of seeking help. By promoting an open and accepting culture that encourages dialogue about mental health, schools can create an environment where students feel comfortable discussing their struggles and seeking support.

Education plays a vital role in mental health promotion. Schools can incorporate mental health education into their curriculum, providing students with knowledge and skills related to emotional well-being, stress management, coping strategies, and building resilience. By integrating mental health education into subjects like health, physical education, or guidance counseling, schools can equip students with the necessary tools to understand, protect, and prioritize their mental well-being.

Prevention efforts are essential in promoting mental health in schools. Schools can implement evidence-based prevention programs that address risk factors and promote protective factors associated with mental health. These programs may focus on topics such as bullying prevention, substance abuse prevention, healthy relationships, and emotional regulation. By targeting these areas, schools can create a safer and more supportive environment that reduces the incidence of mental health problems.

Early intervention is crucial for identifying and addressing mental health concerns at an early stage. Schools can establish mechanisms for early detection and intervention, such as mental health screening tools or referral systems. Trained professionals, such as school counselors or psychologists, can provide support and intervention to students who may be experiencing mental health challenges. Collaborating with community mental health resources can further enhance the support available to students and their families.

Support services are an integral part of mental health promotion in schools. Schools can provide access to a range of support options, such as counseling services, peer support programs, and mental health resources. Having a designated mental health team within the school can ensure that students have a safe space to discuss their concerns, receive guidance, and access appropriate referrals if necessary. Creating partnerships with external mental health organizations can also expand the resources available to students.

Creating a positive school climate that prioritizes mental health is crucial. This involves fostering a sense of belonging, promoting positive relationships, and implementing practices that prioritize well-being. Schools can incorporate strategies such as promoting inclusive and respectful behavior, implementing mindfulness or relaxation techniques, promoting physical activity, and creating opportunities for student engagement and leadership.

Mental health promotion in schools is a comprehensive approach that involves various strategies to enhance the mental health and well-being of students. By creating supportive environments, providing education and prevention programs, implementing early intervention measures, and offering support services, schools play a vital role in promoting positive mental health outcomes for students. By prioritizing mental health in the school setting, we can empower students to thrive academically, socially, and emotionally.

Intersectionality and Mental Health

Intersectionality and mental health refer to the understanding that individuals' mental health experiences are shaped by the intersecting influences of various social identities, such as race, gender, socioeconomic status, sexual orientation, and disability. Intersectionality acknowledges that these identities do not exist in isolation but interact and intersect to create unique experiences of privilege, disadvantage, and discrimination, which can significantly impact mental health outcomes.

The concept of intersectionality recognizes that individuals may face multiple forms of oppression and marginalization, leading to distinct mental health challenges. For example, an individual who identifies as both a racial minority and a member of the LGBTQ+ community may experience unique stressors related to discrimination, identity concealment, or conflicting cultural expectations. These intersecting factors can contribute to increased vulnerability to mental health problems and decreased access to appropriate care and support.

Intersectionality also emphasizes the importance of understanding and addressing the social determinants that influence mental health disparities. Discrimination, stigma, and unequal access to resources and opportunities can disproportionately affect individuals with intersecting identities, exacerbating mental health inequities. For instance, systemic racism, homophobia, or ableism can limit access to quality mental healthcare, lead to increased exposure to trauma, and contribute to the development of mental health challenges.

Additionally, intersectionality highlights the importance of recognizing the strengths and resilience within marginalized communities. Despite facing multiple forms of oppression, individuals with intersecting identities can draw upon their cultural strengths, community support networks, and coping mechanisms to navigate mental health challenges. It is crucial to acknowledge and amplify these strengths and resources when addressing mental health in an intersectional framework.

Intersectional approaches to mental health call for inclusive and culturally competent services. Mental health professionals need to be aware of the unique challenges faced by individuals with intersecting identities and strive to provide care that is sensitive to their diverse experiences. This may involve adopting an intersectional lens in assessment, diagnosis, and treatment planning, as well as fostering a safe and affirming therapeutic environment that recognizes and respects the complexities of identity.

Addressing mental health disparities through an intersectional lens also requires collaborative efforts at the societal level. Policies and programs should be developed and implemented with an understanding of the interconnected nature of social identities and their impacts on mental health outcomes. This includes working towards eliminating systemic barriers, promoting social justice, and creating equitable access to mental health resources for individuals with intersecting identities.

Intersectionality and mental health provide a framework for understanding the complex and interconnected influences of various social identities on mental health experiences. By recognizing and addressing the intersections of race, gender, socioeconomic status, sexual orientation, and disability, we can better understand the unique mental health challenges faced by individuals with intersecting identities. Implementing inclusive and culturally competent approaches to mental health care and advocating for social change can contribute to more equitable and effective support for marginalized communities.

Mental Health of Marginalized and Vulnerable Populations

The mental health of marginalized and vulnerable populations refers to the mental well-being and challenges faced by individuals and communities who experience social, economic, or structural disadvantage. Marginalized and vulnerable populations include groups such as refugees, immigrants, LGBTQ+ individuals, and individuals experiencing homelessness, racial and ethnic minorities, individuals with disabilities, and those living in poverty.

These populations often face multiple intersecting forms of discrimination, stigma, and systemic barriers, which can have a significant impact on their mental health. Marginalized and vulnerable individuals are more likely to experience higher levels of stress, trauma, and limited access to resources, including mental health services. As a result, they may be at a greater risk of developing mental health conditions or experiencing poorer mental health outcomes.

Marginalized and vulnerable populations often face social exclusion, isolation, and limited social support networks. The experience of discrimination, prejudice, and micro-aggressions can contribute to chronic stress, low self-esteem, and a sense of powerlessness, further exacerbating mental health challenges. The cumulative effects of these adversities can lead to higher rates of depression, anxiety, post-traumatic stress disorder (PTSD), substance abuse, and other mental health disorders within these populations.

Furthermore, cultural and linguistic barriers can impede access to appropriate mental health care for marginalized and vulnerable individuals. Limited healthcare coverage, financial constraints, and a lack of culturally responsive services can create significant barriers to seeking and receiving mental health support. Inadequate representation and understanding of diverse experiences within the mental health profession may also contribute to disparities in access and quality of care.

To address the mental health needs of marginalized and vulnerable populations, it is essential to adopt a comprehensive and culturally sensitive approach. This includes:

- Promoting awareness and reducing stigma: Education and awareness campaigns can help challenge stereotypes, reduce mental health stigma, and promote understanding and empathy towards marginalized and vulnerable populations.

- Culturally responsive and accessible services: Mental health services should be tailored to meet the specific cultural, linguistic, and contextual needs of these populations. This includes having diverse mental health professionals, offering interpretation services, and integrating cultural practices and beliefs into treatment approaches.
- Community-based support: Developing community-based mental health programs and support networks can provide a safe and inclusive space for individuals to share experiences, access information, and receive peer support.
- Trauma-informed care: Recognizing the prevalence of trauma within marginalized and vulnerable populations is essential. Trauma-informed approaches focus on creating safe environments, building trust, and understanding the impact of trauma on mental health and well-being.
- Collaborative partnerships: Engaging community organizations, advocacy groups, and social services can facilitate the coordination of care and address social determinants of mental health, such as housing, employment, and access to healthcare.
- Policy and systemic change: Advocacy efforts should focus on addressing systemic barriers and inequalities that contribute to mental health disparities. This includes advocating for policies that promote social justice, equal access to resources, and the reduction of structural discrimination.

By adopting a holistic and inclusive approach that recognizes the unique challenges and strengths of marginalized and vulnerable populations, we can work towards reducing mental health disparities and improving the overall well-being of these communities.

COMMUNITY DEVELOPMENT AND SOCIAL CAPITAL

Community development and social capital are interconnected concepts that involve fostering collective action, building relationships, and mobilizing resources to promote the well-being and empowerment of communities. Community development focuses on improving social, economic, and environmental conditions within a community, while social capital emphasizes the importance of social networks, trust, and reciprocity in facilitating positive community outcomes.

Community development entails a process of engaging community members, organizations, and stakeholders in collaborative efforts to identify needs, set goals, and implement strategies for positive change. It involves empowering individuals and communities to address their own challenges and build capacity to shape their social, economic, and physical environments. Community development encompasses a range of activities such as improving infrastructure, enhancing education and healthcare services, promoting economic opportunities, and strengthening community cohesion.

Social capital refers to the social networks, relationships, and norms of trust and reciprocity within a community. It represents the resources embedded in social connections that can be leveraged for individual and collective well-being. Social capital fosters cooperation, collaboration, and shared values among community members. It includes both bonding social capital, which refers to strong ties within homogeneous groups, and bridging social capital, which refers to connections across diverse groups.

Social capital plays a crucial role in community development by facilitating collective action and resource mobilization. It creates a sense of belonging, shared identity, and mutual support within a community. Trust and reciprocity among community members promote collaboration, cooperation, and the willingness to work together towards common goals. By leveraging social networks and relationships, communities can access resources, expertise, and support that are essential for addressing community challenges and achieving positive outcomes.

Building social capital involves nurturing and strengthening social connections and networks within a community. This can be accomplished through activities such as community events, volunteer initiatives, neighborhood associations, and civic engagement. Building trust, promoting inclusivity, and fostering open communication are fundamental in cultivating social capital. By creating spaces for dialogue and collaboration, communities can facilitate the exchange of ideas, knowledge, and resources, leading to collective empowerment and problem-solving.

Community development and social capital reinforce each other in a reciprocal relationship. Effective community development efforts can strengthen social capital by enhancing community networks, trust, and collective efficacy. Conversely, social capital provides the foundation for successful community development initiatives by fostering collaboration, resource mobilization, and community resilience.

The benefits of community development and social capital are wide-ranging. They include improved social cohesion, increased civic engagement, enhanced quality of life, economic development, and better health and well-being outcomes. Communities with strong social capital and active community development initiatives are more likely to effectively address local challenges, create opportunities for growth, and promote social equity and justice.

Community development and social capital are intertwined concepts that involve empowering communities, building social connections, and mobilizing resources for positive change. Community development focuses on improving conditions within a community, while social capital emphasizes the importance of social networks, trust, and reciprocity. By fostering collective action, collaboration, and shared values, community development and social capital contribute to the well-being, resilience, and empowerment of communities, ultimately leading to sustainable positive outcomes.

Community-Based Participatory Research (CBPR)

Community-Based Participatory Research (CBPR) is an approach to research that emphasizes collaboration and partnership between researchers and community members throughout the research process. CBPR seeks to address community concerns, build trust, and generate knowledge that is meaningful, relevant, and applicable to the community being studied. It recognizes the expertise and lived experiences of community members as valuable contributions to the research process, aiming to create positive social change and improve community health and well-being.

At the core of CBPR is the recognition that communities have unique knowledge, perspectives, and needs that should guide the research agenda. Rather than treating communities as passive subjects or recipients of research, CBPR involves their active engagement and participation from the project's conception to its dissemination. Community members are involved in decision-making, problem identification, data collection, analysis, and the application of findings.

CBPR principles include building partnerships based on trust, equity, and mutual respect. Researchers and community members collaborate as equal partners, with shared power and decision-making authority. Through these partnerships, researchers gain a deeper understanding of community contexts, strengths, and needs, while community members gain research skills and increased awareness of their own health issues.

CBPR is rooted in the belief that research should lead to action and positive change in the community. The knowledge generated through CBPR is intended to inform policies, programs, and interventions that address community needs and improve health outcomes. By involving community members directly in the research process, CBPR helps ensure that the findings are relevant, culturally appropriate, and sustainable.

CBPR also has the potential to build social capital within communities. By fostering collaboration, trust, and shared goals, CBPR strengthens social connections and networks. It promotes community cohesion, empowers community members, and creates opportunities for collective action. The process of CBPR can enhance community capacity, leadership, and advocacy skills, fostering a sense of ownership and empowerment among community members.

CBPR is particularly effective in studying complex social issues, health disparities, and marginalized populations. It enables researchers to understand the root causes of health inequities and work with communities to develop targeted interventions and strategies for change. CBPR has been successfully applied to a wide range of topics, including community health assessments, chronic disease prevention, mental health promotion, environmental justice, and policy advocacy.

However, CBPR also poses challenges and requires careful attention to ethical considerations, power dynamics, and cultural sensitivity. Researchers must be mindful of issues such as informed consent, confidentiality, community representation, and the potential for researcher bias. Building and maintaining long-term partnerships can also require significant time, resources, and commitment.

CBPR is an approach to research that fosters collaboration, partnership, and empowerment between researchers and community members. It aims to generate knowledge that is relevant, actionable, and improves community health and well-being. By involving community members as active participants and recognizing their expertise, CBPR builds trust, social capital, and contributes to positive social change. Through its inclusive and participatory nature, CBPR has the potential to address health disparities, promote community resilience, and create sustainable improvements in community health.

Social Networks and Community Resilience

Social networks and community resilience are interconnected concepts that highlight the role of social connections and relationships in fostering the ability of communities to withstand and recover from adversity. Social networks refer to the web of relationships and interactions that individuals have within a community, while community resilience refers to the collective capacity of a community to adapt, bounce back, and thrive in the face of challenges.

Social networks play a crucial role in community resilience by providing channels for communication, support, and resource-sharing. Strong social connections within a community facilitate the flow of information, enabling individuals to access timely and relevant information during times of crisis. Social networks can also serve as a source of emotional support, fostering a sense of belonging, solidarity, and collective identity, which are essential for coping with stress and trauma.

In times of adversity, such as natural disasters, economic downturns, or social disruptions, social networks can provide practical assistance and resources. Individuals within a community can rely on their social connections to mobilize help, share resources, and collaborate on recovery efforts. Social networks can facilitate the distribution of essential goods, coordinate volunteer efforts, and provide immediate support to those in need.

Social networks also contribute to community resilience through the diffusion of knowledge and skills. Information about effective coping strategies, problem-solving techniques, and community resources can be disseminated through social connections. This shared knowledge enhances the community's collective ability to respond to challenges, adapt to changing circumstances, and develop innovative solutions.

Furthermore, social networks can contribute to community resilience by fostering a sense of trust and cooperation. Trust is a fundamental element of social capital, which refers to the norms, values, and trust within a community that promote cooperation and collective action. Trusting relationships within social networks enable individuals to collaborate, pool resources, and work together towards common goals. This collective effort enhances the community's resilience and its ability to tackle challenges collectively.

It is important to note that the quality and diversity of social networks are critical for community resilience. Networks that are diverse in terms of age, occupation, ethnicity, and socioeconomic status provide access to a wider range of resources, perspectives, and expertise. This diversity enhances the community's capacity to address complex challenges, adapt to change, and promote innovation.

However, it is also essential to recognize that not all social networks are equally beneficial. Some communities may face social disparities, isolation, or limited access to supportive networks. In such cases, efforts should be made to strengthen social connections, bridge social divides, and ensure that marginalized populations have access to supportive social networks.

Promoting social networks and community resilience requires a multi-faceted approach. Community engagement initiatives, such as neighborhood associations, community centers, and social gatherings, can facilitate the development of social connections. Collaboration with local organizations and institutions can provide resources, support, and opportunities for social interaction. Strengthening social networks can also involve promoting trust-building activities, fostering intergenerational connections, and empowering community members to take active roles in decision-making and problem-solving processes.

Social networks are essential for community resilience as they provide a framework for communication, support, resource-sharing, and collaboration within a community. By fostering strong social connections, promoting trust, and enhancing the diversity of networks, communities can enhance their ability to withstand and recover from adversity. Recognizing and nurturing social networks is a critical component of building resilient communities capable of addressing challenges, promoting well-being, and fostering sustainable development.

Community Development and Economic Empowerment

Community development and economic empowerment are interconnected processes that aim to improve the social and economic well-being of communities. Community development focuses on creating positive change and enhancing the quality of life within a community, while economic empowerment emphasizes the ability of individuals and communities to access and control resources, participate in economic activities, and improve their economic circumstances.

Community development initiatives that prioritize economic empowerment seek to address social and economic disparities, promote sustainable economic growth, and enhance opportunities for community members to thrive. These initiatives often involve collaboration between community members, organizations, and local stakeholders to identify and leverage community assets, address economic challenges, and create an inclusive and resilient local economy.

Economic empowerment within community development can take various forms, including:

- Entrepreneurship and Small Business Development: Encouraging entrepreneurship and supporting the establishment and growth of small businesses within the community. This includes providing access to training, mentorship, financing, and networking opportunities to empower individuals to start their own businesses, create employment opportunities, and contribute to local economic growth.
- Skill Development and Job Training: Equipping community members with the necessary skills, education, and training to enhance their employability and access to better job opportunities. This can involve partnerships with educational institutions, vocational training programs, and workforce development initiatives that align training with local labor market needs.
- Access to Financial Services: Promoting financial inclusion and access to affordable financial services, such as banking, savings, credit, and insurance. Ensuring that community members have access to financial tools and resources can empower them to make informed financial decisions, build assets, and participate more fully in the formal economy.
- Local Economic Development: Supporting initiatives that promote the growth and diversification of local industries, businesses, and employment

opportunities. This can include attracting investment, promoting local products and services, fostering innovation and entrepreneurship, and creating an enabling environment for economic activities to thrive.

- Cooperative and Social Enterprise Development: Encouraging the establishment of cooperatives, social enterprises, and community-owned businesses. These models emphasize collective ownership, democratic decision-making, and social impact, providing opportunities for community members to participate in economic activities and benefit collectively.
- Access to Markets and Supply Chains: Facilitating connections between local producers, artisans, and businesses with broader markets and supply chains. This can involve creating platforms, networks, and marketing initiatives that showcase local products and services, and support local businesses to reach wider audiences.

Community development and economic empowerment go hand in hand, as economic empowerment can contribute to broader community development outcomes. By enhancing economic opportunities, individuals and communities can improve their financial stability, access to resources, and overall well-being. Economic empowerment also has a multiplier effect, stimulating local economic growth, job creation, and community investment.

To effectively promote community development and economic empowerment, it is essential to engage community members, foster local leadership, and ensure inclusive decision-making processes. Collaboration with local stakeholders, government agencies, financial institutions, and business networks is crucial for leveraging resources, aligning efforts, and addressing systemic barriers to economic empowerment.

Community development and economic empowerment are intertwined processes that seek to enhance social and economic well-being within communities. By fostering entrepreneurship, skill development, access to financial services, and supporting local economic growth, communities can empower individuals, create sustainable livelihoods, and promote inclusive and resilient economies. Through these efforts, community members can actively contribute to their own economic well-being, enhance their quality of life, and collectively shape the future of their community.

Community Organizing and Advocacy

Community organizing and advocacy are essential approaches that empower communities to address social issues, advocate for change, and promote social justice. These processes involve collective action, mobilization, and engagement of community members to identify and address systemic challenges, create positive change, and amplify the voices of marginalized and vulnerable populations.

Community organizing focuses on building power and capacity within communities to collectively address issues that affect their well-being. It involves fostering relationships, developing leadership, and mobilizing community members to work together towards a common goal. Through community organizing, individuals and groups can come together, share their experiences and concerns, and take action to address the root causes of social problems.

Advocacy complements community organizing by giving voice to community concerns and influencing policies, systems, and structures at various levels. Advocacy involves raising awareness, influencing decision-makers, and promoting policy changes that address systemic inequalities and promote social justice. Advocacy efforts can include grassroots campaigns, lobbying, public education, and coalition building to bring about meaningful and sustainable change.

The processes of community organizing and advocacy often involve the following key components:

- Issue Identification: Community members come together to identify and prioritize the issues that affect their community. This process may involve conducting needs assessments, engaging in dialogue, and collecting data to gain a deeper understanding of the community's challenges and aspirations.
- Building Relationships and Partnerships: Community organizing emphasizes relationship-building within the community and fostering partnerships with other organizations, stakeholders, and allies who share similar goals. By forming alliances and collaborations, communities can amplify their voices, share resources, and leverage collective power.
- Leadership Development: Community organizing nurtures and develops community leaders who can mobilize and empower others. Leadership development programs provide training, mentorship, and opportunities for community members to enhance their skills, knowledge, and capacity to lead and advocate for change.
- Community Mobilization: Through various activities such as community meetings, rallies, campaigns, and grassroots initiatives, community organizing mobilizes community members to take collective action. These efforts can include organizing protests, petition drives, public hearings, or other forms of direct action to raise awareness, apply pressure, and influence decision-making.
- Policy Advocacy: Advocacy efforts focus on influencing policies, laws, and systems to address root causes and promote equitable solutions. This can involve engaging with policymakers, conducting research and analysis, presenting evidence-based arguments, and proposing policy changes that align with community needs and aspirations.
- Evaluation and Reflection: Continuous evaluation and reflection are integral to community organizing and advocacy. By assessing progress, learning from successes and challenges, and reflecting on strategies and outcomes, communities can adapt their approaches, refine their goals, and enhance their effectiveness.

Community organizing and advocacy are powerful tools for promoting social change, advancing social justice, and addressing systemic inequalities. They empower communities to challenge oppressive structures, amplify marginalized voices, and create a more equitable and inclusive society. These processes foster community resilience, build social capital, and enhance the capacity of communities to shape their own futures.

Community organizing and advocacy are transformative approaches that empower communities to collectively address social issues, advocate for change, and promote social justice. By mobilizing community members, building relationships, developing leadership, and influencing policies, communities can create meaningful and sustainable impact. Through these processes, communities can work towards dismantling systemic barriers, promoting equity, and fostering a more just and inclusive society.

Community Gardens and Urban Agriculture

Community organizing and advocacy are essential approaches that empower communities to address social issues, advocate for change, and promote social justice. These processes involve collective action, mobilization, and engagement of community members to identify and address systemic challenges, create positive change, and amplify the voices of marginalized and vulnerable populations.

Community organizing focuses on building power and capacity within communities to collectively address issues that affect their well-being. It involves fostering relationships, developing leadership, and mobilizing community members to work together towards a common goal. Through community organizing, individuals and groups can come together, share their experiences and concerns, and take action to address the root causes of social problems.

Advocacy complements community organizing by giving voice to community concerns and influencing policies, systems, and structures at various levels. Advocacy involves raising awareness, influencing decision-makers, and promoting policy changes that address systemic inequalities and promote social justice. Advocacy efforts can include grassroots campaigns, lobbying, public education, and coalition building to bring about meaningful and sustainable change.

The processes of community organizing and advocacy often involve the following key components:

- Issue Identification: Community members come together to identify and prioritize the issues that affect their community. This process may involve conducting needs assessments, engaging in dialogue, and collecting data to gain a deeper understanding of the community's challenges and aspirations.
- Building Relationships and Partnerships: Community organizing emphasizes relationship-building within the community and fostering partnerships with other organizations, stakeholders, and allies who share similar goals. By forming alliances and collaborations, communities can amplify their voices, share resources, and leverage collective power.
- Leadership Development: Community organizing nurtures and develops community leaders who can mobilize and empower others. Leadership development programs provide training, mentorship, and opportunities for community members to enhance their skills, knowledge, and capacity to lead and advocate for change.
- Community Mobilization: Through various activities such as community meetings, rallies, campaigns, and grassroots initiatives, community organizing mobilizes community members to take collective action. These efforts can include organizing protests, petition drives, public hearings, or other forms of direct action to raise awareness, apply pressure, and influence decision-making.

- Policy Advocacy: Advocacy efforts focus on influencing policies, laws, and systems to address root causes and promote equitable solutions. This can involve engaging with policymakers, conducting research and analysis, presenting evidence-based arguments, and proposing policy changes that align with community needs and aspirations.
- Evaluation and Reflection: Continuous evaluation and reflection are integral to community organizing and advocacy. By assessing progress, learning from successes and challenges, and reflecting on strategies and outcomes, communities can adapt their approaches, refine their goals, and enhance their effectiveness.

Community organizing and advocacy are powerful tools for promoting social change, advancing social justice, and addressing systemic inequalities. They empower communities to challenge oppressive structures, amplify marginalized voices, and create a more equitable and inclusive society. These processes foster community resilience, build social capital, and enhance the capacity of communities to shape their own futures.

Community organizing and advocacy are transformative approaches that empower communities to collectively address social issues, advocate for change, and promote social justice. By mobilizing community members, building relationships, developing leadership, and influencing policies, communities can create meaningful and sustainable impact. Through these processes, communities can work towards dismantling systemic barriers, promoting equity, and fostering a more just and inclusive society.

Community-Based Health Promotion

Community-based health promotion is an approach that focuses on improving the health and well-being of individuals and communities through collaborative efforts at the community level. It recognizes that health is influenced by a range of social, economic, and environmental factors, and aims to address these determinants of health by engaging community members, organizations, and stakeholders in planning, implementing, and evaluating health promotion initiatives.

Key principles of community-based health promotion include:

- Community Engagement: Community members are actively involved in all stages of the health promotion process. Their input, perspectives, and lived experiences guide the development of programs and interventions, ensuring that they are relevant, culturally appropriate, and meet the specific needs of the community.
- Empowerment and Capacity Building: Community-based health promotion aims to empower individuals and communities by building their capacity to address health issues. This involves providing education, skills training, and resources that enable community members to make informed decisions, adopt healthy behaviors, and become advocates for their own health and well-being.
- Collaboration and Partnerships: Community-based health promotion recognizes that addressing complex health issues requires collaboration among various stakeholders, including community

organizations, healthcare providers, government agencies, and other sectors such as education, housing, and transportation. By fostering partnerships, pooling resources, and leveraging expertise, community-based health promotion initiatives can achieve greater impact and sustainability.

- Holistic Approach: Community-based health promotion considers the broad determinants of health, including social, economic, cultural, and environmental factors. It goes beyond individual behaviors and addresses the underlying social, economic, and environmental conditions that influence health outcomes. This approach recognizes the interconnectedness of these factors and the need for comprehensive strategies that promote health and well-being.
- Tailored Interventions: Community-based health promotion takes into account the unique characteristics, assets, and challenges of the community. Interventions are tailored to the specific needs, culture, and context of the community, ensuring that they are effective and meaningful. This approach promotes inclusivity, respects diversity, and recognizes the importance of cultural competence in health promotion efforts.

Community-based health promotion initiatives can encompass a wide range of activities, including:

- Health education and awareness campaigns: Providing information and resources to promote healthy behaviors, preventive measures, and self-care practices within the community.
- Collaborative planning and policy development: Engaging community members and stakeholders in decision-making processes to shape policies, regulations, and initiatives that promote health and well-being.
- Health screenings and preventive services: Organizing health fairs, screenings, and vaccination campaigns to detect and prevent diseases, and improve access to preventive care.
- Physical activity and nutrition programs: Promoting physical activity, healthy eating, and access to nutritious food options through community gardens, walking clubs, cooking classes, or policy changes that support healthy environments.
- Support groups and social networks: Establishing support groups and creating opportunities for social connection and peer support, which can enhance mental health, emotional well-being, and overall community resilience.
- Environmental health initiatives: Addressing environmental factors that impact health, such as air and water quality, safe housing, and access to green spaces.

Community-based health promotion acknowledges the strengths, assets, and resilience within communities and seeks to leverage these resources to improve health outcomes. By empowering communities, fostering collaboration, and addressing the underlying determinants of health, community-based health promotion contributes to building healthier, more equitable, and sustainable communities.

Social Capital in Indigenous Communities

Social capital in Indigenous communities refers to the collective relationships, networks, and resources that exist within these communities. It encompasses the social connections, norms, and trust that facilitate cooperation, mutual support, and the overall well-being of Indigenous peoples. Social capital is deeply embedded in the cultural fabric, traditional practices, and kinship systems that have sustained Indigenous communities for generations.

In Indigenous communities, social capital plays a critical role in promoting resilience, self-determination, and community development. Here are key aspects of social capital in Indigenous contexts:

- Cultural Resilience: Social capital in Indigenous communities is rooted in the preservation and transmission of cultural knowledge, traditions, and values. Strong cultural networks and intergenerational relationships foster a sense of identity, belonging, and cultural pride, which contribute to the resilience of Indigenous communities in the face of historical trauma, colonization, and ongoing challenges.
- Collective Decision-Making: Indigenous communities often have communal decision-making processes that rely on social connections and consensus-building. Through cultural practices such as storytelling, ceremonies, and community gatherings, social capital facilitates the exchange of ideas, the involvement of multiple perspectives, and the participation of community members in shaping the future of their communities.
- Mutual Support and Reciprocity: Indigenous communities emphasize reciprocity and collective responsibility. Social capital facilitates the sharing of resources, knowledge, and support networks, enabling community members to meet their individual and collective needs. Traditional kinship systems, extended family networks, and community-based support structures contribute to the social capital within Indigenous communities.
- Cultural Revitalization and Healing: Social capital plays a crucial role in efforts to revitalize Indigenous cultures, languages, and traditions. Collaborative initiatives, such as language revitalization programs, intergenerational mentorship, and cultural preservation projects, rely on social connections, shared values, and community support to ensure the continuity of Indigenous cultural practices and promote healing from historical trauma.
- Advocacy and Political Engagement: Social capital empowers Indigenous communities to advocate for their rights, assert self-determination, and address social justice issues. Strong social networks and alliances with Indigenous organizations, activists, and allies amplify Indigenous voices, promote collective action, and contribute to positive changes in policy, governance, and Indigenous rights.
- Land-Based Relationships: For many Indigenous communities, social capital is closely tied to their relationship with the land and natural resources. Traditional ecological knowledge, stewardship practices, and

community-based land management systems foster strong connections to the environment and sustainable resource use. These connections contribute to cultural resilience, intergenerational learning, and the well-being of Indigenous communities.

Recognizing and building upon the social capital within Indigenous communities is essential for promoting holistic well-being, self-determination, and positive community outcomes. However, it is important to approach these efforts with cultural humility, respect for Indigenous knowledge and self-governance, and meaningful engagement with Indigenous communities as equal partners. By supporting and amplifying the social capital within Indigenous communities, we can foster Indigenous resilience, promote cultural continuity, and contribute to the well-being and empowerment of Indigenous peoples.

HUMAN RIGHTS AND SOCIAL WORK

Human rights and social work are intertwined fields that share a common goal of promoting social justice, equality, and the well-being of individuals and communities. Human rights provide the ethical foundation for social work practice, guiding professionals in upholding the rights and dignity of all individuals, particularly those who are marginalized, oppressed, or vulnerable.

Human rights, as defined by international declarations and conventions, encompass a range of civil, political, economic, social, and cultural rights that every individual is entitled to without discrimination. These rights include but are not limited to the right to life, liberty, equality, non-discrimination, education, health, and participation in decision-making processes. Human rights serve as a framework for identifying and addressing systemic injustices and violations that hinder individuals from realizing their full potential and accessing essential resources and opportunities.

Social work, as a profession, is committed to advancing social justice and human rights. Social workers work with individuals, families, groups, and communities to address personal and social problems, advocate for their rights, and promote social change. Social workers strive to empower individuals and communities, challenge oppressive systems and structures, and promote equitable access to resources and opportunities.

The integration of human rights principles into social work practice involves several key elements:

- Respect for Dignity and Worth: Social work is grounded in the inherent dignity and worth of all individuals. Practitioners uphold human rights by treating clients with respect, honoring their autonomy, and promoting their participation in decision-making processes that affect their lives.
- Non-Discrimination and Equal Treatment: Human rights require social workers to address discrimination and inequality in all their forms. Social workers are ethically obligated to challenge systemic barriers, biases, and prejudices that perpetuate discrimination based on factors such as race, ethnicity, gender, sexual orientation, disability, or socioeconomic status.
- Empowerment and Self-Determination: Human rights and social work emphasize empowering individuals and communities to exercise their rights and make informed choices. Social workers collaborate with

clients, build on their strengths, and support their self-determination to promote their well-being and enhance their capacity to advocate for their rights.

- Advocacy and Social Change: Human rights principles underpin social workers' commitment to advocating for social justice and systemic change. Social workers engage in policy advocacy, community organizing, and social action to challenge unjust laws, policies, and practices that perpetuate inequality and human rights violations.
- Accountability and Ethical Practice: Human rights provide a framework for social workers' ethical responsibilities. Practitioners must adhere to ethical guidelines and professional standards that prioritize the well-being, rights, and safety of clients, and work within legal and ethical frameworks to protect and promote human rights.
- Intersectionality and Cultural Competence: Human rights and social work recognize the importance of considering intersecting identities and cultural contexts in practice. Social workers strive for cultural competence, acknowledging the diverse experiences and needs of individuals and communities while challenging the structural inequalities and discrimination they face.

The integration of human rights principles into social work practice contributes to the empowerment of individuals and communities, the elimination of systemic barriers, and the promotion of social justice. By embracing human rights as a guiding framework, social workers can advocate for marginalized populations, challenge oppressive structures, and create meaningful change at the individual, community, and societal levels. Human rights and social work are inseparable in their commitment to creating a more just and inclusive world.

Social Work and Refugee Rights

Social Work and Refugee Rights is an important topic that explores the role of social work in advocating for the rights and well-being of refugees. It examines the unique challenges faced by refugees, including forced displacement, trauma, and the need for social integration, while highlighting the ethical responsibilities of social workers in supporting this vulnerable population.

- Trauma-Informed Care for Refugees: Explore how social workers can provide trauma-informed care to refugees, recognizing the impact of pre-migration, migration, and post-migration experiences on their mental health and well-being. Examine interventions and strategies that promote resilience and recovery in refugee populations.
- Access to Social Services and Rights: Investigate the barriers that refugees encounter in accessing social services and their rights in host countries. Explore how social workers can navigate the bureaucratic systems and advocate for the fulfillment of refugees' rights to education, healthcare, housing, and social support.
- Culturally Responsive Practice with Refugees: Examine the importance of cultural competence and sensitivity in social work practice with refugees. Explore strategies for developing culturally responsive interventions that honor refugees' unique backgrounds, experiences, and strengths.

- Integration and Social Inclusion of Refugees: Analyze the role of social workers in facilitating the integration and social inclusion of refugees into their host communities. Explore interventions that promote social cohesion, cultural exchange, and community engagement, while addressing discrimination, xenophobia, and marginalization.
- Refugee Children and Youth: Focus on the unique needs and rights of refugee children and youth. Examine the role of social workers in ensuring their protection, education, and psychosocial well-being. Explore interventions that support family reunification, foster care, and educational opportunities for refugee children and youth.
- Forced Migration and Human Trafficking: Investigate the intersection of forced migration and human trafficking. Explore the role of social workers in identifying and supporting victims of human trafficking among refugee populations, providing trauma-informed care, and advocating for their rights and legal protection.
- Policy Advocacy and Refugee Rights: Analyze the role of social workers in policy advocacy for refugee rights at local, national, and international levels. Explore how social workers can engage in legislative processes, collaborate with human rights organizations, and advocate for policy changes that protect and uphold the rights of refugees.
- Community-Based Approaches for Refugee Support: Examine community-based models of support for refugees, including grassroots initiatives, community organizations, and refugee-led initiatives. Explore the role of social workers in facilitating community empowerment, fostering social networks, and supporting the self-advocacy of refugees.
- Refugee Mental Health and Psychosocial Support: Investigate the mental health challenges faced by refugees and the role of social workers in providing psychosocial support and counseling. Explore trauma-informed interventions, group therapy, and community-based approaches that promote healing and resilience among refugee populations.
- Ethical Considerations in Refugee Work: Analyze the ethical dilemmas and challenges faced by social workers in their work with refugees. Explore issues such as cultural competence, confidentiality, power dynamics, and self-care in the context of refugee rights and social work practice.

Remember to narrow down and refine these topics based on your research interests and the specific objectives of your study. Consider utilizing interdisciplinary approaches, incorporating case studies, and employing appropriate research methodologies to investigate these areas effectively.

Indigenous Rights and Social Work

The topic of Indigenous rights and social work explores the intersection of social work practice and the rights of Indigenous peoples. It delves into the historical and ongoing injustices faced by Indigenous communities, the unique challenges they encounter, and the role of social workers in promoting social justice, cultural responsiveness, and empowerment within Indigenous contexts.

- Cultural Competence and Indigenous Social Work: Examine the importance of cultural competence in social work practice with Indigenous communities. Explore strategies for developing culturally sensitive interventions, recognizing the diversity of Indigenous cultures, and respecting traditional knowledge and practices.

- Decolonizing Social Work Practice: Analyze the need to decolonize social work practice and challenge the oppressive structures that have historically marginalized Indigenous peoples. Explore approaches that prioritize self-determination, community involvement, and Indigenous-led solutions in social work interventions.
- Historical Trauma and Healing: Investigate the impact of historical trauma on Indigenous communities and the role of social workers in promoting healing, resilience, and intergenerational well-being. Explore trauma-informed practices that acknowledge the historical context and foster culturally appropriate approaches to healing.
- Indigenous Child Welfare and Family Support: Examine the overrepresentation of Indigenous children in child welfare systems and the need for culturally responsive approaches to family support and reunification. Explore community-based models, kinship care, and cultural preservation in social work practice with Indigenous families.
- Land Rights and Environmental Justice: Analyze the link between Indigenous rights, land rights, and environmental justice. Explore the role of social workers in supporting Indigenous communities' struggles for land rights, protection of sacred sites, and sustainable resource management.
- Indigenous Youth Empowerment: Focus on the empowerment and well-being of Indigenous youth. Explore the role of social workers in addressing the unique challenges faced by Indigenous youth, including cultural identity, educational disparities, mental health, and community engagement.
- Indigenous Knowledge and Social Work: Investigate the integration of Indigenous knowledge systems and practices into social work. Explore how social workers can collaborate with Indigenous elders, healers, and community leaders to incorporate Indigenous ways of knowing and healing into their practice.
- Indigenous Governance and Self-Determination: Analyze the significance of Indigenous self-governance and self-determination in social work practice. Explore approaches that support community-driven initiatives, Indigenous-led organizations, and the revitalization of traditional governance structures.
- Reconciliation and Truth and Reconciliation Commissions: Examine the role of social workers in supporting truth and reconciliation processes, acknowledging historical injustices, and promoting healing, dialogue, and understanding between Indigenous and non-Indigenous communities.
- Advocacy and Policy Development: Investigate the role of social workers in advocating for Indigenous rights and contributing to policy development at local, national, and international levels. Explore collaborations with Indigenous organizations, engagement in legislative

processes, and efforts to address systemic inequalities and promote social justice.

Remember to narrow down and refine these topics based on your research interests and the specific objectives of your study. Consider utilizing interdisciplinary approaches, incorporating case studies, and employing appropriate research methodologies to investigate these areas effectively.

Gender Equality and Women's Rights in Social Work

Gender equality and women's rights in social work encompass the efforts and responsibilities of social workers to promote gender equality, challenge gender-based discrimination, and advocate for the rights and well-being of women. This topic explores the intersection of social work practice with gender issues, aiming to address the systemic inequalities and social injustices that women face.

- Feminist Social Work Practice: Examine the principles and approaches of feminist social work practice in promoting gender equality. Explore how social workers can adopt a feminist lens, challenge gender norms, and work towards dismantling oppressive structures that perpetuate gender-based discrimination.
- Violence against Women: Analyze the role of social workers in addressing various forms of violence against women, such as domestic violence, sexual assault, and human trafficking. Explore intervention strategies, trauma-informed care, and support services that empower survivors and contribute to prevention efforts.
- Women's Economic Empowerment: Investigate the role of social work in promoting women's economic empowerment, addressing gender pay gaps, and supporting women's entrepreneurship and financial independence. Explore interventions that enhance access to employment, vocational training, and financial resources for women.
- Reproductive Health and Rights: Examine the intersection of social work practice with women's reproductive health and rights. Explore issues such as access to contraception, comprehensive sexuality education, reproductive healthcare services, and advocacy for reproductive rights in diverse cultural contexts.
- Women's Leadership and Political Participation: Analyze the role of social workers in promoting women's leadership and political participation. Explore initiatives that encourage women's representation in decision-making processes, challenge gender biases, and empower women to participate in political and social change.
- Intersectionality and Women's Rights: Investigate the experiences of marginalized women and the impact of intersecting identities such as race, ethnicity, class, disability, and sexual orientation on their rights and well-being. Explore how social workers can adopt an intersectional approach that recognizes and addresses the unique challenges faced by diverse groups of women.
- Engaging Men in Gender Equality: Explore the role of social workers in engaging men as allies and advocates in promoting gender equality and preventing gender-based violence. Investigate strategies for men's

involvement in challenging harmful gender norms and fostering healthy relationships and positive masculinity.

- Gender and Social Policy: Analyze the influence of social policies on gender equality and women's rights. Explore the role of social workers in policy analysis, advocacy for gender-responsive policies, and efforts to ensure the implementation of policies that promote women's rights.
- Women's Empowerment in International Development: Examine the contributions of social work in international development programs that aim to empower women and promote gender equality in various cultural contexts. Explore approaches to community development, capacity building, and gender mainstreaming in international social work practice.
- Ethical Considerations in Gender-Sensitive Practice: Investigate the ethical dilemmas and considerations that social workers face when working with women and promoting gender equality. Explore issues such as confidentiality, informed consent, cultural sensitivity, and self-reflection in gender-sensitive practice.

Remember to narrow down and refine these topics based on your research interests and the specific objectives of your study. Consider utilizing interdisciplinary approaches, incorporating case studies, and employing appropriate research methodologies to investigate these areas effectively.

Human Rights-Based Approaches to Child Protection

A human rights-based approach to child protection is an approach that places the rights and well-being of children at the center of all child protection interventions and policies. It recognizes that children, as individuals with their own rights, should be treated with dignity, respect, and equality. This approach draws upon the principles and provisions of international human rights instruments, such as the United Nations Convention on the Rights of the Child (UNCRC), to guide and inform child protection practices.

At its core, a human rights-based approach to child protection emphasizes the following key elements:

- Respect for the Rights of the Child: It recognizes that children have fundamental rights that must be respected, protected, and fulfilled. These rights include the right to life, survival, development, protection from violence, exploitation, and discrimination, as well as the right to participation, education, and health. Child protection interventions aim to uphold and promote these rights in all aspects of a child's life.
- Non-Discrimination and Equality: It ensures that all children are entitled to the same rights and opportunities, without discrimination based on race, ethnicity, gender, disability, socioeconomic status, or any other grounds. Efforts are made to address structural inequalities and discriminatory practices that prevent certain groups of children from accessing their rights and receiving adequate protection.
- Best Interests of the Child: It places the best interests of the child as a primary consideration in all decisions and actions concerning the child. This principle requires child protection professionals to make decisions that promote the overall well-being, safety, and development of the child,

taking into account their individual needs, experiences, and wishes.

- Participation and Empowerment: It recognizes children as active participants in decisions that affect their lives. Children are encouraged and empowered to express their views, opinions, and concerns, and their participation is sought in matters that affect them. Child protection interventions aim to involve children in decision-making processes, ensuring their voices are heard and their perspectives are taken into account.
- Accountability and Rule of Law: It emphasizes the accountability of duty-bearers, including governments, child protection agencies, professionals, and caregivers, in fulfilling their obligations to protect children's rights. Child protection practices should be guided by clear legal frameworks and adhere to international human rights standards. Monitoring, evaluation, and redress mechanisms are put in place to hold duty-bearers accountable for their actions or inactions.
- Prevention and Systems Strengthening: It recognizes the importance of addressing the root causes of child rights violations and investing in preventive measures. Efforts are made to strengthen child protection systems, including legislation, policies, services, and community support networks, to ensure that children are protected from harm and that their rights are respected throughout their lives.

A human rights-based approach to child protection requires collaboration and coordination among various stakeholders, including governments, child protection agencies, civil society organizations, communities, and children themselves. It emphasizes the need for multidisciplinary and holistic interventions that address not only immediate protection concerns but also underlying social, economic, and cultural factors that impact children's well-being.

By adopting a human rights-based approach, child protection systems and professionals strive to create a protective environment where children can grow, develop, and thrive in a manner consistent with their rights and dignity. It recognizes that children are active rights-holders and that their protection and well-being are inseparable from the promotion and fulfillment of their human rights.

LGBTQ+ Rights and Social Work

LGBTQ+ rights and social work refer to the intersection of social work practice and the promotion of equality, well-being, and social justice for lesbian, gay, bisexual, transgender, and queer individuals and communities. It recognizes the unique challenges and discrimination faced by LGBTQ+ individuals and seeks to address systemic barriers, advocate for their rights, and provide affirming and inclusive support.

A key aspect of LGBTQ+ rights and social work is the promotion of:

- Equality and Non-Discrimination: It acknowledges the fundamental rights of LGBTQ+ individuals and the need to combat discrimination based on sexual orientation, gender identity, and gender expression. Social workers strive to create inclusive environments that value diversity and challenge heteronormative and cisnormative norms.

- Affirmative Practice: It involves adopting affirmative approaches that recognize and validate the identities and experiences of LGBTQ+ individuals. Social workers aim to create safe and supportive spaces, affirm the self-determination and autonomy of LGBTQ+ clients, and provide culturally sensitive interventions that address their unique needs.
- Coming Out Support: It recognizes the significance and complexity of the coming out process for LGBTQ+ individuals. Social workers play a crucial role in providing support, information, and resources to help individuals navigate the challenges of self-disclosure and develop resilience in the face of potential social, familial, and cultural barriers.
- Mental Health and Well-being: It acknowledges the disparities in mental health outcomes faced by LGBTQ+ individuals due to societal stigma and discrimination. Social workers work to promote mental health and well-being by providing counseling, support groups, and advocacy for LGBTQ+-affirming mental health services.
- Family and Relationship Support: It addresses the unique needs of LGBTQ+ individuals and families, including support for same-sex couples, parenting, and adoption. Social workers advocate for the recognition of LGBTQ+ relationships, challenge discriminatory policies, and provide resources to help families navigate legal, social, and psychological challenges.
- Transgender and Gender-Nonconforming Rights: It acknowledges the specific needs and rights of transgender and gender-nonconforming individuals. Social workers play a critical role in providing gender-affirming care, assisting with access to healthcare, advocating for legal gender recognition, and supporting individuals in their journey of self-discovery and self-acceptance.
- Education and Advocacy: It emphasizes the role of social workers as advocates for LGBTQ+ rights and social change. Social workers engage in community education, policy advocacy, and collaborations with LGBTQ+ organizations to challenge discriminatory practices, promote inclusive policies, and work towards legal protections for LGBTQ+ individuals.
- Intersectionality and Multiple Identities: It recognizes the intersecting identities and experiences of LGBTQ+ individuals, including race, ethnicity, disability, and socioeconomic status. Social workers adopt an intersectional approach that acknowledges the unique challenges faced by individuals at the intersection of multiple marginalized identities, promoting inclusivity and equity in their practice.
- Community Building and Empowerment: It supports the formation of LGBTQ+ communities, fostering social connections, and promoting resilience. Social workers facilitate support groups, organize community events, and empower LGBTQ+ individuals to become advocates for their rights and well-being.
- Professional Development and Cultural Competence: It requires social workers to continuously develop their knowledge and skills in LGBTQ+ issues, including cultural competence, understanding diverse gender

identities and sexual orientations, and staying updated on relevant research and best practices in LGBTQ+ affirmative social work.

By embracing LGBTQ+ rights and integrating LGBTQ+-affirming practices into their work, social workers can contribute to creating a more inclusive, equitable, and supportive society for all individuals, regardless of their sexual orientation or gender identity. They play a vital role in advocating for LGBTQ+ rights, promoting resilience, and enhancing the well-being and social integration of LGBTQ+ individuals and communities.

Social Justice and Advocacy in Social Work Practice

Social justice and advocacy in social work practice refer to the principles and actions aimed at addressing systemic inequalities, promoting fairness, and advocating for positive social change. It involves recognizing the structural barriers, discrimination, and injustices that contribute to social problems and working towards creating a more equitable and just society. Social workers play a critical role in advocating for the rights and well-being of marginalized individuals and communities, challenging oppressive systems, and promoting social justice at multiple levels.

At its core, social justice and advocacy in social work practice encompass the following key elements:

- Equity and Fairness: It recognizes that all individuals deserve equal opportunities, resources, and treatment, regardless of their background, identity, or circumstances. Social workers strive to address disparities and promote equity by challenging discriminatory practices and advocating for policies that level the playing field and promote equal access to resources and opportunities.
- Empowerment and Voice: It emphasizes the empowerment of individuals and communities to participate in decision-making processes that affect their lives. Social workers support marginalized individuals in finding their voice, advocating for their rights, and actively participating in efforts to create social change.
- Human Rights and Dignity: It upholds the principles of human rights, recognizing the inherent worth and dignity of every individual. Social workers advocate for the protection and promotion of human rights, challenging violations, and ensuring that individuals' rights are respected, protected, and fulfilled.
- Advocacy at Macro, Meso, and Micro Levels: It involves advocacy efforts at multiple levels. Social workers engage in micro-level advocacy by supporting and empowering individuals directly, while also advocating at meso-level for policy changes, program development, and organizational reform. At the macro-level, social workers engage in broader systemic advocacy to challenge unjust structures and policies that perpetuate social inequalities.
- Collaborative Partnerships: It recognizes the importance of collaboration and partnerships in achieving social justice goals. Social workers work alongside individuals, communities, organizations, and other stakeholders to build coalitions, forge alliances, and create collective strategies for social change.

- Ethical Responsibility: It is guided by ethical principles and professional standards that prioritize social justice and advocate for the well-being of vulnerable and marginalized populations. Social workers adhere to a code of ethics that emphasizes the importance of promoting social justice, challenging oppression, and advocating for social change within their practice.
- Critical Analysis and Reflection: It requires social workers to critically analyze social, economic, and political structures, and reflect on their own biases and privileges. They engage in ongoing self-reflection, examining the ways in which their own values, beliefs, and actions contribute to or challenge social injustice.
- Intersectionality: It acknowledges that individuals and communities experience multiple intersecting forms of oppression and discrimination based on factors such as race, gender, class, sexuality, and disability. Social workers adopt an intersectional lens, recognizing the interconnected nature of oppressions and addressing the unique needs and experiences of individuals at the intersection of multiple marginalized identities.
- Social Change Strategies: It encompasses a range of strategies and interventions to bring about social change. Social workers engage in activities such as policy advocacy, community organizing, grassroots movements, public awareness campaigns, and coalition building to challenge systemic injustices and promote social justice.
- Global Perspective: It recognizes that social justice is not limited to local contexts but also encompasses global issues. Social workers engage in advocacy efforts that address global inequalities, human rights violations, and promote international solidarity in the pursuit of social justice.

By integrating social justice and advocacy principles into their practice, social workers can contribute to the transformation of unjust systems, empower individuals and communities, and work towards a more equitable and inclusive society. They play a vital role in challenging oppression, promoting social change, and advocating for the rights and well-being of those who are marginalized and oppressed.

REFERENCES

1. Austin, M. J. (2009). Community-based research in social work: A framework for practice. Journal of Community Practice, 17(4), 363-386.
2. Gray, M., & Webb, S. A. (2013). The new politics of social work: Power, partnership, and participation. Palgrave Macmillan.
3. Mertens, D. M., &Tarsilla, M. (2013). Research and evaluation methods in social work. SAGE Publications.
4. Morrow, R. G., & Brown, L. (2019). Critical theory and social work: Exploring the links between theory and practice. Routledge.
5. Reisch, M., & Stahl, M. (2019). Contemporary issues in social work practice. Cognella Academic Publishing.
6. Saleebey, D. (Ed.). (2013). The strengths perspective in social work practice. Pearson.
7. Shaw, I., Briar-Lawson, K., &Orme, J. (Eds.). (2016). The Sage handbook of social work research. SAGE Publications.

8. Sheppard, M., Newstead, S., &Caccavo, A. (2017). Social work research and evaluation: Foundations of evidence-based practice. Routledge.
9. Thyer, B. A. (2010). The handbook of social work research methods. SAGE Publications.
10. Trevithick, P. (2012). Social work skills and knowledge: A practice handbook. Open University Press.
11. Walsh, J., &Gowan, T. (2020). Science and social work: A critical appraisal. Springer.
12. Webb, S. A., & Bellamy, C. D. (2018). The Routledge handbook of critical social work. Routledge.

INDEX